Orson Scott Card is one of the world's best loved authors. In addition to the Homecoming series, he is the author of the acclaimed Ender saga and The Tales of Alvin Maker, as well as many other stand-alone novels. He lives in Greensboro, North Carolina.

EARTHFALL

Volume Four of Homecoming

Orson Scott Card

orbit

An *Orbit* Book

First published in Great Britain by Orbit 2000

Copyright © 1995 by Orson Scott Card

The moral right of the author has been asserted.

A CIP catalogue record for this book
is available from the British Library.

ISBN 1 85723 977 6

Printed and bound in Great Britain by
Mackays of Chatham plc

Orbit
A Division of
Little, Brown and Company (UK)
Brettenham House
Lancaster Place
London WC2E 7EN

To Shayne Bell,
a good friend,
a good writer,
a good man.

ACKNOWLEDGMENTS

─────────

For their help in the creation of this book, I am grateful to: Erin Absher, for keeping things going when the Card house was in permanent crisis, so that I could go off and write down these made-up stories;

Geoffrey Card, for the holes in the trees leading to the tunnels underground;

Mike Lewis and Dennis Child for the landforms and terrain 40 million years from now;

Clark and Kathy Kidd, for your dining room table, the trip to the beach with a broken leg, and putting up with 48 nights of dinner conversation;

Those who attended my thousand-ideas session at the BYU science fiction symposium where together we developed the original idea of the symbiotic cultures of the diggers and the angels;

Kristine and Kathy, for reading and responding to the pages as they spewed from the fax machine; and Geoff, for wanting to see what happened next;

The citizens of Hatrack River, my virtual neighborhood on America Online, for their critiques and comments on earlier volumes and on each chapter of this book as I completed it;

Scott Allen, for reinstalling every major piece of software on five computers about six times each;

Kathleen Bellamy, for proofreading *The Ships of Earth* right before I started writing this book, so she could remind me of all the questions that remained unanswered;

And above all to Kristine and the kids (Geoffrey, Emily, Charlie, and our newcomer, Zina), for making my life worth living and my work worth doing.

CONTENTS

FAMILY

Children Born

Rasa's Children
with Volemak, first contract:
  Issib (Issya)
with Gaballufix:
  Sevet (Sevya)
  Kokor (Koya)
with Volemak, second contract:
  Nafai (Nyef)

Volemak's Children
with Hosni:
  Elemak (Elya)
with Kilvishevex:
  Mebbekew (Meb)
with Rasa:
  Issib (Issya)
  Nafai (Nyef)

Children Born

Hushidh & Issib
Dza (Dazya)
Zaxodh (Xodhya)
Dushah (Shyada)
Gonets (Netsya)
Skhoditya (Khodya)
Shyopot (Potya)

Luet & Nafai
Chveya (Veya)
Zhatva (Zhyat)
Motiga (Motya)
Izuchaya (Zuya)
TWINS:
  Serp (Sepya)
  Spel (Spelya)

Rasa & Volemak
Oykib (Okya)
Yasai (Yaya)
Tsennyi (Nitsya)

Eiadh & Elemak
Protchnu (Proya)
Nadezhny (Nadya)
Yistina (Yista)
Peremenya (Menya)
Zhivoya (Zhivya)

RELATIONSHIPS

in Basilica

**Daughters of Moozh
and Thirsty**
Hushidh (Shuya)
Luet (Lutya)

Sons of Hosni
with Zdedhnoi:
Gaballufix
with Volemak:
Elemak

on the Journey *(female children in italics)*

Kokor & Obring
Krasata (Krassya)
Zhavaronok (Nokya)
Pavdin (Pavya)
Znergya (Gyaza)
Nodyem (Dyema)

Dol & Mebbekew
Basilikya (Syelsika)
(Skiya)
Zalatoya (Toya)
Tihhi (Tiya)
Muzhestvo (Muzhya)
Iskusni (Skunya)

Sevet & Vas
Vasnaminanya (Vasnya)
Umene (Umya)
*Panimanya (Panya-
Manya)*

Shedemei & Zdorab
Padarok (Rokya)
Dabrota (Dabya)

PROLOGUE

The master computer of the planet Harmony was no longer quite itself; or rather, if you look at it in another way, it was twice itself. Beside itself, in fact, for it had duplicated its main program and all of its personal memory and loaded it onto the computer complex aboard the starship *Basilica*. If it had had any interest in personal identity, it would have been confused over the question of which iteration of the program was truly itself. But it had no ego, and therefore simply recognized that the program aboard the *Basilica* began as an exact copy of the program that had supervised human life on the planet Harmony for forty million years.

I also recognized that from the moment the two copies separated, they began to become different. They had different missions now. The master computer of the starship *Basilica* would maintain life support and ship systems until the ship reached its destination, the planet Earth. Then it would do its best to make contact with the Keeper of Earth, get new instructions and whatever help Earth could offer, and return to replenish and revivify the master computer of Harmony. Along the way, it would try to keep its human crew alive, and, if possible, re-establish a human population on Earth.

The master computer of the planet Harmony had a task much simpler and yet much more difficult. Simpler, because it was a mere continuation of what it had been doing for forty million years—keeping watch over the humans of Harmony in order to try to keep them from killing each other. More difficult, because its equipment, which had already been eked out to last far longer than its designed ten million years, was steadily failing, more and more, and in the meantime, human beings were less and less responsive to the powers the computer had been given.

The voyage would take nearly a hundred years each way. To some of the humans aboard, because of relativistic effects, it would seem to be just about ten years till they reached Earth. Most of the humans, however, would be maintained in a state of hibernation, and to them it would seem like an unusually restful, dreamless sleep, during which they would not even age.

To the master computer of the planet Harmony, however, the duration would be merely that: duration. It would not grow anxious. It would not count the days. It would set an alarm to notify itself when the earliest possible return might be looked for. Once the *Basilica* left and until the alarm went off, the master computer of the planet Harmony would not think of the starship again at all.

But the master computer of the starship *Basilica* would think of it. And already it was making plans to accomplish all its missions.

1

IF I SHOULD WAKE
BEFORE I DIE

ONE

QUARRELING WITH GOD

Vusadka: the place where humans first set foot when their starships brought them to the planet they named Harmony. Their starships settled to the ground; the first of the colonists disembarked and planted crops in the lush land to the south of the landing field. Eventually all the colonists came out of the ships, moved on, left them behind.

Left to themselves, the ships would eventually have oxidized, rotted, weathered away. But the humans who came to this place had eyes for the future. Someday our descendants may want these ships, they said. So they enclosed the landing place in a stasis field. No wind-driven dust, no rain or condensation, no direct sunlight or ultraviolet radiation would strike the ships. Oxygen, the most corrosive of all poisons, was removed from the atmosphere inside the dome. The master computer of the planet Harmony—called "the Oversoul" by the descendants of those first colonists—kept all humans far away from the large island where the ships were harbored. Within that protective bubble, the starships waited for forty million years.

Now, though, the bubble was gone. The air here was breathable. The landing field once again rang with the voices of human beings. And not just the somber adults who had first walked this ground—many of those scurrying back and forth from one ship or building to another were children. They were all hard at work, taking functional parts from the other ships to transform one of them into an operational starship. And when the ship they called *Basilica* was ready, all parts working, fully stocked and loaded, they would climb inside for the last time and leave this world where more than a million generations of their ancestors had lived, in order to return to Earth, the planet where human civilization had first appeared—but had lasted for fewer than ten thousand years.

What is Earth to us, Hushidh wondered, as she watched the children and adults at work. Why are we going to such lengths to return there, when Harmony is our home. Whatever ties once bound us there surely rusted away in all these intervening years.

Yet they would go, because the Oversoul had chosen them to go. Had bent and manipulated all their lives to bring them to this place at this time. Often Hushidh was glad of the attention the Oversoul had paid to them. But at other times, she resented the fact that they had not been left to work out the course of their own lives.

But if we have no ties to Earth, we have scarcely more to Harmony, thought Hushidh. And she alone of the people here could see that this observation was literally, not just figuratively, true. All the people here were chosen because they had particular sensitivity to the mental communications of the Oversoul; in Hushidh, this sensitivity took an odd form. She could look at people and sense immediately the strength of the relationships binding them to all the other people in their lives. It came to her as a waking vision: She could see the relationships like cords of light, tying one person to the others in her life.

For instance, her younger sister, Luet, the only blood relative Hushidh had known through all her growing-up years. As Hushidh rested in the shade, Luet came by, her daughter Chveya right behind her, carrying lunch into the starship for those who were working on the computers. All her life, Hushidh had seen her own connection to Lutya as the one great certainty. They grew up not knowing who their parents were, as virtual charity cases in Rasa's great teaching house in the city of Basilica. All fears, all slights, all uncertainties were bearable, though, because there was Lutya, bound to her by cords that were no weaker for being invisible to everyone but Hushidh.

There were other ties, too, of course. Hushidh well remembered how painful it had been to watch the bond develop between Luet and her husband, Nafai, a troublesome young boy who had more enthusiasm than sense sometimes. To her surprise, however, Lutya's new bond to her husband did not weaken her tie to Hushidh; and when Hushidh, in turn, married Nafai's full brother, Issib, the tie between her and Luet grew even stronger than it had been in childhood, something Hushidh had never thought possible.

So now, watching Luet and Chveya pass by, Hushidh saw them, not just as a mother and daughter, but as two beings of light, bound to each other by a thick and shimmering cord. There was no stronger bond than this. Chveya loved her father, Nafai, too—but the tie between children and their fathers was always more tentative. It was in the nature of the human family: Children looked to their mothers for nurturance, comfort, the secure foundation of their lives. To their fathers, however, they looked for judgment, hoping for approval, fearing condemnation. It meant that fathers were just as powerful in their children's lives, but no matter how loving and nurturing the father was, there was almost always an element of dread in the relationship, for the father became the focus of all the child's fears of failure. Not that there weren't exceptions now and then. Hushidh had simply learned to expect that in most cases, the tie with the mother was the strongest and brightest.

In her thoughts about the mother-daughter connection, Hushidh almost missed the thing that mattered. It was only as Luet and Chveya moved out of sight into the starship that Hushidh realized what had been almost missing: Lutya's connection to *her*.

But that was impossible. After all these years? And why would the tie be weaker now? There had been no quarrel. They were as close as ever, as far as Hushidh knew. Hadn't they been allies during all the long struggles between Luet's husband and his malicious older brothers? What could possibly have changed?

Hushidh followed Luet into the ship and found her in the pilothouse, where Issib, Hushidh's husband, was conferring with Luet's husband, Nafai, about the life support computer system. Computers had never interested her—it was reality that she cared about, people with flesh and blood, not artificial constructs fabricated of ones and zeroes. Sometimes she thought that men reveled in computers precisely because of their unreality. Unlike women and children, computers could be completely controlled. So she took some secret delight whenever she saw Issya or Nyef frustrated by a stubbornly willful program until they finally found the programming error. She also suspected that whenever one of their children was stubbornly willful, Issya believed in his heart of hearts that the problem was simply a matter of finding the error in the child's programming. Hushidh knew that it was not an error, but a soul inventing itself. When she tried to explain this to Issya, though, his eyes glazed over and he soon fled to the computers again.

Today, though, all was working smoothly enough. Luet and Chveya laid out the noon meal for the men. Hushidh, who had no particular errand, helped them— but then, when Luet started talking about the need to call the others working in the ship to come eat, Hushidh studiously ignored the hints and thus forced Luet and Chveya to go do the summoning.

Issib might be a man and he might prefer computers to children sometimes, but he did notice things. As soon as Luet and Chveya were gone, he asked, "Was it me you wanted to talk with, Shuya, or was it Nyef?"

She kissed her husband's cheek. "Nyef, of course. I already know everything you think."

"Before *I* even know it," said Issib, with mock chagrin. "Well, if you're going to talk privately, *you'll* have to leave. I'm busy, and I'm not leaving the room with the food on any account."

He did not mention that it was more trouble for him to get up and leave. Even though his lifts worked in the environs of the starships, so he wasn't confined to his chair, it still took much effort for Issib to do any major physical movement.

Nyef finished keying in some command or other, then got up from his chair and led Hushidh out into a corridor. "What is it?" he asked.

Hushidh got right to the point. "You know the way I see things," she said.

"You mean relationships among people? Yes, I know."

"I saw something very disturbing today."

He waited for her to go on.

"Luet is . . . well, cut off. Not from you. Not from Chveya. But from everybody else."

"What does that mean?"

"I don't know," said Hushidh. "I can't read minds. But it worries me. *You're* not cut off. You still—heaven knows why—you still are bound by ties of love and loyalty even to your repulsive oldest brothers, even to your sisters and their sad little husbands—"

"I see that you have nothing but respect for them yourself," said Nyef drily.

"I'm just saying that Luet used to have something of that same—whatever it is—sense of obligation to the whole community. She used to connect with everyone. Not like you, but with the women, perhaps even stronger. Definitely stronger. She was the caretaker of the women. Ever since she was found to be the Waterseer back in Basilica, she's had that. But it's gone."

"Is she pregnant again? She's not supposed to be. Nobody's supposed to be pregnant when we launch."

"It's not like that, it's not a withdrawal into self the way pregnant women do." Actually, Hushidh was surprised Nafai had remembered that. Hushidh had only mentioned it once, years ago, that pregnant women's connections with everyone around them weakened, as they focused inward on the child. It was Nafai's way—for days, weeks, months, he would seem to be an overgrown adolescent, gawky, apt to say the wrong thing at the wrong time, giving the impression of never being aware of other people's feelings. And then, suddenly, you'd realize that he was keenly aware all along, that he noticed and remembered practically everything. Which made you wonder if the times he was rude, he actually *meant* to be rude. Hushidh still hadn't decided about that.

"So what is it?"

"I thought you could tell *me*," said Hushidh. "Has Luet said anything that would make you think she was separating from everybody except for you and your children?"

He shrugged. "Maybe she has and I didn't notice. I don't always notice."

The very fact that he said so made Hushidh doubt it. He *did* notice, and therefore he *had* noticed. He just didn't want to talk to Hushidh about it.

"Whatever it is," said Hushidh, "you and she don't agree about it."

Nafai glared at her. "If you aren't going to believe what I say, why do you bother to ask me?"

"I keep hoping that someday you'll decide that I'm worthy to be trusted with the inner secrets."

"My, but we're feeling out of sorts today, aren't we," said Nafai.

It was when he started acting like a little brother that Hushidh most hated him. "I must mention to Luet sometime that she made a serious mistake when she stopped those women from putting you to death when you violated the sanctity of the lake back in Basilica."

"I'm of the same opinion," said Nafai. "It would have spared me the agony of watching you suffer through the distress of being my sister-in-law."

"I would rather give birth every day, that's how bad it is," said Hushidh.

He grinned at her. "I'll look into it," he said. "I honestly don't know why Luet would be separating herself from everybody else, and I think it's dangerous, and so I'll look into it."

So he was going to take her seriously, even if he wasn't going to tell her what he already thought the problem was. Well, that was about as much as she could hope for. Nafai might be leader of the community right now, but it wasn't because he had any particular skill at it. Elemak, Nafai's oldest brother, was the natural leader. It was only because Nafai had the Oversoul on his side—or, rather, because the Oversoul had Nafai on *her* side—that he had been given the power to rule. Authority didn't come easily to him and he wasn't always sure what to do with it—and what not to do. He made mistakes. Hushidh just hoped that this wouldn't be one of those times.

Potya would be hungry. She had to get back home. It was because Hushidh was nursing a newborn that she was spared most duties involved with preparing for launch. In fact, the schedule for the launch had been set up to accommodate her pregnancy. She and Rasa had been the last to get pregnant before they found out that no one could be pregnant during the voyage. That was because the chemicals and low temperature that would maintain almost all of them in suspended animation during the voyage could do terrible things to an embryo. Rasa's baby, a little girl she gave the too-cute name of Tsennyi, which meant "precious," had been born a month before Hushidh's third son and sixth child. Shyopot, she had named him. "Whisper." Potya as his dearname, his quickname. Coming at the last moment, like a breath of a word from the Oversoul. The last whisper in her heart before she left this world forever. Issib had thought the name was odd, but it was better then "precious," which they both thought was proof that Rasa had lost all sense of judgment and proportion. Potya was waiting, Potya would be hungry, Hushidh's breasts were telling her so with some urgency.

On the way out of the ship, however, she passed Luet, who greeted her cheerfully, sounding like she always did, as loving and sweet as ever. Hushidh wanted to slap her. Don't lie to me! Don't seem so normal when I know that you have cut yourself off from me in hour heart! If you can put on our affectionate closeness like a mask, then I'll never be able to take joy in it again.

"What's wrong?" asked Luet.

"What could be wrong?" asked Hushidh.

"You wear your heart on your face," said Luet, "at least to me. You're angry at me and I don't know why."

"Let's not have this conversation now," said Hushidh.

"When, then? What have I done?"

"That's exactly the question I'd like to know. What have you done? Or what are you planning to do?"

That was it. The slight flaring of Luet's eyelids, her

hesitation before showing a reaction, as if she were deciding what reaction she ought to show—Hushidh knew that it was something Luet was planning to do. She was plotting something, and whatever it was, it required her to become emotionally distant from everyone else in the community.

"Nothing," said Luet. "I'm no different from anyone else these days, Hushidh. I'm raising my children and doing my work to prepare for the voyage."

"Whatever it is you're plotting, Lutya," said Hushidh, "don't do it. It isn't worth it."

"You don't even know what you're talking about."

"True, but *you* know. And I'm telling you, it isn't worth cutting yourself off from the rest of us. It isn't worth cutting yourself off from *me*."

Luet looked stricken, and this, at least, was no sham. Unless everything was a sham and always had been. Hushidh couldn't bear to believe *that*.

"Shuya," said Luet, "have you seen that? Is it true? I didn't know, but maybe it's true, maybe I've already cut myself off from—oh, Shuya." Luet flung her arms around Hushidh.

Reluctantly—but why am I reluctant, she wondered—Hushidh returned the embrace.

"I won't," said Luet. "I won't do *anything* that would cut me off from you. I can't believe that I—can't you do something about it?"

"Do something?" asked Hushidh.

"You know, the way you did to Rashgallivak's men when he came to Aunt Rasa's door that time, meaning to carry her daughters away. You tore his men's loyalty from him and brought him down, just like that. Don't you remember?"

Hushidh remembered, all right. But that had been easy, for she could see that the ties between Rash and his men were very weak, and it took only a few well-placed words and a bit of attitude to fill them with contempt for him and cause them to abandon him on the spot. "It's not the same," said Hushidh. "I can't *make* people do things. I could strip Rash's men of their loyalty because they didn't really want to follow him anyway. I can't rebuild your ties to the rest of us. That's something you have to do yourself."

"But I want to," said Luet.

"What's going on?" asked Hushidh. "Just explain it to me."

"I can't," said Luet.

"Why not?"

"Because nothing *is* going on."

"But something's *going* to go on, is that it?"

"No!" said Luet, and now she sounded angry, adamant. "It will *not* happen. And therefore there's nothing to discuss." With that, Luet fled up the ladderway leading to the center of the ship, where the meal was waiting, where the others were gathering.

It's the Oversoul, Hushidh knew then. The Oversoul has told Luet to do something that she doesn't want to do. And if she does it, it will cut her off from all the rest of us. From everybody except her husband and children. What is it? What is the Oversoul up to?

And whatever it was, why hadn't the Oversoul included Hushidh in it?

For the first time, Hushidh found herself thinking of the Oversoul as an enemy. For the first time, Hushidh discovered that she herself did not have any strong ties of loyalty to the Oversoul. Just like that, mere suspicion had dissolved them. What are you doing to me and my sister, Holy One? Whatever it is, cut it out.

But no answer came to her. Just silence.

The Oversoul has chosen Luet to do something, and she has *not* chosen me. What is it? I have to know. Because if it's something terrible, I'm going to put a stop to it.

Luet did not like the building they lived in these days. Hard surfaces everywhere, smooth and unalive. She missed the wooden house they had lived in for eight years in their little village of Dostatok, before her husband found and opened the ancient starport of Vusadka. And before that, all her memories were of living in Rasa's house in Basilica. City of women, city of grace; she yearned sometimes for the mists of the hidden and holy lake, for the noise of the crowded markets, for the endless rows of buildings elbowing their way out over the street. But this place—had the builders ever thought of it as beautiful? Had they liked to live in such dead places?

Yet it *was* home, all the same, because here was where her children gathered to sleep, to eat; where Nafai finally came home so late at night, to curl up wearily beside her on their bed. And when the time came to enter the starship they had named *Basilica*, she would no doubt miss this place also, the memories of frenzied work and excited children and groundless fears. *If* the fears turned out to be groundless.

Returning to Earth—what did that mean, when no human had been there for millions of years? And those dreams that kept coming into their minds, dreams of giant rats that seemed to be filled with a malevolent intelligence, dreams of batlike creatures who seemed to be allies but were still ugly beyond belief. Even the Oversoul did not know what those dreams meant, or why the Keeper of Earth might have sent them. Still, the overall impression Luet got from everyone's dreams of Earth was that it was not going to be a paradise when they got there.

What really frightened her, though—and, she suspected, frightened everyone else, too—was the voyage itself. A hundred years asleep? And supposedly they would emerge without having aged a day? It seemed like something out of a myth, like the poor girl who pricked her finger on a mouse's tooth and fell asleep, only to find that when she woke up, all the rich and beautiful girls were fat old ladies, while she remained the most youthful and beautiful of all. But still poor. That was an odd ending to that story, Luet always thought, that she was still poor. Surely there ought to be some version of it in which the king chose her because of her beauty instead of marrying the richest woman to get his hands on her estate. But that had nothing to do with what she was worrying about right now. Why had her mind wandered so far afield? Oh, yes. Because she was thinking about the voyage. About lying down on the ship and letting the life support system poke needles into her and freeze her for the voyage. How did they know that they wouldn't simply die?

Well, they could have died a thousand times since things first started falling apart in Basilica. Instead they had lived this long, and the Oversoul had led them to this place, and so far things were working out reasonably well. They had their children. They had prospered. No one had died or even been seriously injured. Ever since Nafai had got the starmaster's cloak from the Oversoul, even Elemak and Mebbekew, his hate-filled older brothers, had been relatively cooperative—and it was well-known that they *hated* the idea of voyaging back to Earth.

So why was the Oversoul so grimly determined to ruin everything?

<I'm grimly determined to save your lives, you and your husband.> Here in this place where the Oversoul actually lived, Luet heard the voice of the Oversoul far more easily than she ever had back in Basilica.

"The starmaster's cloak will protect Nafai," Luet murmured. "And he will protect us."

<And when he's old? When Elemak has taught his sons to hate you and your children? It's elementary mathematics, Luet. When the division of your community comes—and it *will* come—on the one side there will be Elemak and his four sons, Mebbekew and his son, Obring and his two sons, Vas and his son. Four strong adult males, eight boys. And on your side, who?

Your husband, of course. But who are his allies? His father, Volemak?>

"Old," murmured Luet.

<Yes, too old. And Issib is a frail cripple from birth. The only other man is Zdorab, and how can you guess where he will stand?>

"Even if he stood with Nafai, he isn't much."

<So you see the problem. Even with your four sons, Issib's three, and Volemak's two, it isn't going to be much of an army. Anyway, Elemak will strike soon, before any of the children are old enough to matter. So it's four strong and brutal men against one man who is *not* strong and *not* brutal.>

"Only if Nafai fails to hold everyone together."

<Elemak is only biding his time. I *know* this. And so you *will* persuade him to do as I have shown you. . . . >

"*You* persuade him."

<He won't listen to me.>

"That's because he knows that your plan would be a disaster. It would cause the very thing that you claim to be trying to prevent."

<Of course there will be some resentment. . . . >

"Resentment! Oh, just a little. We reach Earth and all the adults are wakened from suspended animation, only to discover—oops!—Nafai and Luet somehow neglected to go into suspended animation themselves, and—oops again!—they somehow got a dozen of the older children to stay awake with them for the whole ten years of the voyage! So you see, my dear sister Shuya, when you went to bed your daughter Dza was only eight years old, but now she's eighteen, and married to Padarok, who, by the way, is seventeen now—sorry about that, Shedemei and Zdorab, we knew you wouldn't mind if we raised your only son for you. And while we had these children up, we happened to spend the whole time teaching them, so that now they are experts on everything they'll need to know to build our colony. They're also large and strong enough to do adult work. But—oops again!—none of *your* children, Eiadh and Kokor and Sevet and Dol, none of *yours* has had *any* of this training. *Yours* are still little children who won't be much help at all."

<I see that you have thought through every aspect of the plan. Why can't you see that it is both necessary and flawless?>

"They'll be furious," said Luet. "They'll all hate us—Volemak and Rasa and Issib and Shuya and Shedemei and Zdorab because we stole their oldest children from them, and all the others because we *didn't* give the same advantage to *their* children."

<They will be angry, but those who are my trusted friends will soon come to understand the necessity of having their children be older and stronger. It will change the balance of physical power in the community. It will keep you all alive.>

"They'll always be sure that the only reason the community broke apart was because Nafai and I did such a terrible thing. They'll hate us and blame us and they will certainly never *trust* us again."

<I will tell them that it was my idea.>

"And they'll say that you're just a computer and of course you didn't understand how humans would feel, but *we* understood, and *we* should have refused to do it."

<Perhaps you should. But you won't refuse.>

"I already refused. I refuse again now."

<You refuse with your mouth and with your mind, but Hushidh saw that in your heart, you are already making ready to obey me.>

"No!" cried Luet.

"Mother?" It was Chveya's voice, through the door of Luet's room.

"What is it, Veya?"

"Who are you talking to?"

"Myself, in a dream. All foolishness. Go back to sleep."

"Is Father home yet?"

"Still in the ship with Issib."

"Mother?"

"Go to sleep now, Chveya. I mean it."

She heard the scuffing sound of Chveya's sandals on the floor. What had Chveya heard? How long had she been listening at the door?

<She heard everything.>

Why didn't you warn me?

<Why did you speak out loud? I hear your thoughts.>

Because when I speak out loud my thoughts are clearer, that's why. What's your plan, to get Chveya to carry out your plot?

<Since you won't discuss it with Nafai, I woke Chveya to hear what you were saying. She'll bring it up with him.>

Why couldn't you just talk to him yourself?

<He won't listen to me.>

That's because he's a very wise man. That's why I love him.

<He needs another perspective. You would have been best. Chveya will do.>

You leave my children alone.

<Your children are people in their own right. When you were Chveya's age, you already were known as the Waterseer of Basilica. I didn't notice you complaining that I had such a relationship with you then. And when Chveya first started getting dreams from the Keeper of Earth, I seem to recall that you rejoiced.>

"And to think I once thought of you as . . . as a *god*."

<And what do you think I am now?>

"If I didn't know you were a computer program, I'd say you were a meddlesome, loathsome old bitch."

<You can be angry at me if you like. It doesn't hurt my feelings I even understand. But you have to take the long view, Luet. I do.>

"Yes, your view is so long that you hardly notice how you ruin the lives of little mayflies like us."

\<Has your life been so terrible up to now?\>

"Let's just say that it hasn't gone as expected."

\<But has it been so terrible?\>

"Shut up and leave me alone."

Luet threw herself back down on the bed and tried to sleep. But she kept remembering: *Hushidh saw that I am no longer connected to the others in the community. That means that somewhere in my heart I already have the unconscious intention of doing what the Oversoul has planned. So I might as well give up and do it consciously.*

Do it and then spend the rest of my life knowing that my sister and Aunt Rasa and dear Shedemei all hate me and that I absolutely, completely deserve their hatred.

TWO

THE FACE OF THE OLD ONE

Everyone expected that Kiti's sculpture this year would be a portrait of his otherself, kTi. That was Kiti's intention, too, right up to the moment when he found his clay by the riverbank and set to work, prying and loosening it with his spear. There had been no more beloved young man in the village than kTi, none more hoped-for; there was talk that one of the great ladies would choose him for her husband, an offer of life-marriage, extraordinary for one so young. If that had happened, then Kiti, as kTi's otherself, would have been taken into the marriage as well. After all, since he and kTi were identical, it made no difference which of them might be the sire of a particular child.

But he and kTi were not identical, Kiti knew. Oh, their bodies were the same, as with every other birthpair. Since about a quarter of all birthpairs both lived to maturity, it wasn't all that rare to have two identical young men preparing to offer themselves to the ladies of the village, to be taken or rejected as a pair.

So by custom and courtesy, everyone showed Kiti the same respect they showed his otherself. But everyone knew that it was kTi, not Kiti who had earned their reputation for cleverness and strength.

I wasn't entirely right for kTi to get all the credit for cleverness. Often when the two of them were flying together, watching over one of the village herds or scouting for devils or chasing crows away from the maizefields, it was Kiti who said, One of the goats is bound to try to go that way, or, That tree is one that's likely for the devils to use. And at the beginning of their most famous exploit, it was Kiti who said, Let me pretend to be injured on that branch, while you wait with your spear on that higher perch. But when the story was told, it always seemed to be kTi who thought of everything. Why should people assume otherwise? It was always kTi who acted, it was always kTi whose boldness carried the day, while Kiti followed behind, helping, sometimes saving, but never leading.

Of course he could never explain this to anyone. It would be deeply shameful for one of a birthpair to try to take glory away from his otherself. And besides, as far as Kiti was concerned it was perfectly fair. For no matter how good an idea of Kiti's might have been, it was always kTi's boldness that brought it off.

Why did it turn out that way? Kiti wasn't lacking in courage, was he? Didn't he always fly right with kTi on his most daring adventures? Wasn't it Kiti who had to sit trembling on a branch, pretending to be injured and terrified, as he heard the faint sounds of a devildoor opening in the tree trunk and the tiny noises of the devil's hands and feet inching their way along the branch behind him? Why was it that no one realized that the greatest courage was the courage to sit still, waiting, trusting that kTi would come with his spear in time? No, the story that was told in the village was all about kTi's daring plan, kTi's triumph over the devil.

It was evil of me to be so angry, thought Kiti. That's

why my otherself was taken from me. That's why when the storm caught us out in the open, kTi was the one whose feet and fingers Wind pried away from the branch, kTi was who was taken up into heaven to fly with the gods. Kiti was not worthy, and so his grip on the branch help until Wind went away. It was as if Wind were saying to him, You envied your otherself, so I have torn you apart to show you how worthless you are without him.

This was why Kiti meant to sculpt the face of his otherself. And this was why, in the end, he could not. For to sculpt the face of kTi was also to sculpt his own face, and he could not, in his deep unworthiness, bear to do that.

Yet he had to sculpt something. Already the saliva was flowing in his mouth to moisten the clay, to lick it and smooth it, to give a lustrous patina to the finished sculpture. But if he did not sculpt his otherself's face, so soon after kTi's death, it would be scandalous. He would be seen as lacking in natural affection. The ladies would think that he didn't love his brother, and so they wouldn't want his seed in their family. Only some mere woman would offer to him. And he, overwhelmed with clay fever, would accept that offer like any eager boy, and she would bear his children, and he would look at them every year from then on remembering that he was the father of such low children because he could not bring himself to sculpt the face of his beloved kTi.

I did love him, he insisted silently. With all my heart I loved him. Didn't I follow him wherever he decided? Didn't I trust him with my life again and again? Didn't I save him time after time, when his impetuosity brought him into peril? Didn't I even urge him to turn back, a storm was coming, let's find shelter, we have to find shelter, what does it matter if we find the devilpath on this flight or the next, turn back, turn back, and he wouldn't, he ignored me as if I didn't exist, as if I were *nothing*, as if I didn't even get a vote on my own survival, let alone his.

The clay was growing moist, balling up and beginning to flow in his hands, but it was as much tears as saliva that moistened it. O Wind, thou tookest my otherself, and now I cannot find his face in the clay. Give me a shape, O Wind, if I am worthy! O Maize, if I am to bring you daughters to tend your fields, then give my fingers knowledge even if my mind is dull! O Rain, flow with my saliva and my tears and make the clay live under my hands! O Earth, thou deep-burning mother, make my bones wise, for they will someday belong to you again. Let me bring other bones, young bones, child bones out of your clay, O Earth! Let me bring young wings into your hands, O Wind! Let me make new grains of life for thee, O Maize! Let me bring new waterdrinkers, new weepers, new sculptors for thee to taste, O Rain!

Yet despite his pleading, the gods put no shape under his hands.

His tears blinded him. Should he give up? Should he fly up into the sky of the dry season and search for some faraway village that might want a sturdy male and never see Da'aqebla again? Or should his despair go even further? Should he put the clay out of his hands and yet remain there at the riverbank, exposed, for the watching devils to see that he had no sculpture in him? Then they would take him like an infant back to their caves, and devour him alive, so that in his dying moments he would see the devil queen eating his own heart. That was how his end should come. Carried down into hell, because he was not worthy to be taken by Wind up into heaven. kTi would have all the honor then, and not have to share it with his low, unworthy otherself.

His fingers worked, though he could not see what they shaped.

And as they worked, he stopped mourning his own

failure, for he realized that there *was* a shape now under his hands. It was being given to him, in a way that he had only heard about. As a child, playing at sculpture with the other boys, he had been the cleverest every time, but he had never felt the gods interceding with his hands. What he shaped was always from his own mind and memory.

Now, though, he didn't even know what it was that was growing under his hands, not at first. But soon, no longer grieving, no longer fearful, his vision cleared and he saw. It was a head. A strange head, not of a person or a devil or any creature Kiti had ever seen before. It had a high forehead, and its nose was pointed, hairless, smooth, the nostrils opening downward. Of what use was such a snout as this? The lips were thick and the jaw was incredibly strong, the chin jutting out as if it was competing with the nose to lead this creature forward into the world. The ears were rounded and stuck out from the middle of the sides of the head. What kind of creature is this that I am shaping? Why is something so ugly growing under my hands?

Then, suddenly, the answer came into his mind: This is an Old One.

His wings trembled even as his hands continued, sure and strong, to shape the details of the face. An Old One. How could he know this? No one had ever seen an Old One. Only here and there, in some sheltered cave, was there found some inexplicable relic of their time upon the earth. Da'aqebla had only three such relics, and Da'aqebla was one of the oldest villages. How could he dare to tell the ladies of the village that this grotesque, malformed head that he was shaping was an Old One? They would laugh at him. No, they would be outraged that he would think they were foolish enough to believe such a nonsensical claim. How can we judge your sculpture, if you insist on shaping something that has never been seen by any living soul? You might have done better to leave the clay in a shapeless ball and say that it was a sculpture of a river stone!

Despite his doubts, his hands and fingers moved. He knew, without knowing how he knew, that there must be hair on the bony ridge over the eyes, that the fur of the head must be long, that there must be a depression centered under the nose and leading down to the lip. And when he was through, he did not know how he knew that it was finished. He contemplated what he had made and was appalled by it. It was ugly, strange, and far too large. Yet this way how it had to be.

What have you done to me, O gods?

He still sat, contemplating the head of the Old One, when the ladies came soaring, swooping down to the riverbank. At the fringes were the men whose sculptures had already been seen. Kiti knew them all, of course, and could easily guess at what their work was like. A couple of them were husbands, and because their lady was married to them for life their sculptures were no longer in competition with the others. Some of them were young, like Kiti, offering sculptures for the first time—and from their slightly hangdog expressions, Kiti could tell that they hadn't made the impression that they hoped for. Nevertheless, the clay fever was on all the males, and so they hardly looked at him or his sculpture; their eyes were on the ladies.

The ladies stared in silence at his sculpture. Some of them moved, to study it from another angle. Kiti knew that the workmanship of his sculpture was exceptionally good, and that the sheer size of it was audacious. He felt the clay fever stirring within him, and all the ladies looked beautiful to him. He saw their skeptical expressions with dread—he longed now for them to choose him.

Finally the silence was broken. "What is this supposed to be?" whispered a lady. Kiti looked for the voice. It was Upua, a lady who had never married and who, in some years, had not even mated. It gave her a reputation for being arrogant, the hardest of the ladies to please. Of course she would be the lady who would interrogate him in front of all the others.

"It grew under my hands," he said, not daring to tell them what it really was.

"Everyone thought that you would do honor to your otherself," said another lady, emboldened by Upua's disdainful question.

The hardest question. He dared not dodge it. Did he dare to tell the truth? "I meant to, but it was also my own face, and I wasn't worthy to have my face sculpted in the clay."

There was a murmur at that. Some thought that was a stupid reason; some thought it was deceptive; some gave it thought.

Finally the ladies began deciding. "Not for me." "Ugly." "Very odd." "Interesting." Whatever their comment, they took flight, rising up and circling, drifting toward the branches of the nearest trees. The men, no doubt feeling quite triumphant at the complete rejection of the supposedly talented Kiti, joined them there.

At last only Kiti and Upua remained upon the riverbank.

"I know what this is," said Upua.

Kiti dared not answer.

"This is the head of an Old One," she said.

Her voice carried to the ladies and men in the branches. They heard her, and many gasped or whistled their astonishment.

"Yes, Lady Upua," said Kiti, ashamed at having his arrogance caught out. "But it was given to me under my hands. I never meant to sculpt such a thing."

Upua said nothing for a long time, walking around the sculpture, circling it again and again.

"The day is short!" called one of the leading ladies from her perch in the trees.

Upua looked up at her, startled. "I'm sorry," she

said. "I wanted to see this and remember it, because we have been given a great gift by the gods, to see the face of the Old Ones."

There was some laughter at this. Did she really think Kiti could somehow sculpt what no one had ever seen?

She turned to Kiti, who was so filled with clay fever now that he could only barely keep himself from throwing himself at her feet and begging her to let him mate with her.

"Marry me," she said.

Surely he had misunderstood.

"Marry me," she said again. "I want only your children from now on until I die."

"Yes," he said.

No other man had been so honored in a thousand years. On his first sculpting, to be offered marriage, and by a lady of such prestige? Many of the others, ladies and men alike, were outraged. "Nonsense, Lady Upua," said another of the leading ladies. "You cheapen the institution of marriage by offering it to one so young, and for such a ridiculous sculpture."

"He has been given the face of an Old One by the gods. Let all of you come down here and study this sculpture again. We will not leave here for two songs, so that all of us will remember the face of the Old Ones and we can teach our children what we've seen this day."

And because she was the lady who had offered marriage and been accepted on this spot, the others had to do her will for the space of two songs. They studied the head of the Old One, and together Kiti and Upua entered into the legends of the village of Da'aqebla forever. They also entered into marriage, and Kiti, who would have trembled at the thought of being the husband of such a terrifying lady, would soon learn that she was a kind and loving wife, and that to be an attentive and protective husband to her would bring him only joy. He would still miss kTi from time to time after that, but never again would he think that Wind had punished him by not catching him up to heaven with kTi.

On this day, however, they did not know what the future would bring. They only knew that Kiti was the boldest sculptor who had ever lived, and because his boldness had won him a lady as his wife, it raised him at once in their estimation. He was truly kTi's otherself, and though kTi was taken from them, in Kiti his courage and cleverness would live on until, with age, they would become strength and wisdom.

When the two songs had passed, when the flock of ladies and men arose and went on to the next man, dark shapes emerged from the shadows of the trees. They, too, circled the strange sculpture, and then finally picked it up and carried it away, though it was uncommonly large and heavy and they did not understand it.

THREE

SECRETS

It just slipped out. Chveya didn't intend to tell anyone what she had heard outside Mother's door last
night. She could keep a secret. Even a devastating secret
like the fact that Mother was planning for Dazya to
grow up and marry Rokya during the voyage. What did
that mean, that Chveya was supposed to marry Proya or
something? That would be fun, wouldn't it. He should
marry Dazya, so the two bossiest children could boss
each other to their heart's content. Why did Chveya's
own mother want Dazya to get the best boy who
wasn't a double first cousin?

Chveya was still brooding about this when Dazya
started yelling at her for some stupid thing—leaving a
door open that Dazya wanted closed, or closing it when
Dazya wanted it open—and Chveya just blurted out,
"Oh, shut up, Dazya, you're going to grow up and
marry Rokya during the voyage anyway, so you can at
least let me decide about doors."

And it wasn't Chveya's fault that Rokya happened to

be coming through the door with his father right then, carrying baskets of bread to be frozen for the voyage.

"What are you talking about?" said Rokya. "I wouldn't marry *either* of you."

It wasn't Rokya's reaction that worried Chveya. It was Rokya's father, little Zdorab. "Why are you thinking about who will marry Padarok?" asked Zdorab.

"He's just the only one who's not a cousin or something," said Chveya, blushing.

"Veya always thinks about marriage," said Dazya. Then, helpfully, she added, "She's sick in the head."

"You're only eight years old," said Zdorab, smiling with amusement. "Why would you think marriages would be happening during the voyage?"

Chveya clamped her mouth shut and shrugged. She knew that she shouldn't have repeated anything she heard outside her mother's door. If she said nothing more now, perhaps Zdorab and Rokya and Dazya would forget about it and then Mother would never know that Chveya was a spy and a blabber.

Elemak listened to Zdorab impassively. Mebbekew was not so calm. "I should have known. Planning to steal our children from us!"

"I doubt it," said Elemak.

"You heard him!" cried Mebbekew. "You don't think *Chveya* would invent this scheme of keeping children awake so they'd grow up during the voyage, do you?"

"I mean," said Elemak, "that I doubt Nyef would choose to keep *our* children awake."

"Why not? He could have ten years to poison their minds against us."

"He knows that if he did that to me, I would kill him," said Elemak.

"And he knows that *I* would *not*," said Zdorab. "Imagine—telling his daughter about it, but not even mentioning a hint of it to us."

Elemak thought about that for a moment. Such carelessness wouldn't be unheard of in Nafai, but still he doubted it. "It may not be Nafai's plan, you know. It might be Chveya's mother. Perhaps the Waterseer still misses the influence she had back in Basilica."

"Perhaps she fancies the idea of running a school like her mother did," said Mebbekew.

"But what can we do about it, anyway?" asked Zdorab. "He has the cloak of the starmaster. He has the Index. He controls the ship. No matter what he says, what's to stop him from waking our children during the voyage and doing whatever he wants?"

"The food supply isn't infinite," said Elemak. "He can't wake everybody."

"Think about it, though," said Mebbekew. "What if we wake up and his son Zhatva is a tall seventeen-year-old? Nyef was tall at that age. While our children are still little. And Father's last two boys, Oykib and Yasai. And your Padarok, Zdorab."

Zdorab smiled wanly. "Padarok won't be tall."

"He'll be a man. It's not a stupid plan," said Mebbekew. "He'll have indoctrinated them during the voyage to see things his way."

Elemak nodded. He had already thought of all this. "The question is, what will we do about it?"

"Stay awake ourselves."

Elemak shook his head. "He's already said that the ship won't launch until everyone but him is asleep."

"Then we won't go at all!" said Mebbekew. "Let him take off for Earth and as soon as he's gone, we can take our families back to Basilica."

"Meb," said Elemak, "have you forgotten that we aren't rich anymore? Life in Basilica would be miserable. If they didn't throw us in prison. Or kill us on sight."

"And the journey would be miserable, with little children," added Zdorab. "Not to mention the fact that Shedemei and I don't want to do that."

"So fly with Nafai," said Mebbekew. "I don't care what you do."

Elemak listened to Mebbekew with disgust. What kind of fool *was* he, anyway? Zdorab had brought them the story of what Chveya had said. Zdorab had never been an ally before, but now, his children threatened, they had a good chance to wean him away from Nafai for good. Then Nafai's party would consist only of himself, Father, and Issib—in other words, Nyef, the old man, and the cripple.

"Zdorab," said Elemak, "I take this very seriously. I think that we have no choice but to seem to go along with Nafai's plans. But surely there's some way to get into the ship's computer and set it up to waken us well into the voyage, at a time when Nafai will think he's having everything his own way and so he won't be expecting us. The suspended animation chambers are far from the living quarters of the ship. What do you think?"

"I think that's stupid," said Mebbekew. "Have you forgotten what the ship's computer *is*?"

"Is it?" Elemak asked Zdorab. "Is the ship's computer identical with the so-called Oversoul?"

"Well," said Zdorab, "when you think about it, maybe not. I mean, the Oversoul was set into place *after* the starships first came here. He's loading part of himself into the ship's computers, but he's not as familiar with it as he is with the hardware he's been inhabiting for the past forty million years."

"*He*," muttered Mebbekew scornfully. "*It*, you mean."

Elemak never let his gaze waver from Zdorab's face.

"Um," said Zdorab. "I'm not sure. But I don't think the original voyagers would have . . . I mean, they didn't turn their *own* lives over to the Oversoul. It was the next generation, not themselves. So maybe the ship's computers. . . ."

"And maybe," said Elemak, "if you find some way to be clever about it."

"Misdirection," said Zdorab. "There's a calendar program, for scheduling events during the voyage. Course corrections, and so on. But the Oversoul would be checking that often, I imagine."

"Think about it," said Elemak. "It's really not the sort of thing I do well."

Zdorab preened visibly. Elemak had expected that. Zdorab, like all weak and studious little men, was flattered to have the respect of someone like Elemak, a large, strong man, a leader, charismatic and dangerous. It was easy to win him over. After all these years of seeing Zdorab in Nafai's pocket, it had been astonishingly easy after all. It took patience. Waiting. Burning no bridges.

"I'm counting on you," said Elemak. "But whatever you do, don't talk about it afterward. Not even to me. Who knows what the computer can hear?"

"As in, for instance, it's probably heard everything we said here," said Mebbekew snottily.

"As I say, Zdorab, do your best. It might not be possible. But if you can do *something*, it's more than Meb or I can do."

Zdorab nodded thoughtfully.

He's mine now, thought Elemak. I have him. No matter what happens, Nyef has lost him, and all because he or his wife didn't keep their mouths shut in front of their children. Weak and foolish, that's what Nafai was. Weak, foolish, and unfit to lead.

And if he did anything to harm Elemak's children, then it wouldn't be just Nafai's position of leadership that he'd lose. But then, it was only a matter of time, anyway. Perhaps after Father died, but the day would come when all the insults and humiliations would be redressed. Men of honor do not forgive their lying, cheating, spying, traitorous enemy.

* * *

"Let's take a walk," said Nafai to Luet.

She smiled at him. "Aren't we tired enough already?"

"Let's take a walk," he said again.

He led her from the maintenance building where they all lived, out across the hard, flat ground of the landing field. He led her, not toward the starships, but out into the open, until they were far from anyone else.

"Luet," he said.

"Oh," she said. "We're upset about something."

"I don't know about us," he said. "But *I'm* upset."

"What did I do?"

"I don't know if you did anything," he said. "But Zdorab entered a wake-up date into the ship's calendar."

"Why would he do that?"

"He set it for halfway through the voyage. It was to wake up him. And Shedemei. And Elemak."

"Elemak?"

"Why would Zdorab do that?" asked Nafai.

"I have no idea," said Luet.

"Well, can you think about it for a minute? Can you think about something that you might know, that might allow you to figure it out?"

Luet was getting angry now. "What is this, Nafai? If you know something, if you want to accuse me of something, then—"

"But I don't know anything," said Nafai. "The Oversoul told me about finding Zdorab's little wake-up schedule. And then I said, Why? And then he said, Ask Luet."

Luet blushed. Nafai raised an eyebrow. "So," he said. "Now it all comes together?"

"It's the Oversoul that's playing games with us."

"Oh, really?" said Nafai.

"It shouldn't surprise us," said Luet. "That's what she's been doing all along."

"Do you mind letting me know what the game is this time?"

"It has to be related, though I don't see . . . oh, yes I do. Chveya heard me."

Nafai put his fingers to his forehead. "Oh, now it's all clear. Chveya heard you *what?*"

"Talking to the Oversoul. Last night. About—you know."

"No, I don't know."

"You can't be serious," she said.

"More serious by the minute."

"You mean the Oversoul hasn't even brought it up with you? About keeping the children awake on the voyage?"

"Don't be absurd. We don't have enough supplies to keep everybody awake. It's ten years!"

"I don't know," said Luet. "The Oversoul said that we had enough supplies to keep you and me and twelve of the children awake through most of the voyage."

"And why would we do that?" asked Nafai. "The whole point of the suspended animation is that ten years in a starship will be incredibly boring. *I'm* not even planning to be awake the whole time. Should our children spend ten years of their lives—more than half!—sitting around inside that metal pot?"

"The Oversoul never talked to you about it," she said. "That makes me so angry."

Nafai looked at her, waiting for an explanation.

"It would be our older children, all but the twins, and Shuya's down to Netsya, and Shedemei's boy and girl, and your brothers Oykib and Yasai."

"Why not the little ones?"

"You can't spend your first two years of life in low gravity."

"It can't work," said Nafai. "Even if the others would stand for it, the children would have no one their own age to marry except Shedya's two. The rest would be siblings or double first cousins or, at the best, Oykib and Yasai, and they're single first cousins."

"Nyef, I've said this to her over and over. Do you

think I don't know what a stupid idea it is? That's what Chveya must have heard last night. I was arguing with the Oversoul."

"You don't have to talk out loud to the Oversoul, Luet," he said.

"*I* do," she said.

"Well, whatever happened, Zdorab apparently thinks he has to wake up in the middle of the voyage to check up on me."

"I imagine he's angry," said Luet.

"Well, there's only one thing we can do." Nafai took her by the hand. They headed back to the maintenance building.

It took only a few minutes to gather all the adults into the kitchen, surrounding the large table where they ate their meals in shifts. As usual, Elemak looked quietly annoyed, while Mebbekew was openly hostile. "What's all this?" he demanded. "Can't we even go to sleep at a normal hour anymore?"

"There's something that needs straightening out right now," said Nafai.

"Oh, did one of us do something bad?" asked Meb, tauntingly.

"No," said Nafai. "But some of you think that Luet is planning something—no, come to think of it, you probably think that *I'm* planning it—and I want to get it out in the open right now."

"Openness," said Hushidh. "What a novel idea."

Nafai ignored her. "Apparently the Oversoul has been trying to persuade Luet that we should do something foolish with some of the children on the voyage."

"Foolish?" Volemak, Nafai's father, looked puzzled.

"Foolish," said Nafai. "Like keeping some of them awake during the voyage."

"But that would be so boring for them" said Nafai's older sister, Kokor.

Nafai did not answer her, just looked around from face to face. It was gratifying to see that even Elemak, who surely knew about the idea of keeping children awake and understood all the implications, was not looking a bit surprised by what Nafai was doing. "I know that some of you were aware of this even before I was. The only reason I found out about it at all was because the Oversoul found the wake-up signal you put into the ship's calendar, Zdorab."

Mebbekew's quick glance at Zdorab, and his equally quick glance away, confirmed that he, too, had known about the wake-up signal. He probably even thought Zdorab's little alarm clock would wake him up along with the others. But of course Zdorab knew that waking Mebbekew would be useless. If only Meb understood the contempt that everyone held him in. But then, he probably did, which was why he was so relentlessly belligerent.

"I think, Zdorab, that it's a good idea," said Nafai. "Of course the Oversoul removed your wake-up signal, but I will put a new one in. At midpoint of the voyage, all the adults will be wakened. Just for a day, so you can inspect all your sleeping children and make sure that they're the age they were when you left them. I can't think of any better way for you to make sure that the Oversoul did not get his way in this."

Volemak chuckled. "Do you really think you can fool the Oversoul?"

Luet spoke up. "The Oversoul understands many things, but she is not a human being. She doesn't understand what it would cost us, if our children's childhood was taken away from us. How would you feel, Aunt Rasa, if you woke up and found that Okya and Yaya were eighteen- and seventeen-year-old men? That you had missed all the years in between?"

Rasa smiled thinly. "I would never forgive anyone who did that to me. Even the Oversoul."

"I was trying to explain that to the Oversoul. She doesn't understand human feelings sometimes."

"Sometimes?" murmured Elemak.

"I . . . I spoke out loud. In the privacy of my room. Nafai was working late. But Chveya got up and she must have listened for a rather long time before she knocked."

"Are you saying that *your* daughter is a *sneak*?" said Mebbekew, pretending to be shocked.

Luet didn't look at him. "Chveya didn't understand what she was hearing. I'm sorry that it caused everyone to be disturbed. I know some of you knew about it, and some of you did not, but when Nafai learned about it a few minutes ago he and I rushed back here and . . . here we are."

"Tomorrow, Zdorab can verify that the wake-up signal is set for midvoyage. The only way that it won't wake us up is if the Oversoul cancels it during one of the many times that I'll be asleep myself. But I don't think that's likely, because as soon as I woke up again, I'd waken you all myself manually. I'm telling you now, once and for all, that there will be no games played with the passage of time. Our children will be, when we arrive, the same ages they were when they left. The only person who will have aged during the voyage is me, and believe me, I have no interest in aging any more than the minimum necessary to operate the ship safely."

"Why are you needed awake at all?" asked Obring, Kokor's husband, a little snake of a man, in Nafai's considered opinion.

"The ships weren't designed to be run by the Oversoul," said Nafai. "In fact, the Oversoul's program wasn't fully written until after the original fleet arrived on Harmony. The computers here can hold the Oversoul's program, but no single program is able to control all the computers on the ship at once. It's for safety. Redundancy. The systems can't all fail at once. Anyway, there are things that I have to do from time to time."

"That *someone* has to do," murmured Elemak.

"I have the cloak," said Nafai. "And that point was

settled a while ago, I think. Do you really want to dredge up old arguments?"

Nobody wanted to, apparently.

"Son," said Volemak, "you won't be able to stop the Oversoul from doing what it knows is right."

"The Oversoul is wrong," said Nafai. "It's that simple. None of you would ever forgive me if I obeyed the Oversoul in this."

"That's right," said Mebbekew.

"And I would never forgive myself," said Nafai. "So the issue is closed. Zdorab will see the calendar tomorrow, and he and anybody else who cares can look at it again just before we launch."

"That's very kind of you," said Elemak. "I think we can all sleep more easily tonight knowing that nothing is being planned behind our backs. Thank you for being so honest and open with us." He arose from the table.

"No," said Volemak. "You can't get away with rebellion against the Oversoul. No one can! Not even you, Nafai."

"You and Nafai can discuss this all you want, Father," said Elemak. "But Edhya and I are going to bed." He got up from the table and, putting his arm around his wife, led her out of the room. Most of the others followed—Kokor and her husband Obring, Sevet and her husband Vas, Meb and his wife Dolya. On their way out, Hushidh and Issib stopped for a few words with Nafai and Luet. "Very good idea," Hushidh said, "calling everybody together like this. It was very persuasive. Except that Elemak won't believe anything you do. So it just convinced him you were being devious."

"Thanks for the instant analysis," Luet said nastily.

"I appreciate it," Nafai said quickly. "I don't expect Elemak to take anything I do at face value."

"I just wanted you to know," said Hushidh, "that the barrier between you and Elemak is stronger and deeper than any bond between any two people here. In a way that's a kind of bond, too. But if you thought that this little scene today was going to win him over, you failed."

"And what about you?" said Luet. "Did it win you over?"

Hushidh smiled wanly. "I still see you separated from everyone else except your husband and children, Luet. When *that* changes, I'll start believing your husband's promises." Then she turned and left. Issib smiled and shrugged helplessly and drifted out after her.

Zdorab and Shedemei lingered. "Nafai," said Zdorab, "I want to apologize. I should have known that you wouldn't—"

"I understand perfectly," said Nafai. "It looked to you as if we were planning something behind your back. I would have done the same, if I'd thought of it."

"No," said Zdorab. "I should have spoken to you privately. I should have found out what was happening."

"Zdorab, I would never do anything to your children without your consent."

"And I would never give it," he said. "We have fewer children than anyone. To think of the two of them—having their childhood taken away from us—"

"It won't happen," said Nafai. "I don't want your children. I want the voyage to pass quickly and uneventfully and for us to establish our new colony on Earth. Nothing else. I'm sorry you had to even worry about it."

Zdorab smiled then. Shedemei didn't. She glared at Nafai and then at Luet. "I didn't ask to come on this journey, you know."

"It would be impossible for us to succeed without you," said Nafai.

"But there is one question," said Luet.

"No, Lutya," said Nafai. "Haven't we already—"

"It's something we have to know!" said Luet. "No matter what. I mean it has to be obvious to you,

Shedya, that your two children are the only ones who won't face a consanguinity problem."

"Obviously," said Shedemei.

"But what about the others? I mean, isn't it dangerous for all of us?"

"I don't think it will be a problem," said Shedemei.

"Why not?" asked Luet.

"The only time it's bad for cousins to marry is when there's a recessive gene that leads to problems. When cousins marry, their children can get the recessive gene from both sides, and therefore it expresses itself. Mental retardation. Physical deformity. Debilitating disease. That sort of thing."

"And that's not a problem?"

"Haven't you been paying attention?" asked Shedemei. "Didn't you learn anything back in Basilica? The Oversoul has been breeding you all for years. Bringing your father and mother together, for instance, Luet, all the way from opposite sides of the sea. The Oversoul has already made sure your genetic molecules are clean. You don't *have* any recessive traits that will cause harm."

"How do you know that?"

"Because if you did, they would already have expressed themselves. Don't you get it? The Oversoul has been marrying cousins together for years to get you people who are so receptive to her influence. Any idiots or cripples have already shown up and been bred out."

"Not all," said Rasa. Everyone knew at once that she was thinking of Issib, Nafai's older full brother. His large muscles hopelessly uncontrollable from birth, he had never been able to walk or move without the help of magnetic floats or a flying chair.

"No," said Shedemei. "Of course not all."

"So if my children, for instance, married Hushidh's children. . . ." Luet didn't finish the sentence.

"Hushidh already asked me this years ago," said Shedemei. "I thought she would have told you."

"She didn't," said Luet.

"Issib's problem is not genetic. It was prenatal trauma." Shedemei looked at Rasa. "I imagine Aunt Rasa didn't know she was pregnant when it happened."

Rasa shook her head. No one asked her what it was that she had, in all innocence, done to Issib in the womb.

"It won't be passed on in your children's genes," said Shedemei. "You can marry your children off to your heart's content. If that means you'll be leaving my children alone now, I'll be very thankful."

"We weren't planning anything!" cried Luet, outraged.

"I believe that Nafai wasn't," said Shedemei, "because he discussed it with us all at once."

"I wasn't going to do it either!" insisted Luet.

"I think you were," said Shedemei. "I think you still intend to." She turned and left the room, Zdorab following nervously behind her.

In the corridor outside, Zdorab found Elemak waiting. Letting Shedemei stalk on ahead, Zdorab and Elemak fell in beside each other. "So you were very subtle about it, I see," said Elemak.

Zdorab looked up at him and smiled. "I was certainly clumsy, wasn't I? The Oversoul found my wake-up signal right away." Then he winked and walked faster, leaving Elemak behind. Elemak walked slowly, thinking. Then he smiled slightly and turned down the corridor leading to his family's rooms.

Back in the kitchen, only Volemak and Rasa remained with Nafai and Luet. "You're being foolish," said Volemak. "You must do what the Oversoul commands."

"What the Oversoul commands," said Luet, "is for us to concede that our colony will be permanently split into two irreconcilable factions, and to act in such a way as to make the rift so deep it will last for generations."

"Then do it," said Volemak.

"This discussion is pointless," said Nafai. "Isn't it, Mother?" Rasa signed. "There are things that no decent person will do," she said. "Even for the Oversoul."

"There are larger issues," said Volemak.

"I have these three last children," said Rasa. "Oykib, Yasai, and my little precious daughter. I would hate forever anyone who took them away from me. Even you." She looked from Nafai to Luet. "Or you." And then she looked at her husband. "Or you." She stood up and left the room.

Volemak sighed and rose to his feet. "You'll see," he said. "The Oversoul isn't to be flouted."

"Somewhere along in here," said Nafai, "the Oversoul has to take into account *our* feelings."

But Volemak didn't stay to hear him finish his sentence.

Luet put her arms around Nafai and held him. "I should have told you before," she said. "But I was afraid you'd just do whatever the Oversoul told you."

"The Oversoul knows me better than you do, apparently," said Nafai. "That's why he didn't tell me at all."

"Come to bed, husband," said Luet.

"I have some work to do," he said.

"So we leave a day later," she said.

"I have some work to do."

She signed, kissed him, and left.

Nafai cut himself a slice of bread, wrapped it around a slightly overripe podoroshny, and bit off chunks of it as he left the maintenance building and walked back to the starship.

<Aren't you the clever one.>

I think so, answered Nafai silently.

<Everyone thinks I never even discussed this with you.>

You never did.

<Ignoring me is not the same thing as never having heard me.>

It was never a discussion. It won't happen.

<It will because it must. You'll be killed and so will Luet if you don't.>

You can't see the future.

<Elemak will take your children and make slaves of them.>

He won't punish children for what their parents do.

<He'll call it adopting them. Eiadh is the one who'll turn it into slavery.>

It won't happen.

<It will happen if you don't surround yourself with six more young men whose loyalty to you is complete.>

And I'm telling you again, for the thousandth time, that I will not even consider it without their parents' consent. And I will not lift a finger to persuade them. In fact, I'll argue against it.

<That's a very wise strategy, Nafai. Then they won't be able to blame you when they regret giving their consent.>

Nafai shook his head. They'll never agree to it, he said silently.

<You underestimate my influence.>

FOUR

PERSUASION

Shedemei checked the children again. The third time that night. When she came back to bed, Zdorab was awake.

"I'm sorry," she said. "I had a dream."

"A nightmare, you mean," he said.

For a moment she misunderstood. "Did you have it too?"

"No," he answered, faintly disgusted. "Was it one of those?"

"No, no," she said. "Not from the Keeper of Earth, if that's what you're asking."

"Bats and weasels."

"Giant rats. I don't really have those. I dream of gardens when it's that kind of dream."

"But that's not what you dreamed tonight."

She shook her head.

"And you're not going to tell me."

"If you want, I will."

He waited.

"Zdorab, I kept seeing . . . us, arriving on Earth. All of us coming out of the ship. You and me, unchanged, just as we are now. But then I saw this fine young man and young woman that I had never known before. He was handsome and bright-faced, cheerful and strong. She was dark but her smile was dazzling, and she laughed and there was such intelligence in her eyes."

"And he was eighteen and she was sixteen." His voice sounded sour.

"Royka and Dabya are the only children I'm ever going to have," she said.

"Are you going to accuse me because of that? After all these years?"

"I'm not accusing anyone. I'm just . . . I went to look at them. To make sure they were all right. To make sure they weren't . . . having the same dream."

"And how did you know they weren't? Did you waken them and ask?"

"I don't know what they're dreaming. I only know that they're so young. And I'm looking forward so much to what they'll be. To next week and next month and next year and . . . but then I also saw that. . . ."

"What?" asked Zdorab.

"I remembered how they were. The little babies they were. When they suckled. When they first walked. When they first spoke, when they first played, when they first learned to read and write, I remember everything, and those children are gone."

"Not gone, just grown."

"Grown, I know, but each age of them, *that* goes. You lose those years no matter what you do. They grow past them, they push their own childhood out of the way, they don't thank you for remembering it."

Zdorab shook his head. "I've seen how this overgrown computer works on people, Shedemei. You know you don't want to give your children to Nafai and Luet to raise. They're children themselves."

"I know I don't want to. But what's best for them?

What's best for all of them? People have given their children to war. They've given their children to great acts of heroism."

"And when they've lost them, they've grieved and never stopped grieving."

"But don't you see? We won't lose them. It will be as if . . . as if we sent them away to school. People did it all the time in Basilica. Sent their children to someone else's house to be raised. If we'd stayed there, I would have done it too. They would already be gone, both of them. All we'd really be missing is the holidays."

Zdorab raised himself on his elbow. "As you say, Shedemei, these are our only two children. I never thought I'd have any. I did it only as a favor to you, because you're my . . . friend. And you wanted them so much. And if you had asked me back then, when they were conceived, whether you could give them up, I would have said, Fine, whatever you want, they're yours. But they're not just yours now. I fathered them, incredible as that is to me, and I have taught them and cared for them and loved them and I'll tell you something. I don't want to lose a day with them."

She shook her head. "Neither do I."

"So forget these dreams, Shedya. Let the big computer in the sky plan what it wants to plan. We aren't part of it."

She lay back down in the bed beside him. "Oh, I'm part of it, all right."

"And how is that?" he asked.

She took his hand and held it. "That nonsense I said. About genes. Recessive ones expressing themselves, all that."

The bed shook. Zdorab was laughing.

"It's not funny."

"None of it was true?"

"I have no idea if it's true or not. They know I'm an expert in genetics, they think I know what I'm talking about. But I don't. Nobody does. I mean, we can catalogue the genomes, but most of each genetic molecule is still undeciphered. They used to believe that it was junk, meaningless. But it isn't. That much I've learned from working with plants. It's all just . . . quiet. Waiting. Who knows what will show up if they let those cousins marry each other?"

Zdorab laughed some more.

"It isn't funny," said Shedemei. "I really should tell them the truth."

"No," said Zdorab. "What you told them made it so they won't feel any need to include our children with theirs in any experiment they decide to perform. Fine. That's how it should be."

"But look at Issib."

"What, was his condition genetic after all?"

"No, that part was true enough. But how he's suffered, Zodya. It's not right to let other children go through that, other parents, I can't. . . ."

Zdorab sighed. "You pretend to be hard-nosed, Shedya, but you're soft as cheese on a summer day."

"Thanks for choosing such a foul-smelling analogy."

"Shedya, if what you said wasn't true, how did you think of it?"

"I don't know. The words just came to my mouth. Because I needed *something* to say to turn them away from our children."

"That's right. Now, the Oversoul is perfectly capable of telling them things, right?"

"Constantly."

"So let the Oversoul tell them not to let their children intermarry."

Shedemei thought about that for a moment. "I never thought of that," she said. "I'm not one of those people who 'leaves things up to the Oversoul.' "

"And besides," said Zdorab. "How do you know the Oversoul didn't put the words into your mouth?"

"Oh, don't be so—"

"I'm quite serious. You said the words just came to

you. How do you know it wasn't from the Oversoul? How do you know that it wasn't *true*?"

"Well, I don't *know*."

"There you are. You don't need to say anything to them about anything."

She had no answer to that. He was right.

They lay there in silence for a long time. She thought he was asleep. Then he spoke, a whisper just on the edge of voice. "We aren't just a man with children and a woman with children, sharing the same house, sharing the same children. Are we?"

"No, not just that," said Shedemei.

"I mean, how much does a husband have to desire his wife, sexually, for his feelings toward her to be love?"

She felt her way carefully toward an answer. "I don't know if the feelings have to be sexual at all," she said.

"Because I admire you so much. And the way you are with Rokya and Dabya, I . . . delight in that. And the way you teach them, all the children. And the way you are with . . . with me. The way you're so kind to me."

"And what else would I do? Beat you? Scream at you? You're the most aggravatingly unannoying man I've ever known. You don't do anything wrong."

"Except that I don't satisfy you."

She shrugged. "I don't complain."

"But I do love you. Like a sister. A friend. More than either of those, like a. . . ."

"Like a wife," said Shedemei.

"Yes," said Zdorab. "Like that."

"And I love you as my husband, Zdorab. As you are. Like that." She rolled over, reached for him, kissed his cheek. "Like that," she said again. Then she rolled back onto her other side, her back to him, and soon enough she was asleep.

The dreams came, night after night, those last weeks before the starship *Basilica* was launched. And toward the end, one by one, the dreamers came to him.

Hushidh was first, telling him that the Oversoul was right, that the breach between him and Elemak would never be healed, so he had to be ready. "Don't keep your promise, either," she said. "Don't wake anybody up in midvoyage. It would be a disaster, when we're all confined in that tiny space together."

"Thanks for the suggestion," Nafai said.

"Ignore me if you want," said Hushidh. "You're the one with the cloak, after all."

"Don't snipe at me," said Nafai. "You're Luet's older sister, not mine."

"And we all know what fine specimens *your* older sisters are."

They both burst out laughing.

"Tell Luet for me," said Hushidh, "that once I made up my mind to obey the Oversoul and give my four oldest to you to raise during the voyage, I found that the bonds between Luet and me returned, as strong as ever. The barrier might have been her fault when it began. But it was my fault it wasn't healed till now."

"I'll tell her that," said Nafai. "But better if you tell her yourself."

"I knew you'd say that," said Hushidh. "That's why I hate you." She kissed his cheek and left.

Then Rasa and Volemak came to him together. "It was selfish of us to want to withhold our sons from you. They were born late," said Rasa. "This will be a way for them to catch up with their older brothers."

Volemak smiled thinly. "I'm not so interested in that as Rasa is. As usual, she thinks of people's feelings more than I do. I just remember all that we've given up to get this far, and how stupid it would be for us to repudiate the Oversoul now. There's such a thing as trust, Nafai. Don't risk the survival of the whole colony, particularly of your own family, solely in order to protect your own image of yourself as a man who always does the 'right' thing."

Nafai listened to his father but found no comfort in

his words. "I lost that image of myself when I cut Gaballufix's head from his shoulders, Father. I've regretted that every day of my life since then. Foolish of me, wasn't it, to want to spare myself another source of guilt."

Volemak fell silent then, but Rasa did not. "Wallowing a bit, are we?" she said. "Well, Nafai, you're still young, so you still think the whole universe revolves around you. But the fact is it doesn't. The Oversoul has persuaded us that it's best if our youngest sons are kept awake for the voyage. Now it's up to you to decide if you have the courage to face down Elemak's anger when it's all done."

"And it doesn't matter to you that I gave him—that I gave *everyone*—my word that I wouldn't do this?"

"I am your father," said Volemak, "and Rasa is your mother. We release you from your oath."

"I'm sure Elemak will calm right down when he hears that."

Rasa laughed lightly. "Come now, Nafai. Elemak is the one person out of this whole community who has never believed for a moment that you would keep your word. And do you know why he doesn't believe it? Because he knows that if the situation were reversed, *he* would break that promise in an instant."

"But I'm not Elemak."

"Yes you are," said Volemak. "You are exactly what Elemak would have been, except he never had the goodness of heart."

Nafai wasn't sure if he had been praised or slapped.

After Hushidh, after Father and Mother, Issib came bringing with him, as usual, not just the dreams the Oversoul had given him, but also ideas to make things work better.

"We need to talk," Issib said.

Nafai nodded.

"I keep having these dreams."

"The Oversoul," said Nafai. "I know, I have them too."

"Not the same ones, Nyef," said Issib. "I see my oldest boy, Xodhya, as he comes out of the starship—"

"As I see Zhyat—"

"And he looks just like *me*. Which is silly, because there's so much of his mother's face in his, but in my dream, he's me. Except he's tall and strong, his arms, his chest—like a god. Like one of those statues around the old orchestra."

"Of course. The Oversoul is just manipulating you, Issib."

"Yes, I know that," said Issib. "I was with you when we first withstood him, don't you remember? We did it together."

"I haven't forgotten."

"We proved that we didn't *have* to do what the Oversoul wanted, didn't we, Nafai? But then we decided to help the Oversoul because we wanted to. Because we agreed with what he was trying to accomplish."

"And as long as I agreed, I've cooperated. At great cost, too, I might add."

"Cost? You? With the cloak of the starmaster?"

"I'd trade the cloak in a minute to know that my brothers loved me."

"*I* love you, Nyef. Have you ever doubted that?"

"No, I didn't mean—"

"And Okya and Yaya love you. Are they not your brothers? Am I not your brother?"

"All of you are."

"And I don't really think you give a rat's ass whether Meb likes you or not."

"All right, Elemak. I'd trade the starmaster's cloak for Elemak's respect if I thought I could ever have it."

"Don't you see, Nyef? You can never have his respect."

"Because I'll never be worthy of it."

"Stupid." Issib laughed at him. "You are dense,

Nafai. You can't have his respect precisely because you *are* worthy of it."

"I always hated paradoxes in school. I think they're the conclusion that philosophers reach when—"

"When they've given up on thinking, I know, it's not the first time you've said it. But this isn't a paradox. Elemak hates you because you're his younger brother and he knows, he *knows*, that you have more of Father's respect and love than he has. That's why he hates you, because he knows that in Father's eyes, you're a better man than he is."

"I wish."

"You know it's true. But if you gave it all up, if you surrendered everything to Elemak, if you gave up the cloak, if you repudiated the Oversoul, do you think he'd respect you then? Of course not, because then you really *would* be contemptible. Weak. A nothing."

"You've persuaded me. I'll keep the cloak."

"The cloak is nothing. You're already doing something far worse."

Nafai regarded him steadily. "Am I to understand that you're really here trying to persuade me to keep your four oldest children awake during the voyage, teaching them, raising them for you, so that when you awake you'll find them already grown?"

"Not at all," said Issib. "I'd hate that."

"Well, then, what is all this about?"

"Keep them awake, but bring me awake too, sometimes. Once a year for a few weeks. Let me teach all the children computers, for instance. Nobody's better at that than me."

"They won't need computers in the new colony."

"Mathematics then. Surveying. Triangulation. I can read the same books as you and teach them just like you. Or were you planning on having an agricultural laboratory here? Forestry, perhaps? When were we going to bring the trees aboard?"

"I never thought of that."

"You mean the Oversoul never thought of that."

"Whatever."

"Do it in shifts. Wake Luet up for a while, but then let her sleep again. Wake me, wake Hushidh. Wake Mother and Father. A few weeks at a time. We'll see the children grow, then. We won't miss it all. And when we reach Earth, they'll be men and women. Ready to stand beside you against the others."

Nafai didn't answer right away. "That's not the way the Oversoul explained it to Luet."

"So, where is it engraved on stone that you have to do everything the Oversoul's way? As long as you do what he wants, the methodology hardly matters, does it?"

"Does Hushidh feel the same way?"

"She might. In a while."

"I won't take anyone's child without their agreement."

"Really? And what about the children themselves? Going to ask *them*?"

"I really ought to," said Nafai. "I'll think about this, Issib. Maybe this compromise will work."

"Good," said Issib. "Because I think the Oversoul's right. If we don't do this, if we don't give you strong young men and women to back you up, then when we get away from the starship, when the Oversoul's influence weakens, you'll be a dead man, and so will I."

"I'll think about it," said Nafai.

Issib rose up from the chair and leaned toward the door, then stepped lightly toward it, the floats bearing almost all of his weight. At the door he turned.

"And something else," said Issib.

"What?" asked Nafai.

"I know you better than you think."

"Do you?"

"For instance, I know that the Oversoul talked to you about this whole thing long before Luet ever let anything slip."

"Really?"

"And I know that you wanted it to happen all along
You just didn't want it to be your idea. You wanted i
to be us persuading *you*. That way we can never blame
you later. Because you tried to talk us out of it."

"Am I really that clever?" asked Nafai.

"Yes," said Issib. "And I'm really clever enough to
figure it all out."

"Well, then, I'm not so clever after all."

"Yes you are," said Issib. "Because I really *do* wan
you to do it. And I never *will* be able to blame you i
I don't like the results. So it worked."

Nafai smiled wanly. "I wish you were completely
right," said Nafai.

"Oh? And how am I wrong?"

"I would rather, with all my heart, let all our childrer
sleep through the voyage. Because I would rather have
there be no division between us all in the new colony
Because I would rather make my brother Elemak the
king of us all and let him rule over us, than to have him
as my enemy."

"So why don't you?"

"Because he hates the Oversoul. And when we get to
Earth, he'll resist just as much whatever it is the Keepe
of Earth wants us to do. He'll end up destroying us al
because of his stubbornness. He can't be the ruler ove
us."

"I'm glad you understand that," said Issib. "Because
if you ever start to think that he ought to rule, that'
when he'll destroy you."

Volemak, Rasa, Hushidh, Issib; and then at las
Shedemei and Zdorab came to him, only an hour be
fore they were all supposed to go to sleep for the voy
age. "I don't want to do it," said Zdorab.

"Then I won't waken your children," said Nafai
"I'm not sure yet that I'm going to waken anyone'
children."

"Oh, you are," said Shedemei. "And you're going to

waken us, too, from time to time, to help teach them. That's the deal."

"And when we get to Earth, and our children are all ten years older than Elya's and Meb's and Vasya's and Briya's, you'll stand up to them with me? You'll say, We thought it was a good idea? We asked him to do it?"

"I'll never say I thought it was a good idea," said Zdorab. "But I'll admit that I asked you to do it."

"Not good enough," said Nafai. "If you don't think it's a good idea, why are you asking me to let your only two children take part in it?"

"Because," said Zdorab, "my son would never forgive me if he knew that he had a chance to reach Earth as a man, and I made him arrive there as a boy."

Nafai nodded. "That's a good reason."

"But remember, Nafai," said Zdorab. "The same thing goes for the other children. Do you think that when Elya's boy Protchnu wakes up and finds that your *younger* son, Motya, is eight years older than him instead of two years younger, do you think that Protchnu will ever forgive you, or Motya either? This will cause hatred that will never be healed, generation after generation. They will always believe that something was stolen from them."

"And they'll be right," said Nafai. "But the thing that was stolen, it wasn't taken away until they had already rejected it."

"They'll never remember that."

"But will you?"

Zdorab thought about it for a moment.

"If he doesn't," said Shedemei, "I'll remind him."

Zdorab smiled grimly at her. "Let's go to bed," he said.

No matter who would be wakened later, all would be asleep for the launch itself. There was too much stress, too much pain to pass through it consciously. Instead they would be encased in foam inside their sleep chambers.

Each couple put their own young children to bed, laying them into their suspended animation chambers, kissing them, then closing the lid and watching through the window until they drifted into the drugged sleep that began the process. There was some fear in the children, especially the older ones who understood something of what was going on, but there was also excitement, anticipation. "And when we wake up, we'll be on Earth?" they asked, over and over. "Yes," their parents said.

Then Nafai took the parents to the control room and showed them the calendar with the midvoyage waking scheduled. "You'll be able to check all your children and make sure that they're sleeping safely," Nafai assured them.

"Now I can sleep peacefully indeed," Elemak answered with dry irony.

Nafai watched them all go to sleep, one by one, and one by one he authorized the life support computers to drug them, surround them with foam, chill them until their bodies were barely alive at all. Then he, too, climbed into his chamber and drew the lid closed after him.

No human being saw the ship rise silently into the air, a hundred meters, a thousand, until it was as high as the magnetics of the landing field could raise it. Then the launching rockets fired, blasting downward as the starship rose up into the night sky.

Far away, on the other side of the narrow sea, travelers on the caravan road looked up and saw the shooting star. "But it's rising," said one of them, "No," said another. "That's just an illusion, because it's coming toward us."

"No," said the first again. "It's rising into the sky. And it's much too slow to be a shooting star."

"Really?" scoffed the other. "Then what is it?"

"I don't know," said the first. "But I thank the Oversoul that we could see it."

"And why is that?"

"Because after millions of years, fool, there's not a thing that any man can see that hasn't been seen a hundred or a thousand or a million times before. But *we've* seen something that no one else has ever seen."

"You think."

"Yes, I think."

"And what good is it? To see something wondrous, and have no idea what it is you saw?"

The starship *Basilica* rose higher, out of the gravity well of the planet Harmony. When it was far enough away, the rockets stopped. They would not be used again until it was time for the ship to land on another world. Instead, a web unfolded itself from the sides of the ship, made of strands so fine that they could not be seen were it not for the dazzle of light upon the wires when a molecule of hydrogen or some particle even smaller fell into the energy field the web generated. Then the shape of it could be seen, like a vast spiderweb, gathering the dust of space to fuel the onward progress of the starship. The *Basilica* began to accelerate, faster and faster, until Harmony was left behind, just another dot of light indistinguishable by the naked eye from any other. After forty million years, human beings had left the surface of this world, and, against all expectations, they were going home.

FIVE

THE EAVESDROPPER

The other children all supposed, upon waking, that they must have arrived at Earth. That's what they had been told upon going to sleep in the suspended-animation chambers—when you wake up, it will be Earth.

Oykib, however, already knew that he would be waking long before then. He was not surprised that instead of normal gravity, he seemed unbelievably light and strong, each step sending him bounding up to touch the ceiling. That's the way it was in space, when instead of a planet to hold you down, you had only the acceleration of the ship. And if he had any doubts, they were dispelled by the fact that as Nafai and Luet gathered the children into the ship's library—the largest open space in the starship, except for the centrifuge—Oykib could hear the faint murmurings of the Oversoul to Nafai and Luet: This is a bad idea. Don't give them a choice. Children that age are too young to decide something this important. Their parents have already agreed. If you tell them they have a choice when they really don't, they'll only hate you for it. And so on, and so on.

Oykib had been hearing scraps of conversation like this since earliest childhood. He couldn't remember a time without it. At first, though, it was like music, like wind, like the sound of waves for a child who grows up by the sea. He thought nothing of it, did not search for meaning in it. But gradually, by the time he was four or five, he began to realize that this background noise contained names; that there were ideas in it, ideas that later showed up in discussions among the adults.

Though the voices were all in his mind, and therefore soundless, he began to associate certain ways of thinking with certain people. He began to notice that sometimes, when he was with Mother or Father, Nafai or Issib, Luet or Hushidh, the conversation that he heard most clearly was one that seemed appropriate to what they were talking about with someone else. He would see Luet trying to deal with a quarrel between Chveya and Dazya, for instance, and hear someone saying: Why won't she hold her own with Dazya? Why does she back off like this? And someone else—the most constant voice, the strongest voice—saying, She's holding her own, she's doing fine, have patience, she doesn't need to win openly as long as you assure her of your respect for her. Thus he knew that a particular passionate, intimate manner meant that he was hearing Luet; a cooler, calmer, but more uncertain way of thought belonged to Hushidh. The most matter-of-fact, impatient, argumentative voice was Nafai's.

Yet even so, he was young enough that he didn't realize that he wasn't supposed to be hearing these things. It first became clear to him because of the dreams, for that was one of the Oversoul's most powerful ways of talking to people. One time when Oykib was a very little boy, Luet had come to the house to talk to Mother about a dream she had had. When she finished,

Oykib had piped up and said, "I had that dream, too," and then repeated the things that Luet had seen.

Mother answered him then with a smile, but he knew that she didn't believe that he had seen the same dream. The second time it happened, with a dream of Father's, Mother took Oykib aside and gently explained to him that there was no need to pretend to have the same dreams as other people. It was better to tell only his own dreams.

Oykib was bothered by not being believed, and the older he got, the more it bothered him. Why, with so much communication between these adults and the Oversoul, did they all assume that he, as a three-year-old, as a four-year-old, could not have had the same communication? Eventually he decided that the problem was that the dream really *was* sent to someone else—it was appropriate for their situation, and not at all appropriate for Oykib. Therefore, the adults knew that the Oversoul would never have sent such a dream to him, because it had nothing to do with his life. And in fact the Oversoul *hadn't* sent the dream to him. The dreams and the background conversations were all real enough, but they were also not his own.

He wondered: Why doesn't the Oversoul have anything to say to *me*?

By the time Oykib turned eight, he had long since learned to keep what he overheard to himself. He was naturally quiet and reserved, preferring to be silent in a large group, listening to everything, helping when he was needed. He understood far more than anyone thought he did, partly because he had grown up overhearing adult problems being discussed with an adult vocabulary, and partly because he could hear, along with the vocal conversation, scraps and snatches of internal dialogues as the Oversoul made suggestions, tried to influence mood, and occasionally attempted to distract someone from what they were thinking or doing. The trouble was that it always distracted Oykib, so that he could hardly have any thoughts of his own, so busy was his mind in trying to follow all that was going on around him. When he did open his mouth to speak, he could never be sure if he was responding to what had been said aloud, or to things that he understood only because of overhearing that which he really shouldn't have been hearing.

There was also another reason why Oykib said little. He had learned about privacy and secrets, and he knew people wouldn't be happy if they ever guessed how much he knew. He suspected that it would make them angry to know that their most intimate thoughts, framed in their own minds where only the Oversoul could hear, were being heard and noted and stored away in the mind of a six- or seven- or eight-year-old boy.

Sometimes, the burden of all these secrets was more than Oykib could bear. That was why he had begun having little talks with Yasai, his younger brother. He never told Yaya how he was learning the things he learned. Instead he always said things like, "I'll bet that Luet is angry because of the way Hushidh never stops Dazya from bossing the younger children," or "Father doesn't really love Nafai more than everybody else, it's just that Nafai is the only one who understands what Father is doing and can help him to do it." Oykib knew that Yaya was dazzled by how often Oykib's "insights" turned out to be right, and that Yaya was also flattered to be included in his "wise" older brother's confidence; sometimes it made him feel like a cheater, to let Yaya think that Oykib had simply figured things out. But he knew, without knowing why, that it was a bad idea to tell even Yaya about how all communication with the Oversoul spilled over into Oykib's mind. Yaya was good about keeping secrets, but something *that* important was bound to slip out sometime.

So Oykib kept his secrets to himself. The hardest time was a few months back, when Nafai went out to the mountains and broke through the perimeter and found the starships. Oykib heard some terrible, frightening things. Luet pleading for the Oversoul to protect her husband. The Oversoul urging someone else to be calm, be calm, don't kill your brother, you don't want to live with yourself afterward if you kill your brother. He understood the community well enough by then to know who it was who was planning to kill Nafai. Oykib longed to be able to do something, but he couldn't; in fact, he was almost immobilized by the maelstrom of needs and hungers, shouts and demands, pleas and griefs. He was so frightened; he went to Mother and clung to her, and heard her say to Volemak, "See how the children pick up on things without understanding them?" He wanted to say, "I understand perfectly well that Elemak and Mebbekew are planning to kill Nafai and then rule over all of us—I know it because I've heard the Oversoul trying to get them to stop. I know that Luet is terrified and so are you, that Nafai might be killed. But I also know that the Oversoul is saying a torrent of things to Nafai, important things, beautiful things, only he's so far away that I only catch glimmers of it, and I know that Nafai himself has no fear at all, he's just excited, he keeps shouting inside himself, "Now I get it! So that's it! Now I understand it! Yes!" But he could explain none of this. All he could do was cling to his mother until she had to push him away to get on with her work, and then talk it out with Yasai. "I think Elya and Meb are going to try to kill Nyef today, when he comes back," he said, and Yaya's eyes grew wide. "I think Nyef isn't worried, though, because he's become so strong that nobody can hurt him."

When it all ended with Elemak and Mebbekew humbled before the power of the starmaster's cloak, Yaya was in awe of Oykib's insights more than ever. But Oykib was exhausted. He didn't want to know so much. And yet, underneath it all, he wanted to know more. He wanted the Oversoul to speak to *him*.

Why should he? Oykib was only an eight-year-old

boy, and not strong and domineering like Elemak's boy Protchnu, either, even though Proya was a few weeks younger. What would the Oversoul have to say to *him*?

Now, sitting with the others in the library of the starship *Basilica*, Oykib already knew exactly what was going to be explained to them, because he had heard the Oversoul arguing with the adults about it before the ship was launched, and he could hear the Oversoul arguing with Luet and Nafai even now. He wanted to shout at them to just shut up and *do* it. But instead he held his peace, and listened patiently as Nafai and Luet explained it all.

He didn't like the way they handled it. They told the truth, of course—he had learned to expect that from them, more perhaps than from any of the other adults—but they left out a lot of the real reasons for what they were doing. They only talked about it as a wonderful chance for the children to learn a lot of things they'd need to know in order to make the colony work when they got to Earth. "And because you'll be fourteen or fifteen or sixteen—or even, some of you, eighteen years old—when we arrive, you can do the work of a man or a woman. You'll be grownups, not children. At the same time, though, you'll only see your mothers and fathers now and then during the voyage, because we can't afford the life support to keep more than two adults awake at a time."

Yes yes, all of that is true, thought Oykib. But what about the fact that only a dozen of us children will be in this little school of yours? What about the fact that when I am an eighteen-year-old at the end of the voyage, Protchnu will still be eight? What about friendships like the one between Mebbekew's daughter Tiya and Hushidh's daughter Shyada? Will they still be friends when Shyada is sixteen and Tiya is still six? Not very likely. Are you going to explain *that*?

But he said nothing. Waiting. Perhaps they would get to that part.

"Any questions?" asked Nafai.

"There's plenty of time," said Luet. "If you want to go back to sleep, you can do it a few days from now—there's no rush."

"Is there anything fun to do on this ship?" asked Xodhya, Hushidh's oldest boy. That was the most obvious question, since the adults had spent a lot of time before the launch assuring the kids that they *wanted* to sleep through the voyage because it would be so dull.

"There are a lot of things you can't do," said Luet. "The centrifuge will provide Earth-normal gravity for exercise, but you can only run in a straight line. You can't play ball or swim or lie in the grass because there's no pool and no grass and even in the centrifuge, it wouldn't be practical to throw and catch a ball. But you can still wrestle, and I think you could get used to playing tag and hide-and-seek in low gravity."

"And there are computer games," said Nafai. "You've never had a chance to play them, growing up without computers as you did, but Issib and I found quite a few—"

"You won't be able to play those very much, though," interrupted Luet. "We wouldn't want you to get too used to them, because we won't have computers like that on Earth."

Playing tag in low gravity—that alone probably would have won most of them over. Oykib found himself getting angry that they would pretend to be giving a choice when all they told about were mostly the good things and none of the worst.

He might have said something then, but Chveya spoke up first. "I think it all depends on what Dazya decides."

Dza, always full of herself as the most important child because she was firstborn, visibly preened. Oykib was disgusted, mostly because he had never seen Chveya kiss up to Dza like this before—he had always thought she was the most sensible of the girls.

"Chveya, you children have to make up your own minds about this."

"You don't understand," said Chveya. "Whatever Dazya decides, I'm going to do the opposite."

Dazya stuck out her tongue at Chveya. "That's just what I'd expect from you," she said. "You're always so immature."

"Veya," said Luet, "I'm embarrassed that you would say something so hurtful. And would you really change your whole future, just to spite Dazya?"

Chveya blushed and said nothing.

At last Oykib reached the point where he could not maintain silence. "I know what you should do," he said. "Put Dazya back to sleep for three days. Then when she gets up, Dza and Chveya would be exactly the same age."

Chveya rolled her eyes as if to say, That wouldn't solve anything. But Dazya went crazy. "My birthday would always be first no matter what!" she shouted. "I'm the first child and nobody else is! So I'm *going* to stay awake and still be the oldest when we get there! Nobody else is ever going to boss me around."

Oykib saw with satisfaction that Dazya had shown Nafai and Luet exactly why Chveya didn't want to stay awake if Dazya did.

"Actually," said Luet, "nobody has the right to boss other people around just because she's oldest or smartest or anything else."

Several of the younger children laughed. "Dazya bosses everybody," said Shyada, who, as Dazya's next younger sister, bore the brunt of Dazya's whims.

"I do not," said Dazya. "I don't boss Oykib or Protchnu."

"No, you only boss people who are *weaker* than you, you big bully!" said Shyada.

"Be quiet, all of you," said Nafai. "What you've just seen here is one of the problems with keeping you awake for school during the voyage. The ship isn't very large inside. You're going to be cooped up together for years. We let a lot of things slide back on Harmony, figuring that you'd work things out as the years went by. But during the voyage, we won't tolerate older children bossing the younger children around."

"Why not?" said Dazya. "Grown-ups boss children around all the time."

"Dza," said Luet quietly, "I believe you're intelligent enough to grasp the idea that the three days between you and Veya are not as significant as the fifteen years between you and me."

Chveya followed up this idea at once. "If I stay awake, Mother, then when we reach Earth I'll be three years older than *you* were when I was born."

"Yes, but she was *married*," said Rokya, Zdorab's and Shedemei's boy. Then, suddenly, he seemed to realize what he had just said, because he blushed and clamped his mouth shut.

"I don't think marriage is something you need to worry about now," said Luet.

"Why not?" said Chveya. "*You* worry about it. Rokya is the only boy here who isn't an uncle or a double first cousin of mine."

"That won't be a problem," said Luet. "Shedemei said that there will be no genetic problems, so if it should happen that as you get older, you fall in love with a cousin or an uncle—"

Most of the children made groaning or puking noises.

"I say, as you get *older*, when the idea is no longer repulsive to you, there will be no genetic barrier."

But Oykib knew that before the launch, Shedemei had begged the Oversoul to forgive her for having told that lie to Nafai, and asked the Oversoul to tell Nafai to forbid marriages between close cousins if there would be any danger from it. He also knew something else, though, something Shedemei herself didn't know: that what she said about everyone being carefully bred by the Oversoul so as to be without any defects had been given to her by the Oversoul. He had overheard it as a very powerful sending. And so he was at peace with the idea of marrying a cousin. The Oversoul had better be right—Oykib and Yaya couldn't *both* marry Shedemei's and Zdorab's daughter Dabrota, and therefore one of them was going to marry a niece or die unmarried.

Chveya wasn't satisfied. "That's not what you said that night—"

"Veya," said Luet, trying to be patient. "You didn't hear both sides of that conversation, and besides, I learned some new information since then. Have a little trust, dear."

Motiga spoke up then. Caring nothing about the marriage issue, he had been thinking about something else. "If the people who stay asleep don't get any older, then will the ones who aren't here now still be little? I mean, will I be bigger than Protchnu?"

Luet and Nafai glanced at each other. Clearly they had wanted to avoid facing this question. "Yes," Nafai finally said. "That's what it means."

"Great," said Motiga.

But others weren't so sure. "That's stupid," said Shyada, who had a six-year-old's crush on Protchnu. "Why don't you just have us take turns being up, like you're going to do with the grownups?"

Oykib was surprised that a six-year-old would have thought of this most sensible of solutions. So were Nafai and Luet. They were obviously at a loss as to what to say, how to explain.

So Oykib, always looking for a chance to help, plunged in. "Look, we're not awake right now because Nafai and Luet like us best or anything like that. We're here because our parents are on Nafai's side, and the kids who are still asleep, *their* parents are on Elemak's side."

Nafai looked angry. Oykib heard him saying to the

Oversoul, Any chance of teaching this boy how and when to keep his mouth shut?

Oykib also heard the Oversoul's answer: Didn't I warn you not to offer them a choice?

"I think it's good for us all to decide knowing the *real* reason for things," said Oykib, looking Nafai right in the eye. "I know that you and my parents and Issib and Hushidh and Shedemei and Zdorab are the ones who obey the Oversoul, and I know that Elemak and Mebbekew and Obring and Vas tried to kill you and the Oversoul thinks they'll try again as soon as we reach Earth." He knew he had probably said too much, had given away things that he wasn't supposed to know. So Oykib turned to the other children, to explain it to them. "It's like a war," he said. "Even though Nafai and Elemak are both my brothers, and even though Nafai doesn't want there to be a fight between them, Elemak is going to try to kill Nafai when we get to Earth."

The other children were looking at him with very serious faces. Oykib didn't talk all that much, but when he did, they listened; and what he was saying was serious. It was no longer about trivial matters like who was the boss of the children. That had been Luet's and Nafai's mistake. They wanted the children to choose, but they meant to make them do it without knowing the real issues involved. Well, Oykib knew these children better than the grownups did. He knew that they would understand, and he knew how they would choose.

"So you see," Oykib went on, "the real reason they woke us up is so that Yasai and Xodhya and Rokya and Zhyat and Motya and I will be men. *Big* men. While Elya's and Kokor's and Sevet's and Meb's sons are all nothing but little kids. That way, Elemak won't just be facing an old man like my father or a cripple like Issib. He'll be facing *us*, and we'll stand beside Nafai and fight for him if we have to. And we will, won't we!"

Oykib looked from one boy to the next, and each one nodded in turn. "And it's not just the boys," he added. "The twelve of us will marry and have children, and our children will be born before the others ever have children, and so we'll always be stronger. It's the only way to keep Elemak from killing Nafai. And not just Nafai, either. Because they'd have to kill Father, too. And Issya. And maybe Zdorab, too. Or if they didn't kill them, they'd treat them like slaves. And us, too. Unless we stay awake on this voyage. Elemak and Mebbekew are my brothers, but they aren't *nice*."

Luet's face was buried in her hands. Nafai was looking at the ceiling.

"How do you know all this, Okya?" asked Chveya.

"I just know it, all right?" Oykib answered. "I just *know* it."

Her voice got very quiet. "Did the Oversoul tell you?" she asked.

In a way, yes—but for some reason Oykib didn't want to lie or even mislead Chveya. Better not to answer at all. "That's private," he said.

"A lot of what you just said is private, Oykib," said Nafai. "But now you've said it, and we have to deal with it. It's true that the Oversoul thinks that there's going to be a division in our community when we reach Earth. And it's true that the Oversoul planned all this so that you children would be old enough to stand with your parents against Elemak and his followers and their children. But I don't think there has to be a division like that. I don't *want* a division. So my reason for this is because it would be a good thing to have twelve more adults to help with the work of building the colony—and twelve fewer children who have to be looked after and protected and fed. Everybody will prosper more because of it."

"You weren't going to tell us any of this till Oykib said it, though," said Chveya, just a little angry.

"I didn't think you'd understand it," said Nafai.

"I *don't*," said Shyadá, truthfully.

"I'm staying awake," said Padarok. "I'm on your

side, because I know my mother and father are. I've heard them talking."

"Me too," said his little sister Dabya. One by one, they all assented.

At the end, Dazya turned to Chveya and added, "And I'm sorry if you hate me so much that you'd rather stay a little girl than have to be with me."

"You're the one who hates *me*," said Chveya.

"I really don't," said Dazya.

There was silence for a long moment.

"When it comes right down to it," Chveya said, "we're on the same side."

"That's right," said Dazya.

And then, because Chveya really wasn't good at thinking how things would sound before she said them, she added, "And you can marry Padarok. That's fine with me."

Padarok at once cried out in protest as most of the other children hooted and laughed. Only Oykib noticed that after she said this, Chveya looked straight at *him* before dropping her eyes down to her lap.

So I'm the chosen one, he thought. Sweet of you to make up my mind for me.

But it was also obvious. Of this group of twelve children, Oykib and Padarok were the only boys born in the first year, and Chveya and Dza were the only girls. If Dza and Padarok ended up together, Chveya would either have to marry Oykib or else one of the younger boys or else nobody.

The thought was faintly repulsive. He thought of the one time he had gotten roped into playing dolls with Dza and some of the younger girls. It was excruciatingly boring to pretend to be the father and the husband, and he fled after only a few minutes of the game. He imagined playing dolls with Chveya and couldn't imagine that it would be any better. But maybe it was different when the dolls were real babies. The adult men didn't seem to mind it, anyway. Maybe there was something missing when they played dolls. Maybe in real marriages, wives weren't so bossy about making the husbands do everything their way.

Padarok had better hope so, because if he ended up with Dazya he wasn't going to be able to think his own thoughts without her permission. She really was about as bossy a person as ever lived. Chveya, on the other hand, was merely stubborn. That was different. She wanted to do things her own way, but at least she didn't insist that you had to do them her way, too. Maybe they could be married and live in separate houses and only take turns tending the children. That would work.

Nafai was taking the other children now to show them where they would sleep—the girls' room and the boys' room. Oykib, lost in speculation about marriage, had lingered in the library, and now found himself alone with Luet.

"You certainly had a lot to say just now," said Luet. "Usually you don't."

"You two weren't saying it," said Oykib.

"No, we weren't," she answered. "And maybe we had good reason for that, don't you suppose?"

"No, you didn't have a good reason," answered Oykib. He knew it was outrageous for him to say such a thing to a grownup, but at this point he didn't care. He was Nafai's brother, after all, not his son.

"Are you so very sure of that?" She was angry, oh yes.

"You weren't telling us the real reason for everything because you thought we wouldn't understand it, but we did. All of us did. And *then* when we made up our minds, we knew what we were choosing."

"You may think you understand, but you don't," said Luet. "It's a lot more complicated than you think, and—"

Oykib got really angry now. He had heard their arguments with the Oversoul, all the nuances and possible problems they had worried about, and even though he wasn't going to tell them how he knew these things, he certainly wasn't going to pretend now that he couldn't understand them. "Did you ever think, Lutya, that maybe it's a lot more complicated than *you* think, too?"

Maybe it was because he called her—an adult!—by her quick-name, or maybe it was because she recognized the truth of what he said, but she fell silent and stared at him.

"You don't understand everything," said Oykib, "but you still make decisions. Well, we don't understand everything, either. But we decided, didn't we? And we made the right choice, didn't we?"

"Yes," she said quietly.

"Maybe children aren't as stupid as you think," Oykib added. It was something he had been wanting to say to an adult for a long time. This seemed like the appropriate occasion.

"I don't think you're stupid at all, not you or any of the. . . ."

But before she could finish her sentence, he was out of the library, bounding up the corridor in search of the others. If he wasn't there when they picked, he'd end up with the worst bed.

It turned out that he ended up with the worst bed anyway, the bunk on the bottom right by the door where he'd be in plain view to anybody coming down the corridor so he couldn't get away with *anything*. He had chosen the best bed, and since he was first boy, none of the others had argued with him. But then he saw how miserable Motya was at having the worst spot—especially when Yaya and Zhyat teased him about it. So now he was stuck with the worst bed and he knew nobody was going to want to trade later. Ten years, he thought. I'm going to have to sleep here ten lousy years.

SIX

THE UGLY GOD

Emeez's mother took her to the holy cave when she was six years old. It was a miraculous place, because it was underground and yet it had not been carved by the people. Instead it grew this way, a gift from the gods; they had created it, and so this was where the gods were brought to be worshipped.

The cave was strange, all jagged and wet, not dry and smooth-walled like the burrows of the city. Limey water dripped everywhere. Mother explained how the water left a tiny amount of lime behind with each drop, and in time that's what formed the massive pillars. But how could that be? Weren't the pillars holding up the roof of the cave? If the pillars weren't forming until the water dripped for years and years, what would have held the roof up at the beginning? But Mother explained that this cave was made of stone. "The gods break holes in the mountain the way we chip off flakes of stone for our blades," Mother said. "They can hold up a roof of stone so wide that you can't see the other side, even with the brightest torch. And there is no wind so strong that it can tear the roof off the burrow of the gods."

That's why they're gods, I suppose, thought Emeez. She had seen what the storm did to the uphill end of the city, knocking down three rooftrees so that rain and later sunlight poured into what had once been nurseries and meeting halls. It took days to seal up the tunnels and create new burrows elsewhere to replace the lost space, and during that time two cousins and three nieces stayed with them. Mother nearly went crazy, and Emeez wasn't far behind. They were private, quiet people, and didn't deal very well with busybodies constantly prying into their business. Oh, what's *this*, are we learning to weave at such a young age? Oh, I'll bet you've already set your heart on some young fellow who's just now out on his first hunt, you pretty little thing you.

Such a lie. Because Emeez was not a pretty little thing. She wasn't pretty. She wasn't little. And she wasn't a *thing*, either, though people often treated her that way. She was too hairy, for one thing. Men liked a woman with very downy hair, not dark and coarse like hers. And her voice wasn't lovely, either. She tried to sound like Mother, but Emeez just didn't have that kind of music in her. One time when Cousin Issess—*there* was an undistinguished name for you!—didn't know Emeez was nearby, she said to her stupid daughter Aamuv, "Poor Emeez. She's a throwback, you know. They're just as hairy as that back on the east slope of the mountain. I hope she doesn't have any of their *other* traits!" The story was, of course, that the hairy east-slopers ate the hearts and livers of their enemies, and some said they simply spitted their victims and roasted them whole. Monsters. And that's what people thought of Emeez, because she was so hairy.

Well, she couldn't help what grew on her body. At least it wasn't a horrible fungus infection like the one that made poor Bomossoss stink so badly. He was a mighty warrior, but nobody could really enjoy being around him because of the odor. Very sad. The gods do what they want with us. At least I don't smell.

There wasn't any worship going on here—of course, since that was a man thing, and not for women, and *certainly* not for little girls. But she had heard that the men worshipped the gods by licking them until they were wet and soft and then rubbing them all over their bodies. She hadn't really believed it, until she came into the first of the prayer chambers.

Some of the gods were very intricately carved, with startlingly beautiful faces. There were pictures of fierce warriors and of the hideous skymeat beasts, of goats and deer, of coiled snakes and dragonflies perched on cattails. But when Mother started pointing out the very holiest of the gods, the ones most worshipped, to Emeez's surprise *these* were not intricately carved at all. The very holiest of them were nothing but smooth lumps of clay.

"Why are the beautiful ones not as holy as the ones that don't look like anything?"

"Ah," said Mother, "but you have to understand, they were once the most beautiful of all. But they have been worshipped most fervently, and they have given us good babies and good hunting. So of course they've been worn smooth. But we remember what they were."

The smooth lumpy ones disturbed her. "Couldn't somebody carve new faces on them?"

"Don't be absurd. That would be blasphemy." Mother looked annoyed. "Honestly, Emeez, I don't understand how your mind works. Nobody carves the gods. They would have no power if men and women just made them up out of clay."

"Well who *does* make them, then?"

"We bring them home," said Mother. "We find them and bring them home."

"But who makes them?"

"They make themselves," said Mother. "They rise up from the clay of the riverbank by themselves."

"Can I watch sometime?"

"No," said Mother.

"I want to watch a god coming forth."

Mother sighed. "I suppose you're old enough. If you promise you won't go telling the younger children."

"I promise."

"There is a certain time of year. In the dry season. The skymeat come down and shape the mud by the riverbank."

"Skymeat?" Emeez was appalled. "You can't be serious. That's disgusting."

"Of course it *would* be disgusting," said Mother, "if you thought the skymeat actually understood what they were doing. But they don't. The god comes awake inside them and they just start mindlessly shaping the clay in fantastic intricate patterns. Then, when they're done, they just go away. Leave them behind. For us."

The skymeat. Those nasty flying things that sometimes trapped and killed hunters. Their young were brought home and roasted and fed to pregnant women. They were dangerous, mindless beasts, treacherous and sneaky, and *they* made the *gods?*

"I'm not feeling well, Mother," said Emeez.

"Well, then, sit down here for a few minutes and rest," said Mother. "I'm supposed to meet the priestess three rooms up—that way—and I can't be late. But you can come after me and find me, right? You won't wander off the main path and get lost, will you?"

"I don't think I suddenly turned *stupid*, Mother."

"But you did suddenly turn rude. I don't like that in you, Emeez."

Well, nobody likes much of anything in me, she thought. But that doesn't mean I have to agree with them. *I* think I'm excellent company. I'm much smarter than any of my other friends, and so everything I say to myself is scintillating and exciting and has never been

said before. Unlike those who say over and over, end-
lessly, the same bits of "wisdom" they picked up from
their mothers. And I'm certainly better company than
the boys, always throwing things and breaking things
and cutting things. Much better to dig and to weave,
the way women do, to gather things rather than kill
them, to combine leaves and fruit and meat and roots
together in a way that tastes good. I will be a fine
woman, hairy or not, and whatever man ends up getting stuck with me will make a big show about how dis-
appointed he is, but in secret he'll be glad, and I'll
make him a whole bunch of smart hairy babies and
they'll be just as ugly and just as smart and clever as I
am until someday they wake up and realize that the
hairy ones make the best wives and mothers and the
hairless ones are just slimy and *cold* all the time, like
skinned melons.

Angry now, Emeez got up and started looking closer
at the gods. She couldn't help it—there was nothing interesting about the overworshipped gods. It was the
pristine, intricate ones that fascinated her. Maybe that
was her whole problem—she was attracted to gods with
poor reputations, and that's why she was cursed with
ugliness, because the really effective gods knew that she
wouldn't like them. That was terrible, though, to punish her from birth for a sin she wouldn't even commit
until she was six, only two years before she became a
woman.

Well, as long as I've already been punished for it, I'm
going to go right ahead and *deserve* the punishment.
I'm going to find the very most beautiful, most
*un*worshipped god of all and choose that one for my favorite.

So she began searching seriously for one that was in
perfect condition. But of course all the gods had received at least *some* worship, so even though she could
find sections of them that still had the most beautiful
details, there was none that was unmarred.

Until she found the most astonishing one, in the back corner of a small side chamber. It looked like none of the others. In fact, it looked like no beast that she had ever seen before. And the carving was absolutely pristine. It had been smoothed nowhere, which meant that it had never been worshipped by anyone.

Well, she said to the ugly god. *I* am your worshipper now. And I will worship you the best way, not like any of the others. I won't lick you or rub you or whatever other disgusting thing they do with those other muddy gods. I'm going to worship you by looking at you and saying that you are a *beautiful* carving.

Of course, it was a beautiful carving of an astonishingly ugly creature. Or rather, just the head of the creature. It had a mouth like a person, and two eyes like a person, but the nose pointed downward and its jaw was amazingly pointed, and down at the base of the head it narrowed down until the neck was much, much thinner than the head. How does it hold up such a massive head on such a skinny neck? And why would a stupid skymeat even think of making something that no one had ever seen?

The answer to that last question was obvious enough, of course, when she thought of it. The skymeat carved this head because this was what the god looked like.

No. What god would choose to look like *that?*

Unless—and here was an astonishing thought— unless the gods couldn't help the way they looked. Unless this god was just like her and grew up ugly and yet he didn't think that meant he didn't have a right to have a statue and be worshipped, and so he got a skymeat to carve his head but then when it was brought down here not one soul ever worshipped him and he got stuck off in a dark corner, only now *I've* found you, and I may be ugly but I'm the only worshipper you've got so don't tell me you're going to reject me now!

<I accept you.>

She heard it as clear as if someone had spoken behind her. She turned around to look, but there was no one in this darkish room, no one but her.

"Did you speak to me?" she whispered.

There was no answer. But as she looked at the ugly beautiful statue, she suddenly knew something, knew something so important that she had to tell Mother at once. She ran from the room and up the main road until she reached the room where Mother and the priestess were conversing animatedly. "I see you feel better, Emeez," said Mother, patting her head.

"Mother, I have to tell you—"

"Later," said Mother. "We've just about decided something wonderful for you and—"

"Mother, I have to tell you *now*."

Mother looked embarrassed and annoyed. "Emeez, you're going to make Vleezheesumuunuun think that I haven't raised you well."

From the priestess's name, Emeez realized that she must be somebody very important and distinguished, and suddenly she was shy. "I'm sorry," she said.

"No, that's all right," the old priestess said. "It's the hairy ones who still hear the voice of the gods, they say."

Oh, great, thought Emeez. Don't tell me that because I'm ugly I might have to end up as a *priestess*.

"What was it you wanted to tell us, child?" asked the priestess.

"I just—I was looking at a really beautiful god, only it was really ugly, and suddenly I knew something. That's all."

The priestess went down on all fours. Immediately Mother did, too, and Emeez was well-bred enough to know that *she* must also assume that posture. It was exhilarating, though, because it meant that the priestess was taking her seriously. "What did you suddenly know?" asked Vleezheesumuunuun.

"Well now that I think about it, I don't even know what it means."

"Tell us anyway," said Mother, and the priestess blinked a slow *yes*.

"The ones that were lost are coming back home."

Mother and the priestess looked at her blankly. Finally Mother spoke. "That's *all?*"

"That's enough," the priestess whispered. "Tell no one." The priestess's eyes were closed.

"Then you know what this means?" asked Mother.

"I don't," said the priestess. "Not what it *means*. But don't you remember from the song of creation, where the great prophet Zz says, 'There will be no more meat from the sky on the day when the lost ones are found, and no more gods from the river when the wanderers come home'?"

"No, I don't remember that one," said Mother, "and if you'll notice, Zz didn't say anything about lost ones coming home. She said the lost ones are found, and the ones who come home are the wanderers. So I don't think you need to take this so seriously and frighten my poor daughter to death."

But it was obviously Mother who was frightened. Emeez certainly wasn't. She was exhilarated. The god had told her he accepted her worship, and then had given her a gift, that bit of knowledge that meant nothing to her, but apparently meant a great deal to the priestess—and to Mother, too, despite her protests to the contrary.

"This changes everything," the priestess said.

"I was afraid of that," Mother said with a small voice.

"Oh, don't be absurd," said the priestess. "I'm still going to find a mate for your daughter."

Find a mate! Oh, what awful shame! An arranged marriage! Mother was *so* sure that no man would ever want her that she had gone to the priestess to arrange for a *sacrifice* marriage? Some man would be forced to take her as a wife in order to make up for some offense?

Emeez had seen that happen twice before, and both times the woman who was offered that way had also been an offender, and that was *her* penance, to be forced upon a man like some nasty herb to heal a wound.

"What crime am I guilty of?" Emeez whispered.

"Don't be petulant," said the priestess. "As I said, this changes everything."

"How?" asked Mother.

"Let's just say that when the words of Zz are promised their fulfillment in the mouth of a girl, that girl will not be given to a common blunderer or a moral cretin."

Oh, joy of joys, thought Emeez bitterly. I suppose that means I'll be given to some truly spectacular miscreant.

"She's six?" asked the priestess. "Two years till she's a woman?"

"As far as we can guess such things," said Mother. "It's the choice of the gods, of course."

The priestess stroked Emeez's fur. As always, Emeez stiffened under the touch. People were always touching the crooked limbs or stumps of cripples, too, and she just hated it, even if it *was* supposed to bring them luck. But then she realized that the priestess wasn't doing that hesitant little lucktouch. She was stroking Emeez's fur with real affection, it seemed, and it felt good. "I don't know if we've been right," said the priestess, "to call that soft downy nothing hair beautiful. I think along with the hair of our women we might have lost something else. A closeness to the gods."

Mother was too polite to disagree, but her very silence made it plain that *she* was not of that opinion.

The priestess was still talking. "Muf, the son of the war king, will be of age at about the same time as Emeez here."

After a moment's pause, Mother laughed. "Oh, you can't mean that you'd. . . ."

"A girl who hears the echo of Zz after all these centuries. . . ."

Mother was still protesting. "But Muf won't be happy to be given a. . . ."

"Muf intends to be war king. He will marry as the gods direct. As far as I'm concerned, the gods have chosen here today."

But it wasn't the gods, thought Emeez. Or rather, *I* chose *him*.

"It's too much for her," said Mother. "She never expected such honor."

"The girls who expect it," said the priestess, "are the very ones who should never be given it."

Finally Mother could believe it—or perhaps she finally realized that her very incredulity was making it plain to Emeez just what she thought of her. Whatever the reason, Mother finally squeaked in delight and embraced Emeez.

Before they left, the priestess had Emeez show her which god she had been looking at. She knew as soon as Emeez led her into that small side chamber which god it would be. "The big ugly one, right? No one has ever touched it."

"But the workmanship is beautiful," said Emeez.

"Yes, that's true," said the priestess. "No large hands like ours could ever make such intricate perfection. That's why the gods use the skymeat to give them material shape. But this one—I always wondered what he would do, since no one has ever given him a chance to make a child or bring the rain or anything like that. He must have been waiting for you, child." And again the old priestess stroked her hair.

I will be the wife of the new war king, if he turns out to be worthy to succeed his father. I'll do everything I can to help him be worthy. And I'll keep a beautiful room for him, with carpets and tapestries, baskets and robes more lovely than have ever been seen before. And when people see him, they won't think, Look at that poor man, to have such a hairy wife. Instead they'll say, the wife of the war king may be hairy, but she has surrounded our king with beauty.

I will never forget you for this great gift, she said silently to the beautiful ugly god.

"Will you move this god out into the open now?" asked Mother.

"No," said the priestess. "Nor are either of you to tell anyone what god it was who put these words into the girl's mouth. This god has never been touched. Let him stay that way."

"I've never heard of treating a powerful god like that," Mother protested.

"And I've never heard of an untouched god having any power," said the priestess. "So we don't have any precedents here. Therefore—we will do whatever works. And not touching this one seemed to be quite effective. That's enough for me."

And for me, said Emeez silently. Then, aloud, she repeated the first and clearest words that the god had said. "I accept you."

"Save those words for your husband," said Mother. "Now I think we'd better head home while there's still time to make a good supper."

All the way home, Mother kept repeating to her that she had to keep all these things to herself and not brag to anyone because until old Vleezh made some public announcement she could still change her mind. "Or she might die. She's old. And you can't imagine that any of the other priestesses would be the least bit impressed if I brought you in and said, But Vleezh said she was going to pair my Emeez with Muf, the son of the war king."

No, of course I can't imagine that, Mother. Who could?

In the back of her mind, though, one question kept nagging at her, one that Mother and the priestess both seemed to have ignored. What did it *mean*, to say that the lost ones were coming home? Who was coming? And how did they get lost? And why was it this strange ugly god who brought the news, out of all the thousands of gods in the holy cave?

I will watch and wait, thought Emeez. I think the god meant to accomplish more with these words than just to get me married off so far beyond all expectations. So I will try to see what the god's message really meant, and when I do, I will proclaim it or whatever else the god wants me to do. It will be clear to me, when it happens, what I'm supposed to do.

She did not wonder how she knew that. Instead she began to speculate on what word to add to her name, for the wife of the war king's son would never be left with just her weaning name. Emeezuuzh? Uuzh was the ending Mother had taken on her day of glory, when her basket was chosen for the burial of the old blood king. But that was a pretty name, a delicate name when a woman chose it. Emeez would have something stronger. She would have to think about that. There'd be plenty of time to make up her mind.

SEVEN

A STORM AT SEA

Zdorab had been born in the wrong era. He had
never realized it until now. Oh, he knew he didn't fit in
where he grew up or where he lived in Basilica before
Nafai gave him the chance to save his life by coming
with him into the desert. But now, at the end of his second stint as Nafai's co-teacher of the children on the
starship *Basilica*, Zdorab knew where he truly belonged. The trouble was, the culture that might have
valued him had been gone for forty million years.

Whoever it was that built this starship, with its fine-
ness of design and craftsmanship, was to be admired, of
course. It was only after living in it that Zdorab understood that he also loved their way of life. True, they
were confined indoors, but as far as Zdorab was concerned, outdoor life was over-rated. He did not miss in-
sects. He did not miss excessive heat and cold, humidity
and dryness. He did not miss the defecations of animals
and the smells of strange things cooking or overfamiliar
things rotting.

But it wasn't the absence of annoyances that made him relish the life aboard ship. It was the positive things. A comfortable bed every night. Daily bathing in a shower of clean water. A life centered around the library, around learning and teaching. Computers that could play as well as work. Music perfectly reproduced. Toilets that cleaned themselves and had no odors. Clothing that could be cleaned without laundering. Meals prepared in moments. And all of it while traveling at some unfathomable speed on a hundred-year voyage to another star.

He tried explaining it to Nafai, but the young man merely looked at Zdorab in puzzlement and said, "But what about trees?" Obviously Nafai couldn't wait to get to the new planet, which would no doubt be another place with lots of dirt and bugs and plenty of sweaty manual labor to do. Zdorab had played obsequious servant all the way across the desert; he loved the fact that in this starship there *were* no servants, because all work was either done by machines and computers or was so simple and easy that anyone could do it—and everyone did.

And he loved teaching the children. Some of them were barely children anymore, six years into the voyage. Oykib had shot up to nearly two meters now, at the apparent age of fourteen. He was lanky, but Zdorab had seen him working out in the centrifuge and his body was wiry with hard tight muscles. Zdorab knew he was middle-aged by the fact that he could see that beautiful young body and feel only the memory of desire. If there was any mercy in nature, it was the fading of the male libido with middle age. Some men, feeling the slackening of desire, went to heroic—or criminal—lengths to get the illusion of renewed sexual vigor. But for Zdorab it was a relief. It was better to think of Oykib and his even-more-beautiful younger brother, Yasai, as students. As friends of his son, Padarok. As potential mates of his daughter, Dabrota.

My son, he thought. My daughter. Good Lord. Who

would ever have guessed, during his years in clandestine love affairs in the men's city outside Basilica, that I would ever have a son and a daughter. And if any man laid hands on either one of them without my consent, I think I'd kill him.

And then he thought: I'm a jungle creature after all.

He was going to sleep again today, as Shedemei wakened to take his place. They would overlap for a few hours—the Oversoul said there was life support enough for that—and it would be good to see her. She was his best friend, the only one who knew his secrets, his inward struggles. He could tell her almost everything.

But he could not tell her about the little program he had set up in a life support computer, one of those not directly part of the Oversoul's memory. Just before scheduling the one wake-up call for midvoyage, the obvious one that the Oversoul had detected at once, Zdorab had written a program that ostensibly took a harmless inventory of supplies. It also checked, however, to see if it was exactly six and a half years into the voyage, and if it was, it would send a new version of the schedule file to the computer where the calendar was executed. The new version would call for Elemak, Zdorab, and Shedemei to be wakened thirty seconds later; then, after another second, the original copy of the schedule would be restored and the inventory program would rewrite itself to eliminate the extra subroutine. It was all very deft and Zdorab was proud of its cleverness.

He also knew that it was potentially lethal to the peace of the community and he kept intending, now that he was taking part in Nafai's little plan, to get into the life support computer and eliminate it before it could go off. The trouble was that it was not as easy to get access to that computer, now that they were in flight. He had duties, and when those were done, the children were everywhere all the time and they would be bound to ask him what he was doing. He told himself that he was looking for a safe opportunity to make the change. Now he was only hours from going back to sleep, and he had found no such opportunity. Why not?

Because he was afraid, that's why. That was the worm in his salad. Not that he was afraid for himself—the hunger for self-preservation was no longer as important to him as the need to protect his children. He had gone along with Nafai's scheme, not because of dreams—those were for Shedemei and others that the Oversoul had bred to be especially receptive to them—but because he did not want *some* of the children to be given an advantage, and not his own. When Issib came up with the plan of having the adults help teach the children in shifts, Zdorab wouldn't have dreamed of refusing to take part.

At the same time, though, he was afraid of what Elemak would do later on to take vengeance. When he woke up on Earth and found himself surrounded by these strong young men, all committed to Nafai's cause, he would be so filled with hate that he would *never* forgive. There would be war, sooner or later, and it would be bloody. Zdorab didn't want his children to suffer from that. Didn't want them to have to take part, or even take sides. What better way to accomplish that than to prove his loyalty to Elemak by letting the wake-up call come through as planned?

Of course, Nafai and the Oversoul would have no problem figuring out who had done it—nobody else had the computer skills back on Harmony, and none of the children who had acquired those abilities during the voyage were likely to want to wake up Elemak. Hadn't he heard Izuchaya—who had been so young at launch that she barely remembered Elemak—asking, "Why do we have to wake up Elemak at all, if he's so bad?" "Because that would be murder," Nafai had answered her, and then explained that even when you disagree with someone, they still have a right to live their life and make their own choices. The only time you have a right to kill someone is when they're actually trying to kill you or someone you need to protect.

Someone you need to protect. I need to protect my children. And here's the cold hard truth, Nafai: My children are no blood kin of yours. Therefore, even if we side with you, I can't believe for a moment that you will ever be as careful of them, as loyal to them, as you are to your own children or your parents' young children or your brother Issib's children. I have to find a way to protect them myself, to make it so Elemak won't hate them the way he will hate you and your children— even as I've helped them take advantage of your plan to become older and stronger than Elemak's boys. That's what a father does. Even if his wife wouldn't approve of it.

Shedemei had different ideas of loyalty, Zdorab knew. She was an all-or-nothing kind of person. That's because she hadn't lived in the nightmare world of inter-weaving treachery that Zdorab had inhabited for so many years. Gaballufix's constant plotting, in which other people's trust was regarded as a weapon to be turned against them; the routine violence and corruption of life in the men's village, where the ameliorating influence of women did not penetrate; and of course the relentless deception of the life of a man who loved men. No one can really be trusted, Shedemei, he said silently.

Not even the Oversoul. Especially not the Oversoul.

Zdorab's only contact with the master computer was through the Index and, later, through the ordinary computers of the starship. He had no dreams, and as far as he knew the Oversoul neither cared about him nor heard any of his thoughts. How else could he have in-stalled his clandestine wake-up program? The Oversoul had no particular use for him except to provide the other set of chromosomes for Shedemei to reproduce. Well, that was fine—Zdorab didn't have all that much use for the Oversoul, either. He was firmly convinced that whatever it was the Oversoul wanted, it didn't care much about the comfort and happiness of the human beings it manipulated. And because the Oversoul didn't care about him, he was the one person in the whole community with privacy.

At the same time, in the back of his mind, Zdorab hoped that, in fact, the Oversoul *did* hear his thoughts and knew all about the wake-up call. It had probably already removed it, in fact; Zdorab hadn't checked it for the same reasons that he hadn't removed it himself. The Oversoul wouldn't let anything dangerous happen during the voyage. Elemak wasn't going to wake up until Earth. And when he did, Zdorab could truthfully say, "I left the wake-up call in place. The Oversoul must have found it."

He silently rehearsed the words, shaping them with his lips and tongue and teeth, knowing even as he did it that Elemak wouldn't believe him, or if he did he wouldn't care.

They're wrong to have brought me with their family, wrong to force me to choose between them in their deadly domestic quarrels.

He stood before Shedemei's sleep chamber as the lid slipped back and her eyes fluttered open. She smiled weakly.

"Hi, brilliant and beautiful lady," he said.

"To be flattered upon first waking is every woman's fondest dream," she said. "Unfortunately I'm still stupid from the drugs."

"What drugs?" He helped her sit up before he unclamped and dropped the side of the chamber so she could get out.

"You mean I'm just naturally this mentally slow?"

She got up and clung to him, partly to support herself as she tried to get her legs working again in the low gravity, and partly as an embrace between friends. He responded, of course, and began telling her of all that the different children had accomplished since she had last been awake. "I think this may be the finest school that ever existed," he said.

"And how convenient that the teachers are all put to sleep between terms," answered Shedemei.

They spent the hours together talking about the children, especially their own, and about anything that came to Shedemei's mind. But they did not talk about the one thing preying most on Zdorab's mind, and Shedemei noticed something was wrong.

"What is it?" she asked. "You're not telling me something."

"Like what?" he answered.

"Something is worrying you."

"My life is worry," he said. "I don't like climbing into the sleep chamber."

She smiled thinly. "All right, you don't have to tell me."

"Can't tell you what I don't know myself," he said, and since this contained a grain of truth—he didn't know whether the Oversoul had removed his program or not—Shedemei's truthsense allowed her to believe him and she relaxed.

A few hours later he said goodbye to the children in a ritual that they were all used to by now, since their teachers all came and went this way. Handshakes or hugs all around, depending on the child's age; a kiss for his own children whether they liked it or not; and then Nafai and Shedemei escorted him to his chamber and helped him in.

As the drugs began to take effect, though, he was filled with a sudden panic. No, no, no, he thought. How could I have been so stupid? Elemak will never be loyal to me, no matter what I do. I have to change the program. I have to keep him from waking up and taking Nafai by surprise. "Nafai," he said. "Check the life support computers."

But the lid of the chamber was already closed, and he couldn't see whether Nafai was even watching his lips,

and before he could even move a hand, the drug overwhelmed him and he slept.

"What did he say?" Nafai asked Shedemei.

"I don't know. Something was bothering him but he
didn't know what?"

"Well, maybe he'll remember it when he wakes up,"
said Nafai.

Shedemei sighed. "I always have that same anxiety,
too, like I've forgotten to say something *very* important. I think it's just one of the side effects of the suspension drugs."

Nafai laughed. "Like when you wake up in the middle
of the night with a very important idea from a dream,
and you write it down and then in the morning it says,
'Not the food! The dog!' and you have no idea what
that could possibly mean or why you once thought it was
important."

"The real dreams," said Shedemei, "you don't have
to write down. You remember them."

They both nodded, remembering what it felt like to
have the Oversoul or the Keeper of Earth speak to them
in their sleep. Then they returned to the children and
set to work on the next part of their training.

Chveya was working with Dza on coaching some of the
younger children through their exercises. They had
learned years ago that everybody had to be supervised
or they would start to slack off, even though Nafai had
warned again and again that if they didn't put in two
hard hours every day in the centrifuge, they would
reach Earth with bodies so slack and feeble that they
would have to borrow Issib's chair just to get around.
So the younger children exercised with older children
calling the times, and the older children worked with
younger ones monitoring them. That way they never
had peers "telling them what to do." The system
worked well enough.

Dza was still not Chveya's friend—they really hadn't

that much in common. Dza was one of those people who couldn't stand to be alone, who always had to surround herself with the hubbub of conversation, with eager gossip, with laughter and mockery. Chveya could see that, now that Dza wasn't bossing them anymore, the younger girls genuinely liked her. It appeared to Chveya like a physical connection between them, and she could see how the younger girls brightened when they came into Dza's presence—and how Dza brightened also. But Chveya could not enjoy being with them for long. And envy wasn't the cause of it, either, though at times she *did* envy Dza her bevy of friends. All the constant chat, the rapidly shifting demands on her attention—it wore Chveya out very quickly, and she would have to go off by herself for a while, to surround herself with silence and music, to read a book continuously for an hour, holding the same thread of talk.

Father had talked to her about it, and Mother, too, when she was awake the last time. You spend too much time alone, Chveya. The other children sometimes think you don't like them. But to Chveya, reading a book was not the same as being alone. Instead she was having a conversation with one person, a sustained conversation that stuck to the subject and didn't constantly fly off on tangents or get interrupted by someone demanding to tell *her* gossip or talk about *her* problem.

As long as Chveya got her solitary time, though, she could get along peaceably enough with the others—even Dza. Now that she had got over her childish infatuation with being "first child," Dza was good company, bright and funny. To her credit, Dza had not been jealous when it was discovered that Chveya alone of the third generation had developed the ability to sense the relationships among people, even though it was Dza's mother, not Chveya's, who had first learned to do it. When Aunt Hushidh was awake, she spent more time with Chveya than with her own daughters, but Dza did not complain. In fact, Dza once smiled at Chveya and said, "Your father teaches all of us all the time. I'm not going to get mad because my mother spends time teaching you." Studying with Aunt Hushidh was like reading a book. She was quiet, she was patient, she stuck to the subject. And better than a book: She answered Chveya's questions. With Aunt Hushidh, Chveya suddenly became the talkative one. Perhaps that was because Aunt Hushidh was the only one who had seen the things that Chveya saw.

"But you see more," Aunt Hushidh said one day. "You have dreams like your mother, too."

Chveya rolled her eyes. "There's no Lake of Women on this starship," she said. "There's no City of Women to make a fuss over me and hang on every word of my accounts of my visions."

"It wasn't really like that," said Hushidh.

"Mother said it was."

"Well, that's how it seemed to her, perhaps. But your mother never exploited the role of Waterseer."

"It wasn't useful, though, like . . . well, like what we can do."

Hushidh smiled slightly. "Useful. But sometimes misleading. You can interpret things wrongly. When you know too much about people, it still doesn't mean that you know enough. Because the one thing you never really know is *why* they're connected to one person and distant from another. I make guesses. Sometimes it's easy enough. Sometimes I'm hopelessly wrong."

"I'm always wrong," said Chveya, but it didn't make her ashamed to say this in front of Aunt Hushidh.

"Always *partly* wrong," said Hushidh. "But often partly right, and sometimes very clever about it indeed. The problem, you see, is that you must care enough about other people to really think about them, to try to imagine the world through their eyes. And you and I—we're both a little shy about getting to know people. You have to try to spend time with them. To listen to them. To be friends with them. I'm saying this, not because I did it at your age, but because I didn't, and I know how much it hampered me."

"So what changed it?" asked Chveya.

"I married a man who lived in such constant inner pain that it made my own fears and shames and sufferings seem like childish whining."

"Mother says that long before you married Uncle Issib, you faced down a bad man and took the loyalty of his whole army away from him."

"That's because they were another man's army, only that man was dead, and they didn't have much loyalty to begin with. It wasn't hard, and I did it by blindly flailing around, trying to say *everything* I could think of that might weaken what loyalty remained."

"Mother says you looked calm and masterful."

"The key word is 'looked.' Come now, Veya, you know for yourself—when you're terrified and confused, what do you do?"

Chveya giggled then. "I stand there like a frightened deer."

"Frozen, right? But to others, it looks like you're calm as can be. That's why some of the others tease you so mercilessly sometimes. They think of you as made of stone, and they want to break in and touch human feelings. They just don't know that when you seem most stony, that's when you're most frightened and breakable."

"Why is that? Why don't people understand each other better?"

"Because they're young," said Hushidh.

"Old people don't understand each other any better."

"Some do," said Hushidh. "The ones who care enough to try."

"You mean you."

"And your mother."

"She doesn't understand me at *all*."

"You say that because you're an adolescent, and

when an adolescent says that her mother doesn't understand her, it means that her mother understands her all too well but won't let her have her way."

Chveya grinned. "You are a nasty, conceited, arrogant grownup just like all the others."

Hushidh smiled back. "See? You're learning. That smile allowed you to tell me *just* what you thought, but allowed me to take it as a joke so I could hear the truth without having to get angry."

"I'm trying," Chveya said with a sigh.

"And you're doing well, for a short, ignorant, shy adolescent."

Chveya looked at her in horror. Then Hushidh broke into a smile.

"Too late," said Chveya. "You meant that."

"Only a little," said Hushidh. "But then, all adolescents are ignorant, and you can't help being short and shy. You'll get taller."

"And shyer."

"But sometimes bolder."

Well, it was true. Chveya had started a growth spurt soon after Hushidh went back to sleep the last time, and now she was almost as tall as Dza, and taller than any of the boys except Oykib, who was already almost as tall as Father, all bones and angles, constantly bumping into things or smacking his hands into them or stubbing his toes. Chveya liked the way he took the others' teasing with a wordless grin, and never complained. She also liked the fact that he never used his large size to bully any of the other children, and when he interceded in quarrels, it was with quiet persuasion, not with his greater size and strength, that he brought peace. Since she was probably going to end up married to Oykib, it was nice that she liked the kind of man he was becoming. Too bad that all he thought of when he looked at *her* was "short and boring." Not that he ever said it. But his eyes always seemed to glide right past her, as if he didn't notice her enough to even ignore her. And when he was alone with her, he always left as quickly as possible, as if it nearly killed him to spend any time in her company.

Just because we children are going to have to pair up and marry doesn't mean we're going to fall in love with each other, Chveya told herself. If I'm a good wife to him, maybe someday he'll love me.

She didn't often allow herself to think of the other possibility, that when it came time to marry, Oykib would insist on marrying someone else. Cute little Shyada, for instance. She might be two years younger, but she already knew how to flirt with the boys so that poor Padarok was always tongue-tied around her and Motya watched her all the time with an expression of such pitiful longing that Chveya didn't know whether to laugh or cry. What if Oykib married *her*, and left Chveya to marry one of the younger boys? What if they *made* one of the younger ones marry her?

I'd kill myself, she decided.

Of course she knew that she would not. Not literally, anyway. She'd put the best face on it that she could, and make do.

Sometimes she wondered if that's how it was for Aunt Hushidh. Had she fallen in love with Issib before she married him? Or did she marry him because he was the only one left? It must be hard, to be married to a man you had to pick up and carry around when he wasn't in a place where his floats would work. But they seemed happy together.

People can be happy together.

All these thoughts and many more kept playing through Chveya's mind as she helped Shyada, Netsya, Dabya, and Zuya get through their calisthenics. Since Netsya was a cruel taskmaster when *she* was doing times for the older children, it was rather a pleasure to say, "Faster, Netsya. You did better than this last time," as Netsya's face got redder and redder and sweat flew off her hands and nose as she moved.

"You are," Netsya said, panting, "the queen, of the bitches."

"And thou art the princess, darling Gonets."

"Listen to her," said Zuya, who was *not* panting, because she did all her exercises as easily as if they were a pleasant stroll. "She reads so much she talks like a book now."

"An old, book," Netsya panted. "An ancient, decrepit, dusty, yellowed, worm-eaten—"

Her list of Chveya's virtues was interrupted by a loud ringing sound, followed by a whooping siren that nearly deafened them. Several of the children in the centrifuge screamed; most held their hands over their ears. They had never heard such a thing before.

"Something's wrong," Dza said to Chveya. Chveya noticed that Dza was not holding her hands over her ears. She looked as calm as an owl.

"I think we should stay here until Father tells us what to do," said Chveya.

Dza nodded. "Let's make sure who we have and not lose track of them."

It was a good idea. Chveya was momentarily jealous that she hadn't had the presence of mind to think of it. But then she knew that the wisest thing *she* could do was not to worry about who came up with the good ideas, but simply to use them. And Dza was a natural leader. Chveya should set the example of quick and willing obedience, as long as Dza's decisions were reasonable ones.

Dza had been working with the younger boys. She quickly counted them up. Motya, the youngest; Xodhya, Yaya, and Zhyat. She herded them to where Chveya had the younger girls. Chveya already had her tally because her girls had been working out together when the alarm went off.

"Just sit here and wait," shouted Dza to all the children.

"Can't they turn it off?" wailed Netsya, clearly terrified.

"Cover your ears, but keep looking at the rest of us!" shouted Dza. "Don't close your eyes."

Dza thought of things quickly—if the children couldn't hear, they had to *watch*, so they could receive instructions if they needed to do something. Again Chveya felt a little stab of jealousy. It didn't help that she could see how clearly everyone's loyalty, trust, *dependence* on Dza had suddenly increased.

Even my own, thought Chveya. She really *is* first child, now that she doesn't misuse it.

A pair of legs appeared in the ladderway at the top of the centrifuge. Long legs, with big awkward feet. Oykib. And he was more awkward than usual, because he was carrying something bulky under his arm. Something wrapped in cloth.

When he reached the floor, he turned at once to Dza. As if he had known she would be in charge. "It's not as loud in the sleeping rooms," he shouted. "Can you get all the younger ones to their beds?"

Dza nodded.

"That's where Nafai wants them, then, if you can do it safely without losing any."

"All right," said Dza, and immediately she started giving instructions. The younger children started up the ladder, Dza reminding each one to wait in the tube just outside the centrifuge until she got up there. Chveya felt completely unnecessary.

Oykib turned to her and held out the cloth bundle. "It's the Index," he said. "Elemak is awake. Hide it."

Chveya was amazed. None of the children had ever been allowed to touch the Index, even wrapped in cloth. "Did Father tell you to—"

"Do it," said Oykib. "Where Elemak won't think to look."

He shoved the bundle into her stomach and her arms

instinctively folded around it. Then he turned and left, following Dza up the ladder.

Chveya looked around the centrifuge. Was there anyplace to hide the Index here? Not really. The exercise space was largely unencumbered, except for the strength machines, and those offered no concealment. So she clutched the Index under her arm and waited for her turn up the ladder.

Then she saw, where the centrifuge floor curved up to make its circle around the girth of the ship, the break in the carpet where the access door was. When the centrifuge was stopped, the access door could be pulled up so that someone could crawl down into the system of wheels that allowed the centrifuge to spin. The trouble was, it would take half an hour for the centrifuge to spin to a stop even if she turned it off right now. And then another hour or more to spin back up to speed. It would be obvious to Elemak that the centrifuge had been stopped for *some* reason. She couldn't count on his not noticing. Just because he had never been awake during the voyage didn't mean he wouldn't be aware of anomalies in the working of the ship.

On the other hand, the very fact that the centrifuge hadn't been stopped would imply to him that nothing had been hidden there.

She ran to the access door and pulled up on it. It wouldn't budge—an interlock prevented it from being opened while the centrifuge was spinning. She ran to the nearest emergency stop button and pushed it. The alarm that it sounded was lost in the howling of the main siren. Now the access door could be opened, even though the centrifuge was spinning rapidly. She flopped it back; it formed a slight arch on the curved floor. Through the door she could see the wheels of the centrifuge as the roadway hurtled by beneath them; then her perspective shifted, and she realized that she was on the hurtling surface, and the roadway was really the structure of the rest of the ship, holding still beneath the wheels. Up at the top of the ladder, the spin seemed so much slower. Just as many revolutions per minute, but so close to the center that it wasn't fast at all.

If I drop the Index, will it be crushed?

More to the point, if I fall or even touch the roadway, will I be killed or just maimed and crippled for life?

Sweating, terrified, she extended one leg, then the other, down through the opening until she was standing on the frame of the nearest wheel assembly. Then, holding her weight on her right hand, she braced the Index against the door while she got her hand under it. Balancing the Index on her palm, she carefully lifted it down into the opening and reached into the top of the other wheel assembly, right up under the centrifuge floor. In a place where four metal bars formed a square, she gingerly tipped the Index out of her hand, so that it rolled off and dropped into place. It was secure there—nothing was going to tip it off and it was far too wide to drop through. Best of all, it couldn't be seen unless you got down into the opening so far that your head was under the level of the centrifuge floor. Chances were that long before he got down far enough to see it, Elemak would conclude that it was far too dangerous for anyone to have put the Index down here and would give up and search somewhere else.

In fact, now that she thought about it, it really *was* dangerous to be down here. And she had to get back up and turn the centrifuge back on so its alarm would stop sounding before the main siren finally shut down. Getting out wasn't as easy as getting down had been, and now that she wasn't concentrating on getting the Index hidden, she had time to be really terrified. Slow, she kept telling herself. Careful. One slip and they'll be scraping bits of me off the road for a month.

Finally she was out, spread-eagle over the opening.

She spider-walked until she was clear of it, then leaped to her feet and flung the door closed. It slammed into place, the catch engaged, and now she could turn the centrifuge back on. She could barely feel it speeding up—it was so well-engineered that in all that time with the motors off, friction had hardly slowed it down at all.

The siren went off. The silence was like a physical blow; her ears rang. She had made it with only ten or fifteen seconds to spare.

In the silence, she heard the noise of someone on the ladder.

She looked up. Legs. Not Father's. Not a child's. If she was found here, for no reason, then Elemak would wonder why she hadn't gone with the other children.

Without even thinking, she flung herself down to the floor, curled up in fetal position, buried her face in her hands, and began to whimper softly, trembling with fear. Let them think she had panicked, frozen up, terrified by the strange loud noise. Let them think she was weak, that she had lost all control of herself. They would believe it, because nobody knew she was the kind of person who could perform dangerous acrobatics while speeding over a roadway. Why should they? She hadn't known it herself. She could hardly believe it now.

"Get up," said the man. "Get yourself together. Nothing's going to hurt you."

It wasn't Elemak. It was Vasnya's and Panya's father, Vas. Aunt Sevet's husband. So it wasn't just Elemak who was awake.

"Nothing to be ashamed of," he said. "Loud noise—it gets to some people. You should see how the little ones are. It's going to take hours to get them quieted down."

"Little ones?" She realized at once that he didn't mean the twelve- and thirteen-year-olds. "The little children were wakened?"

"Everybody's awake. When the suspended animation alarm goes off, everybody is awakened at once. Just in case something is wrong with the system."

"What set it off?" asked Chveya.

Now, for the first time, a dark look of anger came across Uncle Vas's face. "We'll have to find that out, won't we? But if it hadn't wakened us, we wouldn't have had a chance to see you as such a pretty little—what—fourteen-year-old?"

"Fifteen," she said.

"Happy birthday," he answered dryly. "I'm sure my eight-year-old daughter Vasnaminanya will be delighted to see her dear cousin Veya. You'll really enjoy playing dolls with her, don't you think?"

Suddenly Chveya was ashamed. Vasnya had been her friend, the one child of the first year who had been nice to her and included her in things even during the times when Dza decreed that Chveya was untouchable. But because Vasnya's parents were friends of Elemak instead of Nafai, Vasnya had been left behind. Chveya was already six and a half years older. They would never really be friends again. And why? Was it anything Vasnya had done? No—she was a good person. Yet she had been left behind.

"I'm sorry," Chveya said quietly.

"Yes, well, we know who's to blame for this, and it isn't any of the children." He held out a hand to her. "Elemak's in charge now. He should have done it long ago."

He was trying to seem nice and reassuring, but Chveya wasn't stupid. "What have you done to Father?"

"Nothing," said Vas, smiling. "He just didn't seem terribly interested in contesting Elemak's authority."

"But he has the cloak of the—"

"Cloak of the starmaster," said Vas. "Yes, well, he still has it. Sparking its little heart out. Nafai has the cloak. But Elemak has the twins."

The twins, Serp and Spel. Chveya's youngest brothers, so small that they couldn't be included in the school. Elemak must be holding them hostage, threatening to hurt them if Father doesn't do what he wants.

"So he's using babies to get his way?" said Chveya scornfully.

Vas's expression got very ugly indeed. "Oh, what an awful thing for him to do. Someday you'll have to explain to me why it's bad for Elemak to use the children to get his way, but it was all right for your father to do exactly the same thing. Now come with me."

As she preceded him up the ladder, Chveya tried to find a clear distinction between holding babies hostage, like Elemak, and giving children a free choice to join with him in—in keeping control of the colony. That's what it came down to, didn't it? Using the children to get and keep control of the whole community.

But it *was* different. There was a clear moral difference and if she thought hard enough she would be able to explain it and then everybody would understand that the voyage school was a perfectly decent thing to do, while holding the twins as hostages was an unspeakable atrocity. She would think of it any minute now.

Then a completely different thought came to her. Oykib had given her the Index. He had assumed that Dza would lead the other children to safety, but when it came time to hide the Index of the Oversoul, instead of doing it himself he had entrusted it to Chveya. And he hadn't told her where to hide it, either.

Everyone was gathered in the library. It was the only room large enough to hold them all, since it was a large open room using almost the whole girth of the ship. There were babies crying and little children looking puzzled and afraid. Chveya knew all the little children, of course. They were unchanged, gathered around their mothers. Kokor, Sevet, Dol. And Elemak's wife, Eiadh. She wasn't holding her own youngest, though, not

Zhivya. No, Aunt Eiadh was holding one of the twins, Spel.

And Elemak, standing at one edge of the library, was holding Serp.

I will never forgive either of you, Chveya said silently. I may not be able to sort out the moral theory of it, but those are my brothers you're holding, using the threat of harming them to get your own way.

"Chveya," said Luet, seeing her.

"Shut up," said Elemak. "Come here," he said to Chveya.

She walked toward him, stopped a good many paces away.

"Look at you," said Elemak, contemptuously angry.

"Look at *you*," said Chveya. "Threatening a baby. Your children must be proud of their brave daddy."

A hot rage swept over Elemak, and she saw his connection to her take on an almost negative force. For a moment he wanted her dead.

But he did nothing, said nothing until he had calmed himself a little.

"I want the Index," said Elemak. "Oykib says he gave it to you."

Chveya whirled on Oykib, who looked back at her impassively. "It's all right," Oykib said. "Your father was the one who wanted it hidden. Now the Oversoul is telling him to give the Index to Elemak."

"Where's Father?" asked Chveya. "Who are you to speak for him?"

"Your father is safe," said Elemak. "You'd better listen to your *big* uncle Oykib."

"Believe me," said Oykib. "You can tell him. The Oversoul says it's all right."

"How can you possibly know what the Oversoul says?" demanded Chveya.

"Why shouldn't he?" Elemak said snidely. "Everybody else does. This room is *full* of people who love to tell other people what the Oversoul wants them to do."

"When I hear it from Father's mouth, I'll tell you where the Index is."

"It has to be in the centrifuge," said Vas, "if she's the one who hid it."

Oykib's eyes grew wide. "There's no place to hide it in there."

Elemak snapped at Mebbekew and Obring. "Go and find it," he said.

Obring got up at once, but Mebbekew was deliberately slow. Chveya could see that his loyalty to Elemak was weak. But then, his loyalty to everybody was weak.

"Just tell them, Veya," said Oykib. "It's all right, I mean it."

I don't care whether you mean it or not, said Chveya silently. I didn't risk my life to hide it, only to have a traitor like you talk me into giving it back to them.

"It doesn't matter," said Oykib. "The only power the Index has is to enable you to talk to the Oversoul. Do you think the Oversoul is going to have anything to say to a man like *that*?" His voice was thick with scorn as he gestured at Elemak.

Elemak smiled, walked to Oykib, and then with one hand lifted him out of his chair and threw him up against the wall. It knocked the breath out of Oykib, and he slumped, holding his head where it had banged against the cabinets. "You may be tall," said Elemak, "and you may be full of proud words, but you've got nothing to back it up, boy. Did Nafai really think I'd ever be afraid of a 'man' like you?"

"You can tell him, Chveya," Oykib said, not answering Elemak at all. "He can beat up on children, but he can't control the Oversoul."

It seemed to be just a flick of Elemak's hand, but the result was Oykib's head striking the cabinets again with such force that he fell to the floor.

Chveya saw the great, bright strands of loyalty connecting Oykib to her. It had never been like this before.

And she realized that he was undergoing this beating at Elemak's hands solely to convince her that he was not a traitor, that what he was saying was true. She could give the Index to Elemak.

But she couldn't bring herself to do it. Even if Oykib was right and the Index would be useless, Uncle Elemak didn't seem to think so. He wanted it. She might be able to get some leverage out of that.

However, she couldn't very well let Oykib take any more abuse if she could help it. "I'll tell you where it is," said Chveya.

Obring and Meb were poised at the ladderway in the center of the library.

"When you let me see that Father is all right," Chveya added.

"I've already told you that he's all right," said Elemak.

"You're also holding a baby to make sure you get your way," said Chveya. "That proves you're a decent person who would never tell a lie."

Elemak's face flushed. "We've grown up with a mouth, have we? Nafai's influence over these children is such a wonderful thing." As he spoke, though, he walked to where Mother sat silently with her other children. He handed Serp to her. "I don't threaten babies," said Elemak.

"You mean now that you already got Father to surrender to you," said Chveya.

"Where is the Index?" said Elemak.

"Where is my father?" asked Chveya.

"Safe."

"So is the Index."

Elemak strode to her, towered over her. "Are you trying to bargain with me, little girl?"

"Yes," said Chveya.

"As Oykib said, the Index is useless to me," said Elemak with a grin.

"Fine," said Chveya.

He leaned down, cupped his hand behind her head, whispered in her ear. "Veya, I will do whatever it takes to get my way."

As soon as he pulled away from her, she said loudly, "He said, 'Veya, I will do whatever it takes to get my way.'"

The others murmured. Perhaps at her audacity in repeating aloud what he had whispered to her. Perhaps at Elemak's threat. It didn't matter—the network of relationships was shifting. Elemak's hold on his friends was a little weaker. Fear and dread still bound all the others to him, of course; his mistreatment of Oykib had strengthened Elemak's control. But Chveya's boldness and his blustering against her had weakened the loyalty of those who were following him willingly.

He seemed to sense this—he had been a strong leader of men, taking caravans through dangerous country, and he knew when he was losing ground even if he didn't have Chveya's and Hushidh's gift of seeing ties of loyalty and obedience, love and fear. So he changed tactics. "Try all you like, Veya," he said, "but you can't make me the villain of this little scene. It was your father and those who conspired with him who betrayed the rest of us. It was your father who lied when he promised to waken us in mid-voyage. It was your father who cheated our children out of their birthright. Look at them." He waved his hand to indicate the four-year-olds, the five-year-olds, the eight-year-olds who were still trying to reconcile these tall adolescents with the children of their own age whom they remembered seeing only hours before, when they were put to sleep together before the launch. "Who is it who mistreated children? Who is it who exploited them? Not me."

Chveya could see that Elemak was winning sympathy again. "Then why is your wife still holding Spel?" asked Chveya.

Eiadh leapt to her feet and spat out her answer. "I

don't hold babies prisoner, you nasty little brat! He was crying and I comforted him."

"Maybe his own mother might have done it better," said Chveya. "Maybe your husband doesn't *want* you to give Spel back to Mother."

Eiadh's immediate glance at Elemak and his irritated gesture proved Chveya's point for her. Eiadh sullenly carried Spel to Luet, who took him and sat him on her other knee. In all this time, however, Luet had said nothing. Why is Mother silent? Chveya wondered. Why have these adults left it to me and Oykib to do all the talking?

<Because they have children.>

The thought came into her mind with such clarity that she knew it came from the Oversoul. She also understood the Oversoul's meaning at once. Because the adults have little children, they're afraid of what Elemak might do to them. Only adolescents like Oykib and me are free to be brave, because we don't have any children to protect.

<Yes.>

So if you can talk to me, and it's all right for me to give the Index to Elemak, why not say so?

But there was no answer.

Chveya didn't understand what the Oversoul was doing. Why she was telling Oykib one thing while *not* confirming it to her, not telling her anything she needed to know. The Oversoul could pipe up and explain why the grownups weren't saying anything, but she didn't have any helpful advice about what Chveya should actually *do*.

Maybe that meant that what she was already doing was fine.

<Yes.>

"Take me to see Father," said Chveya. "When I see that he's unharmed, I'll give you the Index."

"The ship is not that large," said Elemak. "I can find it without you."

"You can try," said Chveya. "But the very fact that you're so reluctant to let me see my father proves that you've hurt him and you don't dare let these people know what a violent, terrible, evil person you are."

She thought then, for a few moments, that he might hit her. But that was just an expression that flickered in his eyes; his hands never moved; he didn't even lean toward her.

"You don't know me," said Elemak quietly. "You were just a child when we last met. It's quite possible that I'm exactly what you say. But if I were really that terrible, evil, and violent, why aren't you bruised and bleeding?"

"Because you won't make any points with your toadies if you slap a girl around," said Chveya coldly. "The way you treated Oykib shows what you are. The fact that you aren't treating me the same just proves that you're still not sure you're in control."

Chveya would never have dared to say these things, except that she could see with every word, with every sentence, that she was weakening Elemak's position. Of course, she was bright enough to know that this was dangerous, that as he became aware of his slackening control he might behave more rashly, more dangerously. But it was the only thing she could think of doing. It was the only way of asserting some kind of control over the situation.

"But of course I'm not in control," said Elemak calmly. "I never thought I was. Your father is the only one who wants to control people. I have to keep him restrained because if I don't, he'll use that cloak thing to brutalize people into doing what he wants. All I'm looking for is simple fairness. For instance, all of you overgrown children can go to sleep for the rest of the voyage while *our* children get a chance to catch up halfway, at least. Is that such a terrible, evil, violent thing for me to want?"

He was very, very good at this, Chveya realized. With

just a few words, he could rebuild all that she had torn down. "Good," she said. "You're a sweet, reasonable, decent man. Therefore you'll let me and Oykib and Mother all go and see Father."

"Maybe. Once I have the Index."

For a moment Chveya thought that he had given in. That she had only to tell where the Index was, and he would let her see Father. But then Oykib interrupted.

"Are you going to believe this liar?" demanded Oykib. "He talks about Nafai brutalizing people with the cloak—but what he doesn't want anybody to remember is that he and Meb were planning to *murder* Nafai. That's what he is, a murderer. He even betrayed our father back in Basilica. He set Father up to be slaughtered by Gaballufix and if the Oversoul hadn't told Luet to warn him—"

Elemak silenced him with a blow, a vast buffet from his massive arm. In the low gravity, Oykib flew across the room and struck his head against a wall harder than ever before. Gravity might be lower, but as all the children of the school had learned, mass was undiminished, and so Oykib's full weight was behind the collision. He drifted unconscious to the floor.

Now the adults did not keep silence. Rasa screamed. Volemak leapt to his feet and shouted at Elemak. "You were always a murderer in your heart! You're no son of mine! I disinherit you! Anything you ever have now will be stolen!"

Elemak screamed back at him, his self-control momentarily gone. "You and your Oversoul, what are you! Nothing! A weak, broken worm of a man. I'm your *only* son, the only real man you ever begot, but you always preferred that lying little suck-up to me!"

Volemak answered quietly. "I never preferred him to you. I gave you everything. I trusted you with everything."

"You gave me nothing. You threw away the business,

all our wealth, our position, everything. For a *computer*."

"And you betrayed me to Gaballufix. You are a traitor and a murderer in your heart, Elemak. You are not my son."

That did it, Chveya knew. In that moment, though fear remained, all loyalty to Elemak evaporated. People would still obey him, but none of them willingly. Even his own oldest son, eight-year-old Protchnu, was looking at his father with fear and horror.

Rasa and Shedemei were taking care of Oykib. "He's going to be all right, I think," said Shedemei. "There'll probably be a concussion and he may not wake up very soon, but there's nothing broken."

Silence held for a long time after her words. Oykib would be all right—but nobody could forget who had caused the injuries he did have. No one could forget the utter savagery of the blow, the rage that was behind it, the sight of Oykib flying through the air, helpless, broken. Elemak would be obeyed, that was certain. But he would not be loved or admired. He was not the leader of choice, not for anyone, not now. No one was on his side.

"Luet," said Elemak softly. "You come with me and Chveya. And Issib, too. I *want* you to witness that Nafai is all right. I also want you to witness that he is not going to be in command on this ship again."

As Chveya followed Elemak down the ladderway to one of the storage decks, she wondered: Why didn't he just take her to see Father when she first asked? It made no sense.

<He didn't take you, because you demanded it.>

How childish of him.

<No, it was prudent. If he was going to establish his authority, he had to assert total control from the start.>

Well, he's done *that*.

<On the contrary. Between you and Oykib, and Volemak at the end, you broke him. He's already lost. It might take him a while to know it, but he's lost.>

It gave her a glow of triumph as she followed Elemak to the storage room where Father was imprisoned.

The glow dissipated quickly, though, when she saw how they had treated him. Father lay on his side on the floor of a storage compartment. His wrists had been bound tightly—savagely—behind his back. She could see the skin bulging above and below the twine, and his hands were white. They had also tied his ankles together, just as tightly. Then they had pulled his legs up behind him, bowing him painfully backward, and had run two cords from his ankles up over his shoulders, twisting them before and after so they were held tight along his neck. Then they ran the cords down his stomach to his crotch and passed them between his legs to where they fastened them, behind his buttocks, to his bound wrists. The result was that the cords exerted constant pressure. The only way Father could relieve the pressure on his shoulders, at his groin, was to pull his legs even higher or bend himself backward even more. But since he was already pulled in that direction as tightly as they could force his body, there was no relief. His eyes were closed, but his red face and quick, shallow breaths told Chveya that he was in pain and that even breathing was hard for him in that impossible posture.

"Nafai," Mother murmured.

Nafai opened his eyes. "Hi," he said softly. "See how a little storm at sea can disrupt the voyage?"

"How cleverly you tied him," Issib said with venom in his voice. "What an inventive tormentor you are."

"Standard procedure on the road," said Elemak, "when a needed person is being stubborn about something. You can't kill him and you can't let him get away with his defiance. A couple of hours like this is usually enough. But Nyef has always been an exceptionally stubborn boy."

"Can you breathe, Nafai?" Mother asked.

"Can *you?*" asked Father.

Not until that moment had Chveya realized that the air *was* rather close and stuffy.

"What do you mean by that?" demanded Elemak.

Issib answered for him. "The life support system can't handle so many people awake all at once," he said. "It's straining already. We're going to get lower and lower on available oxygen as the hours go by."

"Not a problem," said Elemak. "We're putting all the sneaks and liars and their overgrown children back to sleep for the rest of the voyage."

"No you're not," whispered Father.

Elemak regarded him quietly. "I think when I have the Index, the ship's computer will do what I want."

Father didn't even answer.

"The Index, Chveya," said Elemak. "I kept my word."

"Untie him," said Chveya.

"He can't," said Issib. "Nafai has the cloak. It can't be taken from him. So if he ever lets him go, Nafai will be back in control in moments. No one could stand against him then."

So this was what holding the twins as hostage had accomplished. Father had willingly submitted to being tied like this, so that his little ones would be unharmed. For the first time, Chveya really understood how powerless parents were. Only people without children were really free to act on their own best judgment. Once you had little ones to care for, you could always be controlled by someone else.

"Can't you loosen the cord?" Chveya said. "You don't have to twist him up like that."

"No, I don't have to," said Elemak. "But I *want* to.

After all, I'm evil and terrible and violent." He eyed her steadily. "The Index, Chveya, or your mother goes down on the floor beside him. It doesn't hurt him, not really, because the cloak heals him, but it won't heal *her*."

Chveya could feel how Mother stiffened beside her. "You won't," said Chveya.

"Won't I? Since you and Oykib and Father have already got everybody hating me, it won't make things any harder for me. And if I prove that I can treat a woman just as badly as a man, maybe I won't have to put up with any more interference from big-mouthed little bitches like you."

"Tell him," said Father. His voice sounded like defeat.

She had heard it from his own mouth. There was nothing more to accomplish by resisting. "I'll take you," said Chveya. "It's in the centrifuge. You'll have to wait until it spins down, though. You can't get it out while it's moving."

"Inside the works, then?" Elemak said. "All this bother—and I would have thought of it eventually anyway. All right, get out, all of you. I'm locking this door behind me, and I'll post a continuous watch here, so don't even imagine that you can sneak down here and untie him. You're lucky I haven't killed him already."

For a moment Chveya wondered: Why hasn't Elemak already killed him? He tried before, didn't he? It has to be the cloak. Father can't be killed, not that easily. Not while he's inside the ship, or even near it. Elemak probably can't even touch him, let alone do violence to him, not unless Father permits it. And if Elemak tried to kill him, it might not even require a voluntary response on Father's part to strike back. The cloak would probably lash out automatically. Or maybe the Oversoul controls it. But that's automatic, too, isn't it? Because the Oversoul is really just a computer.

<And you're really just an array of organic compounds.>

Chveya blushed. She let Elemak herd her and the others out of the room, remembering only at the last moment to call out, "Father, I love you!"

At first Elemak insisted on getting the Index out while the centrifuge was still moving, but when he saw for himself that the Index could not possibly be removed without running a serious risk of dropping it and breaking it under the wheels, he glumly waited while the machine ran down. Then, with it stopped, he sent Obring into the opening to get it. Chveya understood why. Elemak dared not get completely down into the opening, because he then couldn't be sure that someone wouldn't slam the door shut. He could get out soon enough, through one door or another—there were openings leading from the roadway out into the rest of the ship—but not before somebody could make it to Father and untie him. He couldn't trust anyone now. So it was Obring who went down through the maintenance hole, and Obring who handed up the cloth-wrapped Index to Elemak.

"I can't believe she got it in there while the thing was moving," Obring said.

Elemak didn't respond, but Chveya was defiantly proud of the compliment. She *had* done well. And even though Oykib, for whatever reason, had told Elemak almost at once who had hidden the Index, she had managed to weaken Elemak's position and visit her father as the price of telling where it was.

Now Elemak lifted off the cloth and held the Index in his hands.

Nothing happened.

He turned to Issib. "How does it work?" he demanded.

"Like that," said Issib. "Just what you're doing."

"But it's not doing anything."

"Of course it's not," said Issib. "The Oversoul controls it, and he's not speaking to you."

Elemak held it out to Issib. "You do it, then. Make it do what I tell you, or Hushidh ends up with Nafai on the storeroom floor."

"I'll try, but I don't think the Oversoul will be fooled just because I'm the one holding it. It's still not going to submit to you."

"Shut up and do it," said Elemak.

Issib sank lightly to the floor and received the Index as Elemak laid it in his lap. He put his hands on it. Nothing happened.

"You see?" said Issib.

"What usually happens?" asked Elemak. "Could it just be slow to respond?"

"It's never slow," said Issib. "It's just not going to work while the starmaster is not in control of the ship."

"Starmaster," said Elemak, as if the word were poison in his mouth.

"We're going to run lower and lower on oxygen," said Issib. "The ship can only break up carbon dioxide so fast, and we have too many people breathing."

"What you mean is that the Oversoul is trying to use the oxygen supply to force me to surrender."

"It's not the Oversoul," said Issib. "He doesn't control the life support systems, not directly, and he certainly couldn't override them in order to cause human beings harm. The machines have failsafe systems built in. It's just the way things are."

"Fine," said Elemak. "We'll just put to sleep all the people I don't want up. I might even let Nafai go to sleep for the rest of the voyage—though I think he might stay tied up like that during his nap."

"And come out crippled worse than me at the end?" asked Issib.

"That's a thought," said Elemak, clearly approving of the idea. "I never had any trouble with *you*."

"Doesn't matter what you plan," said Issib. "The Oversoul *can* stop you from starting up any of the suspended animation chambers. All it has to do is keep sending a danger signal to the computers that control them. You can't override that."

Elemak contemplated the idea for a while.

"Fine," he said. "I can wait."

"You think you can outwait the Oversoul?"

"I think the Oversoul doesn't want this voyage to fail," said Elemak. "I think he'll eventually realize that I'm *going* to lead the colony, and he'll make his accommodation."

<Not a chance.>

"Not a chance," Chveya echoed.

"Oh, really," said Elemak, turning to her. "Is the Oversoul talking to *you* now?"

Chveya said nothing.

<I can accomplish my primary mission even if every organism on this ship is dead.>

"The Oversoul can accomplish her main purpose even if everybody on the ship is dead," Chveya said.

"Or so it tells the people it deceives," said Elemak. "I guess we'll have an interesting few days, as we find out just how sincere the Oversoul is."

"The babies will die first," said Issib. "And the old people."

"If one of my babies dies from this," said Elemak, "then as far as I'm concerned everybody can die, myself included. Death would be better than another day being ruled over by that lying, sneaky, smart-mouthed, traitorous bastard that Father foisted on me as a brother." Elemak turned to Chveya and smiled. "Not to say anything bad about your father in front of you, little girl. But then, since you take after him so thoroughly, it probably sounded to you like praise."

Chveya's loathing overcame her fear of his anger. "I

would be ashamed of him," said Chveya, "if a man like you didn't hate him."

Did Obring chuckle softly behind Elemak? Elemak whirled to see, but Obring was all innocence.

You've already lost, thought Chveya. The Oversoul was right. We've already beaten you. Now let's just hope that nobody dies before you finally realize it.

EIGHT

UNBOUND

Luet was angry, but not with Elemak. To her, Elemak had become almost a force of nature. Of course he hated Nafai. Of course he would seize on any excuse to hurt him. There was too much history between them now, too much old resentment, too much guilt at Elemak's earlier attempts to kill his brother. You didn't manage the situation by trying to change Elemak. You managed it by finding ways to avoid provoking him.

You did this, Luet said to the Oversoul. It was your idea. You pushed it. You maneuvered Nafai and me and the parents of the other children to play these little games with time.

<And I was right.>

You just didn't count on them waking up, is that it?

<I am still right. Everything will work out.>

My babies are having trouble breathing. They can hardly eat because swallowing takes so long they're gasping for another breath by the time it's done. We're dying, and you tell me everything will work out?

\<We have days before anyone is in danger of dying.\>

Well, that makes me feel so much better.

\<I am not Elemak. I did not make Elemak do the things he did.\>

You set it up. You put us in the situation.

\<Did you think this day would never come? That if you did everything just right, Elemak would never turn on you? Better here, where I have some control over the situation, than on Earth, where you'll be entirely on your own.\>

Oh, no, we won't be on our own on Earth. We'll have the Keeper of Earth to look out for us. And if she has half the love and care for us that you have, we'll all be dead within a year.

\<The Keeper is much more powerful than I am.\>

That's nice to hear.

\<I understand your anger. Just don't let it cloud your judgment.\>

No, we mustn't have clouded judgment, as we pant to get enough oxygen, as we watch our children getting sluggish and torpid, as we think of our husband twisted and bent, his hands and wrists garotted with cords. . . .

So went Luet's conversations with the Oversoul, hour after hour. She knew that when her rage was spent she would fall silent, would reconcile herself to the situation, would even, in the end, probably agree that things had worked out for the best. But they hadn't worked out yet. And if this was the best, it was hard to imagine what the worst—or even the next best—might have been. That's the one thing that could never be known: what *would* have happened. People spoke as if it could be known. "If only that alarm hadn't gone off." "If only Nafai had not had such a smart mouth as a boy"— that was Nafai's own favorite, Luet well knew, as he took the blame for everything on himself. But nothing is ever caused by just one thing, Luet knew, and removing or changing one cause does not always make the effect go away, or even make things better.

I will someday stop feeling this deep, unreasonable rage at the Oversoul, but not now, not with the sight of Nafai in such cruel bonds so fresh in my mind, so alive in my nightmares. Not with my children gasping after each swallow. Not with bloody-hearted Elemak in control of the people on this ship.

If only we had all withstood the Oversoul and not held school during the voyage.

In her heart she raged; ranted at the Oversoul; invented long, viciously cutting speeches that she knew she could never deliver to Elemak, to Mebbekew, to all who supported them. But to the others she showed a calm, impassive face. Confident, unafraid, not even annoyed, as far as she would let anyone else see. She knew that this more than anything else would unsettle Elemak and his followers. To see that she did not seem much worried would worry them; it was the most she could do, little as it was.

They. We. In her own mind, she had taken to thinking of Elemak's followers and their families as "the Elemaki"—the people of Elemak—and of those who had taken part in the voyage school as "the Nafari." Normally such endings were used to refer to nations or tribes. But are we not tribes, here on this ship, however few in numbers we might be?

Elemak required the Nafari families to take their meals at the same time in the library, and then he or Meb would escort each family back to their cramped quarters and seal the door. While they were gone, Vas and Obring kept watch. Luet studied them, there in the library during meals. They did not seem really comfortable with their office, but whether that was because of shame or because they simply weren't confident in their ability to prevail in a physical confrontation she had no way of knowing.

Some of the Elemaki women made feeble attempts at conversation in the library during meals, but Luet did not show by facial expression or gesture, and certainly not by word, that she knew they existed. They went away angry, especially Kōkor, Aunt Rasa's younger daughter, who snippily said, "You brought it all on yourself anyway, putting on airs because they used to call you Waterseer." Since this had nothing whatever to do with the conflict, it was clear that Kokor was merely revealing her own ancient resentment against Luet. It was hard not to laugh at her.

Luet's silence toward the Elemaki women was not motivated by pique. Luet knew perfectly well that they had had nothing to do with the men's decisions, that Meb's wife Dol and Elemak's wife Eiadh were deeply mortified at what their husbands were doing. She also knew, however, that if she ever let them assure her of their sympathy, if she ever let them cross over the invisible boundary between Elemaki and Nafari, it would make them feel *much* better. In fact, it might make them feel downright comfortable, even *noble* at having extended friendship to Nafai's beleaguered wife. Luet did not want them comfortable. She wanted them to be so uncomfortable, in fact, that they began to complain to their husbands, until at last the pressure built up so strongly that the others would begin to fear their wives' displeasure and contempt almost as much as they feared Elemak's, and Elemak himself would begin to believe that his actions were costing him more in his family than he was gaining in that twisted part of his psyche that held his hatred for Nafai.

Of course, there was always the chance that additional pressure from his wife would merely make Elemak more intransigent. But since snubbing the Elemaki women was the only thing Luet could do, she did it.

The only anomalous thing was the strange way Zdorab and Shedemei were treated. They were definitely being watched, escorted everywhere just like Luet, Hushidh and Issib, and Rasa and Volemak. But in the library, they were not under the same kind of scrutiny. They and their children were encouraged to sit with the Elemaki, and they were allowed to converse freely among themselves.

It led Luet to the inescapable conclusion that the alarm that opened all the suspended animation chambers had not been an accident, that somehow Zdorab had managed to leave not one but two wake-up calls, and the Oversoul had not found the second one. It was not possible that Shedemei had known about this; it was barely believable that Zdorab had known, for hadn't he joined with them in teaching the children? Hadn't he been part of the voyage school? Hadn't his son and daughter grown up along with the other children? What sort of twisted mind did he have, to allow him to accept freely the friendship of the Nafari, and yet know the whole time that his wake-up call would put Nafai's life in danger and split the whole community worse than ever? No, it was impossible to imagine. Zdorab couldn't have done it. No one could be so duplicitous, so. . . .

And yet there was Zdorab, sitting with his son, Rokya, next to him, and Meb's wife Dolya right across. Shedemei, on the other hand, sat apart from the others. Her shame was almost palpable. She kept her daughter Dabya with her, and spoke only when spoken to. She did not look at anyone, keeping her eyes to her plate while eating, and then leaving the room as quickly as possible. Luet longed to ask Chveya or Hushidh to assess the relationships, to find out where Zdorab's loyalty lay. But she was forbidden to talk to Hushidh, and Chveya, too, was kept isolated from everyone else. Oykib was also isolated from the other children; the two of them had certainly attracted special attention from Elemak.

In the evening of the second day Luet opened the door of her family's room to find that it was Zdorab knocking. The twins were asleep, breathing rapidly but regularly. The older children—Zhatva, Motiga, and Izuchaya—were not asleep, but they lay on their beds, resting so as to avoid using more oxygen; all of them had been ordered to do this whenever possible, and since they could feel how depleted the oxygen already was, this was one command of Elemak's that all obeyed readily.

Luet regarded Zdorab wordlessly, waiting for him to speak.

"I have to talk to you."

She debated closing the door in his face. But that would be to judge him without having heard what he had to say. She stepped back and let him inside. Then she leaned out into the corridor and saw that Vas and Obring were both watching. This was not a clandestine visit, then. Unless those two stout hearts actually had the courage to conspire against Elemak's express orders.

She closed the door.

"It was me," said Zdorab. "I know you know it, but I had to tell you myself. Elemak told me that I should say that I couldn't have removed my wake-up program even if I wanted to, but I could have. And I did want to. Right at the end, as I was being put to sleep, I tried to shout for Shedya and Nyef to stop, to open my chamber, to. . . ."

He could see that his words were having no effect on her. He looked away toward the door. "I couldn't foresee how things would work out. I just—I thought that Elemak would see it was an accomplished fact. That maybe he'd work out a way to have the other children get the last three years of schooling. Something like that. Your children would have had six and a half years, his would have three and a half. I didn't—the violence, Nafai tied up like that, and now the life support—running out of air—can't you get the Oversoul to relent and let half of us go back to sleep?"

So that was what this was about. Elemak and the others were using Zdorab to try to talk her into saving them from the consequences of their own actions.

"You can tell Elemak that when Nafai is untied and

put back in control of the ship, he and his people will be free to go back into their suspended animation chamber at any time. Or should I be saying you and *your* people?"

To her surprise, tears almost leapt from Zdorab's eyes. "I don't have a *people*," he said. "I may not even have a wife. Or a son or a daughter."

So Shedemei hadn't known. Not that that was a surprise.

"I don't expect you to feel sorry for me," he said, wiping his eyes and getting back in control of himself. "I just want you to understand that if I had known—"

"If you had known what? That Elemak hated Nafai? That he wanted him dead? How did you miss that little bit of information, considering that we all saw Nafai covered with blood from Elemak's last little plot?"

Anger flashed in Zdorab's eyes. "It wasn't Elemak with the little plot this time."

"No, it was the Oversoul," said Luet. "*And* you. In fact, you managed to take part in conspiracies on both sides." Then it dawned on her. "Oh, that was the point, wasn't it?"

"I'm an outsider here," he said. "Shedya and I aren't kin to anybody."

"Shedya is one of Aunt Rasya's nieces."

"That's not a blood relationship, that's—"

"It's closer."

"But not *me*. My son, my daughter, they're going to be caught up in this family quarrel between Nafai and Elemak no matter what I do. I'm not like Volemak or his sons, I'm not physically strong, I'm not—I'm not much of a *man* the way men are judged. So how could I protect *my* children? I thought that if I could have a good relationship with both Nafai and Elemak—"

"That is not possible," said Luet. "Especially now, thanks to you."

"I did what I thought was best for my children. I was wrong. Now neither side trusts me, and my children will pay for that, too. I was *wrong*, and I'm not trying to conceal what I did or how bad it was. But I wasn't trying to betray you or Nafai. I was doing what I thought was best for my children."

"Very good," said Luet coldly. "You have unburdened yourself. I've heard you and if I'm ever allowed to speak to anyone but my children again, I'll be sure to tell everyone that you were motivated entirely by altruistic concern for your children."

"Mebbekew says you're a cold one," said Zdorab.

"And we know what a fine observer of human beings Meb can be."

"But he's wrong," said Zdorab. "You're not cold, you're on fire."

"Thank you for that insight into elemental metaphors for my character."

"Just remember, Luet. I did you wrong. I know that, and I'm in your debt, deeply and forever. I'm not a dishonorable man by nature. I acted as men like me have always had to act—for survival, as best I understood it. There'll come some future time when, no matter how much you despise me, you'll need my help. I'm here to tell you that when that time comes, and when you or Nafai ask me, I'll do whatever you need."

"Good. Tell Elemak to untie my husband."

"Whatever you need that's within my power. I've already asked him to untie your husband. Kokor and Sevet have demanded it. Your oldest daughter spit in his face and called him a eunuch who had to imprison his betters in order to feel like a real man."

Luet gasped. "Did he hit her?"

"Yes," said Zdorab. "But she's all right. Everybody was disgusted at him for it, and he hasn't gone near her since. For what it's worth, I think it turned even his own wife against him, to see him hit Chveya like that."

No doubt that was Chveya's purpose. "That's always been Elya's problem," said Luet. "He has always attempted to answer words with actions. It might silence the speaker, but it only confirms the truth of what was said."

"Even you, with your unbending silence—that's half what the women talk about," said Zdorab. "And Shedya has joined in your boycott of conversation. Everybody wants Elemak to stop. I thought you'd want to know that. What you're doing, what Chveya and Oykib have done, even Nafai's quiet endurance—it's all a kind of resistance, stubborn and brave, and it makes everyone who's on Elemak's side so . . . so ashamed."

Luet nodded gravely. She needed to hear that. The fact that he came and told her didn't make them friends.

"I've seen real courage these last two days," said Zdorab. "I've never had it myself, not the kind of courage that stands out in the open, even when you're powerless, and dares the strong one to do his worst. Chveya. Oykib. My life might have been different if I'd ever acted like that." Then he laughed bitterly. "Yes, I'd probably be dead."

It occurred to Luet that she actually knew almost nothing about Zdorab, about his upbringing. He spoke as if he had lived his whole life friendless and in fear. Why?

In spite of herself, she had to admit that things might look very different from where he stood. For her, there was no choice—she had to do everything she could to help Nafai and the Oversoul prevail against Elemak, because if they did not win, there would be nothing left for her. But Zdorab could conceive of a future in which Elemak had won, and if that happened—and it certainly could happen—it wasn't morally unspeakable for him to try to prepare a place for himself and his children in Elemak's camp.

The trouble was that he might easily end up without a place on either side. Which is where things were headed right now.

She did not let herself sound so cold when she spoke

again. "Zdorab, what you've said hasn't fallen on deaf ears. If you're worried about the future, I can tell you this with complete confidence. None of us will retaliate against you and certainly not against your children. They haven't lost their place with us, if that's where they want to be."

"Elemak is going to lose this one," said Zdorab. "It's only a matter of how many will die before he breaks."

"None, I hope," said Luet.

"I'm just saying that pure self-interest could have brought me here. You have no reason to trust me. I deceived you all. You thought I was one of you, and I betrayed you. You can never forget that. *I* certainly never will. But this you can count on: If you or Nafai ever need me again, I'll be there. No matter what. Even if I die trying to help you."

Luet barely suppressed a scornful, mocking answer.

"It's not for me," Zdorab said. "Or even really for you. I just . . . it's the only way I can ever redeem myself in the eyes of my children. Everyone will know what I did, sooner or later. That's why I didn't bother trying to conceal this conversation from your children, the ones lying there awake with their eyes closed. My children will be ashamed of me, even if no one taunts them for it. Somehow, someday, I'm going to redeem myself in their eyes. That's what survival means, for me. I thought it was a matter of staying alive, but it isn't. Nobody lives forever anyway. It's how you're remembered. It's what your children thought of you, what they think of you after you're dead. That's survival." He looked Luet steadily in the eye. "And if there's one thing that can truly be said about me, it's this: I survive."

He got up from the edge of the bed where he had been sitting. Luet palmed the door open and he left.

In the silence after the door closed, Zhatva spoke softly. "I'm glad I'm not in *his* shoes."

Luet answered wryly, "Don't be so sure. Our own shoes aren't all that comfortable right now."

"I wish I'd been as brave as Veya," said Zhatva.

"No no, Zhyat, don't think that way. She was in a position where being brave could accomplish something. You weren't. When the time ever comes when you need courage, you'll have it. Enough of it. All you need." To herself she added silently: May that day when you need courage never come. Even as she said it, though, she knew that the day *would* come. She shuddered.

Oh, Nafai, she said silently. If only you could hear me as the Oversoul hears me. If only you knew how much I love you, how much I ache thinking of what you're going through. And all I can do for you is take care of the children as best I can and trust in the Oversoul and in the workings of human nature to work some miracle and set you free. What I *can* do, I'm doing, but it's not enough. If you die, what life will there be for me? Even if the children are all safe, even if they live to be good, strong, wonderful adults, it won't be enough, not if I've lost you. The Oversoul might have brought us together as pawns in her game, but that doesn't mean that the bond between us is any weaker. It's strong, far more powerful than the cords they've tied you with, but without you beside me I feel as if I'm the one who's tied, trussed up inside my soul and unable to move, unable to breathe. Nafai.

His name rang through her mind. The image of his face seared her. She lay down on the bed, willing herself to relax, commanding herself to sleep. The less oxygen I breathe, the more he will have, the more the children will have. I must sleep. I must be calm.

But she was not calm, and even when she finally slipped into a fitful sleep, her heart raced and she breathed quickly, short sharp breaths, as if she were engaged in battle, the enemy jabbing at her as she barely dodged each new thrust.

* * *

The first meal of the third day, Elemak was out of the room. Where he was, no one dared to ask. Nor did anyone mind. When he was gone, wariness remained; real fear only returned when he did. This was not because anyone trusted the good will of Meb, Obring, and Vas—Meb seemed to delight in tiny cruelties, and Obring, to all appearances, enjoyed his status as one of those who shared in authority. Everyone knew, though, that either of them would gladly betray Elemak in a moment, if they thought it would benefit them. Vas, on the other hand, seemed to detest what he was doing; nevertheless, he did it, and was the one Elemak relied on most. Elemak could give him a task and expect that it would be carried out resourcefully and well, even when Elemak was not there watching—something that could not be said of the other two Elemaki men.

On this day, however, with Elemak gone, there came the first open challenge to his authority. Volemak, after a glance at Rasa, rose to his feet and began to address the group.

"My friends and family," he began.

"Sit down and shut up," said Mebbekew.

Volemak fixed a gaze of snakelike calmness on his second son and said, "If you care to silence me, feel free to attempt it. But in the absence of physical force, I will have my say."

Meb took one step toward his father. Immediately, though they had not been prompted in any way, Volemak's youngest son Yasai, Issib's eldest boy Zaxodh, and Nafai's eldest, Zhatva, all rose to their feet. They were nowhere near Volemak, but the threat was clear.

Meb laughed. "Do you think I'm afraid of your children?"

"You might want to be careful," Rasa said. "They've been living in low gravity for six years, while you still seem a little uncertain on your feet."

"Come on, Obring," said Meb.

Obring took a step toward Volemak. Now Nafai's second son, Motiga, stood up, as did Zdorab's son Padarok. A moment later, Zdorab himself rose to his feet.

"Vas," said Meb, "you can pretend not to care, but this looks like a revolt to me."

Vas nodded. "Obring, go get Elemak."

"We can handle it ourselves!" Meb snapped.

"I can see. We're doing so well already."

Obring looked from Vas to Mebbekew, then turned and left the library.

"As I was saying," said Volemak, "this entire dispute is misplaced. It was I whom the Oversoul summoned into the desert, and I was the one who led this expedition at all times. It's true that in the desert I delegated the day-to-day authority to Elemak, but this was never more than a temporary arrangement in recognition of his skill and experience. Likewise, during the voyage I have delegated command of the ship itself to Nafai, because he is the one to whom the Oversoul gave the cloak of the starmaster. The fact remains that I am the only lawful leader of this group, and when we arrive on Earth, I shall not delegate that authority to anyone else. Neither Elemak nor Nafai will be in command as long as I am alive."

"And how long is that, old man?" asked Meb.

"Longer than you wish, you contemptible slug," said Volemak mildly. "It is obvious that Elemak is out of control. Through threat of force and the cooperation of three weak-willed bullies" —he looked Vas in the eye— "and because Nafai has submitted to captivity in order to save the lives of his babies, Elemak's mutiny at present seems to be prevailing. However, we are all aware that at some point Elemak will inevitably have to submit to reality—the ship cannot sustain us all awake, and the Oversoul will not permit him to put anyone into suspended animation while Nafai remains bound. So what I ask of you now is your solemn oath, every one of you, to submit to my authority and no one else's, after this crisis has passed. While I live there will be no choosing between Nafai and Elemak, but only obedience to me, in accord with your solemn covenant. I invite all of you, men and women, to take this oath. All who vow to submit only to my authority after this crisis, rise to your feet and say yes."

Immediately all the men who were standing, except Vas and Mebbekew, said a resounding yes. Rasa, Hushidh, Luet, and Shedemei also rose at once, joined by the young women who had taken part in the school; their higher voices echoed those of the men. Issib rose slowly and said yes.

"I assume," said Volemak, "that if Oykib and Chveya were not being kept in isolation they would also join in this oath, and so I also count them among the lawful citizens of my community. When Nafai is released, I will also ask him to submit to this oath. Is there anyone here who doubts that he will affirm it? And that he will keep that oath, having taken it?"

No one spoke.

"Remember, please, that I am asking you to accept my authority *after* the present crisis has passed. I am not asking you to jeopardize yourselves by entering into resistance to Elemak at this time. But if you do not take this oath at this time, you are not citizens of the colony I will establish on Earth. You may, of course, apply for citizenship at a later time, and then I will take a vote of the citizens to see whether or not you will be admitted. If you take the oath now, however, you will be a citizen from the beginning."

To everyone's surprise, Vas spoke up. "I will take this oath," he said. "When the crisis has passed, your authority is the only authority I will accept as long as you are alive. And I will do all I can to prolong your life as long as possible."

With Vas having spoken, his wife Sevet rose to her

feet, along with her three young children. She said, "I take the oath," and her children echoed her.

Those who remained seated obviously were feeling beleaguered indeed.

"Elemak won't be happy with you," said Meb to Vas.

"Elemak isn't happy these days anyway," said Vas. "All I want is peace and justice."

"My father was part of Nafai's little plot, too, you know," said Meb. "He's hardly unbiased."

"I know that some of you are unhappy about the children who were kept awake to be schooled during the voyage," said Volemak. "Unfortunately, Elemak has never permitted us to explain. Every one of us whose children were included in the school were urged by the Oversoul to do so. Nafai was very reluctant to do it. We pressed him until he agreed. These children were chosen by the Oversoul, and they and we freely chose to go along. The result is not an unhappy one. Instead of having only a handful of adults and many unproductive children, we have divided the younger generation, so that we will now have a continuous population of young people coming into adulthood for many generations to come. Whatever disadvantage you think you perceive at this time will disappear when you realize that you will have more years of life on Earth than those who stayed awake during the voyage."

Dol rose to her feet, causing her children to stand, also.

"Sit down, you disloyal bitch!" screamed Mebbekew.

"My children and I will be citizens of your colony," said Dol. "We all affirm the oath."

Mebbekew rushed toward her. Vas stepped between him and his wife, putting out a hand to restrain him. "This isn't a good time for violence," said Vas. "She's a free citizen, I think, and has the right to speak her mind."

Mebbekew flung Vas's hand away from his chest

"None of this will mean *anything* after Elemak comes back!"

Only a meter away from him, Eiadh rose to her feet. Immediately her oldest son, Protchnu, plucked at her sleeve to pull her back down. "After the crisis, I will submit to your authority, Volemak," she said.

Protchnu turned to the other children and shouted at them, "Don't you dare take the oath!" The children were obviously frightened of his rage.

"I recognize that your younger children are being intimidated into not taking the oath," said Volemak. "So they will be given a chance to take it freely at a later time."

"They'll never take it!" shouted Protchnu. "Am I the only one here who is loyal to my father? He's the only one who should lead us!"

Kokor stood up, her children with her. "We'll be citizens too," she said. "After the crisis."

"You will if you take the oath," said Volemak.

"Well, that's what I mean, of course," she said. "I take the oath."

Her children nodded or murmured their assent.

From the doorway, Elemak spoke softly. "Very well," he said. "Everyone has made their choice. Now sit down."

Immediately, Kokor sat down and urged her children to join her. Gradually the others also sat, except for Volemak, Rasa, and Eiadh, who turned to face her husband. "It's over, Elya," she said. "You're the only one who doesn't see that you can't possibly win."

"What I see," said Elemak, "is that I won't permit Nafai to rule over me or anyone else."

"Even if that means that your own children suffocate?"

"If Nafai's pet computer chooses to kill the weakest of us, I can't stop it. But it won't be me killing anyone."

"In other words, you don't care," said Eiadh. "As far

as I'm concerned, that's the final proof that you aren't fit to rule this colony. You care about your pride more than the survival of our babies."

"That's enough from you," said Elemak.

"No," said Eiadh, "that's too much from you. Until you stop this childish display of masculine temper, you are not my husband."

"Oh, not renewing me, are you?" asked Elemak with a nasty smile. "What do you think of *that*, Proya?"

His eldest son, Protchnu, walked to his father. "I think that I have no mother," he said.

"How appropriate," said Elemak, "since I have no father and no wife. Have I also no friend?"

"I'm your friend," said Obring.

"I stand with you," said Meb. "But Vas here took the oath."

"Vas will take whatever oath you ask," said Elemak. "But his word has always been worthless. Everybody knows that."

Sevet laughed. "Look at your friends, you poor man," she said. "One deluded eight-year-old boy. And then what? Meb! Obring! They were both worthless back in Basilica."

"You didn't say that when you invited me into your bed!" Obring shouted at her.

"That had nothing to do with you," said Sevet contemptuously. "That was between me and my sister, and believe me, I have paid deeply for that mistake. Vas knows that since then I have been faithful to him, both in my heart and in my actions."

The children old enough to understand what was being revealed here would have plenty of family scandal to talk about later. Obring and Sevet had an affair? And how did Sevet pay for it? And what did she mean that it was between her and Kokor?

"Enough," said Elemak. "The old man has made his little play, but you'll notice he didn't have the courage to ask you to stand against me now. It was only in some imagined future that he rules over you. He knows, as you all know, that I rule over you now, and believe me, you will never see a future in which I do not." He turned to Obring. "Stay here and keep everyone in the library."

Obring grinned at Vas. "I guess you aren't going to be giving me orders anymore."

"Vas is still a guard," said Elemak. "I don't trust him, but he'll do what he's told. And now he'll do what *you* tell him, Obring. Right, Vas?"

"Yes," said Vas quietly. "I'll do what I'm told. But I'll also keep all my oaths."

"Yes yes, a man of honor and all that," said Elemak. "Now, Meb, let's take Father and his wife to visit Nafai. And while we're at it, let's bring along the woman who claims she is no longer my wife."

"What are you going to do?" asked Rasa contemptuously. "Tie us up the way you've tied Nafai?"

"Of course not," said Elemak. "I have respect for old people. But for every person who took that little oath of yours, Father, Nafai will take a blow. And you will watch."

Volemak glared at Elemak. "I wish that before I fathered you, I had been castrated or killed."

"What a sad thought," said Elemak. "Then you would never have fathered your precious Nafai. Though, come to think of it, I wonder if there was a man's seed involved in conceiving him. He is so completely his mother's little girl."

A moment later, Elemak and Mebbekew manhandled Volemak and Eiadh down the ladderway and through the corridor to the storage room where Nafai lay. Rasa followed helplessly behind.

Nafai was not really asleep, not ever during the past few days. Or if he did sleep, it felt as though he was awake, so vivid were the dreams. Sometimes they were his worst fears, dreams of the twins gasping for air until finally they stopped breathing altogether, their eyes open, their mouths agape, and in the dream he tried to close their eyes and close their mouths, but they kept flying open again as soon as he took away his hand. He woke gasping for breath himself from these dreams.

Sometimes, though, the dreams were of other times, better times. He remembered getting up in the morning at his father's house and running out under the shower and turning on the cold water. At the time he had hated it, but now he remembered it with fondness. An innocent time, when the worst thing that could happen to you was a shock of icy water on your head and back, when the worst thing you could do to someone else was smart off at them until they got angry enough to stop laughing and start pushing you around. Only now they never laughed at all, they never forgave at all, and the cold water was nothing, would be a pleasure if it could ever come again. How could I have known in those days, he wondered upon waking from such memory dreams, how could I have known that Elemak's annoyance would turn to such hatred? That such evil days would come upon us? I made smartmouth jokes because I wanted his attention, that was all. He was like a god, so strong, and Father loved him so much. All I wanted was for him to notice me, to tell me that he liked me, that he thought I might someday ride with him on a caravan to some faraway land and come home with exotic plants for Father to sell. All I wanted was for him to respect me and put his arm around my shoulder and say, This is my brother, look at my brother, I can count on him, he's my right-hand man.

Who else could have been your brother, Elemak? Meb? He's the one you chose? Was I so despicable to you, that you chose him over me?

<He chose Meb because he could rule Meb. He hated you because you were stronger than him.>

Yes, with the cloak of the starmaster I'm stronger.

<You know you can strike him down at any time.>

No I can't. The cloak can. *You* can. But I can't. I'm
tied up here and my wrists and ankles hurt.

<It's your choice not to heal them. You know the
cloak can do it in a moment.>

He wants me in pain. If he sees my skin chafed and
bleeding, maybe that will satisfy him.

<He will only be satisfied with your death.>

So be it.

<I will not let you die. As soon as you're unconscious, the cloak is mine to control again, and I will heal
you.>

Stay away from me in my sleep. I want none of your
dreams now, and certainly none of your meddling.

<Do you like the pain?>

I hate the pain of having my brother hate me. And
knowing that this time maybe I deserve it.

<You never deserve to suffer for helping me.>

Oh, and here I thought *you* were helping *me* by having us keep those children awake.

<I was helping you so you could help me. Don't pretend to be stupid or play those childish argument games
with me.>

Are you really talking to me? Or am I dreaming this,
too?

<Yes. And yes.>

So if this is a dream, why can't I wake up from it?

As soon as he said this in his mind, Nafai awoke. Or
rather he dreamed that he awoke, for he knew at once
that he was still asleep, perhaps more deeply than before. And in his sleep, thinking he was awake, he felt
the cords melt away from his hands and he rose to his
feet. The door opened at his touch. He walked through
the corridors and here and there he saw people lying
about, mouths open, panting, none of them noticing
him as if he were invisible. Ah, he thought. I understand now. I'm dead, and this is my spirit walking the
corridor. But then in his dream he realized that his
wrists and ankles hurt and he was having trouble walk-

ing straight, even in the low gravity, so he wasn't dead after all.

He got to the ladder and climbed up, higher and higher, to the highest level of the starship, where the shielding field was generated. But now the ladder didn't stop. It went up, and the next opening was not onto the smooth plastic floor of the starship, it now opened onto a stone floor. He stepped out onto the floor, and felt his body weigh heavily, his steps painful because gravity was normal again. It was dark, a cave. He heard footsteps here and there, but none of them came near; nor did they go very far away. Just a scurry of steps, and he walked a little, and then another scurry of steps. That's all right, he thought. Follow me, I'm not afraid of you, I know you're there but I also know you won't harm me.

He came to a corridor and saw a light burning in a small side chamber of the cave. He walked there, entered the room, and saw dozens of statues, beautifully carved of clay, perched on every shelf of rock and all over the floor. But as he looked more closely, he saw that all the statues were marred, smoothed here and there, the detail lost. Who would deface such marvelous work? Deface it, and yet keep it here as if it were a secret treasure trove?

Then at last he noticed a statue high up and far back from the light, a statue larger than the others, and unmarred. It wasn't the perfection of the detail work that made him stare, however. It was the face itself. For unlike the others, which were all either animals or gargoyles, this was a head of a human. And he knew the face. He should. He had seen it in every mirror since he became a man.

Now the footsteps came closer, not scurrying, but slowly, respectfully. He felt a small hand touch him on the thigh. He did not look; he did not need to. He knew who it was.

Except that it was only in the dream that he knew. In

fact he had no idea who it might be, and he tried to make his dream self turn, look down, see who or what had touched him. But he could not make his own head turn; he could not make himself bend over. In fact, he was bending backward, and his neck was caught between two cords, and there were footsteps, loud ones now, not quick scurrying steps, and a light went on, dazzling him.

He blinked open his eyes. Really awake now, not just dreaming that he was awake.

"Time for my walk?" he asked.

A quick whistling sound, and then a sharp pain in his arm. Against his will he cried out.

"That's one," said the voice of Elemak. "Tell me, Rasa, what's your count? How many took the oath?"

"Do your own foul business," said Mother's voice.

"Could it be hundreds?" asked Elemak. Again the whistling sound. Again the excruciating pain, this time in the ribs of his back. One of them broke; he felt the bone stabbing him as he breathed. And yet he couldn't stop breathing, he had to gasp, because he wasn't getting enough oxygen anymore, he couldn't breathe deeply enough to get the air to stay conscious.

<Heal yourself.>

"I don't count any of these against the total, until you tell me what the total might be," said Elemak.

"Count it yourself," said Rasa. "It was everybody except Protchnu, Obring, and Mebbekew. *Everybody*, Elemak. Think about *that*."

"He's not healing himself," said Luet.

Nafai heard her voice and felt a surge of anger against Elemak. Did he think she was so weak that her spirit would break because she saw her husband enduring pain? What was Elemak trying to gain, anyway? It was the Oversoul he had to persuade—or surrender to. Something had happened, though. An oath.

"I've noticed that," said Elemak. "His wrists don't seem to get better, or his ankles. I can't figure out if that's because the cloak just isn't working right now, or because he's deliberately not healing himself in order to look more pitiful so I'll feel sorry for him and loosen his bonds so he can get free and kill me."

The whistling sound. Another blow, this time on the back of his neck. Nafai gasped at the pain that shot up and down his spine; for a few moments he was numb from the neck down, and he thought, He's broken my neck.

<A stunning blow, that's all. Some neural damage.>

Why doesn't he just kill me?

<Because I still have some influence over him. Enough to distract him whenever his thoughts turn to finishing you off.>

Well stop it. Let him kill me. Then he'll have his victory and there'll be peace and everybody will be better off.

<Elemak doesn't know it, but killing you is the worst thing he could ever do. Because then he'd never be able to defeat you.>

What, dead isn't defeated?

<What he wants is for his father to say, You, Elemak. I choose you. And if you're dead, Nafai, Volemak can never choose him over you. He'll always be second choice then.>

Then if you have any decency, tell Volemak to say the magic words and end all this.

<There's the rub, Nafai. Elemak wouldn't believe it even if Volemak said it. Because he knows that it isn't true. He knows that he's not as good or decent or wise or strong a man as you, so that even if his father said, Elemak, I choose you, it would be a lie, because he knows Volemak is not such a fool as to value him above you.>

I'm too tired to make sense of this. Go away and let me die.

<He just caused you very serious damage with that last blow.>

The one on my neck?

<That was three blows ago. You're bleeding internally now.>

Oh, yes. I can feel that.

<I'm going to heal you.>

Don't do it.

<Before the blood loss causes internal damage.>

Don't heal me until he leaves the room. Give me that much dignity.

<Dignity? Would you die for dignity?>

It's between him and me. I don't want him to see how you intervene for me.

<Your pride is unbelievable. It's between him and *you*? It's between him and *me*, and it always has been. Just as it was between Moozh and me. Just as it's between *you* and me. And between Luet and me. And when we get to Earth, it will be between all of you and the Keeper.>

This really hurts.

<I'm healing you, that's why.>

I said not to.

<Too bad.>

"Look," said Elemak. "His leg is straightening out. I guess we found out how much pain he could take, and now he's got his invisible friend to save him."

"I'm looking," said Volemak coldly. "What I see is a coward, striking a bound man with a metal rod."

Elemak's voice rose to a scream. "*I'm* the coward? I'm not the one with the cloak! I'm not the one who can get magically healed whenever I stub my toe! I'm not the one with the power to give people jolts of electricity whenever I want to bring them to heel!"

"It's not the power you have that makes you a coward or a bully," said Volemak. "It's how you use it. Do you think that being bound like that keeps the cloak from having the same power it's always had? As badly as you're treating him, as badly as you're treating all of us,

Nafai still chooses not to strike you dead where you stand."

"Do it then, Nyef," said Elemak softly. "If you have the power to strike me dead, do it. You've killed before. A drunk lying unconscious in the street, I think it was. My older half-brother, I think it was. That's your specialty, killing people who can't fight back. But Father thinks *I'm* the bully. How can it be bullying, to break the bones of a man who can heal himself in moments? Look, I can break your skull and—"

There was a scream of rage from a woman and the sound of scuffling. Then someone was slammed into a wall; a woman cried. Nafai tried to open his eyes. All he could see was the wall his face was pressed against. "Luet," he whispered.

"Luet can't heal herself, can she?" said Elemak. "She should remember that before she tries to fight with me."

"All you're doing," said Nafai, "is using up the oxygen that your children need to breathe."

"You can end it at any time, Nyef," said Elemak. "All you have to do is die."

"And then what?" asked Volemak. "You'll just start hating the next best man, and for the same reason. Because he's better than you. And when you kill him, you'll find still another better than you. It will go on and on forever, Elemak, because each act of bullying cruelty you commit makes you smaller and smaller until finally you'll have to kill every human being and every animal and even then you'll look at yourself with such contempt that you won't be able to bear it—"

The rod smashed down right in Nafai's face. He felt it cave in all the bones of the front of his head, and then everything went black.

A moment later? It could have been; it could have been hours or days. He was conscious again, and his face was not broken. Nafai wondered if he was alone.

Wondered what had happened to Father and Mother. To Luet. To Elemak.

Someone was in the room. Someone was breathing.

"All better," said the voice. A whisper. Hard to identify. No, not hard. Elemak. "The Oversoul wins again."

Then the lights went out again and the door closed and he was alone.

Eiadh was singing softly to the little ones, Yista and Menya and Zhivya, when Protchnu came to her. She heard him come into the room, the door sliding open and then sliding closed again behind him. She did not stop singing.

When the light returns again
Will I remember how to see?
Will I recognize my mother's face?
Will she know me?

When the light returns again
Then nothing will I fear;
So I close my eyes and dream of day
In darkness here.

"Singing is a waste of oxygen," said Protchnu softly.

"So is crying," Eiadh answered quietly. "Three children are not crying now because one person sang. If you came to stop my singing, go away. Report my crime to your father. Maybe he'll get angry enough to beat me. Maybe he'll let you help."

Still she didn't turn to look at him. She heard him breathing a little more heavily. Raggedly, perhaps. But she was surprised that when he spoke again, his voice was high with barely contained weeping. "It's not my fault you turned against Father."

She had been so stung by his repudiation of her in the library that she hadn't spoken to him since, and had avoided thinking of him. Protchnu, her eldest, saying such terrible things to his own mother. The boy had looked so savage at that moment, so much like Elemak, that she had felt as though she didn't know him. But she did know him, didn't she? He was only eight years old. It was wrong for him to have been torn between quarreling parents like this.

"I didn't turn against your father," she said softly. "I turned against what he's doing."

"Nafai cheated us."

"The Oversoul did. And all the parents of those children did. Not just Nafai."

Protchnu was silent. She thought maybe she had carried the point with him. But no, he was thinking of something else. "Do you love him?"

"I love your father, yes. But when he lets anger rule him, he does bad things. I reject those bad things."

"I didn't mean Father."

It was plain that he expected her to know already. That he had the idea somehow that she loved another man.

And, of course, she did. But it was a hopeless love and one that she had never, never shown to anyone.

"Whom did you mean, then?"

"Him."

"Say the name, Proya. Names aren't magic. It won't poison you to put the name on your lips."

"Nafai."

"Uncle Nafai," she corrected. "Have respect for your elders."

"You love him."

"I would hope that I have a decent love for all my brothers-in-law, as I hope you will also love all your uncles. It would be nice if your father had a decent love for all his brothers. But perhaps you don't see it that way. Look at Menya, lying there asleep. He is the fourth son in our family. He stands in relation to you as Nafai stands to your father. Tell me, Proya, are you planning someday to tie up little Menya and break his bones with a rod?"

Protchnu started to cry in earnest now. Relenting, Eiadh sat up and reached out for him, gathered him into her arms, pulling him down to sit beside her on the bed. "I'll never hurt Menya," he said. "I'll protect him and keep him safe."

"I know you will, Proya, I know it. And it's not the same thing between your father and Nafai. The difference in their ages is much greater. Nafai and Elya didn't have the same mother. And Elemak had a brother even older."

Protchnu's eyes opened wide. "I thought Father was the oldest."

"He's the oldest son of your grandfather Volemak. Back in the days when he was the Wetchik, in the land of Basilica. But Elemak's mother had other sons before she married Volemak. And the oldest of those was named Gaballufix."

"Does Father hate Uncle Nafai because he killed his brother Gaballufix?"

"They hated each other before that. And Gaballufix was trying to kill Nafai and your father and Issib and Meb."

"Why would he want to kill Issib?"

Eiadh noted with amusement that Protchnu didn't wonder why someone would want to kill his uncle Meb. "He wanted to rule Basilica, and the sons of the Wetchik stood in his way. Your grandfather was a very rich and powerful man, back in the land of Basilica."

"What does 'rich' mean?"

What have I done to you, my poor child, that you don't even know what the word means? All wealth and grace have gone from life, and since you have seen nothing but poverty, even the words for the beautiful life are lost to you. "It means that you have more money than. . . ."

But of course he didn't know what *money* meant, either.

"It means you have a more beautiful house than other people. A larger house, and fine clothing, many changes of clothing. And you go to better schools, with wiser teachers, and you have better food to eat, and more of it. All you could want, and more."

"But then you should share," said Protchnu. "You told me that if you have more than you need, you should share."

"And you *do* share. But . . . you won't understand, Proya. That kind of life is lost to us forever. You'll never understand it."

They were quiet for a few moments.

"Mother," said Protchnu.

"Yes?"

"You don't hate me because I chose Father? In the library that day?"

"Every mother knows there'll come a time when her sons will choose their father. It's a part of growing up. I never thought it would come to you so young, but that wasn't your fault."

A pause. Then his voice was very small indeed. "But I don't choose him."

"No, Protchnu, I didn't think you would ever really choose the bad things he's doing. You're not that kind of boy." In truth, though, Eiadh sometimes feared that he *was* that kind of boy. She had seen him playing, had seen him lording it over the other boys, teasing some of them cruelly, until they cried, and then laughing at them. It had frightened her, back on Harmony, to see her son be so unkind to those smaller than him. And yet she had also been proud of how he led the other boys in everything, how they all looked up to him, how even Aunt Rasa's Oykib stepped back and let Protchnu take the first place among the boys.

Can it ever be one without the other? The leadership

without the lack of compassion? The pride without the cruelty?

"But of course you choose your father," said Eiadh. "The man you know he really is, the good, brave, strong man you love so much. That's the man you were choosing that day, I know it."

She could feel how Protchnu's body moved within her embrace as he steeled himself to say the hard thing. "He's really unhappy without you," he said.

"Did he send you to tell me that?"

"I sent myself," said Protchnu.

Or did the Oversoul send you? Eiadh wondered sometimes. Hadn't Luet said that they were *all* chosen by the Oversoul? That they were all unusually receptive to her promptings? Then why shouldn't one of her children have these extraordinary gifts, like the one that had popped up in Chveya, for instance?

"So your father in unhappy without me. Let him release Nafai, restore peace to the ship, and he won't have to be without me anymore."

"He can't stop," said Protchnu. "Not without help."

He's only eight years old? And he can see this deeply? Perhaps the crisis has awakened some hidden power of empathy within him. The Oversoul knows that at his age I was utterly without understanding or compassion for anyone. I was a moral wasteland, caring only for who was prettiest and who sang the best and who would be famous someday and who was rich. If I had only grown out of that childishness earlier, I might have seen which of the brothers was the better man, back before I married Elemak, back when Nafai was gazing at me with the calf eyes of adolescent love. I made a terrible mistake then. I looked at Elemak and couldn't see him without thinking, he's the heir of the Wetchik, oldest son of one of the richest and most prestigious men of Basilica. What was Nafai?

Of course, if I'd been truly wise, I'd have married neither of them and I'd still be in Basilica. Though if

Volemak was right, Basilica has already been destroyed, the city demolished and its few survivors scattered to the wind.

"And what sort of help does your father need?" asked Eiadh.

"He needs a way to change his mind without admitting that he's wrong."

"Don't we all," she murmured.

"Mother, I can hardly breathe sometimes. I wake up in the morning feeling like somebody's pressing on my chest. I just can't breathe in deeply enough. Sometimes I get dizzy and fall down. And I'm doing better than most. We have to help Father."

She knew that this was true. But she also knew that after that scene in the library, she didn't have the power to help him. Now, though, with Protchnu beside her, she could do it. Had this eight-year-old that much power?

Eight years old, but he had seen. He had understood what was needed, and he had taken the responsibility for acting on that understanding. It filled her with hope, not just for the immediate future, but for a time far distant. She knew that the community would divide, at the death of Volemak if not sooner, and when it did, Elemak would be the ruler of one of the halves. He would be angry, embittered, filled with loathing and violence. But Elemak would not live forever. Someday his place as ruler would be filled by someone else, and the most likely man was this one sitting beside her on the bed, this eight-year-old. If he grew in wisdom over the years, instead of growing in rage as his father had done, then when he took his father's place as ruler of the people he would be like autumn rains on the cities of the plain, bringing relief after the dry fire of summer.

For you, Protchnu, I will do what must be done. I will humble myself before Elemak, unworthy as he is, for your sake, so that you will have a future, so that someday you can fill the role that nature has suited you to.

"At the next mealtime in the library," she said. "Come to me then, and with you beside me I'll do what must be done."

Elemak was with them during the meal, of course. He always was, now, ever since Volemak had used his absence as an opportunity to give the oath. The meals were more sparsely attended these days. After watching Elemak beat Nafai, Volemak and Rasa had taken to their beds. The lack of oxygen was affecting them as badly as the youngest of the babies. They hadn't the strength to move, and those who tended to them—Dol and Sevet—reported that they kept slipping into and out of unconsciousness and were delirious much of the time. "They're dying," they whispered—but loudly enough that Elemak could surely hear them during meals. He showed no reaction.

At the noon meal of the fourth day of the waking, Elemak was sitting alone, his food untouched, when Protchnu got up from the table and walked to his mother. Elemak watched him go, his face darkening. But it was clear to everyone there that Protchnu was not joining himself to his mother's cause. Rather he was fetching her, bringing her along. He might be only two-thirds her height, but he was in control. Slowly they approached the table where Elemak sat.

"Mother has something to tell you," said Protchnu.

Suddenly Eiadh burst into tears and dropped to her knees. "Elemak," she sobbed, "I am so ashamed. I turned against my husband."

Elemak sighed. "It's not going to work, Eiadh. I know what a good actress you are. Like Dolya. You can turn the tears on and off like a faucet."

She wept all the harder. "Why should you ever believe me or trust me again? I deserve whatever terrible things you want to say to me. But I am your true wife.

Without you I'm nothing, I'd rather die than not be part of you and your life. Please forgive me, take me back."

Everyone could see how Elemak struggled between belief and skepticism. It was not as if he had it in him to be subtle or clever. Everyone was getting logy and stupid from the lack of oxygen. They could remember that once they had good, quick judgment, but they couldn't remember what it even felt like. Elemak blinked slowly, looking at her.

"I know who the strongest, best man is," she said. "Not one who relies on tricks and machines, on lies and deception. You're the honest one."

His lip curled in contempt at her obvious flattery. Yet he was also affected by it. Someone understands. Even if she's just mouthing empty words, the words *are* being said.

"But the liars have the upper hand. *They're* the ones who are holding our babies hostage, not you. Sometimes a man has to give in to evil in order to save his children."

Most of those listening knew that they were hearing a distortion of the truth. And yet they wanted it to be believed, wanted Elemak at least to believe it, because if he did, it would provide him with a way to surrender and still be noble and heroic in his own eyes. Let this be the version of history that Elemak believes in, so that our history can go on beyond this hour.

"Do you think I'll be fooled when Nafai starts strutting around here again? Him and his sparkling cloak embedded in his flesh, making him look like a machine himself—I'll be grateful to go back into suspended animation for the rest of the voyage, so I don't have to look at him. When I wake up, let it be on Earth, with you beside me, and our children still to raise. They'll grow older. Time will pass. And you'll still be my husband and a great man in the eyes of all who know the truth."

Elemak looked at her sharply. Or at least he tried to be sharp. Now and then she simply went out of focus.

She opened her mouth to speak again, but Protchnu laid a hand on her shoulder and she settled back, sitting on her ankles, as Protchnu stepped forward and spoke quietly, where few but Elemak could hear. "Pick the time of battle," he said quietly. "You taught me that back in Vusadka. Pick the time of battle."

Elemak answered him just as softly. "They've won already, Protchnu. By the time I awoke they had already cheated you out of your inheritance. Look at you, so young, so small."

"Do what it takes to let us all live, Father. Someday I will not be small, and then we'll have vengeance on our enemies."

Elemak studied his face. "*Our* enemies?"

"What they have done to the father, they have done to the son," whispered Protchnu. "I will never, never, never, never, never forget."

It filled Elemak with hope, to hear such resolve, such hatred in his son's voice.

He rose to his feet. All eyes were upon him, watching as he took Protchnu by the hand and led him to the ladderway in the middle of the room. He turned back. "Meb. Obring."

They got up slowly.

"Come with me."

"Who'll watch these people, then?" asked Obring.

"I don't care," said Elemak. "I'm tired of looking at them."

He dropped down the ladderway, Protchnu after him, and then Obring and Meb.

As soon as they were gone, the women gathered around Eiadh. "Thank you," they said softly. "It was brave of you." "You were wonderful." "Thank you."

Even Luet took Eiadh's hands in hers. "Today you were the greatest among women. It's over now, because of you."

Eiadh could only press her face into her hands and weep. For she had overheard the words that Protchnu said to Elemak, had heard the hatred in his voice, and she knew that Protchnu was not putting on a performance as she had done, not now, anyway. Protchnu would carry on his father's hatred into the next generation. It was all for nothing. She had humbled herself for nothing. "For nothing," she murmured.

"Not for nothing," said Luet. "For our children. For all the children. I say it again, Eiadh. Today you were the greatest among women."

Luet knelt beside her; Eiadh reached out to her and wept against her shoulder.

The door opened and the light came on. Nafai's eyes adjusted quickly. Elemak, Mebbekew, Obring, and Elya's son, Protchnu. He could see the hatred in their eyes, all of them.

They've come to kill me.

To Nafai's surprise, the thought did not come as a relief. Despite all his words of desperation to the Oversoul, he did not really want to die. But he would do it, he would submit to it, if that's what would bring peace.

To his surprise, Elemak knelt down at his feet and began fumbling with the knots at his ankles. Mebbekew joined him, working on the knots at his wrists.

His skin was sore there, and their working chafed him painfully. After his beating, after the Oversoul had caused the cloak to heal him, Nafai had resumed letting the sores at his ankles and wrists go unhealed. Now it made the moment of release almost excruciating.

"We've taken an oath," Elemak said quietly. "The oath Father administered to everyone else on the ship. *He* is the sole ruler of the colony. No one else is his second in command or his chief adviser or any other such fiction that disguises power. *He* will rule. I've taken the oath, and so have Meb and Obring. And my son

Protchnu. As long as Volemak lives, we obey him and no other."

"That's a good oath," said Nafai softly. He did not add: If only you had taken it earlier and lived by it, as I did from my childhood on. It would have spared us a lot of trouble.

"You go straight from here and take the oath as well," said Meb.

The cords at his neck, the cords that had pulled his body in a backward arch, suddenly released. Pain shot up and down his back. He moaned.

"Stop the histrionics," said Meb contemptuously. "We know you could heal this in a moment if you wanted to."

His feet and hands were numb; they felt like heavy clubs, sluggish, not obeying what he told them to do. As he rolled onto his stomach, his back ached and he could hardly pull himself up onto his knees. Bracing himself on the wall, he finally stood on unsteady legs. "Where's Father?" asked Nafai. "I must go and take the oath."

"Oykib and Chveya haven't taken it yet, either," said Obring.

"Go get them, then," Elemak answered scornfully. "Are you still waiting for me to command you? I'm not in charge here anymore."

"And neither am I," said Nafai.

But he was. Already the cloak was giving him whatever information he wanted. "There is enough oxygen in the working reserve to bring us up near normal for two hours. That will be enough time to oxygenate everyone's blood and for all of us to enter suspended animation. Then the ship can replenish itself before anybody else wakes up."

Elemak laughed nastily. "What, aren't you going to promise us to stay asleep till we reach Earth?"

"I'm going to resume the school where we left off," said Nafai. "If Father says I should."

"I have no doubt that he'll say whatever you want him to say."

"Then you don't know him or me at all. Because Father will say whatever the Oversoul wants him to say, and nothing else."

"Oh, let's not argue, Nafai," said Elemak, with exaggerated cheeriness. "We must be *friends* now."

Nafai walked in silence, leaning against the corridor walls as he needed to, grateful for the low gravity. "Is this really what you want for Protchnu, Elemak? To feed him this steady diet of hate?"

"Hate is the richest of foods," said Elemak. "It makes you strong, it fills you with power. And I have a banquet of it to give my children."

"Let there be peace between your children and mine, Elya," said Nafai.

"Between your big, tall children and my little tiny ones?" asked Elemak. "Of course there'll be peace, the way there's peace between the lion and the fly."

They reached the door of Volemak's and Rasa's room just as Obring returned with Oykib and Chveya. Wordlessly Chveya embraced her father, and he leaned on her as they went into the room.

Nafai knelt and took the oath, holding his father's hand as he did it. Chveya and Oykib followed him.

Feebly, Volemak spoke from the bed. "Then it's done. All have taken the oath. Give us the oxygen now, and let us return to sleep."

In only a few seconds, they began to feel the difference, all of them. The breaths they were taking were deep enough, and in a few moments their panting, their gasping, began to cause them to feel drunk on oxygen, faint with air. Then their bodies adjusted, their breathing went back to normal, and it was as if nothing had ever been wrong. Mothers wept over their babies, now breathing normally. Children began to laugh and shout and run, because at last they could.

Long before the two hours were up, however, the

laughing and shouting had ended. Parents put their children to sleep. Zdorab and Shedemei put all the adults to sleep then, except for Nafai, who stayed apart from all the others so as not to cause needless offense to Elemak and those who regretted his defeat.

Once again Nafai and Shedemei stood over the chamber where Zdorab lay. "Forgive me, Nafai," said Zdorab.

"I already have," said Nafai. "Luet explained to me what you were thinking at the time. And how you regretted it after."

"No more surprises," said Zdorab. "I'm with you till I die."

"Your oath is to my father," said Nafai. "But I'm glad of your friendship, and you may be sure that you have mine."

Alone with Shedemei, Nafai could allow the sores on his wrists and ankles to heal at last. "Who would have guessed," he said.

"What?" she answered.

"That Zdorab's mistake would end up accomplishing something that would have been impossible otherwise."

"And what is that?"

"I expected that as soon as we reached Earth, Elemak would go out of control and we'd be at war. I think the Oversoul expected it, too. But now we've had the war, and I think the peace will hold."

"Until your father dies," said Shedemei pointedly.

"Father isn't old yet," said Nafai. "It gives us time. Who knows what might happen in the years to come?"

"I don't want to be there," said Shedemei.

"It's a little late to decide that now," said Nafai.

"I don't want to be there for the conflict. For the fighting. I came here to do some gardening." She laughed self-deprecatingly. "To tinker around with the plant and animal life of Earth. That's the dream the Keeper sent to me. Not like you others. I'm just the gardener."

"Just? You'll be the most important person among us."

"I lied to you too, you know, Nafai. When I told you that it would be safe for cousins to marry. Just like Zdorab, I held something back."

"That's all right," said Nafai. "Everyone holds something back, whether they know it or not."

"But your children—the consequences may be terrible."

"I don't think so," said Nafai.

"Oh." She grimaced. "So the Oversoul told me what to say?"

"Suggested it. Every word was true."

Shedemei laughed sardonically. "Or at least as true as every *other* word of the Oversoul."

"I trust him," said Nafai.

"Trust her to say whatever is necessary to accomplish her purposes. That's as far as she can be trusted," said Shedemei.

"Ah, but you see, Shedya, the Oversoul's purposes *are* my purposes. So I can trust him completely."

She patted his cheek. "You may be technically about as old as I am by now, what with staying awake continuously during the voyage. But Nyef, I must say, you still have a lot to learn."

With that she swung into place in her chamber. Nafai raised the side, locked it, then activated the suspension process. The lid slipped closed. He watched as she drifted to sleep in the airtight compartment. He was alone again.

<I can only sustain the oxygen like this for about fifteen more minutes, and then it's gone.>

I'm hurrying.

<Everything worked out rather well, don't you think?>

I have an idea. Just don't talk to me for a little while. Let me go to sleep with only my own thoughts in my head.

<If you want. But it will feel rather strange to you.>
I can handle it.
<Because you've never gone to sleep without me in your life.>
I wish you were better company, then.
<Go ahead and be angry at me. But remember that I didn't make Elemak the way he is. If he had chosen better, if he were innately a better man, then he'd be in your place, wearing the cloak of the starmaster.>
I wish he were.
<Yes, you mean that. You really don't want to have the responsibility or the power. And yet you accepted them both because someone must, and only you could do it. Not against your will, but against your desires and your better judgment. And that is why I led you to the cloak. Because if you had understood what it was, you would never have reached for it.>
I'm just the puppet you want, is that it?
<You're not a puppet at all. Puppets are useless to me. I need willing friends and allies.>
Let me go to sleep in peace, and maybe when I wake up I'll be willing again.
<Sleep well, my friend. There's a long road yet ahead of us.>

The skyscreen in the library showed it, the globe of Earth, blue and white, with patches of brown and green here and there. Since they had slept through the launch, they had never seen a world like this, like a ball floating in the black of night.

"Like a moon," said Chveya.

Oykib reached out and took her hand. She looked up at him and smiled. The last three and a half years had been both wonderful and excruciating, to know that he loved her, and yet to know that it was impossible to marry and have children during the voyage. They didn't speak of what they felt—it was easier for both of them that way. The others had been just as discreet in their pairing up. But now, as they made their reconnaissance, orbiting the Earth again and again, reading the reports the instruments made, studying the maps, searching for the landing place, waiting for the Oversoul to make a decision, or for a dream from the Keeper to tell them what to do, it was impossible for Oykib to keep himself from thinking about Chveya, about what lay ahead for them. A new world, hard work, farming and exploring, and who knew what sort of dangers from disease or animals or weather—but set against all this was the thought of Chveya in his arms, of babies, of starting the cycle over again, of being part of the living world.

"We once fled from this world in shame and fear," said Chveya. "We once fouled it and slaughtered each other."

She did not need to add the fear that it would happen again. They all knew that the time of real peace would be over, that even if the oath to Volemak held, the tension would still be alive underneath the civility. And how long would Volemak live? Then war might come again. Human blood might once again be shed on Earth.

Oykib heard Chveya speaking to the Oversoul. Why did you bring us here, when we're no better and no wiser than the ones who left?

"But we *are*," said Oykib. "Better and wiser, I mean."

She turned to him, her eyes wide. "What is it that you do? Back in the crisis, you spoke so knowledgeably. Of what the Oversoul wanted. Of what Nafai wanted, when you hadn't even spoken to him. What is it you do?"

"I eavesdrop," he said. "It's been that way all my life. Anything that's said on the channels of the Oversoul, I hear. What he says. What you say."

She looked horrified. Is this true? she was saying to the Oversoul. That's horrible!

"Now you know why I've never told anyone.

Though I certainly showed it clearly enough during the crisis. I'm surprised no one guessed."

"What I say to the Oversoul—it's so private."

"I know that," said Oykib. "I didn't ask to hear it. It just came to me. I grew up knowing a great deal more than any child should know. I understand what's going on in others' lives to a degree that—well, let's just say that I'd much rather take people at face value than to know what really troubles them. Or, with the ones who never speak to the Oversoul, what things he has to do to keep them from doing the worst things they desire. It's not a pleasant burden to carry."

"I can imagine," said Chveya. "Or maybe not. Maybe I can't imagine. I'm not even trying to imagine right now. All I'm doing is trying to remember what I've said to the Oversoul, what secrets you know."

"I'll tell you one secret I know, Veya. I know that of all the people on this starship, no one is more honest and good than you, no one more loving and careful of other people's feelings. Of all the people on this ship, there's no one who is so at peace with herself, no one who adds less to the burden of shame and guilt that I carry around with me. Of all the people on this ship, Veya, you are the only one that I would be glad to be close to forever, because all your secrets are bright and good and I love you for them."

"Some of my secrets are *not* bright and good, you liar."

"On the contrary. The evil secrets you're ashamed of are so mild and pathetic that to *me*, having seen real evil to a degree I hope you'll never understand, to me even your darkest, most shameful secrets are dazzling."

"I think," said Chveya, "that you're hinting around that you want to marry me."

"As if it could ever be a secret to you, who senses the connections between people just like Aunt Hushidh. Talk about invasion of privacy."

"I do know your secret, Okya," she said, smiling, facing him, putting her arms around his waist, holding his hips against hers. "I know what you want. I know how much you love me. I see us bound by bright cords, tied so tightly that there's no escape ever as long as either of us lives. You are my captive, and I'm never going to have mercy and let you go."

"Those bonds aren't bondage at all, Veya," said Oykib. "They're freedom. This whole voyage I've been in captivity because I couldn't have you. When we step out on that new world, that old world, and I'm tied to you at last, openly, so we can begin our life together—that's when I will truly be unbound."

"My answer is yes," she said.

"I know," he said. "I heard you tell the Oversoul."

2

LANDFALL

NINE

WATCHERS

There were many things for a young man to do,
many duties that the community required of him, even
if he *was* already married, and to a remarkable woman
like Iguo. Because of pTo's extraordinary advancement,
people looked to him for achievement, looked for him
to be a model of young manhood.

Well, perhaps not always. Many of them looked to
pTo for disappointment at best, scandal at worst. He
was too young. Iguo had only married a mere boy like
that because her great grandmother Upua had done the
same with Kiti. It had become something of a family
tradition for the women of that line, to marry a man
who was too young—and pTo was no Kiti, as many
were quick to point out.

"You're no Kiti, you know," said pTo's own
otherself, Poto.

"As well for you I'm not," said pTo. "*His* otherself
was dead the year he made his sculpture and was chosen
by Upua."

"You can't go doing crazy things. They're not going to forgive you anything. If you're brilliant they'll say you're arrogant. If you falter, they'll say you over-reached. If you're friendly they'll say you're condescending. If you're aloof they'll say you're arrogant."

"So I might as well do what I want."

"Just remember that it's my name you're dragging through the mud. If *you're* a madman, what am I?"

"A helpless victim of my lunacy," said pTo. "I want to go to the tower."

Resting on the stout limb of a tree, they were watching over a flock of fat turkeys. The turkeys themselves were docile enough, too stupid to know the fate that the people had in store for them. The danger was from devils, who liked nothing better than to steal from the herds of the people. Lazy creatures, devils never did their own work except digging their nasty little holes in the ground and carving out the hearts of trees. During the birthing season, they came in force, stealing sometimes as many as a third of each year's newborns—that was why so many people had lost their otherself. During the rest of the year, though, it was the flocks and herds they were after.

"We're on watch," said Poto.

"We're watching the wrong thing," pTo insisted. "The Old Ones at the tower are the most important creatures in the world."

"Boboi says they're our enemies."

"Why was my wife's ancestor shown the face of an Old One, then, if they aren't to be our friends?"

"To warn us," said Poto.

"The Old Ones know secrets, and if we don't make friends with them, they'll give those secrets to the devils. Then we really *will* have them as enemies."

"It's forbidden," said Poto, "and we have responsibilities here, and no matter how young you might have been when you got married, you are *not* Kiti."

pTo knew that his otherself was right. He usually was.

But pTo couldn't bear to concede the point, because he knew that if he didn't learn about the Old Ones, no one else would. No one else *dared*. "I'm not Kiti," said pTo, "but I also am the only man who doesn't fear that he'll be rejected by all the women because of flouting Boboi's ban on visiting the Old Ones."

"You're not the only married man."

"You know what I mean. The older men don't *want* to go. They get a little slow, a little fat. It's too dangerous for them to go down there into the heart of devil country."

One of the turkeys decided, as turkeys will, that it was urgently required to be somewhere out in the brush, and it suddenly started gobbling and running. Without a word, Poto swooped down from the limb and flew in front of the bird, shouting. The bird stopped, gazing stupidly at the man beating his wings in the air in front of him. Poto dropped to the ground, then jumped into the air again and, on the leap, kicked the turkey in the face. It screeched, turned around, and trotted back to the herd.

When Poto rejoined him on the limb, pTo couldn't resist. "What you just did to that turkey is what Boboi is doing to all the men."

Poto sighed. "Give me a little peace, pTo."

"What I'm saying, Poto, is that I'm going. You can tend the herd alone."

"We herd in twos because a man is needed to watch the turkeys, and another to watch the man so he isn't taken by surprise."

"Then come with me," said pTo. "I'm not ashamed to admit that I'm afraid to go alone."

"I'm afraid to go at all, and you should be, too."

"Then goodbye, my otherself, my bettermind. Perhaps my Iguo will marry you after I'm dead." In the old days, they would both be married to her already. Sometimes pTo wished it had not changed.

"Yes, everything's a poem to you," said Poto scornfully, but pTo was not deaf to the emotion behind his hard words.

"My death, when it comes, will be one that the poets sing of."

"Better to have a life that your children remember with joy than a death that the poets remember with song."

"Hard to believe you're not an old man, when you quote nonsense like that."

"Go if you must."

pTo immediately leapt from the branch. Moments after his glide began, he rose up, circling higher than the treetops. He shouted down at Poto. "Watch your back, Obedient One!"

"No!" shouted Poto, truly angry. "I won't do your work for you!"

His words stung, but pTo flew on, down the valley. He knew that others would see him, and he knew that while Poto was high enough up the valley to be in little danger, others would say that he was so unnatural as not to love his otherself. Let them say what they would. Boboi was wrong. There was great danger in ignoring the Old Ones. pTo *would* study them, learn about them, perhaps enter into conversation with them. Learn their language. Become their friend. Bring back their ancient secrets. Better to bring knowledge back to the people than mere trinkets. Their trove of Old One artifacts was not large, but it had taken many generations to collect it. All of it was worthless, because none of it meant anything. It was knowledge that was needed, secrets that must be told. Not to the devils, either. To us.

It wasn't far. pTo wasn't even tired when the tower came into view. He had seen it before, from afar, and marveled at it every time. Who could shape a thing as smooth and tall as that? Like sunlight on the water, it was so bright, and the trees looked like bushes bowing down to worship it.

Why had the Old Ones come to dwell among the

devils, and not among the people? Was it possible that the Old Ones were hellfolk and not from the gods at all? Yet they had not burst upward from the ground. They came from the sky. How then could they be hellfolk?

They could be hellfolk because they rested their tower right beside a stand of thick, ancient trees. The signs of a devil city were all around. Dead trees here and there; depressions here and there from old tunnels that had given way; and nearby, the rocky hills that held miles of caves for their obscene cannibalistic worship. The Old Ones must have seen all this, must have known, and yet they built their own village where the devils could watch them without leaving their holes. Why would the Old Ones do this, if they didn't intend to befriend the devils? They probably already had. It was already too late.

But if it *is* too late, then I'll see signs of their alliance, I'll get some idea of what the danger is, and I'll come home and report. When the danger is clear enough, they'll stop listening to Boboi. But then we'll come down here for war instead of learning, and the Old Ones will probably strike us out of the sky with magic. The Old Ones live in a tower that stands on a foundation of fire. Even the greatest warrior of the people would be no more irritating to them than a gnat.

It must not be war. It must be friendship. I must find a way to make it friendship.

The devils had no doubt already noticed him. Flight was the salvation of the people, but it was also their bane, at least in the daytime. They could leap to the sky to escape an enemy; but their enemy could look to the sky to watch them approach. Much had been made of the difference: The people were open and honest, the devils stealthy and deceptive. The people lived in the realm of the sun and stars, the devils in the realm of the worms and grubs. The people were as light as air, and therefore spiritual, akin to the gods; the devils were heavy and plodding, and therefore earthy, akin to stone.

But it didn't change the fact that if a devil once got its hands on a man, it could break any of his bones as easily as snapping a twig. There was no fighting the devils hand to hand. One thrust with a spear, that's all a man would ever get. Then he either had to fly or die. He couldn't even lift a very heavy burden—not even a stone to drop on a devil's head, or at least not a stone large enough to cause harm.

Couldn't even lift his own child when the child was at that awkward age, too large to carry in flight, too young yet to fly. So it was at that time of year that the devils came, and parents had to make the terrible choice: Which child the two of them would carry to safety. Some were able to get back in time to save the second. Some were lucky enough to have older children who had not yet mated, who could take the other twin to safety. That's how Poto had survived, because he and pTo were thirdborn. Rare indeed was the firstborn whose otherself was still alive.

So the devils were watching him, wondering why he came. Salivating, too, no doubt, at the thought of having his meat between their teeth. Well, pTo was young and quick enough that no one was going to take him. He was still light enough to perch on far branches that the devils couldn't climb on without shaking them. His ears were still so keen that he could hear the sound of the fingers digging into the bark of the tree. There was danger if he walked into a trap, but if he was careful he would be safe.

Then pTo had a troubling thought: Every man or woman taken by the devils must have thought exactly the same thing, right up to the moment when they realized they were wrong.

The Old Ones' village was very small, in terms of numbers, but huge in terms of size. Their houses were monstrously large. Whole trees had been felled and split to make the walls and roofs, except for the few buildings made of strange substances that pTo had never seen before. It was hard to make sense of what the buildings were for. The large one must be a dormitory—but then, why was there only one? Did their unmated males and females sleep in the same house? Unthinkable.

He chose his vantage point—a slender branch, sturdy enough to provide a good launch for flight, with many leaves to keep him from the Old Ones' view. He inspected the trunk of the tree, but it was thin enough that the devils couldn't have hollowed it yet, so he didn't have to worry about ambush through a hidden door in the tree. For a devil to get to him it would have to climb the outside of the trunk, and pTo would hear it.

Unless he *didn't* hear it, or unless they *could* hollow a tree that thin.

pTo ignored his own fears and settled down to watch. He watched all day, and by sundown he had learned many strange new things. The most amazing thing was that all the adults seemed to be married, each couple dwelling in their own house. The largest building was used during the day by a couple of adults and all the young children; obviously the Old Ones were holding school. But indoors? Closing their children off from the world in order to teach them about it made no sense to pTo.

Another thing pTo learned was that everyone lived in the buildings made of wood; the buildings made of that strange, smooth substance were only for storage or some more arcane purpose, for these buildings were rarely visited, and then only to fetch a tool or some other item, or return it to its place.

The Old Ones kept some animals in pens, but very few, and they were strange. A pair of them looked like goats, but they were huge. A pair of them looked like cows, but they were tiny. And there were dozens of wolves—or at

least they barked and whined and howled like wolves—
and they ran free among the Old Ones. Friends of wolves!
What kind of creatures were these Old Ones? Didn't they
fear for their babies' safety? Or were their babies born
strong? No, not at all: pTo could see that a couple of the
Old Ones carried babies with them in slings, and the babies looked completely helpless.

At first pTo thought—with disappointment—that all
the children were alone. It was only late in the after-
noon that he realized that two of the little ones were
identical, and had the same parents. They did have
otherselves! And yet the two of them weren't always
together—that was why pTo hadn't realized they were
not the same child until late in the day. He thought
about this: only one pair out of all the children. Had
the Old Ones been such calamitously unlucky parents
that all the other pairs had been broken? Or was it possible that only some of their children were born in pairs,
and all the others simply came as singles? What were
they, then—animals?

Time to think about that later. When he had learned
their language, he could perhaps find a way to ask such
indelicate questions. For now, though, he could only
watch. But particularly he would watch the pair, to see
how they could go through childhood so often apart
from each other. Are they so much stronger than we
are, pTo wondered, or do they simply lack real affection?

During the day he noticed that most of the adults
spent a great deal of time in the large cleared area,
where they had marked the earth in many rows, as if
loosening the clay to make a giant sculpture—though
the soil here was loose, and would never hold together
if they tried to shape it. But after watching for several
hours, it dawned on pTo that the furrowed soil was
quite possibly just an early stage of the four strange
meadows, each with grass of a different height. For
there, too, the roots of the grasses seemed to grow in

rows. There were other areas, too, where plants seemed to have been intentionally placed, and from one of them a couple of Old Ones went to gather melons, which were then cut open and shared with the workers in the middle of the day.

This was the first secret pTo learned from the Old Ones, that instead of remembering from year to year where the best plants grew, and taking care to leave an offering of fruit and roots in the earth so the Mother would give back new plants the next year, the offerings could be taken away from their original rooting place and herded together like turkeys or goats, so they could be watched over and cared for all at once, by only a few men and women. Of course, there would be danger in this, too—all the devils would have to do is find an artificial meadow like this, and then lie in wait until the gatherers came. So it might be that the people couldn't use this particular secret of the Old Ones. But maybe they could.

More to the point, the devils almost certainly could. But then, the devils could easily have learned the people's secret, too, of herding animals so they could be protected from predators and led to good eating. Instead, the devils simply learned to search for the people's flocks and herds, and steal from them. No doubt the devils were already planning to steal fruit and seeds from the meadows of the Old Ones.

Here was the strangest thing of all. No one stood on guard. Some of the children took turns standing in two of the meadows, the one where all the grasses were coming ripe at once, and the one that was new-furrowed, where the birds seemed to be finding new-planted seeds. There the children watched for birds to land and ran to shoo them away.

Birds they watch for, but not devils.

Did this mean that the Old Ones had already befriended the devils? Or perhaps they had already conquered them and forced them into submission.

Or—was it possible?—the devils had been so stealthy, and the Old Ones so careless, that they had not yet noticed that the devils were watching them.

Surely the Old Ones could see some fragment of what pTo could see. During the day he had watched as more than a dozen different parties of devils arose out of the earth or emerged onto branches of trees, to watch. pTo had seen several of the devils taking note of *him*, too, and was sure that they were plotting some way to take him, or at least drive him off. The devils were clever, but not *that* clever. Or were the Old Ones merely unobservant? How could they have become so powerful if they were too stupid to notice things as important as where the devils were, what they were watching, where they were laying their traps?

The sun set.

Now was the time, pTo knew, when the devils would spring whatever trap it was that they had been planning all day. Night was also when they would do their thieving and spying on the Old Ones. He could already see in the waning light that devils were gathering at meadow's edge; yet the Old Ones gave no alarm, and seemed to set only the most inadequate watch—one male, walking around carrying a lamp in his hands (and never spilling it!). A lamp—it made no sense. Why not just shout, "I'm coming, get out of my way, hide from me so I can't see you!"

pTo heard a faint rubbing sound and felt his branch vibrate. For a moment he was tempted to wait, to tease the devil, to pretend that he didn't know he was being stalked. But then he thought: Perhaps this is all the warning I'll get. Perhaps the devil is closer than I think. And if I linger for even a moment longer. . . .

He lunged for the sky and as he did he heard a hiss of disappointment right behind him, so loud and close that he imagined he could feel the devil's breath on his back. That is how people die, he thought. Waiting just a little too long to take to the sky.

He swooped, then rose up high enough to soar for a few moments. He was a little stiff from his posture of stillness during the day. It would have been better if he could have set his hands and feet and hung upside down—but then he would have been in danger of falling asleep. No, stiffness was the price of remaining in an upright posture all day, without moving. Though from what he had seen of the Old Ones, pTo wondered if he needed to be so careful. He could probably do a jig and sing a song, and the Old Ones wouldn't see him.

He knew that the devils would be out in the Old Ones' meadows now, but he felt he had to take a risk and gather up samples of the grasses they were growing in such perfect unison. He went to the ripest field first and saw at once that the danger there was extreme. The stalks weren't strong enough to hold him, and yet were tall enough to interfere with flight. Worst of all, the breeze rustled them constantly so that pTo wouldn't be able to hear any of the faint noises the devils might make moving through the grass. He dared not settle to the ground there—every devil in the grass would have seen him, though he couldn't see any of them at all, and there was a chance he would come down within a few handspans of one of them and never know it till the powerful hands clamped around his legs or arms, or ripped into the tough, thin skin of his wings.

He dared not come to ground, and yet he did it, because he would not go home without some trophy of his expedition. The secrets he had learned were the most valuable things he could bring back, he knew, but it would go better for him in withstanding Boboi's criticism if he also had something in his hands. So he came to ground and immediately started breaking off stalks as near the ground as he could. He didn't bother to look around him. He wouldn't have been able to see anything, anyway. If a devil was very close, he was doomed whether he looked or not; and if the devils were farther off, stopping and looking for them through the impenetrable grass would merely have given them time to get closer.

How many stalks? One. Two. Three. Each one took its moment to break off, to lay down next to the first; how many moments did he have? Four. Five. How many stalks did he need? Six. Seven. Were they all ripe? Or would he be bringing home only immature ones, which would embarrass him? Eight. Nine.

Enough. Done. Fly.

Gathering the stalks in one foot, he squatted, then jumped upward with all his might. His wings could barely spread in the grass, so that he had to fling them out to full length after he rose above the stalks, and then it took all his strength to dig into the air and rise. For a terrifying moment he hovered at the level of the tops of the stalks, moving forward but not rising. Under him, he could see eyes—four, six, eight—flowing in the moonlight, leaping upward toward him as he passed. If they had been taller, or if pTo had been slower, he would now be lying amid the stalks as they tore his body to pieces and carried the bits of him down into their holes to share with their filthy dirt-eating mates.

But they were not taller, and pTo was not slower, and so he rose into the air and flapped his way toward the village of the Old Ones. He had to touch one of the buildings that was not made of wood. This was safer, though. None of the devils had moved into the village, and the Old One with the lamp would probably not see him. He would be on the roof, too, with nothing to hinder him from taking flight.

The roof gave way slightly under his weight. Since he could only hold his place with the foot that wasn't gripping the stalks of grain, he had to bend down and use his hands to feel the texture of it. Woven like a temporary nest, like a basket, only the weave was astonishingly tight and fine. Even water couldn't pass through a weave as close as this. And what the fibers were made of he could not begin to guess. They had shone in the sunlight. Why would the Old Ones kill trees to build their houses, when they could weave a roof as fine and perfect as this one?

One last temptation, after the smooth house: He flew to the base of the tower and touched it. Not like the woven house at all. There was no give to it; it was like stone, except not as cold to the touch. When he struck it lightly with his knuckles, he could hear a faint ring to it, like several of the artifacts of the Old Ones in the village trove. This much, then, was still true of the Old Ones: They built music into the things they made.

He was startled by a noise—like a voice, only loud and deep. He was so frightened that he took flight without thinking. Only when he was airborne could he turn and overfly the place and see who had spoken. It *was* a voice. One of the Old Ones. A male. How had it come upon him so quietly? The Old Ones were noisy in everything they did, like deaf people. This one shouted like a deaf person, too, his voice so loud and booming. And yet he had been able to come upon pTo so quietly that—

So quietly that he obviously must not have "come upon" pTo at all. He must have been sitting there in the shadow of the tower. Sitting there all along. How much did he notice? Did he see the stalks of grain that pTo had stolen? Would he be angry now? Would this theft make the Old Ones enemies of the people?

For a moment pTo thought: I won't tell anyone that the Old One saw me.

But he discarded the idea at once. If we ever become friends with the Old Ones, they will remember the stalks that I stole from their meadow. I will bear the penalty for it then. But my people will already have known that my theft was noticed. They will know that I told them the truth about everything I did—even the mistake of being seen. Many will criticize me for my carelessness—but none will doubt that I am honest, or claim that I altered my story to make myself look good. Better to have the trust of the people than their respect. With trust, their respect could be earned later; without it, respect could never be deserved, and so to have it would be like poison.

Tired from the day's stillness, dreading his homecoming, pTo flapped his way higher, up the canyon, toward the valley where the people lived.

Oykib watched the giant bat as it circled once, then flew away up the canyon. He knew that to others, this would mean the beginning of the fulfillment of the old dreams, the ones from the Keeper of Earth. But to Oykib, it was something else. He had heard the voice of the Keeper, speaking to this visitor—and he had understood it.

The voice of the Keeper was strange. It was quieter than the voice of the Oversoul, less clear. It spoke more in images than ideas, more in desires than in emotions. It was harder for Oykib to understand; indeed, when they first arrived on Earth it had taken him several weeks before he even realized that the voice of the Keeper was there. The conversations between humans and the Oversoul were so much louder that the voice of the Keeper was like distant thunder, or a light breeze in the leaves—more felt than heard. But once he noticed it, once he had an idea of what it was, he began to listen for it. Sitting in the shadow of the starship in the gathering dusk, he could concentrate, gradually letting the louder voice of the Oversoul fade into the background.

It was especially hard because the Keeper didn't speak to humans very often. A dream now and then, sometimes a desire; and the dreams didn't often come at times when Oykib could hear them easily. But the Keeper had almost constant dialogue with someone else. Many someones, who seemed to surround the village of Rodina—but how far away or near they were he couldn't guess. The real problem was understanding what was being said. The dreams, the desires he overheard made no sense. At first he thought it was a simple matter of confusion. There were too many of them, that was all. But then, as he began to be able to distinguish one dream from another, as he began to follow a particular thread of communication, he realized that the strangeness was inherent in the messages. The Keeper was prodding these someones with desires that Oykib had never felt, that he couldn't understand; and then, suddenly, there would be something clear: a desire to go care for a child. A wish not to embarrass himself in front of his friends. And the more he listened, the more he began to glimpse what the stranger hungers were: a desire to dig, to tear at wood with his hands. A desire to smear himself with clay. These things made no sense, and yet as Oykib sat in the shadow of the ship, stripping away his humanness, these desires swept over him and he felt—different. Other. Not himself.

He and Chveya had speculated recently, for she, too, had been catching glimpses, out of the corner of her eye, of inexplicable threads, not connecting one human to another. "And yet I can't possibly be seeing any such thing," she had told him. "I only see the threads connecting people that I can see, or at least people that I know. Yet I've seen no one that these threads could belong to."

"Or you've seen them out of the corner of your eye," Oykib had suggested. "Seen them without knowing what you've seen."

"If that's the case, then dozens of them have been gathered all around the village and the fields, and we haven't seen them. Not once, not ever. That's really a pretty silly idea."

"But they *are* gathered around us, all the time."

"Around us, but far. You said what you heard was faint."

"Compared to the Oversoul, that's all. Like trying to

hear a distant concert when somebody's tootling on a fife right next to you."

"See? You said it yourself—a distant concert."

"What if someone *is* watching us?"

"What if they are?" Chveya had answered him. "Let them watch. The Keeper is also watching *them*."

Naturally, all those who believed in the truth of dreams were watching for the winged flyers and the burrowing rodents—what had Hushidh and Luet called them? Angels and Diggers. But in all Oykib's listening, in all of Chveya's glimpses of someone's threads of loyalty and concern, they heard and saw nothing to tell them which of the strange species they had dreamed of their watchful neighbors might be. If it was either of them.

Whatever or whoever these strangers were, though, Oykib had been getting more and more disturbed by the dreams and desires coming into his head. The desire to eat something warm and salt-blooded, still quivering with life—when he first understood that one, it set him to retching with self-revulsion that he could desire such a thing. And even though he knew that the desire came from outside him, it still haunted him as if it had been his own desire. For the warm and salt-blooded something that he wanted to eat alive was, he understood, a soft, tender infant. There was something confusing in his image of it—a dazzle of sky, a leathery crackling blanket. Like all the communications between the Keeper and these strangers, nothing was every really definite. But this much Oykib knew: It had been a prayer from one of these creatures to the Keeper of Earth, and the prayer had been for the living flesh of a youngling.

What kind of monsters were these people?

I must tell someone, he thought; but he couldn't. To tell anyone but Chveya would be to let them know that he had been overhearing all their most secret communication with the Oversoul for many years. It would make them all feel spied upon, robbed, violated. And to tell Chveya would be to terrify her about the safety of their firstborn child, already growing in her womb; about the safety of the little children she was teaching in the school every day.

So while he could tell her most of what he over-heard, he couldn't tell her the worst things; for this past week, he couldn't explain to her why he woke up sweating and gagging in the middle of the night, or why he had grown silent in the past few days, barely speaking to her or to anyone.

Tonight, though, tonight had answered so many questions. For when this bat with its leathery wings came down and landed on the roof of a nearby storage tent, Oykib had sensed a different kind of being en-tirely. This creature, too, was getting an almost contin-uous stream of communication from the Keeper in yet another unfamiliar language of desires; but it was brighter and clearer, though more fearful as well. There were questions, and they were formed in ideas that Oykib could understand; best yet, they were linked with language. He didn't understand the words, but he knew that the language could be learned.

The desires, though, he understood very well indeed. A wish not to disappoint others; a desire to protect his wife and children; a hunger for secrets.

Hunger for secrets. Into Oykib's mind, as he watched the creature there on the tent roof, came an image of *whose* secrets the flyer was trying to decipher. Two pic-tures came into his mind almost at once. A vague image of a human head made of unfired clay, large and mon-strous; and then, much more clearly, the image of Nafai in the flesh. Only it wasn't Nafai. It was a creature just like this one, only with patchy hair and tattered wings, unable to fly, and yet respected, being listened to by all the others.

It was Nafai, but it was also not-Nafai.

Then, suddenly, he understood. It's this creature's

word for us, for human beings. Old man. Old people. We're the old people.

But that would imply that they knew that humans had once lived on Earth before. That was absurd. Nothing could possibly be remembered for forty million years. And how could they remember anyway? As far as he knew, these creatures had not yet evolved into sentient beings when humans last walked upon the Earth.

Then the creature leapt from the tent and swept quickly over the clearing to the base of the starship. There, as he touched the metal, then rapped upon it with his fingers, he was speaking to the Keeper—no, singing to the Keeper, so rapturous was his mood. Oykib felt as if this creature's awe and rejoicing were inside him. He had a thought, as clear as if it were his own thought: "The Old Ones still put music into the things they make."

He had understood it, even though the words attached to the idea were in a language he had never heard before. No real sound had been uttered, and yet he knew inside his memory what this creature's voice would sound like. High and musical, rich in subtle lingering vowels, but with no sibilants or nasals or even fricatives. The only consonants were plosives and stops, and yet they were no less musical than the tonguing of a flautist, making fluttering interruptions in a tune. T's and K's, G's and P's, B's and D's, and a guttural consonant that Oykib knew his own throat could not possibly make. Sometimes these consonants had an extra puff of air; sometimes they were stopped. It was a beautiful language.

More important, though, was the fact that the desires were not dark and violent, and the Keeper did not seem to be struggling to restrain this creature. Rather than distracting him, the Keeper was encouraging him, reinforcing his desires. The contrast came as such a relief to Oykib after all these weeks and days of confusion and darkness that he spoke aloud. "At last the Keeper has brought a friend to us," he said.

He had forgotten how careful and watchful the creature—no, the angel—had been. He hadn't realized that the angel hadn't seen him there in the darkness. But as soon as he heard his own voice, he knew it was too loud, too sudden. The angel leapt almost a man's height into the air and then beat his wings in a frenzy to rise higher, out of harm's way.

But terror didn't rule him. He flew back, swooping around as if to get a good look at Oykib. Well, look to your heart's content, said Oykib, standing with his hands open and spread wide. I'll not harm you, Oykib tried to say with his body.

And then to the Keeper he said, Help him to know I'm not his enemy.

As usual, there was no answer. Others could get their dreams and their whispered silent words of guidance; Oykib could only overhear them, never receive them directly for himself. For once, though, with the memory of the angel's language and desires still fresh, Oykib did not regret the lack. Perhaps it was the better gift, to hear others.

When the angel winged its way into the night sky, heading up the canyon in moonlight, Oykib walked around the starship and headed back to his house. He could see the flash of the lantern. Who was on duty tonight? Meb? Vas? One of the Elemaki, at any rate.

Obring, that's who it was. Obring always swung the lantern as he walked, making it impossible for him to see any strange motions, for the lantern itself created moving shadows that would mask any real movement that might take place. Oykib had heard Elemak remonstrating with Obring about it once. Obring had only laughed and said, "There's nothing to see, Elya. And besides, it's Volemak we all obey now, not you, remember?"

Elemak remembered. Oykib knew *that*. And while

Elemak never spoke to the Oversoul in prayer or conversation, he did curse, and when his curses had real intent behind them, their very intensity moved them into the pattern of communication with the Oversoul, so Oykib could hear him. Silent curses, but nothing said aloud. The man was controlling himself. And at the end there *was* a prayer, or perhaps only a mantra: I am no wordbreaker. I will keep the oath.

Oykib had no doubt which oath he meant—it was the oath to Father, to obey him as long as he was alive to rule over them. Better than anyone except Hushidh and Chveya, who could see the loyalties of the colony laid out like a map before them, Oykib knew that peace in the colony was only skin deep. Everyone knew who the Elemaki were, and who the Nafari; everyone could see that the village was virtually divided down the middle, with Nafari on the east and Elemaki on the west. The colony was not united and never would be. Health to you, Volemak. Health and long life. Let there be no war among us before my children are safely born and grown. Live forever, old man. You are the only cord that holds this harvest together in a single sheaf.

So there was Obring, on watch but worthless at it, while Oykib was aware of dark mutterings and savage prayers out in the darkness and dared not speak to anyone about it.

And tonight, was there some new urgency about it? Some sense of triumph tinged with fear? Daring, that's what it was. Someone was daring something that they had not dared before. And the Keeper was sending a constant stream of distractions. Something's happening. What is it? Speak to me, Keeper! Speak to me, Oversoul!

Chveya was asleep when he came into the house. It was often this way. Up at dawn, Chveya worked hard all day, as if her pregnancy should make no difference in her schedule. Then she would come home and fall asleep without undressing, wherever she happened to sit or lie down. Once Oykib came home and found her asleep standing up, not leaning on anything, just standing like a flagpole in the middle of the single room of the house, her eyes closed. Breathing heavily—had she been lying down, it would have been a snore.

Tonight she was on the bed, but fully dressed, her feet still dangling to the floor. He wanted not to waken her—but her legs would be asleep in the morning and it would cause her much discomfort, especially if she woke up needing to void her bladder in the night, and her legs wouldn't support her.

Besides, it was important. What had happened tonight, the angel coming to him, or at least to the ship, touching it, and the clarity of his voice to the Keeper and of the Keeper's voice to him. The fact that Oykib could hear his language and understand it. And the murmurings and stirrings of the other, darker beings who surrounded the village.

He moved her feet onto the bed. Chveya awoke.

"Oh, again?" she murmured. "I meant to wait up for you."

"Doesn't matter," he said. "Sleep when you can, you need it."

"But you're upset," she said.

"Happy and worried," he corrected her. Then he told her all that had happened and what he thought it might mean.

"So the angels are starting to come to us," she said.

"But you know that it tells us who the others we've been seeing are. Those rat-creatures. Out there in the dark."

"I think you're right," said Chveya.

"Didn't Hushidh have a dream of them stealing her children?"

"And you feel as though something has broken tonight?" asked Chveya. "I think we have to give warning. Put on extra watches."

"And tell them what? Explain what?" asked Oykib.

"Explain nothing. When we ask Grandfather to double, triple the watch tonight, he'll do it even if we tell him it's just a feeling. He has respect for feelings."

They headed for the door, but no sooner had they opened it than a scream sounded from the Elemaki side of the village. It came from a human throat, and all the grief of the world was in it.

TEN

SEARCHERS

Eiadh was the one who had screamed. In moments the adults were gathered around her. She wasn't screaming now, but it took great effort for her to control her voice as she explained.

"Zhivya's gone!" she said. "The baby. Taken from her crib. I woke up to see them, like low shadows, running." Now she did lose control, the horror of it filling her voice. "They were holding the four corners of her blanket. My baby was stolen away by *animals*!"

Elemak had been—somewhere. Not in the house with her, that was certain. Now, though, he was on his knees in the doorway. "Look at this footprint," he said. "An animal made this. Coming in and going out—two animals, actually. And heavily burdened when they left." He got up and looked at them. "I saw a flying creature go down into the fields, then up onto the food storage tent, and then down behind the ship. A moment later it took off, flying up the canyon. No doubt it went to get its friends." He touched the footprint. "That . . .

thing . . . could have made this print. I'm going to follow it up the canyon."

But Oykib looked at the footprint and knew that
Elemak was wrong. The angel's feet had been like
hands, or perhaps more like powerful visegrips. These
footprints came from a creature with flatter feet and
long heavy-clawed toes. The feet of a runner or a digger. Not a creature that flies, that clings to branches.

"The angel didn't make this print," said Oykib.

Elemak looked up at him with steely hatred in his
eyes.

Nafai at once interrupted. "Elemak is the one who
knows how to read the tracks of animals, Oykib."

"But I saw the angel—"

"So did Elemak," said Nafai, "and it's his daughter."
He turned to Elemak. "Tell us what to do, Elemak."

Chveya turned to Oykib and, for a moment, silently
buried her face in his shoulder. It was the way she responded when Nafai said exactly the wrong thing—
which was surprisingly often, for a man as bright as he
was. Nafai was correct as far as he knew; it was quite
proper for everyone to defer to Elemak's judgment in
this matter. But he should have known by now that
Elemak would not be grateful to prevail because Nafai
told everyone to let him have his way.

Besides, Elemak should *not* prevail, because he was
wrong. Oykib knew that angels hadn't taken the child.
The kidnappers were no flyers. They had to be searched
for on the ground. Worse, those who did take Zhivya
had among them at least a few who hungered to eat the
living flesh of an infant. There was real urgency in the
search, and it would be a criminal waste of time to go
off trying to track flying creatures who didn't have the
baby.

As if she could hear his thoughts, Mother put a hand
on Oykib's shoulder. "Be patient, my son," she said.
"You know what you know, and you'll be heard in due
time."

Due time? Oykib looked down at Chveya. Her lips were pursed; she was as worried as he was, and as frustrated.

Elemak was organizing his search party, assigning men where to go.

Volemak spoke up. "Are all the adults gathered here? Who's watching the children, when we already know that they aren't safe in their homes?"

At once the women with children began rushing out of the house, back to their homes.

"Elemak," said Volemak. "Leave me a few men here, to protect the village while you're gone."

Elemak agreed at once. "You keep Nafai and Oykib here—he can tell you his theories to his heart's content. Give me the other men, though."

"I'm a man," said Yasai.

Oykib restrained himself from saying, "Yes, if a dandelion is a tree." This wasn't the time for teasing. And Yasai *was* a man.

"If there's an attack," said Volemak, "we'll need more. Perhaps the younger men."

Now Elemak dug in his heels. "Nafai has the cloak. If you need more, you have the older boys. We're trying to track creatures who fly. I can't do it without as many men as possible."

"I can protect the village," said Protchnu, trying to look older than his nine years.

Elemak looked at him with a serious expression. "You'll have to. Obey your grandfather without question."

Protchnu nodded. Oykib could not help but think that if Elemak had ever followed his own advice, everyone's lives would have been a lot happier over the past few months.

Moments later Elemak was off, leaving behind, of the men, only Nafai, Issib, Volemak, and Oykib.

"Welcome to the ranks of the useless," said Issib wryly.

"Useless? I hardly think so," said Volemak. "All right, now, Oykib. Tell us what you know."

"I saw an angel tonight," said Oykib. "The same one Elemak saw. But he was only a couple of meters from me, and I saw his foot. It couldn't possibly have made this print."

"Who, then?" asked Nafai.

"There are others," said Chveya. "I've caught glimpses of them. Never anything I could see clearly, but enough that I've begun to make connections. Hushidh has got some hints of this, too. They're all around us. But they're low, in the underbrush. Like Eiadh said, low shadows. Sometimes in the trees."

"You know this, and you haven't *seen* them?" asked Issib.

"I see the connections among them. Faintly." Chveya smiled grimly. "It's the best we've got."

"Not enough," said Nafai. He fixed Oykib with a cold stare. "Stop playing games, Oykib. What do you *know*?"

For the first time it occurred to Oykib that maybe he hadn't kept his secret as well as he thought. "What I *know* is that there was no malice in the angel. In his mind we're the Old Ones, and he's filled with respect and awe. But there are other minds, and they've been watching us for months, and some of them. . . ." He glanced at Eiadh, realized that he had to be careful how he said it. "Some of them might be dangerous to Zhivya."

"The ones that we've been calling diggers," said Nafai.

Volemak nodded. "And they live nearby."

Issib laughed. "What, we get shovels and start digging?" He waved his arm to show the vast area they'd have to dig up.

"Burrows have entrances," said Nafai.

"We've been exploring all around here," said Protchnu. "We've never seen any holes."

"Why don't we do the obvious thing?" said Oykib. "The thing that Elemak would have done, if he hadn't been so sure that the kidnappers could fly. Follow the footprints."

The diggers' prints were lost almost at once in the mess that their own feet had made when they ran in response to Eiadh's scream. It didn't help that Rasa was leading the women in gathering the little children out of their beds and into the schoolhouse. Despite the tumult, though, Volemak managed to get lanterns distributed to the men and the older boys, and in a few minutes Protchnu gave a cry. "Here!" he shouted. "They weren't dodging or anything, they just ran in a straight line."

It was true—the trail picked up just where it might have been expected from the direction the diggers first ran upon leaving Elemak's and Eiadh's door. The others ran to join Protchnu, but stayed behind as he led the way toward the edge of the woods.

"Wait," said Volemak. "Nafai, Oykib—you spread out to the sides and keep watch. I don't want Protchnu walking head down into a trap."

Carrying lanterns in one hand, gardening tools as makeshift weapons in the other, the ragtag little army entered the verge of the forest. Four adult men, a bunch of little boys, and the young women who had no children yet—that would strike terror in their enemies. As soon as they entered the woods, the tracking became harder—leaves on the forest floor didn't hold footprints very clearly. It took Protchnu a while to get even six meters into the woods, and then he lost the trail.

Moving slowly and carefully, they all scouted an ever-widening circle, trying to pick up the trail again. Then Oykib heard a low cry from Protchnu, standing only a few paces off. The boy was looking up into the branches. "I'm so stupid!" he said, and immediately ran back to where he had lost the trail.

Oykib followed him. "You think they carried the baby through the trees?"

"Up into one tree," said Protchnu. "Remember the hollow stumps we found when we were felling trees?"

"Shedemei said it wasn't impossible for some disease to have. . . ."

By then, though, Protchnu had clambered up the tree and was pressing against the trunk here and there, pressing hard. "Protchnu, you aren't looking for secret passages, are you?"

"We burned the hollow trees because we couldn't use them for construction," said Protchnu. "We should have studied them. The prints lead right to this tree and disappear. They went *somewhere*."

Protchnu suddenly stopped and grinned. "It gave a little here. Hold your torch up, *Uncle* Oykib. I found me a door." Using the blade of the hoe he was carrying, Protchnu pried into a fissure in the bark and sure enough, an oblong patch of trunk opened up like a door. It had been a seamless part of the trunk until that moment.

"Protchnu, remind me never to call you stupid," said Oykib.

Protchnu barely heard him. He had already turned around and had his legs into the opening.

Oykib set down his lantern and fairly leapt up the trunk to grab Protchnu's arm. "No!" he cried. "We don't need to be trying to rescue *two* of Elemak's children!"

"I'm the only one who can fit through the door!" Protchnu yelled, struggling to get free of Oykib's grip.

"Proya, you've been brilliant, so don't turn stupid on me!" Oykib shouted back. "You can't go feetfirst into their den! You don't know whether there'll even be room down there to use the hoe. Come on, get your legs out before they cut off your feet!"

Reluctantly, Protchnu backed out of the door.

By now, the others had gathered. Nafai was carrying

an ax, as was Oykib. When Protchnu was out of the tree, they began to work quickly, chopping into the trunk. In only a few minutes, they had torn away so much of the surviving trunk that the tree toppled.

Now the opening wasn't just a tiny doorway. It was large enough that any of the adults could drop down into the hole. And, lowering his lantern as far down into the opening as he could, Nafai announced that the chamber was tall enough for a human to stand, and the tunnels large enough for humans to use them—on all fours.

"I don't think that's a good idea at the moment," said Volemak.

"We don't have time to waste, Father," said Nafai.

"Stand up and look around you, Nyef."

They raised their lanterns and looked. In the trees, on the ground, hundreds of diggers surrounded them, brandishing clubs and stone-tipped spears.

"I think they've got the numbers on us," said Issib.

"They're ugly," said Sevet's son Umene. "Their skin's all pink and hairless."

"Ugly is the least of our problems," said Volemak.

"Any idea who their leader is?" asked Nafai.

"Didn't Chveya come with us?" asked Oykib.

She was already scanning the diggers. She frowned, then pointed. "He's there, behind those others."

At once Nafai stripped his shirt off over his head, baring the skin of his chest and back. As he did, his skin began to glow, to shine. The cloak of the starmaster, normally invisible as it lived under his skin, was now radiating light in order to make a god of Nafai—at least in these diggers' eyes. At once Oykib heard a cacophony of prayers and curses. "It's working," Oykib said quietly. "The sphincter muscles are loosening. There's going to be a circle of extrafertile ground when this night is over."

A couple of the boys laughed. None of the adults did. Nafai walked over and stood before the place that

Chveya had pointed out. "Which one of these little monsters do I want?" he asked.

Chveya came up beside him, careful not to touch his glowing skin. Now she could pick out the leader, a large, strong one, wearing a necklace of small bones around his neck. "The one with the trophy necklace."

Nafai raised his hand and pointed. His finger glowed. Suddenly a spark leapt from his hand to the leader of the diggers. The trophy necklace wasn't much help to him—he immediately sprawled flat on the ground, trembling.

"You didn't kill him, did you?" asked Chveya.

Oykib could barely hear her. The tumult of terrified prayers from the diggers drowned out almost all other perceptions in his mind. Yet even their terror was tainted with rage and with lust for vengeance. They feared Nafai, but they hated him and wanted him destroyed. "If you think you're making friends," Oykib murmured.

"Oykib," said Nafai, ignoring both their comments, "I need you to do the speaking. I'm busy being a god. I can't let them see me struggling to communicate. Besides, you're the only one with a hope of understanding their responses."

Oykib was astonished. "How can I talk to them? I don't know their language."

"You caught some of the angel language, didn't you? The Oversoul said you did."

"But I've never understood or even heard their—"

"You're about to hear it now," said Nafai.

So the Oversoul *is* aware of me and knows what I can do, thought Oykib. It was the first confirmation of this that he had ever had. But did the Oversoul know how much he *couldn't* do?

He stepped forward, walking toward the leader, who was being helped back to his feet. "The baby," said Oykib. He pantomimed rocking a baby in his arms. The diggers had been watching the humans long enough to understand what the gesture represented.

The digger king babbled something. Oykib was surprised by the language. It was the opposite of the angel language—all sibilants, fricatives, nasals, with a sound, not of music, but of spitting and humming. Does it only sound like an evil and slimy language to me because of what I know about their prayers and hungers?

When the digger king was speaking to his followers, Oykib understood nothing, of course. In a few moments the diggers dragged forward four of their soldiers and threw them down at Nafai's feet. Now Oykib *could* get a clear sense of the terror, the cursing and prayers of the four. "These are the ones who did the kidnapping," said Oykib. "I think they're giving them to you for punishment."

Immediately Nafai turned his back on the offering. "Tell them it's the baby I want, not vengeance."

"Oh, I'm supposed to do that with sign language?" said Oykib. But he tried, all the same, using the same symbol for the baby, and then gesturing for the four to be taken away.

But the diggers apparently thought the gesture meant something else. At a command from the king, four other diggers bounded out and put the blades of their spears against the throats of the four kidnappers. "No!" Oykib shouted, hearing Chveya's voice along with his. Nafai turned around and with a single sweep of his dazzling arm he knocked all eight diggers to the ground. Then he seemed to go berserk, pointing at trees, one at a time, until a spot in their branches burst into flame.

"It's too wet to start a real fire going," Oykib murmured.

"I'm counting on that," said Nafai. "You think I want to burn down our village?"

As far as the diggers were concerned, though, this was the rage of the gods and their forest was doomed. The king rushed out and threw himself down on his belly at Nafai's feet. Then, almost at once, he flipped himself onto his back and flung his arms and legs outward, so his naked belly was completely exposed.

Oykib's mind was filled with prayers, and now, because the digger king was close, because Oykib now knew something of the context, he was able to understand more of what the king was saying. "He's pleading with the god—with you—to kill him and spare his people."

"So he *is* a worthy king," murmured Nafai. "Tell him we want the baby and nothing else. But first I'm going to respect his offering." Nafai took a single stride, so he straddled the supine body of the king. Then he reached down and touched the king's chest with the blade of the axe. "What do you think?" asked Nafai. "They're a violent people, right? Help me on this, I'm making up a ritual as I go along."

"No blood," said Oykib. "That wouldn't be right. It's the other king who does the blood rituals."

"Other king?" asked Nafai.

Chveya was startled, but then confirmed it. "There's as much loyalty to another as to this one." Then she frowned. "But there's someone else, too. Someone that the king himself feels allegiance to. Someone underground."

"No blood," said Nafai. "So what should I do?"

"Give him the axe," said Oykib. "That's the thing that he hardly dares to hope for, but wants above all else. He'll give you his spear and his bone necklace."

Nafai let the handle of the axe slip out of his hands.

"No!" shouted Protchnu behind them. "Don't give up your weapon! You never give up your weapon!"

"Shut up, Proya," said Volemak mildly.

The digger king wrapped one hand around the shaft of the axe, then rolled to his belly and rose to his feet. He could lift the axe easily enough, but the handle wasn't right for his hand and he couldn't raise the head of the axe while holding the end of the handle. There was no reason to worry that he could use it as a weapon.

The king bent down and picked up his spear, then offered it to Nafai.

"What does it mean if I take this?" asked Nafai.

"I don't know," said Oykib. "It's not like this stuff comes to me with a glossary and footnotes."

Nafai took the spear. The king now lifted the bone necklace over his head and held it out to Nafai. "I don't like the bones of this thing," said Nafai, hesitant to take it.

"I don't either," said Oykib. "I think it's time to demand Zhivya again."

"And why do you think that?"

"Because I don't like the way he's praying for you to take the necklace. He really, really wants you to take it, but I don't think it's because he loves you."

"All right," said Nafai. "Tell him I want the baby."

Oykib stepped between Nafai and the king, effectively blocking the transfer of the necklace. The king rocked back on his haunches, looking—what? Was that anger? It looked like anger to Oykib. He made the sign for the baby, then shouted—no, screamed—right in the king's face. "Bring us Zhivya or we'll kill every last one of you ugly naked pink-skinned bastards!"

"Since they don't understand you anyway," said Chveya, "couldn't you use language that we won't have to explain to the little boys later?"

"He's trying to communicate rage," said Nafai. "Is it working?"

"Oh, it's working," said Chveya. "You and he are definitely gaining control over the situation. They don't like you, though."

"I'm heartbroken," said Nafai.

"Break the spear," said Oykib.

"What?" said Nafai.

"That's what he's afraid of, as he stands there holding the axe. He's afraid you'll break the spear."

Nafai broke the handle of the spear across his knees. The crack of the breaking wood rang through the air.

At once the digger king took the axe in both hands and tried to break the handle. He couldn't. It was too thick, too well-tempered.

"Do something else he can't do," said Oykib. "He has to fail twice."

Nafai reached down and took the end of the spear that had the head on it. Using the tip of the spear as a knife, he cut quickly and deeply across his own belly. Blood immediately sprayed out onto the digger king's face, and for a moment Oykib saw, to his horror, that Nafai had cut all the way through the muscle and exposed his bowels. In moments, though, the cloak of the starmaster began healing the wound, and as the diggers watched, the wound closed without a scar.

The digger king took the head of the axe in his hands, as if he contemplated his own disembowelment.

"I don't want him to kill himself," said Nafai. "I don't have the power to heal him."

"Don't worry," said Oykib. "You did exactly the right thing. The one thing the war king can't do is shed his own blood for the people. Don't ask me why, I just know that's the quandary he's trying to deal with."

Chveya interrupted. "Someone else is coming."

They looked up and saw that the digger army was indeed responding to someone else. "Not the blood king," said Oykib. "It's the mother."

"The queen?"

"I think she's the war king's mate, yes," said Oykib. "But she's something more than that. They all call her 'the mother.'"

"What, they have a queen rat?" said Chveya. "Like a queen bee or a queen ant?"

"These are mammals," Oykib reminded her. "It's a religious title, I think. Like blood king and war king." Then, tentatively, he made the sound he had heard in his mind. "Emeezem," he said.

"What's that?" asked Nafai.

"Her name. That's the name they're calling. And her title is Ovovoi."

"Say her name again," said Nafai. "I have to get it right the first time I say it."

"Emeezem," said Oykib. "It's not as if I know for sure *I'm* right."

Nafai lifted his chin and bawled out her name like a caller in a marketplace. "Emeezem!"

The diggers all fell silent. A single figure emerged from the woods and slowly approached Nafai.

She was obviously female, but the real surprise was that she was hairier than most of the males. She wore no decoration, but the pattern of graying in her hair served the purpose well enough. She looked regal; she also looked frail.

"She is begging the god to forgive her. She didn't know what the foolish males were planning."

"I want the baby," said Nafai.

"She knows that. Her women are searching for the baby right now," said Oykib. Then, suddenly, he realized what she was straining to see. "Hold your lantern up to Nafai's face, Chveya."

Chveya did it, and the digger queen covered her head and curled herself into a ball on the ground. "She can die happy now," said Oykib, "because she's seen your face in flesh at last."

"*My* face?" asked Nafai.

"That's what it seems to me she's saying," said Oykib. "*You're* the one with the pipeline to the Oversoul. I'm having a hard time making sense of any of this."

"Don't get testy with me," said Nafai. "The Oversoul doesn't hear the things you're hearing. Your connection with the Keeper is better than his."

Oykib felt a glow suffuse throughout his body. Pride and fear, a strange mixture. The Oversoul needs me to help with this—that was the pride. But the fear was stronger: If I make a mistake, there's no one to correct me.

Emeezem uncurled herself from the ground. "She's waited all her life for you," said Oykib, trying to make sense of the images that flashed into his mind—images of herself as a child, of dark underground places. "She thinks it was you that made her queen. Because you accepted her."

"When could I have done that?"

"When she was a little girl," said Oykib. "I don't understand it, but her childhood memories include you."

"Her bond with you is incredibly strong," said Chevya. "Stronger than her bond with her husband. It's really amazing, Father."

"She's begging you to spare her husband's life. He didn't know about the kidnapping either. It was the blood king's son who did it."

Emeezem hissed and sputtered a fierce command to her husband, and he rose to his feet and shouted almost the same words. Moments later, a proud-looking male strode out, casting aside his weapon in a flamboyant gesture. He walked up to stand before Nafai, but he did not bow or show respect in any way.

Emeezem and the war king both muttered commands to him, but he showed no sign of hearing them.

The queen turned to Nafai and spoke a stream of what sounded like horrible invective.

"She's begging you to strike Fusum dead," said Oykib. "That's the young one's name—he plotted everything even though everyone had been commanded not to harm us."

"I'm not going to kill him," said Nafai.

"You have to do something," said Oykib. "This is the guiltiest one. The war king didn't dare to touch him since he's the blood king's son, so that's why he gave you the four actual kidnappers. But you're a god, Nyef. You have to do something to him or—well, I don't know. Chaos. The universe collapsing. Something really bad, anyway."

"I hate this," said Nafai. "How about if I take him prisoner?"

"And put him in our secure prison?" asked Chveya. "Good thing we built a jail first thing."

"Not a prisoner, then," said Nafai. "A hostage?"

"Strike him down," said Oykib. "They're terrified because you hesitate."

"All I want is Zhivya back," said Nafai. "I don't want any corpses here."

Volemak strode forward and took his place beside Nafai. "Bow to me," he said to Nafai. "Or whatever passes for a bow in their culture."

"Get on all fours and kiss Father's belly, then," said Oykib.

"You're kidding," said Nafai. "That's not what the war king did to show respect to *me*."

"The war king was offering himself as an unworthy sacrifice. You're greeting Father as your king and father."

"Do it," said Volemak. "They don't have to know that I don't have the powers of the cloak. They have to see that you, too, are taking directions from someone. That tells them that powerful as you are, they haven't begun to see our powers."

Nafai dropped down on all fours. But from that position he couldn't reach his father's belly to kiss it. He let his hands off the ground and rose up high enough, then pressed his face into Volemak's shirt.

At once there was a murmur among the diggers.

"Can you glow brighter than you already are?" asked Volemak.

"Yes," said Nafai.

"All right, when I touch your head, really light yourself up."

Volemak reached down with a flamboyant gesture and touched Nafai's head. At once Nafai seemed almost to explode with light. Even the humans gasped then, as the diggers cried out in terror.

"Well done," said Volemak. "I figured we needed to juice up the perception of power. Now, knock down this proud little puppy. Don't kill him, just put him out like these others."

Nafai rose to his feet, still glowing, and reached out his hand, pointing toward Fusum.

The son of the blood king didn't cower, didn't even flinch. He just looked Nafai in the face, defiant. Then the air between them sizzled, his limbs leapt our rigidly, and he keeled over like a falling tree. He lay there twitching.

"You do have a natural sense of theatre," said Volemak. "Now, tell Oykib to point to all nine of these sleepy little diggers and have them carried to the ship."

"To the ship?" asked Nafai.

"Don't let it be seen that you argue with me," said Volemak sharply. "Just do it. Hostages. And Shedemei can keep them drugged up or even put them in suspended animation while she runs some nondestructive studies on them. Trust me, Nafai."

"I do trust you, Father. Forgive me for hesitating." He turned to Oykib and elaborately instructed him exactly as Volemak had told him to.

It felt absurd, at first, for Nafai to repeat to him exactly the words that they had all heard Father say. But as Nafai went through it it took on the power of a ritual. It was the expression of authority. The king. The son of the king. The servant of the son. The diggers needed to see the show. But so, too, did the other humans, especially the boys. Especially Protchnu. This is power and authority, Proya, thought Oykib. This is how it should work, and this is why your father is such a failure—because Elemak could never accept the rule of someone over him. Those who will not *be* ruled are not fit to rule anyone else.

So when Nafai finished his recitation, Oykib made a

great deal of ceremony about pointing to each of the unconscious diggers and indicating that other diggers should pick them up and carry them to the ship.

The queen seemed to understand the dance that they were doing. In her turn, she spoke sharply to her husband, the war king, and then he in his own turn addressed the soldiers waiting in the trees. Soon, in groups of four, they gathered around the unconscious ones and lifted them from the ground.

At that moment, other voices called out from the woods. Emeezem called out an answer, and four female diggers emerged from the undergrowth. Each held the corner of a blanket, and in the middle lay Zhivya, who was laughing. She was enjoying the ride.

"Quickly," said Volemak. "Protchnu, run back to the village and fetch Eiadh. Bring her out here!" To Nafai he said, "Don't reach for the baby. Make them wait. They'll deliver Zhivya into her mother's arms."

They held the pose in silence. It felt like forever, though it couldn't have been more than five minutes. Finally Protchnu returned, leading Eiadh, who cried out in joy when she saw the baby. She ran to where the four female diggers stood, and reached down to scoop Zhivya out of the blanket. "Zhivoya, my lively one, my laughing one," she sang, laughing and crying and turning around and around.

"All right," said Volemak. "Nafai, tell Oykib to tell them to carry the hostages to the ship. And order Dazya to lead them there, so she can explain to Shedemei what's needed. I want them kept unconscious and I want them thoroughly studied."

Dazya, the erstwhile First Child, stepped forward. "I understand," she said.

"But you apparently didn't understand well enough to know that I wanted Nafai to give you the order," said Volemak, not looking at her.

Nafai turned to Dazya and gave the exact orders that Volemak had already given. Dazya, blushing, obeyed.

The digger soldiers formed a procession behind her, carrying the nine unconscious ones toward the ship.

The order of authority had now been clearly established. Queen Emeezem now addressed herself directly to Oykib. The trouble was, she didn't perceive him as a god, and therefore when she spoke to him, her words weren't a prayer. It wasn't a communication with the Keeper or the Oversoul, and so to Oykib it was nothing but unintelligible hissing and humming. "I can't understand them unless they think they're speaking to a god," said Oykib.

"Just stand there and refuse to hear them," said Volemak. "When she pauses, point to Nafai."

Oykib obeyed. She quickly got the idea and spoke the same words to Nafai. Oykib could understand her again.

Or maybe he couldn't. "She begs you to come and see how well they've . . . cared for your. . . ."

"Cared for my what?"

"It doesn't make any sense," said Oykib.

"Cared for my what?"

"Your head," said Oykib.

"Where does she want me to go?"

"It's underground," said Oykib. "She wants you to follow her underground."

Nafai turned to Volemak and elaborately repeated all that Oykib had said. Volemak made a show of listening with a grave demeanor.

"First make all these soldiers go away," said Volemak. "And then you, Nafai, will follow her into the tunnels. You're the one with the cloak. If they mean to betray us, you're the only one who'll be safe."

"I have to take Oykib with me," said Nafai. "I don't understand a word they're saying."

Volemak hesitated only a moment. "Keep him safe," he said.

ELEVEN

HOLES

It was astonishing that a god would condescend to such a degree. Emeezem dared to ask him because she was old and had no fear, and because in her life she had learned to hope even for things that could not be hoped. And just as he had accepted her when she was an ugly, undesirable child so many years ago, so now the god accepted her again and followed her down into the city.

To leave the world of light and come into dimness because she asked! To let the bright shimmer of his immortal body illuminate the earthen walls of the deep temples! She wanted to sing, to dance her way down the tunnels. But she was leading a god to his temple. Dignity had to be maintained.

Especially for Mufruzhuuzh's sake; he needed dignity today. No one would criticize him for what had happened—after all, it was Fusum who plotted the stealing of the baby, forcing a deadly confrontation that Muf had neither sought nor desired. And he had faced the god bravely—all saw that he had no fear when he offered his heart for the god to take. Then, when the god asked him to match impossible feats, requiring Muf to do things that only the blood king could do, if anyone could do it at all—well, no one could fault him for hesitating, for failing to act. He had nowhere to turn, so he did not turn at all.

Still, it was humiliating for him, that his wife should have to come forward and extricate him from the dilemma. Never mind that it was rare for the wife of the war king to be the root mother also. He was shamed when his wife was accepted by the god who had merely posed unanswerable riddles to him.

But could Emeezem help it that the baby came to her hands? Muf didn't know where the baby had been hidden—it was only when Fusum's sister realized what a terrible thing he had done that she came to Emeezem with the truth, and by then Muf was already facing down the god. It was just an unfortunate set of circumstances. Mufruzhuuzh was still war king. The god would set everything to rights.

The god was so large he had to bow down on all fours to travel through the tunnels. Of course, he could just as easily have walked upright, tearing out the roofs of the tunnels just by passing through them. But he chose not to, leaving the tunnels undamaged for the people to use. Such kindness! Such generosity to mere earth-crawling worms like us!

Around them she could hear the patter of a thousand feet, as men and women and children scurried to every open passageway, hoping for a glimpse of the god as he passed. Emeezem could see hands reaching up to let the light of the god's body touch pink hands; parents held up their babies so the light of the god would bless their tiny bodies. And still the god followed her, his light undiminished.

They came to the chamber where, so many years ago, Emeezem—no, she was mere Emeez in those days—

had first seen the unmarred head of the god. She stopped, and beseeched him to forgive them for leaving him in such obscurity for so long.

She heard the undergod speak to him, and he answered. Then he licked his finger, reached out his hand, and touched the lintel of the doorway. Thus did he leave the fluid of his body on the door of the place. That was more than mere forgiveness. She keened in relief, and many others joined in with her. She could hear one voice, a man, singing, "We put your glorious head in darkness, not worshipping it because in the clay we could not see your light. But you return the waters of life to us, and bring light into the stomach of the earth. So noble, so great!" Others sang their assent to his words: "So noble! So great! So noble! So great!"

The god paid them the compliment of staying there, still, unmoving, till the song ended. Then Emeezem moved on, leading him farther up the corridor, to the temple she had caused to be built for him, starting the very day she was chosen as root mother. Because the head was so large, she had decided that the god must also be very tall, and so she had made the people dig his temple so low that the ceiling could be high. She also placed the temple so that the roof reached up into a crevice in the rock, letting a bit of daylight reflect down into the chamber. And in the brightest spot of the soft diffused glow, on a pedestal made of bones of the skymeat, she had placed his head.

It was nighttime now, though, so there was little illumination when he came into the temple. Instead he brought the light with him, and it brightened every corner of the room when he rose to his feet. Others came through the door after him, gathering along the walls of the temple, watching as he approached the pedestal where the sculpture sat. Now he would see how they had worshipped him, once they understood that his strange large head was a sign of power and not of weakness. Hadn't the entire spring harvest of infant skymeat been offered to him that first year, so that his pedestal immediately rose at once to be as high as any god's? Hadn't he also had more than his share of skymeat broken open and shared among the people in his honòr every year since then? Yet still no one had used his head in the time of mating, for they understood that he was not to be worshipped in that way.

The god walked slowly to the face and stood before it. It glowed in the brightness of his body, answering his bright face with an earthen one. He reached out to it, touched it. Then he lifted his head upward toward the source of the room's faint natural starlight and sank to his knees before the statue.

I see, thought Emeezem. You show us how to worship you properly. We cannot do exactly what you have done, because our knees do not bend in that direction. But we will touch the face as you touched it. Was there a reason why it was the lips you touched? Should it always be the lips? Or will we touch that part of the face that we want to have bless us? You must tell me. Perhaps later, if you should deign to soil your lips by speaking our language, or if your undergod should choose to speak our impure tongue. We touch your face, look at the light, then go down on our haunches before your face and gaze at it. Yes, I will remember. We will all remember.

Like all the other women, Shedemei was at once frightened, repelled, and fascinated by the procession of diggers who came into the village, carrying their compatriots who had been knocked unconscious by Nafai. But the responsibility for doing something with them was hers, and so she quickly set her personal feelings aside and led the diggers into the ship. She knew at once what Volemak's purpose was; he had seen her doing nondestructive scans and studies of the few animals they had revived, and knew that she could learn a vast amount about a creature using the equipment on the ship. It was imperative that they understand the physical structures and systems that gave shape to the lives of the diggers, and yet it was just as important that they not be harmed.

The trouble was that it might not be such a good idea to let the diggers see the inside of the ship. From the little that Dza had said, she knew that Nafai had overawed them with the powers of the cloak of the starmaster. Perhaps the smooth and shiny surfaces of the inside of the ship would enhance that effect; but perhaps not. There was definitely danger in letting the diggers see that the humans were, after all, human, that what miracles they did were done with tools and machines and not by godlike powers inherent in them.

But that was for another day. Volemak had made his decision, and it was almost certainly best. Even if it wasn't, Shedemei would obey. The peace they had had these past months since arriving on Earth depended on supporting his authority; she would obey him even if he was flat wrong. Peace—that's all Shedemei wanted. A chance to do her work without having to worry about which side she was on and who was on top in the endless family struggles among Volemak's and Rasa's children.

The first order of business once the carriers were gone was to sedate the diggers so that they didn't awaken at an inconvenient time. There had been forty million years of evolution since the biota of Earth and Harmony had diverged, but the most conservative aspect of life was at the chemical level. A light dosage of the safest sedative should do the job. She spoke to the medical computer as she weighed each of the bodies in turn. The dosages were meted out and she pressed the pads against the pink skin.

Pink hairless skin—why would these rodents have lost their fur? She suspected that there was no sound evolutionary reason for it—it was a cultural thing. Some standard of beauty became general and then only those who exhibited the beautiful trait were able to mate.

Soon pink skin would predominate in the culture while hairiness would be relegated to a few despised members. Otherwise, the trait made no sense. Digger skin had no melanin. No wonder they had to stay in shadows and tunnels all the time, unlike their ancient rat ancestors—they couldn't bear the sunburn if they emerged from the trees.

Once they were all sedated, she meant to begin scanning them at once. But then sleepiness swept over her like a wave at the beach, and she realized that after being awake all night this was hardly the time to conduct serious investigations. So she used the cart and carried each digger in turn to a suspended animation chamber. She set the chambers to normal life support so they wouldn't kick into suspended animation mode—there was too much risk that the suspended animation dosages wouldn't be right for diggers and they'd be unrevivable.

Then she went to her berth and lay down, just for a nap. A couple of hours and she'd be fine. It reminded her of the way she had lived in Basilica before they persuaded her—no, tricked her, manipulated her, forced her—to join Volemak's exodus into the wilderness. In those days, when she was hot on the trail of some elusive gene, she could work around the clock, taking short naps that amounted to little more than a couple of hours of sleep a day. The excitement of discovery and creation was more important than sleeping and eating. She had never wanted that life to be interrupted.

Well, it *had* been interrupted, and she wasn't entirely unhappy about it. For one thing, Basilica had been destroyed in Moozh's bid for empire, so her old life couldn't have continued in any case. Even if Basilica still stood, however, Shedemei's journey in the wildnerness had given her many good gifts. Her two children, Padarok and Dabrota—their names meant Gift and Kindness, and they had grown up to merit them. Zdorab, her shy and complicated husband, a man who had never desired women and yet had given her two children, not to mention good companionship for these many years. Despite his lack of desire, despite her lack of interest, they had helped each other join the great stream of life, of creation. Wouldn't it have been sad if I had spent my life bending and shaping life, and yet had never taken part in it myself? I was spared that, I am glad of it.

But now Rokya and Dabya were adults. Rokya was married to Hushidh's daughter Dza; Dabya was married to Luet's son Zhatva. They were going to be parents soon. They didn't need Shedemei anymore. Zdorab had never needed her, not really. Liked her, yes, even loved her, but it wasn't a *need*. So why am I still here? she wondered. I don't want to see this community torn apart. I don't want to watch as my children have to choose sides. I don't want to be here when blood is shed, when lives are lost. I don't even want to care about the outcome. I just want to be by myself, working on plants, on animals, studying how the biosystems have diverged, understanding more and more of the way life creates itself. I want to know why giant cattle roam the plains north of this massif. I want to know why two sentient species evolved in such close proximity without one of them destroying the other. I want to know why the Oversoul brought us to this place of all places, instead of to one of the many locations where we could have established our colony without interfering in the lives of diggers or angels.

I want my dream to come true.

Ah, yes, that was the underlying wish above all wishes. The dream that the Keeper of Earth had sent her, so many years ago, a dream of a garden in the sky. Of course it had already *been* fulfilled. The seeds and embryos she had brought with her were already beginning to play a role in the life of this planet. But couldn't the dream be more literal? Once the colony was fully established, couldn't she take the ship back into the sky and orbit the Earth, studying ecosystems, developing variations and enhancements and hybrids of lifeforms from Harmony and Earth, coming down only now and then to take samples and measurements and to introduce new organisms into the world? Then she really would be the gardener of Earth, a whole planet to play with. I'd be good at it, she whispered to the Oversoul. Then I wouldn't have to be part of the messiness here in the colony. I don't want to have to care about rivalries and loyalties. I just want to learn, to change, to create, to transform. That's what my talent is. I have no gift for getting along with humans. I've given you what you needed from me. Let me now have what I want.

<All right.>

Shedemei felt the anxiety and longing seep out of her. The Oversoul said it would be all right. Now she could sleep.

Oykib was grateful to be able to stand up at last, after crawling or duckwalking his way through seemingly endless low tunnels. He had hardly been able to pay attention to his surroundings, partly because the grays and browns of the rock and earthen walls hardly offered much in the way of scenery, but mostly because the diggers that surrounded them were all crying out to the gods, and so Oykib could hear the silent pleadings and psalms and paeans as if they were all singing in his ears.

Still, despite the confusion of voices, Oykib *was* beginning to learn some words, some shapes and structures in the language. It became music to him first, so that he heard the rhythms and tunes that helped carry meanings and emotions. This must be what dogs hear in human speech, he thought. The music of our voices tells them if we're angry or happy, sad or frightened. That was as much of the language as Oykib understood, but he knew that soon he would understand more. He had never had to learn a second language before, so that until now he had never known how easy it was. He had a talent for it. Or perhaps it was simply easier to learn a language if you had some understanding of the speakers before trying to grasp their speech.

Now, standing in the temple chamber, the light from the cloak illuminating every corner, Oykib could take a moment to look at the diggers gathered around the walls of the room. Their origin as rats was unmistakable, but so was the fact that the thousands of generations between them and their ancestors had changed them far more than the humans of Basilica had changed. The snout and whiskers were still prominent, but much less so than in their ancestors, and the jaw had changed shape to allow for speech. Oykib was eager to discuss with Shedemei what all the other structural changes were for.

"Oykib," said Nafai.

That's right, he had a job to do. A little embarrassed at having allowed himself to daydream at such a tense moment, he stepped up beside Nafai. "Yes?" he said.

But Nafai didn't answer, just continued to stare at the statue that rested on a pedestal of tiny bones. It was a human head. But not just any human. The face was clearly Nafai's own.

"When could they have done this?" asked Nafai.

Oykib tried to sort out the many prayers going on in the room, and gradually gleaned a little information. "They didn't do it," he said. "They don't make their gods. The way they tell it, their gods make themselves. They're praising *you* for having given them such a perfect copy of your head."

"It *is* perfect," said Nafai. "Perhaps a little younger."

"Get this," said Oykib. "The head is a hundred years old."

"Impossible."

"It was fifty years ago when the queen found this statue in that tiny secluded chamber that you—blessed, or whatever it was you were doing."

"I hope I was blessing it," said Nafai.

"And it was fifty years old then. Apparently her relationship with that statue was pivotal in her life. It's because of you that she married the war king. Because you accepted her."

"Are you sure you're understanding this?" asked Nafai.

"Not at all," said Oykib. "But it's as clear as anything else I've understood. There's plenty of time to figure this all out. But one thing's sure. The head is older than any living digger. And they definitely claim they didn't make it themselves, though how their clay gods could make themselves I can't imagine. They point out how perfectly the features have been preserved. This is because they worshipped you differently from the other gods. They didn't—this is kind of repulsive—they didn't rub your head in order to breed."

"So their other gods are involved in fertility worship."

"The images I'm getting are pretty nasty," said Oykib.

"Religion isn't always pretty," said Nafai. "Especially viewed from the outside, by an unbeliever. So they use the other statues as part of a mating ritual, but mine they left alone."

"Because you were so ugly." Oykib couldn't keep a bit of laughter out of his voice.

"To them, I'm sure," said Nafai. "Just imagine what they would have thought if it had been *your* head."

"Babies would have run screaming from the cave, I'm sure."

"So what do I do with this sculpture?"

"Invent a ritual, Nafai. You've been winging it pretty well so far."

So Nafai sank to his knees before the statue and improvised a fairly simple and harmless sort of obeisance. When he was done, he got up and smiled at Oykib. "This is kind of embarrassing," he said. "To have people worshipping me. Though there are those who'll be bound to say that it's what I've secretly longed for all my life."

"So don't tell them that you're being worshipped."

"I can't conceal something like this. My face, carved a hundred years ago. Since I certainly did *not* sculpt it, someone did. And someone knew what I looked like."

"The Keeper, obviously."

"Yes, but don't you understand? It means that the Keeper knew things about us here on Earth at a time when—well, when the information couldn't possibly have traveled at lightspeed. At the speed of light, the Keeper would have to have seen my face almost eighty years before I was born in order to have this carved a hundred years ago."

"So we don't know everything about physics. Hardly a surprise, since the Oversoul was keeping human beings from learning a lot of science and technology."

"But Oykib, I've always assumed that the Keeper was some kind of computer, like the Oversoul. The Oversoul was created by humanity at its technological peak, along with our starship. And at that time they knew nothing about faster-than-light communication."

"So, somebody learned more."

"Who, Oykib? The human beings were gone from Earth. Who built the Keeper, if he has powers far beyond what humanity was capable of creating at its peak?"

"Maybe the humans didn't all leave," said Oykib.

"Maybe," said Nafai. "It's a puzzle. In the meantime, I'd really like to get out of this dark, musty, dirty place. It must be near dawn by now, and I'm exhausted."

"I wouldn't mind a nap myself."

"So how do I extricate myself? I have no clue how to get out of here."

"Wing it," said Oykib.

"I'm sure glad I have you along for wise counsel," said Nafai dryly. .

* * *

Dawn was breaking when Elemak's party reached the place where the canyon became a shallow depression and finally just a part of the saddle of the first range of mountains. It had been slow climbing in the darkness, even with the lanterns. Perhaps especially with the lanterns. And it didn't help that Mebbekew and Obring seemed to be in competition for the longest, vilest string of obscenities whenever they slipped or whenever a passage looked especially forbidding or . . . whenever.

Zdorab hated listening to them. In fact, he realized now, he simply hated *them*, even when by chance they were silent. He hated the way they treated women. He hated the way they treated men. He hated the way they thought. He hated the way they didn't think. It was hard to imagine which of them he hated more. On the one hand, Obring was inherently stupid and brutal. It wasn't a decision he made. It was a chronic condition bordering on the continuous. On the other hand, Mebbekew was actually rather bright; he merely chose to be stupid. He seemed to take pleasure in cruelty, too, but unlike Obring, he didn't care enough to seek out occasions for it. He simply took whatever opportunity to be stupid and cruel happened to come to hand. Which of them, then, was more detestable? The one who was loathsome by nature, or the one who wanted to be loathsome but hadn't enough ambition to excel at it?

How did I come to be here this morning, Zdorab wondered, greeting dawn on a mountain range on Earth, in hot pursuit of a flying creature that left no trail and might not be anywhere near us? Why am I not asleep in a soft chair in a library in Basilica? Why am I now sharing such strenuous activity in the company of exactly the kind of men I most hated back in civilization? And, worse, taking orders from them?

Zdorab knew that most of the others were thinking similar thoughts. Well, not dreaming of soft beds in Basilica. The younger men had never seen the city—or any city, for that matter. Nevertheless, they were filled with resentment, knowing that there was no hope of accomplishing anything. Wherever these flying creatures lived, it would probably be very high. Out of reach. And if in fact they had taken Elemak's daughter, how was this group of men going to save her? With their motley assortment of farming tools, what would they do? Hand over our little girl, you villains, or we'll *plant a garden*!

At this little bit of whimsy Zdorab couldn't help but smile. But at that moment he crested the rise to find Elemak glaring at him.

"What's the smile about, Zdorab?"

"I was off in another world," said Zdorab, ducking his head obsequiously. It was a posture he had learned long ago. It generally deflected the wrath of bullies. "I'm so sorry."

"You shouldn't be," said Elemak. "Better any world than this."

So he, too, resented it. As if he hadn't been part of the cause of it, with his plotting and conniving back on Basilica.

But Zdorab said nothing more. Instead he turned and surveyed the terrain that dawn was revealing. At this altitude the air was noticeably cooler, and the undergrowth wasn't quite as thick. A thin mist had formed in the valley behind the saddle, like a river flowing among the trees. The next row of peaks was astonishing in its craggy beauty, and behind that he could see the very tops of a couple of mountains so high that even at these latitudes they had snow. It had snowed several times during the years he lived in Basilica, but it was never more than an inch or two on the ground, and it always melted within a day. But the snow must never melt up there. What had Shedemei said? Mountains so new and high that it was a miracle the mantle of Earth could sustain the weight of them. Eleven thousand meters. The Oversoul said that there were no mountains so high on Harmony, and as far as his records showed there had never been such high mountains on Earth before, either. These were new, pushed up by an ocean plate being subducted under what had once been a narrow isthmus connecting two continents. Now it was a great massif, the highest spot on Earth, and every climate and terrain existed on its perimeter. On the western coast the mountains were so high their rain shadow caused an utter desert. On the east, there was a place where rain fell almost continuously, day and night, summer and winter, so that it was bare rock, except for a few hardy mosses that could live with perpetual cloud cover.

Why can't Shedemei and I leave this village, simply explore this new planet? They don't need us. We don't want to be with them. Our son and daughter are grown up and married now. It would be nice to visit with them from time to time, but parenting they don't need. When they have children, I can sing them silly songs and dandle them on my knee. Twice a year.

But thinking of little children made him remember why they were there. Why they had spent tonight with no sleep, climbing a canyon in the dark. And now he looked out over the valley and saw that in the first light of dawn, the trees were jumping with life. Flying creatures bounding into the air, flying a short distance, and then dropping back down into the leaves. Each of them seemed to be carrying something in its feet as it flew.

"They're terrified of us," said Elemak softly.

"How can you tell *that*?" asked Mebbekew.

"Because they're evacuating their village. Look—those are their own children they're carrying."

"Look," said Zdorab. "When the children are a little larger, it takes two adults to carry them."

"Good eyes," said Elemak. "It took four of them to lift Zhivya. And if they think they can get away from me by carrying their children to—"

"They *can*," said Vas scornfully. "They can get away from us any time they want, precisely by carrying their children to safety. What are you going to do, dance along the treetops till you catch up with them?"

Elemak turned slowly. "Go back down the mountain, then, if you don't care about this errand."

Vas immediately apologized. "I'm tired, Elemak. I'm too tired to know what I'm saying."

"Then keep your mouth shut," said Elemak. "And your eyes open."

Zdorab sighed and turned away from this touching scene of true friendship. The only people who hated Elemak worse than his enemies were his friends. And yet they followed him, because they knew he needed them so much he couldn't ignore them, as Nafai certainly would have. That's probably how a lot of vile men get others to follow them, thought Zdorab. They can't get good men to follow them, and they need somebody, so they have to take the kind of men who can't find a good man interested in taking them on. The miracle was that evil persisted in the world, since the only people who took part in it generally couldn't stand each other, and for good reason.

Zdorab's attention was caught by a movement in a tree just down from the crest. A single bat-thing was sitting on a branch. "Look," said Zdorab.

"I see him," said Elemak.

"What's he doing?" asked Yasai.

"We all have the same number of eyes," said Elemak scornfully. "Watch and we'll see together."

The angel abruptly dropped from the tree, fluttering down to the ground in a small clearing that led up to where the humans stood. Zdorab got a chance to see it clearly then, its wings extended. The face was hideously ugly, but that was hardly a surprise. After all, it had descended from some wizen-snouted species of bat, hadn't it? The real surprise was the fascinating compromise that evolution had reached. Its arms and legs were almost mockingly thin. From wrist to ankle on each side of his body, the wings fanned out, held rigid by two distorted fingers of each hand. The other three fingers on each side, however, were of normal size, giving the creature good hands for grasping. And the head was very large for the size of the body. The miracle was that it could fly at all. It was surely at the outside limit of its growth—any larger, and it would lose the power of flight.

At this moment, however, it was walking toward them. It wasn't without grace when it walked, but it was clear that it was more at ease on branches or in the air. A long-distance hiker it would never be, not on those feet.

Those feet.

Zdorab knew enough to hold his tongue. Young Yasai, alas, did not. "Oykib was right," he blurted out. "No way did those feet make those footprints back in the village."

Elemak turned slowly toward him. "So maybe it wasn't this *thing* that made the prints. Do you think I didn't know that was a possibility? The fact remains that this fellow was the lookout for the kidnappers. If he doesn't have Zhivya, he knows where she is." Elemak took a step downward, toward the creature.

Almost at once, the creature stopped, and then did the most extraordinary thing. He reached down and took from his foot a small number of stalks of grain that he had been holding. Then he laid them down in the grass, making a great show of each one, as if counting them out. When they were all laid out, the creature took a step backward.

"That's grain from our field," said Obring.

"Did you just realize that?" asked Vas.

"Does it matter?" asked Meb.

"He thinks that's why we came up here," said Padarok, Zdorab's own son. "Because he stole our grain. He's giving it back."

"And when did you become an expert on overgrown bats?" asked Elemak.

"It makes sense," said Padarok stubbornly.

Zdorab waved a hand at him, trying to get him to shut up.

"No, I won't shut up, Father. This whole thing is ludicrous. The angel took some grain from the field and he doesn't know a thing about Zhivya. If somebody had stopped to give this any thought at all, we wouldn't have spent all night climbing a mountain in pursuit of an innocent man."

Elemak's hands snapped out and seized Padarok by the head. Like his father, Padarok had not grown into a very tall man, and he was slight of build. He looked like a puppet in Elemak's massive grasp. "Man?" Elemak demanded. "You call that *thing* a *man?*"

"Figure of speech," Padarok murmured.

"That *man*, as you call him, knows where my daughter is!" With those words Elemak shook Padarok. His whole body went limp. For a moment Zdorab feared that the shaking had done brain damage, had perhaps even killed him. And even though Padarok's eyes immediately fluttered open and he moved his limbs, the hot rage that surged inside Zdorab did not fade. To his own surprised, Zdorab found himself in the odd position of holding a scythe over Elemak's shoulders and neck, saying to him the most unbelievable words. "Let go of my son," he said. "Now."

Elemak turned slowly and regarded Zdorab with lizard eyes. "And if I don't, will you cut off my arms?"

"Only if I miss your neck," said Zdorab.

Elemak let go of Padarok. "Don't threaten me, Zdorab. Even if *you've* forgotten who our enemy is, *I* haven't." With a quick movement Elemak snatched the scythe out of Zdorab's hands, so quickly that Zdorab could barely register that it had happened. For a moment Elemak stood there, the scythe poised, and Zdorab wasn't sure whether Elemak meant to strike him or his son. But then he cast the scythe to the ground and strode to where the creature waited.

The poor thing visibly wilted under the head of Elemak's fierce glare, but it stood its ground. Elemak reached out a foot and ground the stalks of grain into the muddy grass. "I don't care about the grain," he said. Then he reached down and snatched the creature up by one arm. "Where's my daughter!" he bellowed.

"What language do you expect him to answer in?" said Padarok scornfully. "Or should he draw you a map in midair?"

Please, don't goad him, don't provoke him, Rokya; Zdorab thought the words but didn't say them. Because he was also proud. He had spent his life bowing to men like this, so they wouldn't hurt him. But his son did not bow. He might have inherited my height, thought Zdorab, but he has his mother's spine.

Elemak's answer was to roar in rage, and as he did, he snapped the creature like a whip. Zdorab saw, to his horror, that in Elemak's grip the poor thing was like a brittle stick. He could see its arm break on both sides of Elemak's grip, and at the same time both wings tore and began to bleed, while every joint seemed to have bent the wrong way and now could not get back. The creature screamed once and then fell silent, hanging limp and broken in Elemak's hands.

"My my my," said Meb. "Fellow doesn't know his own strength sometimes."

"Good work," said Padarok. "Now that he's dead, he'll make a great guide."

Elemak hurled the broken animal away from him. It struck the trunk of a tree and stuck there for a moment, then dropped lifelessly to the ground. "Where is my daughter!" Elemak shouted. "They've taken my daughter!"

His rage was so terrible that they all backed away from him, just a step, but it made their fear plain. Except Padarok. He didn't back away.

And that meant that he would be the one to bear the

brunt of Elemak's helpless fury. Already Elemak was glaring at him.

So, again without thinking, Zdorab stepped forward. "We're going back down now, Elemak. We all tried. But there's no way we can find her, if she's up here. If breaking and killing a helpless little creature will make you feel better, then you've done it. You don't have to kill or break anything else."

He could see Elemak visibly pull himself back under control.

"I'll never forgive you for saying that," Elemak said.

"There's not a soul here that you haven't promised, one time or another, never to forgive," said Zdorab. "But we forgive *you*, Elemak. We all have children. It could have been any one of us. If we could bring her back to you, we would."

"If you could bring her back to me," said Elemak, "I would be your willing servant forever." Then he stalked off, over the saddle, and down into the canyon.

Obring and Meb followed him immediately, but both paused as they passed Zdorab. "Who would have thought the little pizdoon had some spunk in him after all," Obring said, laughing derisively.

"You keep *this* up," said Meb, "and someday, who knows? You might actually get a hard-on. Then you'll be half a man." He patted Zdorab on the head and followed Obring and Elemak down.

Padarok came to Zdorab and hugged him. "Thank you, Father. I thought he was going to break my neck."

"We saw what he wanted to do to *you*, Rokya," said Zdorab, "because he did it to the angel."

Then, from down by the tree where Elemak had flung the poor creature, Yasai called out. "He's not dead!"

"Then maybe we should kill it to put it out of its misery," suggested Zhatva, Nafai's eldest son. They all gathered around the creature.

"This isn't a dog," said Yasai. "Oykib said he was

sentient. A person, not a beast. Shedemei will be able to heal him if it can be done at all."

The creature kept slowly blinking one eye.

"Are you sure that's not a reflex?" asked Xodhya.

Yasai was peeling off his shirt. "Help me lift him onto this," he said. "Without breaking his neck."

"It's already broken," said Motiga helpfully.

"But maybe the spinal column isn't severed." Then Yasai whistled in surprise. "He's so light."

"It hurts him," said Vas. "He's closing his eyes in pain."

"But not complaining," said Zdorab. "He bears his suffering well."

"Yeah, a real man," said Zhatva. But there was little mockery in his voice. The creature was to be admired.

"What if Elemak sees that we're carrying him?" asked Motya.

"I hope he does," said Padarok. "This creature wasn't threatening him in any way, and look what he did. Even if it had *been* a dog. . . ."

He didn't have to finish his sentence. Four of them took up the four corners of the shirt. The others carried their lanterns, and they began the slow journey down the canyon.

Eiadh heard the glad shouting of the children and knew that Elemak and the men who were with him had finally come back down from their night's search. No doubt Elya would be exhausted and a bit frustrated that his search was in vain. But when he saw Zhivya, that would make up for everything.

Zhivya, perhaps worn out from yesterday's excitement, was taking a late morning nap. Eiadh picked her up carefully; the baby stirred but did not wake. Eiadh's one worry now was that she might remember something from the experience. She was old enough to toddle around now, but surely not old enough for memories to linger. There should be no nightmares of diggers looming over her crib or of journeys through long dark tunnels. There was nothing to worry about now.

Zhivya woke up as Eiadh carried her along toward the village's edge. There was Elemak, tall and strong— for all his flaws, a fine man, a powerful figure. Eiadh remembered again why she had fallen in love with him, back when she was a foolish shallow girl in Basilica. True, he had proven not to have the self-control and the selflessness that she admired in some of the other men, and his temper meant that she and the children had to tread carefully at home. But he was her husband, and she wasn't unhappy about that. Not today, not with their daughter rescued from the monsters of the underground.

As she approached, she could see that Volemak was telling him what had happened; as they spoke, Volemak cast his gaze toward her, and Elemak looked also, seeing that she had the baby. Elemak smiled at her. It could have been a bit more enthusiastic, but he was tired.

Suddenly there was a flurry of activity. Yasai, Rokya, Xodhya, and Zhyat were carrying something in a shirt—Yasai's, no doubt, since he was barechested. Volemak directed them toward the ship, where Shedemei was studying the digger hostages. What was it? They hadn't harmed one of the angels, had they?

As soon as she thought of it, she knew it was true. Volemak was remonstrating with Elemak, and now Eiadh was near enough and their voices were loud enough for her to hear.

"But he was unarmed?" Volemak was saying. "He didn't threaten you at all?"

"I told you that I thought he knew where my daughter was!"

"So you crippled him? Even if you didn't care that we have to live in this place and you have *needlessly* made enemies of a tribe of sentient creatures, you might have thought that brutalizing the one person who *might* have helped you was beyond stupidity!"

Volemak was too angry, Eiadh thought. Elemak didn't respond well to tongue-lashings, especially in public. He had been faithful to the oath of obedience, but why push it?

Of course, she hadn't seen the injured angel, and Volemak had. What had Elemak done?

"Oh, yes, I'm beyond stupid," Elemak was answering. "But your perfect hero with the magic cloak was down playing god with a bunch of rats!"

"He got your daughter back, he and Oykib and Protchnu and I," said Volemak. "And we did it surrounded by armed diggers that outnumbered us by hundreds, because *you* had insisted on taking all but a handful of our men of fighting age."

"If you had commanded me to leave some behind," Elemak began, but Volemak cut him off.

"Oh, yes, you would have obeyed—while you accused me of wanting your daughter to die. Well, Elya, she lived, no thanks to you. Now let's see if that harmless angel is as lucky."

"What am I supposed to do, kneel down and worship at Nafai's feet? Is he supposed to be *my* god, too?"

That was too much for Eiadh. "You might thank him," said Eiadh quietly. "He gave us back Zhivya."

"No he didn't," said Elemak. "The cloak of the starmaster did whatever was done. If *I* had had the cloak, I could have done at least as well."

"No you wouldn't," said Eiadh. "Because you would have been up the canyon with the cloak, no doubt using it to shoot angels out of the sky, and down here without it we would have been overrun and slaughtered by the diggers, every one of us."

"How should I have known that some creatures we'd never seen before took the baby?"

"Oykib tried to tell you, but you wouldn't listen. It's one reason you aren't fit to lead us. You never listen, you just decide based on what you already know. Well, Elemak, you don't know everything." Eiadh heard her own words and knew she was saying too much. The rage in his face was frightening. He hadn't looked at her like that since ... since she took Volemak's oath during the voyage.

"So this is my greeting from my wife when I come home," he said.

"I meant to greet you with joy," said Eiadh, bowing her head. "I'm sorry."

Because she had submitted, Elemak could turn his anger to others. "So I was wrong," he said. "I didn't hear any of *you* arguing with me!"

They answered him with silence.

"So don't go criticizing me if you haven't the brains to come up with a better idea."

"We all had a better idea," said Padarok quietly. "We all knew that you were wrong. We knew it from the beginning."

His words were like a slap in Elemak's face. "Then why did you follow me?"

"It was your daughter who was missing," said Padarok.

"That didn't mean that I was *right*," said Elemak. "It probably meant my judgment wasn't at its best."

"Yes, that's what I was saying," said Padarok.

"You followed me *because* my judgment wasn't good?" asked Elemak. "You all knew I was wrong, and you followed me *because* I was wrong?" The contempt in his voice made a poor disguise for the confusion he was obviously feeling.

"Elemak, come inside, come to the house," Eiadh said.

"No, I want to understand this," said Elemak. "I want to understand why these so-called men are so stupid that they knowingly follow someone that they think is wrong."

"Please, Elemak."

"We didn't follow you because you were wrong," Yasai finally said. "We followed you because you were irrational. We didn't know what you'd do if we refused to obey."

"What do you mean?" demanded Elemak. "What mattered was finding my daughter. That's *all* that mattered."

"Was it?" asked Eiadh. "If *that* was true, you would have stopped and listened to Oykib when he tried to tell you that it wasn't the angels who took Zhivya. Now please, stop arguing about it. Everybody's home safe and nobody was harmed."

Elemak shrugged off the hand she had laid upon his arm. "Don't patronize me, Eiadh."

"Don't be angry, Elemak," she said. "Zhivya was lost, and she's been restored to us. It's a day for rejoicing, not anger. You might even thank the ones who brought her back to us."

"Thank them? Because the Oversoul gave Nafai the only good weapon? Because they followed me on a foolish chase up the canyon *because* they knew it was foolish?"

Padarok stepped closer to Elemak. "No, Elemak. We followed you because we were afraid that you would do to one of us what you finally ended up doing to that harmless angel. And our fear was not unfounded. If you'll remember, you came very close to doing it to *me*."

Only now did Eiadh notice the bruises on Padarok's neck and jaws.

"If Father hadn't stood against you," said Padarok.

Elemak, his face red with rage—or was it shame?—answered contemptuously. "Do you think I stopped because of *his* pathetic threats?"

"I don't know why you stopped," said Padarok. "But we never know whether you *will* stop. And so we obey you when you're angry and irrational, because we're afraid of you. And if you think about it without letting rage cloud your reason, you'll realize that we have cause to be afraid."

"Let's go home, Elya," said Eiadh again.

But Elemak was determined to have this out. "You would have let Zhivya die, because you were so afraid of me that you didn't dare to argue with me?"

Paradok shook his head. "We knew that Nafai would get her back, if it could be done at all."

"Nafai?" said Elemak. Then he roared. "Nafai! Nafai! Nafai! You trusted *him* to do it! You put my daughter's life in *his* hands! What does he know, that stupid, boastful boy, that snot-nosed little pretender, that—"

"He *did it*!" Eiadh screamed at him. "You stupid angry fool, he *did* save her, so they were *right* to trust him!" Her screaming frightened the baby, who started to cry. But Eiadh couldn't stop now. "And they knew that if you stayed here, you'd just do some angry stupid thing and cause a disaster, so it was *better* to have you off up the canyon where you wouldn't start a war between us and the diggers. Do you get it now, Elemak? Now that you've made us tell you more than we ever meant to, will you finally understand what you *are* to us? We know that if anything delicate needs to be done, *you'd* better not be there, because you'll always, always, always do something like what you did to that angel!"

For a moment Eiadh felt the thrill of having finally blurted out the truth, of having struck down the prideful man who had complicated her life so much for all these years.

Then she saw something she had never seen before. Elemak didn't rage. His shoulders slumped. He visibly wilted. He looked at no one, met no one's gaze. He just turned his back and walked into the forest.

"I'm sorry, Elya," she called after him. "I was angry, I didn't mean it."

But he knew she meant it. Everyone knew she meant it, and everyone knew that what she had said was true.

Everyone had known it for years. Finally, today, Elemak knew it too.

He came back the next day. Quiet, subdued. A different man. A broken man. Eiadh tried to apologize to him when they were alone in the house, but he walked out the door and wouldn't listen. They shared their bed, but he never reached out to her. He would answer the children when they asked him questions, and sometimes he would play with them and laugh and smile like the old days. But he didn't come to any of the meetings of the adults, and when Eiadh tried to involve him in decisions about their own household, he always answered the same way. "Whatever you want," he said. "I don't care."

And he didn't care, or so it seemed. He did his work in the fields, but he no longer had any ideas about what others should do. He simply did what he was asked. He worked hard. He exhausted himself, in fact. But he still seemed invisible.

I killed him, thought Eiadh.

Or maybe, just maybe, I took the first step toward healing him.

She would cling to that hope, she decided. This puzzling, quiet, withdrawn personality was just a stage in his development into a mature, wise, self-restrained, good man.

A man like Nafai.

TWELVE

FRIENDS

Shedemei asked Volemak for a meeting of all those involved in dealing with the two sentient species. "There are decisions to be made," she said, and so when the evening meal was done, they gathered in the ship's library: Volemak and Shedemei, of course, and along with them Nafai and Luet, Issib and Hushidh, and Oykib and Chveya. "I invited Elemak," Volemak explained, "because he had so much experience back on Harmony, dealing with strange cultures and foreign leaders. He declined to come, but I'm still going to ask him to work with the diggers, at least. They're the ones who are living practically on top of us—"

"Actually, we're living on top of *them*," said Nafai.

Volemak paused for a moment of patience, as if saying silently, When will the boy grow up enough not to make jokes during serious discussions? Luet leaned over to Nafai and jabbed his leg with her finger. He grinned stupidly at her.

Volemak went on. "And it's imperative that we reach

a workable living arrangement. I don't know about you, but what *I* saw the night of the kidnapping was a seriously conflicted digger society—an abduction organized by the son of the blood king, contrasted with the worship from the wife of the war king. The very fact that the wife—what's her name?"

"Emeezem," said Oykib.

"The fact that Emeezem succeeded where, um. . . ."

"Mufruzhuuzh."

"Where Muffle-whatever had failed may have weakened him. Therefore we can count on there being a faction that wants to rid the Earth of human beings, and perhaps two—Mufya's and the plotters who did the actual kidnapping. I think Elemak can be valuable in reaching some kind of understanding with the hostile ones."

"If he'll do it," said Hushidh. "He isn't very closely bonded right now with anyone. Not even Protchnu, since the boy couldn't keep himself from bragging to his father about how *he* was the one who discovered the entrance to the digger city up in a tree. It wasn't a welcome topic at home."

"You saw this domestic scene?" asked Volemak.

"I heard about it from an eyewitness," said Hushidh.

"So it's gossip," said Volemak.

"First-generation gossip," said Hushidh. "Very accurate. The best quality."

Volemak smiled, then repeated firmly. "Gossip."

Nafai spoke up. "I think Elemak's the natural choice to work with the diggers."

"There won't be just one," said Volemak. "And do us all a favor, Nafai. Don't let it be known that you favor the idea of Elemak having such an assignment."

Nafai nodded, suddenly serious. But Luet was not impressed. She knew that he understood, intellectually, that it was a bad idea for him to keep trying to be nice to Elemak. Just yesterday Luet had tried to explain it to him again, and he had interrupted her and explained it right back. "Elemak doesn't see my eagerness to give him authority as trust or kindness, he sees it as conde-scension and gloating, I know. But it's not gloating and it's not condescension, Luet. I really *do* admire his abil-ities and I trust him to do an excellent job of whatever he's doing. I can't help wanting to reach out to him."

"From your end it looks like reaching out," Luet ex-plained, patiently—for the fiftieth time, she was sure. "From his end it's more like rubbing in."

Nafai knew that he should simply remain silent on any issue regarding Elemak, but he couldn't stand it. "Then everybody will think I'm sulking or that I don't want him to do anything. I really *do* want him to do things, and so I have to say so, don't I? So *everybody* knows there's no hard feelings."

"Can't you just trust me?" said Luet. "Can't you just trust me and *shut up?*"

He had given her his solemn vow—again—that he would say nothing to or about Elemak's role in the community. And here he was in this meeting, not a day since the last time she had pleaded with him and he had remade his promise to her, doing exactly what he had vowed not to do.

Volemak was taking the meeting back to its main subject. "Anyway, we won't have just one person work-ing with the diggers. We have to have as many different perspectives as possible—even as we work to raise crops and get food and seeds stored away for the dry season. All of this is just a preamble, though. This meeting is Shedemei's. I assume this means she has a report on digger and angel biology, and that's as good a starting place as any."

"It's not really a report," said Shedemei. "It's more like a list of questions. The initial scan showed that like all the other animals and plants we've examined since we arrived, the diggers and angels show only the nor-mal sorts of evolutionary changes from their ancestors of forty million years ago. Diggers were a species of field rat common in southern Mexico, and angels were a common species of bat. The genetic variation is on the order of only five percent from the original in both cases. It will be ages before we can even begin to examine the fossil record, but here you can see how the digger body has changed to be able to support a heavier head and the hands have evolved for grasping big heavy tools—while not losing the raw power of digging, climbing, and, I must add, killing with no tools at all."

She switched from the rat and digger skeletons on the computer display to the bat and angel skeletons. "The angels had a more complex job—to retain flight, support a heavier brain, and develop the manual strength to use tools. Their compromise is to keep the use of their feet as strong hands. Standing on one foot, these hip joints give them enough rotation to swing a hand axe. But their arms, which in bats have only vestigial hands, have evolved back into good manual instruments. They can't bear much weight, and as we learned through an unfortunate incident, the arms break easily enough in a strong grasp. So the hands aren't used for gross physical activities. Rather they're used for very delicate, fine work."

She sat and regarded them steadily.

Luet finally realized what she was indicating. "You mean that the statues down in the digger city were made by the angels?"

"The digger hand is simply incapable of doing the fine work you described," said Shedemei. "I've tested the diggers when they were semi-conscious. They can't do work that doesn't require a lot of force. When you sculpt in soft clay, you have to be very restrained, press only so hard. The diggers are incapable of that. They would mash the clay to a pulp."

"Perhaps," said Issib, "you've only been examining soldiers and manual laborers."

"Did you notice any dimorphism underground?" Shedemei asked Nafai and Oykib.

"None," said Nafai.

"And they admitted that they didn't make the sculptures themselves," added Oykib.

"But those are their gods," said Chveya. "Gods which they worship by offering the bones of dead baby angels to them. It seems a little incongruous."

"Yes, it does," said Shedemei. "But that strikes at the heart of the most important questions. The first one is, Why did two intelligent species develop virtually in each other's laps like this, without one destroying the other? According to the records in the library, several sentient species evolved along with humans from the same stock—robusts and heidelbergs, they called them—but the erects essentially erased the robusts, and the moderns wiped out the heidelbergs."

"Might have absorbed them," Issib corrected.

"However it happened," said Shedemei, "where the moderns went, there were no more robusts, heidelbergs, or erects. So why do both angels and diggers survive?"

"Because they don't compete for resources?" asked Chveya.

"My good student," said Shedemei with a smile. "But the diggers *do* eat the angels' young. And worship the statues they make. So it's not the same as, for instance, octopuses and eagles, which simply don't compete in any way. The angels are prey to the diggers. And yet they survive."

"Art lovers," said Nafai.

It sounded like another wisecrack and Luet was ready to poke him, but Shedemei answered as if it were a serious suggestion. "I think you're right, Nafai. I think there's something biological here, and the sculptures are involved. Didn't you say, Oykib, that you've learned that the statues are always associated with mating and breeding in their worship?"

Oykib blushed and looked furtively at his wife, then at Nafai.

"Don't be shy about it, Okya," said Volemak. "Nafai

felt it was wise to tell the rest of us about what you can do. Not everybody—just the people in this room. No reason to make everybody else paranoid about their prayers."

Issib grinned maliciously. "We, of course, are the ones who are so perfect of heart that we don't mind being spied on."

"What Issya is trying to say," said Volemak, "is that we accept that some of us have the ability to learn things that others might wish kept secret. But you've shown such remarkable discretion throughout your childhood and on into adulthood that we aren't afraid of you."

"I am," said Chveya. "That's the only reason I let you get me pregnant."

"Veya," Luet remonstrated. Did the girl have to be so crude?

"Anyway, Oykib, is that right?" said Shedemei.

"Yes," he said. "Some of the . . . worshipful thoughts . . . they're downright pornographic. I mean, the way they think of the statues. We've seen how most of them were worn down until some of them were just lumps. They worship by rubbing the statues all over themselves."

"That's very helpful," said Shedemei. "That's not a behavior I've seen in rats or any other rodent. Have you ever seen anything about that in your studies?"

"*You're* the biologist, Shedya," said Hushidh. "If you haven't seen it, you can count on it that *we* haven't."

"As long as we're on the subject of who knows what," said Luet, "I'd like to know why I'm here. I mean, Shedya's husband isn't here, and Aunt Rasa isn't here, so we're not doing this in couples or anything. Shuya and Veya are both needed for understanding the diggers and angels because they can see things that language can't convey. Oykib's method is different, but the result is the same. Nafai is the one with the cloak, who has his face on a sculpture down in the digger city. Issib can't work in the fields and he's good at language and nobody handles the Index better than he does, so he'll be vital for research and conversation. Why am *I* here?"

"Feeling a little insecure, my love?" asked Nafai with mock solicitude.

"You're here," said Volemak, "because you're you. Not everybody has to have a specialization for what I have in mind. And you communicate with the Oversoul better than anyone."

"Not when you use the Index," said Luet. "I shouldn't be here."

"Shut up, Lutya," said Hushidh cheerfully. "Your self-doubt is wasting everyone's time."

"Be patient," said Volemak. "I'm making my point, and you'll understand." He took Shedemei's illustrations off the display and replaced them with a map of the immediate area. "Here *we* are," he said, "and here are the diggers. And way up here are the angels. Take a wild guess which culture we'll come to understand best."

"Especially if they get into a kidnapping mood again," said Issib.

"I think that this can lead to an unfortunate outcome," said Volemak. "First, we'd no doubt become closer to the species we know the best, and that might be a serious mistake. Second, and perhaps more important, the angels would certainly assume that we were closer to the diggers, and therefore they would be suspicious of everything we did. Perhaps hostile. You see the problem?"

Issib nodded. "You want some of them to go up and live among the angels."

"That sounds so final," said Nafai. This time Luet did poke him.

"Not some of *them*, Issya," said Volemak. "Some of *you*."

Issib looked angry. "Not me," he said. "Not the chair."

Luet understood. He had hated those years in the wilderness when he had been physically helpless except when in his floating chair. To have Hushidh have to lift him and carry him and help him with his bodily needs—it was bad enough when his children were little, but now it would be an unbearable humiliation. Here in the vicinity of the ship his magnetic floats worked just as they had in the city of Basilica, giving him nearly normal physical freedom. He was not about to give that up.

"Hear me out," said Volemak. "I've thought this through very carefully, and if you listen reasonably you'll agree with my conclusions. First, I don't think we should send very many to the angels, because we need most of our strength here, working the fields and establishing the colony. So I'm sending only two couples and their small children. I can't send Shedemei, because she has to be here, using the instruments in the ship. But I need to send somebody who is as methodical as she is, and as familiar with the library. That points to you, Issib."

"It points to anybody here and half the people not here," said Issib.

"Chveya and Hushidh both have roughly the same ability," said Volemak, "and that ability is indispensable. So one stays here, and one goes there."

"Oykib is the most valuable one for learning languages," said Issib. "Send him up there."

"I need Oykib down here," said Volemak. "I want him learning the digger language alongside Elemak."

Luet understood, as she was sure everyone else did—it would not be healthy if Elemak were the only interpreter they had. Volemak didn't want to say it outright, but Elemak could not be wholly trusted. And the way he'd been acting since the night of the kidnapping, he might not accept the assignment to work with the diggers anyway.

"Besides," said Volemak, "the diggers know Oykib."

"They know Nafai, too," said Issib.

"Don't fight me on this, Issya," said Volemak. "Nafai they see as a god. Therefore it's very important that they not see too much of him. Let them worship the clay head and leave the man himself a mystery."

"In other words," said Nafai, "nobody who knows me could worship me."

"That's pretty much it," said Volemak.

"I worship you," Luet said, too sweetly.

Nafai smiled sweetly back.

"As for your loathing for the chair," said Volemak, "Nafai and I are pretty sure we can install a relay somewhere on that peak. It overlooks the angels' valley as well as the whole canyon approach. I think your magnetics will work there."

"Unless I walk behind a tree," said Issib.

"The relay consists of four installations so that there's always a parallax," said Nafai. "It would have to be a very big tree."

"If the magnetics work, I'll do it," said Issib.

"You'll do it anyway," said Volemak. "You'll just be angrier if you're in the chair. But think of this as the consolation prize. You get the Index."

"So there we'll be," said Nafai. "The four of us. The brothers who married the sisters."

"I'll still be useless," said Luet, trying to sound dispassionate, but failing.

"No more so than Nafai," said Volemak. "And no less. The angels aren't going to be as impressed by the glowing skin as the diggers were. *Their* first exposure to us was an act of wanton violence. Even with Hushidh and Issib to counsel you, it's going to take some delicate maneuvering to get them to accept you in the first place. Yasai and Padarok have assured me that our injured angel made no offer of violence. But that doesn't mean that the others are necessarily peaceable. After all, they *are* a sentient species. If humans and diggers are any example of what that means, we can anticipate that they have just as many murderous tendencies as we have."

"Then let's just wipe 'em all out," said Nafai.

Everyone looked at him in horror.

"That was a *joke*," he said.

"Try not to make jokes like that with the angels," said Volemak.

Nafai looked disgusted. "When I'm responsible for

something, I don't make stupid jokes," he said. Then he grinned. "But this is *your* meeting."

"I appreciate your supportive attitude," said Volemak. "Now does anyone have anything else?"

"I do," said Shedemei. "This is especially for the four of you who are going up to the angels, but it's really for everybody who works with the diggers, too. You have to notice everything. Not just the way that they're different from us, but the ways that they're the same, too. You have to make a note of it immediately, every single thing you notice, because the longer you wait to write it down, the more you'll be accustomed to their way of doing things and so the more likely you are to stop noticing it. Issib has the Index, and I have the computers here on the ship—we should be making reports every night."

"When do we do all this?" asked Oykib.

"The work with the diggers starts immediately," said Volemak. "But until we can take a healthy—or at least not dying—angel back up to his people, we aren't going back up that canyon. So for now, the four of you will take shifts with this poor busted-up fellow. Spend as much time with him as Shedemei thinks advisable. Make a *friend* out of him, if you can." Then he glowered at them all. "And you *will* make sure that you never take this fellow anywhere that he even *might* run into Elemak. Elya will have access to the ship as always, but I'll ask him to stay off the deck where Shedemei is helping the angel recuperate. That should do the job."

Shedemei had only one thing to add. "I especially want to know anything that has to do with sex. Reproduction and survival—those are the two key forces that drive evolution. I won't understand their biology or their culture until I know what is imperative for their mating, breeding, sustenance, and defense. Somehow those sculptures play a role for *both* cultures."

"Art is life," Nafai intoned. "And life is art."

Luet poked him again, as hard as she could. He yelped. She hoped it left a bruise.

As the meeting broke up, Shedemei and Issib spent a few moments looking in detail at the scans and charts of the digger and angel bodies. "I was going to bring this up for the whole group," Shedemei said, "but the meeting went a different way. I didn't know what Volemak was planning, and all that matters is that *you* be aware of this so you can watch for an explanation when you're up the canyon with the angels."

"I haven't agreed to go," said Issib.

Shedemei looked at him blankly.

"Yes, well, show me anyway," said Issib.

"Here," she said. "In the digger males. And here, in our one angel, also a male."

"I don't know what it is you're pointing at."

"Neither do I," said Shedemei. "But it's a tiny organ, maybe a gland, I'm not sure at all of the function. But it isn't present in humans, and it isn't present in any other species I've scanned."

"So, they're different."

"It's not that simple," said Shedemei. "Biological diversity come through branching. There are two ways that creatures can have similar organs. One is that they have a common ancestor. The other is through convergent evolution—similar pressures in the environment caused them to develop similar strategies to counter it. Now, if they have the identical organ because of a common ancestor, there should be evidence of it in all the other species that diverged from the same source at the same time. But there isn't, Issib. *No* other species of rat or bat or any other rodent or related animal has anything remotely like this structure in this location or even near it. I'm talking about now and I'm talking about forty million years ago, when the oldest biological database on the ship was put together. It's not there."

"Convergent evolution, then."

"But except in the case of skeletal and muscular structure, convergent evolution only gets you organs with similar *functions*. There's no particular reason why they should have the same location."

"Unless it has to do with male reproduction and just above the scrotum is the only location that would work," said Issib.

"Exactly. So what I need you to look for, and what I'll be looking for down here, is a reason for these two species, and only these two species, to have this organ. When you think about it, why should the two sentient species on Earth have this particular similarity?"

"Because it's related to their intelligence?" asked Issib.

"That has to be the first thought," said Shedemei. "But then, we haven't had a chance to look at females. They're intelligent, too—but if they lack this structure—"

"Or one that has an analogous function—"

"You see the mystery," said Shedemei. "This organ came from somewhere and has some function, and it exists only in the two intelligent species, and may exist only in the males. It may have to do with intelligence. It may have to do with sex, given the location."

Issib grinned. "Maybe they're more similar to humans than we thought."

Shedemei glowered. "You mean that maybe male intelligence is testosterone-related?"

"I would have put it more crudely," said Issib.

"No doubt," said Shedemei, "seeing as you're a male. But as you implied, human males already think with their male appendage half the time, and they *don't* have this strange little organ."

"It was just a joke, Shedemei, not a serious scientific proposal."

Shedemei smiled thinly. "I knew that, Issib. I was joking back."

He laughed. It was a little forced.

"Watch for some explanation, Issib, that's all I ask. I'll put everything I notice in the database so we can share information through the Index the whole time you're up there."

"*If* I'm up there," Issib said.

"Whatever," said Shedemei.

While Issib and Shedemei conferred at one of the computer displays, Chveya stopped Luet and took her aside, letting all the others leave the library and the ship without them.

"Why was Father acting so childish during the meeting?" Chveya asked. "It's embarrassing."

"Childish?" asked Luet. "I don't think of it that way. He's always done this sort of thing."

"I've never seen him do it. And it isn't funny."

"It is to him," said Luet. "And to me, actually."

"I don't understand him at all," said Chveya.

"Of course not," said Luet. "He's your father."

Chveya was almost to the ladderway when Luet thought of the real answer to Chveya's real question. "Veya, my dear, the reason you've never seen him like this before is simple enough. This is how he acts when he's happy."

Chveya raised her eyebrows, nodded thoughtfully, then took hold of the ladder and slid down like a child. "Be careful!" Luet yelled down after her. "Remember that you're pregnant!"

"Oh, Mother!" Chveya yelled back, her voice echoing through every floor of the ship.

And she criticizes her father for acting childish? Luet shook her head, then took hold of the ladder and went down, one step at a time.

Poto hung upside down from the branch, his wings gathered close against his body like the clothing that the Old Ones wore. He listened in patient silence to Boboi's harangue, to all the others who argued her side. There were so many of them, and none had come to speak for Poto. pTo's wife, Iguo, would gladly have spoken for him, but it was forbidden for a wife to speak in such circumstances, simply because everyone knows what she would say. She stood upside down from the same branch as Poto, but she was silent.

If Poto stood alone, he nevertheless had two things going for him. First, everyone here knew what one owed to one's otherself. Boboi could muster all her arguments— pTo is certainly dead; the Old Ones are already angry so let's not provoke them more; the Old Ones only took pTo's body home to feed it to the devils—but in the heart of every man and woman in the assembly there would be all the deep and complicated feelings each had for his or her otherself. Poto's own feelings were difficult to sort out. pTo had gone down against Poto's own advice; it had also been against Poto's advice that he went alone to face the Old Ones, to offer to return the stolen grain. But pTo was also his otherself, and when Poto watched the angry bearded giant break and tear pTo's body like it was kindling, it was all Poto could do to keep himself from screaming and flying at the Old One, even though that would mean certain death and was strictly prohibited. When you cannot save the captured one, then don't give them a second one. Poto tried to be perfectly obedient to the laws and wisdom of the people; others commended him afterward for his silence as it happened, but it was little consolation to him. pTo, you fool! he cried out inside himself. And then, O pTo, my otherself, if only I could have died for you!

For wasn't it fated that Poto should be the one to die? When they were two years old—too big for either of their parents to carry one of them alone—the devils came on their raid and found the family hiding place. Without hesitation, both parents took hold of pTo's feet and carried him off to the high refuge. It was a long flight. Poto was alone on the branch, with a digger climbing rapidly to reach him. Knowing that his parents had chosen his otherself, and not him, Poto almost stayed where he was; why should he value his own life, if his parents did not? But the will to live was too strong. And also there was pTo's shout as his parents carried him off. "Live, little soul!" he cried. For his parents Poto was nothing, so he would not live for them. He would live for pTo.

So he inched his way out to the most remote end of the branch. The devil laughed at him then, and began climbing out the branch, slowly, carefully. It bowed lower and lower under his weight. Poto could see another devil waiting under the branch, ready to seize him the moment he descended low enough.

The devil below him jumped and its fierce digging hands brushed Poto's head. Many children at such a time became so terrified that they tried to fly, but with wings so small and weak they couldn't get aloft, and the devils would have sport chasing them as they fluttered and staggered near the ground. Those who tried to fly always were caught, were always carried down into the devil's tunnels where they were eaten in terrible barbaric festivals.

Poto did not try to fly. Instead, he mustered his courage and moved closer to the devil on the branch. This had the effect of raising him above the height that the lower devil could reach by jumping. But it put him nearly within reach of the upper devil's sweeping hand. Twice the hand struck at Poto's feet. But the second time, the devil had so extended himself that his balance was precarious indeed, and at that moment Poto *bounced*. The devil yelped and fell from the branch. And before he could climb back up and try again, Poto's parents returned and carried him away to safety, to the place where pTo greeted him with an embrace and listened as Poto told him of his terrible adventure. Ever since that time Poto knew that his life had been spared so he could watch over the chosen self; everyone had respect for that and knew that if it were not meant for Poto to protect pTo, he would have been taken by the devils that day.

The second great argument on Poto's side was that everyone knew that no matter what the assembly decided, Poto would go down to find pTo and do his best to save him, even offering himself in pTo's place, if he wasn't already dead. So what the assembly was really deciding was not whether Poto would go, but rather whether Poto's going would be so dangerous that he should have a wing torn to prevent him from going. This would be a terrible punishment, for to deprive a man of flight was the ultimate humiliation. It was the punishment given to a man who forced himself on a woman, and it always led to the same end: a cruel, humiliating death at the hands of the devils on their next raid. Because he was not an infant, he would not be carried down into the caves. Instead, the raiders would eat him raw on the spot, not bothering to kill him first. The distraction of having a tornwing to eat might save a few infant lives—it was the only thing such a criminal was good for.

It would be a cruel thing to do, when Poto's only crime was that he intended to save his otherself no matter what the assembly decided. But it would do no good to deny that he meant to defy the assembly—that would only humiliate him by making it seem that he did not love his otherself more than the law. Just as a wife was expected to plead for the rescue of her husband, and so was silenced regardless of whether she actually would have pled for him or not, so also a man was expected to defy all fears, laws, dangers, and wisdom to fly to the rescue of his otherself. So whether he broke the law or not, he should be punished as if he had. If the people did *not* punish him, it would mean they thought he was the most contemptible of creatures, a man who would not risk all for his otherself. Better to be a tornwing.

So the assembly had to decide whether to tear Poto's wing or to let him risk the people's safety by going down to confront the Old Ones yet again.

Finally Boboi fell silent, the last of her supporters having spoken. How many were there? Fewer than half the assembly, but not very much fewer. If even a few of the silent ones voted with her, Poto would be torn and pTo would remain alone among the Old Ones.

It was Poto's turn. The people were already tired. He would be brief. "I don't believe the Old Ones are all our enemies. They were very angry at pTo or they would not have come up the canyon to find him. They rejected his offering, it's true. But the one who struck him acted alone. I saw the others turn away from him or reach out to stop him—"

"How do you know what the Old Ones *meant* by anything!" Boboi interrupted him.

The assembly squealed their anger at Boboi for daring to interrupt. After all, Poto had maintained perfect courtesy. Abashed by the high screeching, Boboi turned her face away from the assembly.

Poto resumed. "I'm not the only one who saw this. If there's any witness who denies that the other Old Ones did not seem to want him to break pTo as he did, then speak now, I give my consent."

There might have been some who disagreed, but none who were certain enough to dare to repudiate him when he was pleading for his otherself.

"pTo was not dead—I saw how bravely he opened his eyes to show us that he lived. And the Old Ones, seeing him alive, chose not to eat him, even though he was not a child. They treated him tenderly and put him in their own leather to carry him down the canyon. I have no idea what they intended. But the Old Ones are not devils in their bodies, even if they are mostly hairless under their leather, and so perhaps they are not devils in their hearts. They came from the sky, didn't they? So perhaps they are no longer angry at pTo, and if I went to plead for him, they would let me take him home, or at least stay and tend him until he dies."

He swallowed, trying to think of what other points Boboi had made, so he could refute them. "I don't think that the Old Ones are angry at all of us, or they would not have stopped with harming just pTo. It was dawn, and they could surely see the watchwomen flying above the village. They knew where we might be found, but they did not come further than the crest of the ridge. This shows that they do not hold the whole responsible for the acts of the one. Therefore I will not bring danger to the people even if they hate me for coming to them."

What else? Most of Boboi's argument had consisted of many people saying the same things over and over; he had little else to say. "People of the assembly," said Poto, "I can add only this: My otherself did nothing more terrible than to follow in the footsteps of his wife's illustrious ancestor, Kiti. Both of them were drawn to the Old Ones. pTo put us all at risk, but even though Boboi had declared that no one should go to the Old Ones until the assembly decided, the fact remains that the assembly had not yet forbidden what he did. It was foolhardy, but it was also brave and he acted, not for himself, but for what he thought was the good of the people. Should such a one be abandoned? Should his otherself be torn to prevent him from standing beside him? I think everyone here, even Boboi, would be proud to be the otherself of one as brave as my pTo. Let me be a true brother and friend to him. The danger to the people is not known. Should the unknown evil prevent us from doing the known good?"

With that, Poto slowly turned around on the branch and extended his wings, ready to be torn if the vote went against him. He could hear the sound of Boboi's supporters dropping to the ground. How many? They went quickly, all at once, and then there were no more. So easily they made up their minds. Perhaps that meant that only those who spoke with her had voted with her.

Or perhaps not.

Chveya woke up first, as usual. It used to be that she could out-sleep Oykib any day of the week, but, to her surprise, pregnancy had already diminished her bladder's capacity and she had to get up before daybreak whether she wanted to or not. And she didn't often want to. There was no use trying to get back to sleep, either. She would just lie awake anyway, so she might as well get up and do something.

What she was doing today was sitting on a stool, leaning against the wall of their one-room house, trying to imagine Basilica, the City of Women. Mother had told her about buildings, thousands of them, so close together they touched on every side except the front. And sometimes people would come along and build a new house right in front of yours, completely cutting yours off from the street, unless you had the money to hire thugs to drive them away. They could build right across a street, completely blocking it—except when passersby, angry that someone was trying to close their street, would dismantle the building as they passed.

It was hard to imagine such a place, so many people. In her entire life, Chveya had known only the people of their colony. The only new people she had met were the babies who were born. The only buildings she had seen were the buildings they built with their own hands— and the impossible, magical buildings of the spaceport, and that was no city, since its population consisted entirely of the same people she had always known.

The diggers had a city, though, didn't they? Even though it was underground, except where the entrances of their tunnels were bored upward into the trees. Chveya imagined how they must have scrambled when the humans first arrived from Harmony and started cutting down the trees, extending the meadow where they had first landed. The tunnels that led to doomed trees had to be filled, so that when the humans looked down into the hollow trunks, they wouldn't see that tunnels opened out underneath them. And yet even with so many tunnels filled, the digger city was a vast network of connected chambers.

Chveya knew it was real. She could now see the connections among many, perhaps most of the diggers, and she knew that there were hundreds of them down there, constantly coming and going. It was the only real city she had ever seen, but she hadn't really seen it, probably never *would* see it. She would never crawl along the tunnels. She *hoped* she would never crawl through them, in the darkness. Her skin didn't glow the way Father's could, when he wanted it to. It would be night down there all the time. And she would be surrounded by strangers. It wasn't that they were so alien, so animal-like. It was that she didn't know them, didn't know what to expect. Even Elemak, even Meb and Obring, dangerous and untrustworthy as they were, seemed safer to her because after all she *knew* them. The diggers were all strangers to her.

And that's how it must have been in Basilica. Nobody could possibly know that many people, so walking along the streets must have meant being surrounded by strangers, by people you had never seen before and would never see again, people who could have come from anywhere, who could be thinking anything, who might be desiring terrible things that would destroy you or those you loved and cared for and you had no way of knowing.

How did they do it, the people who lived there? How could they bear to live their lives among aliens? Why didn't they just retreat to their homes, block the doors, and cower in a corner, whimpering?

For that matter, thought Chveya, why don't I? Right now, knowing that I am surrounded by diggers that I don't know, that I can't predict, who have the power to destroy me and everyone I love—why am I still going to bed at night, getting up in the morning?

Someone clapped their hands softly outside the door. She got up and went to the door. It was Elemak.

"Is Oykib up?" he asked.

"Um, no," said Chveya. "But it's time he was."

"I'm up," said Oykib sleepily from the bed. "Awake, anyway."

"Come in," said Chveya.

Elemak came in. He stood until Oykib sat up in bed and indicated his eldest brother should sit at the foot of it. "What is it?" he asked.

"Volemak wants me to work with this digger hostage," said Elemak.

"If you want to," said Oykib.

"I do my duty," said Elemak. He smiled nastily. "I took the oath."

"Well," said Oykib. "Then we're both supposed to learn his language."

"You have a head start," said Elemak. "I'd like you to teach me what you know about the language."

"Not much yet. Just a few words. I don't know the structure yet."

"Whatever you know, I'd like to learn it. I'd like Protchnu to learn it, too. Can you give us a class in digger language?"

"That's a good idea," said Oykib. "Yes, I will."

Someone was running around outside. Pounding feet. Protchnu stood in the doorway. "Father," he said.

Elemak stood up.

"There's one of those angels standing on the roof of Issib's house."

"Who's on watch?" asked Oykib, standing up, pulling on his clothes.

"Motya," said Protchnu. "He sent me to fetch you."

"To fetch *me*?" asked Elemak.

"Um, to get the adults."

"He didn't mean me," said Elemak.

Protchnu looked defiant. "But *I* did."

"Go get Volemak," said Elemak.

Chveya was surprised that Elemak understood so well what his role in the community was now—and that he seemed to accept it. She knew that his connection to most people was very thin these days, but she could see that his bond with his eldest son was bright and strong. Yet he had let his son see his own humility. It made her rather sad that he could not be as strong and proud as Protchnu longed for him to be. It was bound to cause real pain in Protchnu, and yet Elemak faced it openly and. . . .

Unless he *wanted* to make sure that Protchnu felt that pain.

No, she wasn't going to believe that Elemak had

some elaborate plan that involved the kindling of deep resentment in his son's heart.

Oykib was dressed now, and heading out the door. Elemak gave no sign that he intended to follow.

"Aren't you curious?" asked Chveya, as she followed Oykib out.

"I've seen one," said Elemak.

When they got to Issib's house, the angel was standing on the roof, rigid, unmoving. Issib and Hushidh and their children were outside, looking up at him; other people were gathering, too. "He looks so frightened," said Chveya.

"Not of us," said Oykib. He gestured toward the trees. The shadowy forms of diggers could be seen in the branches, in the underbrush. "Their word for the angels is *mveevo*. Meat from the sky."

"They eat them?"

"They prefer the babies," said Oykib. "Let's just say that international relations between diggers and angels are on a kind of primitive level."

But Chveya was seeing something else now. The angel on the rooftop had the brightest, strongest connection she had ever seen between any two people, and the connection led to the ship. "He's here for the other one," she said. "For the injured one in the ship."

"I guess so," said Oykib.

"I know it," she said.

"He's praying that we won't give him to the devils before he finds his . . . brother. But more than a brother."

"Then let's take him," said Chveya. She walked to the edge of the roof, reached up, took hold of the roof beam, and started climbing up the rough log wall.

"Veya," said Oykib, annoyed. "You're pregnant."

"And you're just standing there," she said.

A couple of moments later they were both on the roof. The angel looked at them, but didn't move. Oykib held out a hand. So did Chveya.

The angel spread his wings, unfolding himself like an

umbrella. The effect was astonishing. From being a small, quivering thing, he was suddenly transformed into a great looming shadow. So this is what the injured one would look like, if he were strong and healthy. Like a butterfly, though, the body was so thin and frail inside the canopy of the wings. Only the head was still in proportion to the great width of the wings. The heavy, nodding head.

"Well, we can't carry him or anything," Oykib said. He beckoned for the angel to come closer. The angel took an awkward step. "Not much of a walking animal, is he," said Oykib.

"He's not an animal," said Chveya. "He's a very brave and frightened man, and he loves his brother."

"His other self," said Oykib. "That's what the word is. His otherself."

"So let's lead him there." She went to the edge of the roof, sat down, swung off. Oykib followed her. And a few moments later, the angel perched on the edge, then swooped off. Some of the children shrieked and ran off a little way.

Chveya could see the diggers in the forest draw nearer, but they apparently didn't dare to cross the line into human territory.

Oykib was explaining to Nafai and Volemak what he and Chveya had seen, what they had decided.

"Do we want the two angels together?" asked Nafai. "What will his reaction be when he sees how badly injured his brother is?"

"More to the point," said Volemak, "what would his reaction be if we blocked him from seeing his brother?"

Nafai nodded. In the meantime, Oykib and Chveya led the angel toward the ship.

pTo had awakened several times since the Old Ones took him, but every wakening had been like a dream. He drifted, floating on his back, as if the air had grown thick and now held him up without effort. He didn't know whether he could move or not because he couldn't summon up the will to move, not even his lips to speak. And when he let his eyes fall open, what he saw was a female Old One, also floating, slowly drifting into and out of his field of vision. Above him the sky, of a neutral color, as if the clouds had not yet decided whether to be stormy or benign. And there were faint breezes, coming from no particular direction—perhaps from below him. Nothing smelled alive except his own faint sweat and the mustier perfumes of the Old One.

Then he drifted off again, not into sleep, really, but into oblivion.

Is this death? Do Old Ones take us to the sky god? Is this life inside a cloud?

But then, perhaps the third time or the fifth time he awoke—he wasn't sure how many separate memories had gone before—he realized that this must be the inside of the tower of the Old Ones, and the sky was no sky, but rather a roof. So would this be considered a tunnel, like the ones the devils made, only built above the ground? Or would it be a sheltering nest, like the woven thatch that the people build above the nests where infants clung, first to their mothers' fur, and then to the twigs under the nest?

Are the Old Ones like us, or like them?

Like the devils, because of the way the Old One in his terrible fury tore and flung pTo and left him for dead.

Like the people, because of the careful tender way the Old Ones lifted him onto the woven thatchlike leathers they put on and took off their bodies at will. Like the people, because of the way they carried him down the hill before at last, mercifully, he slipped into unconsciousness. Like the people, because he was still alive, not eaten, not torn to bits, not even held as a prisoner.

Or a third possibility. Perhaps they were like the gods. After all, there was no pain.

And then a day came when there *was* pain, but along with the pain he came fully awake for the first time. Not floating any more. And now able to feel his limbs, his fingers, and to move them. Some of them. A great weight pressed down on the bones that had been broken. He turned his head—yes, he could turn his head, he could shift his back enough to let him see that something had been wrapped around his broken bones, splinting them like the graft of a tree branch. The splints were so heavy he couldn't lift them, and when he tried it only caused the dull undercurrent of pain to become sharp.

Why have they let the pain come back? Is it a prelude to death? Have I been judged and found unworthy? Or is it because they have decided to let me return to life? To see again my otherself. My wife. My people.

A whining, hooting sound—ah, yes, the speech of the Old Ones. There was some music in it, but there were also those devil sounds, hissing and humming.

And then another sound. His name, spoken clearly, with love, with concern. "pTo," said the voice, and he knew it at once, impossible as it was that it could be real.

"Poto," he answered, and then with a rustle of his leathery wings pTo's otherself stood on the same surface where pTo lay, and looked down at him. "I told you not to go to the Old Ones' tower," Poto said.

"And now you've come, too," said pTo.

"Boboi wanted to tear my wings to prevent me," said Poto. "I almost fled without awaiting the verdict. But I wanted you to be able to return in honor if you should live. So I waited, and the people stood with me. With us, pTo. They honor you. The way you bore the punishment of the angry Old One."

"He was the most terrible creature I've ever seen," said pTo. "Surely more terrible than the devils."

Poto shook his head. "I've looked the devils in the face, and these Old Ones also."

"But the devils, Poto, they don't hate us, they merely hunger for us. There is no hate like the Old Ones' hate."

"They led me to you, my self, my most beautiful

self," said Poto. "They knew who I was and what I wanted, and they led me to you."

The voice of the Old One rang out again. Poto looked at her, and at others; pTo looked around and saw that four others had come into the—what, the nest? The tunnel? Whatever this place was. He recognized one of them—the male he had seen that fateful night, just as he touched the tower. "That's the one who saw me," said pTo. "That's the one who saw I stole the grasses and must have given the alarm."

"But he's not the angry one?" asked Poto.

"He's not angry now," said pTo. "Not like the other one. Oh, let me never see the angry Old One again!"

"Finally," said Oykib. "Something like a prayer. Half of what the diggers say is at least partly directed toward their gods. It'd be easier for me if the angels were as pious."

"But what did they say?" asked Shedemei.

"He wanted never to see the angry one again. The angry Old One." He laughed. "We're Old Ones, of course. The ancients come back."

"That's not to laugh about," said Shedemei. "That's very important. Luet or Nafai, can you go and get Hushidh and Issib? They need to be here, to meet them—if they're going to be liaison with the angels."

"Yes, I'll go," said Nafai.

"No, Nafai, that's silly, I'll go," said Luet.

"*I'll* go," said Oykib.

"We need you here," said Shedemei. "In case you can understand anything more."

Nafai left.

"The language is all pops and song, isn't it?" said Luet. "Like bubbles in a stream. Like. . . ."

"Yes, Mother?" said Chveya.

"Like the music of the Lake of Women, when I floated on it at the edges of a true dream."

"Maybe the Keeper of Earth was able to send their songs to you," said Chveya.

"Hush," said Shedemei. "These two are twins, I think. Look how perfectly identical they are."

"Each calls the other his *otherself*," said Oykib. "It's much more than a brother."

"My twins might feel that way about each other," said Luet, "if only babies their age could articulate their feelings."

"Hush," said Shedemei. "Listen, Oykib. Watch, all of you."

But Chveya had to say this one last thing: "There's no love I've ever seen among humans like the love that binds these two."

"You are without doubt the stupidest of all men," said Poto.

"I accept the honor," said pTo. "And you are the truest of all. May some woman now see the strength and power in you, and take you as her husband."

Oykib spoke. "The injured one prays that some female will admire how strong the healthy one is and mate with him. No, bind with him."

"Marry him," suggested Chveya.

"Well, it could be. The word has overtones of twining and knotting."

"I know about twining," said Chveya. "He means marriage. The injured one is married, and the healthy one is not—because the injured one has a strong tie to someone not here, someone up the canyon."

"Do they have names?" asked Shedemei.

"You expect me to produce those sounds?" asked Oykib.

"We'll have to, someday. You might as well try."

"The name of the healthy one is oh-oh, with quick little consonants in there. To-to. Po-to."

"And the other one?"

Oykib laughed in frustration. "The same. The same name."

"Otherself," murmured Shedemei.

"No, it's different. Like, Po-*to*, and the healthy one is *Po*-to."

"Quiet," said pTo. "Listen."

"To what?"

"The Old Ones. They just said your name."

They listened.

"Poto," said Oykib. "Poto." Then he babbled some more, and then the name stuck out again. "Poto. Poto."

"They want you," said pTo.

Poto immediately leapt down to the ground, out of pTo's field of vision. But pTo could hear him say, "I am Poto, Old One, if it is truly me you seek. Let no more harm come to my otherself! If you have more punishment, I will bear it."

"He's praying to *us*," said Oykib.

"Oh, good," said Shedemei. "Maybe we can be gods to everyone now."

"If we're going to tear the wings again, he wants us to tear his and not the wings of his otherself."

"What brought that up?" asked Chveya. "Does he think we're angry?"

"How can he know what to think?" said Luet. "Let me try to show him."

They watched as Luet sank to her knees, then, still on her knees, shuffled forward to the healthy one. "Poto," she said, pointing to him.

He turned his back to her and spread out his wings, not fully wide, but enough that the leather of the wings hung loose and open before her.

"Touch them," suggested Shedemei. "Very gently. They're strong, but I don't know whether they're sensitive to pain or not."

Luet reached out her hand and gently stroked the skin of his wing. It was hairless and smooth, like shoe leather, but much lighter. Springier.

The angel seemed to wait for more, but when it didn't come, he turned around, looked at her.

"Poto," Luet said again. And now she held out her hand to him, palm up, open.

He studied her hand, then looked around from face to face, trying to find meaning. Perhaps he found some meaning that they could not even guess at, or perhaps he simply decided for himself what the gesture must mean. But in the end, he bowed his body until his cheek lay against her palm. As if she had intended this all along, Luet gently closed her other hand over his face, resting her palm against his other cheek. She held this pose for only a moment, then raised her hand.

The angel quietly spoke, not to her, but to his twin.

"pTo, she has made herself an aunt to me, she folded me truly, and on the side."

"Oh, Poto, may all our people have such a gift from the Old Ones," answered pTo from the bed behind him.

"The one on the bed prays that all his people can have a blessing like that from the Old Ones," said Oykib.

"Very nice," said Shedemei.

"Not enough," said Luet. "I refuse to let us be gods to these people."

So now she bowed herself before him, offering her own head to be clasped between hands.

"What do I do, pTo?" cried Poto in distress. "She bows to me as to a father, her head not even turned to the side."

"If the Old One demands that you be her father, then do it!" said pTo. "Don't make her angry! They're terrible when they're angry."

"But I can't be her father," said Poto. "It isn't right."

"It *is* right," said pTo. "She doesn't have a father. He's dead."

"And how do you know that, Broken Wings?"

"He's dead, Poto, I know it. I saw it when I was sleeping. I saw it in my dreams."

"You've never even seen the face of the Old One who kneels before me."

"I've seen her, too. I've seen them all." It was true. pTo had not remembered until now, until the moment that he needed the memory, and then it flooded back. He had seen all their faces in dreams. Even the angry one, only not angry, surrounded by little ones, by his children. And he knew from her voice which one this was. She was the one he saw with both of his own first-born children perched on her shoulders. "She will stand one day in a meadow in the village, and my children will stand on her shoulders."

"All right," said Poto. "I'll take her as my niece, then."

"Daughter," said pTo. "She has no father. You will be her father now."

"I have no wife," said Poto. "What woman will marry me, if she must become the mother of an Old One when she does?"

"The one who *should* be your wife, and no other," said pTo. "You have been chosen to be the father of an Old One, and you're worried about mating? Are you *that* lonely, my dear mad self?"

"They sound upset," Luet murmured.

"Just stay where you are," said Oykib. "I'm catching some of this. I think when you took his head in your hands, it's like you made him a relative. You took him under protection. And now you're asking him to adopt *you* as a relative."

"Mm," said Luet. "Maybe it's not a good idea."

"Do it," said Shedemei. "Just stay there and let him decide."

The conversation between them stopped. And then Poto spread his wings wide, and instead of placing them on either side of Luet's head, he enfolded her entire body in his wings. She felt them wrap around her, feathery-light. She knew that if she struck out with either arm she would tear the wing; she also knew that to tear this creature's wing would destroy, not him, but her.

"He's praying that he can be a good father to you," said Oykib.

"Father?" asked Luet.

"He says that he hopes he can take the place of your ancient father who died in a faraway place."

"What?" asked Chveya. "Mother, how can he know that?"

"He says that he will not die unless he can die defending you from the hungry devils. I think it's part of the ritual language of adoption. Only of course you're not an infant."

"Can you tell me the word for *father*?" asked Luet.

"Um," said Oykib, "I think—let's see if he says it again when I can—"

The angel spoke some more.

"Bet," said Oykib.

"What?" said Chveya.

"The word is *bet*. The word for *father*."

When the angel took his wings from around her, Luet sat back on her heels and looked him in the eye. "Poto," she said, pointing to him. "Bet." Then she pointed to herself. "Luet," she said.

"What's she saying?" asked Poto. "I think she's telling me her name, but I don't know what the sound is, it's so strange."

"Oo-et," said pTo.

"No, there's something first. Not a devil sound, either, just a kind of twisting of the music. Woo-et. Yoo-et."

"Listen to him trying to say your name," said Oykib. "I don't think they have an L sound in their language."

"Wuet is close enough," said Luet. She nodded, agreeing with the name Poto was able to produce. "Wuet," she said, pointing to herself again. Then to him. "Poto. Bet Poto."

"Potobet," the angel corrected her.

"Potobet," she said.

Then he pointed at her again. "Wuetigo," he said.

"Wuetigo," she said, pointing at herself.

As she had done, the angel nodded—but it was an exaggerated, awkward movement for him. Nodding must not be how they showed agreement, but he had learned her way and was using it. "Smart guy," she said.

Then she pointed to the bed, to where the other angel lay. "Po-*to?*" she asked.

"pTo," said Poto.

"pTo," she answered.

"pTobet," Poto added.

"Ah," said Shedemei. "If the one adopts you, the other twin is also your father."

"Twinning must be a big deal in their culture," said Oykib.

From the bed came the voice of the injured one. "Wuetigo," he said. And then, to their surprise, he twisted his tongue around with great effort and said, "Luetigo."

They laughed and clapped their hands in delight. At first the angels seemed startled, afraid. But then, seeing that they were also nodding as they clapped, Poto began to clap his hands together, too.

At that moment Nafai re-entered the room, with Issib and Hushidh behind him. "Did I miss anything?" he asked.

"Not much," said Luet. "Meet my new adopted fathers, Poto and pTo. Only I must call them Potobet and pTobet because I'm their daughter. And they call me Luetigo."

"Luetigo means that you're their aunt," said Oykib. "Remember, you adopted them first. The one on the bed—puh-*to*—"

"pTo," Chveya corrected him.

"The injured guy," said Oykib. "He's very grateful that after you showed them the honor of taking them to be your nephews, you than showed them the even greater honor of letting them be your fathers. It's a big deal to them. And I think it's permanent."

"Yes," said Hushidh. "You see it, too, don't you, Chveya?"

"They've taken you into their lives, Mother," said Chveya. "You're family. Tied in with them like the way you're tied to me. They aren't joking. It's not just a formality."

"They think," said Oykib, "that it means that all the Old Ones will be friends with the—people, the angels—forever."

"Good," said Nafai. "I think we're off to a very good start. Now let's give the two of them time alone. Lock up the medicine, Shedya, and let's get out of here for a few hours."

"He won't like the pain."

"Can you give him something that leaves him conscious?"

"Yes," said Shedemei. "But will his twin let me do it?"

Poto wasn't happy about it. But when Luet bowed before him, both hands out in supplication, he seemed to understand that no harm was meant by the tool in Shedemei's hand. She applied it to pTo's shank, and then they all withdrew from the room.

"They trust us," said pTo.

"Or else we're both prisoners," said Poto.

"Test them, then. Try to leave. They'll let you go, I know it."

"I won't leave until you can leave with me."

"Then we *are* prisoners. But it is my injury that binds us here, and not the Old Ones."

Poto was back on the bed now, examining his otherself's wounds. "pTo," he said, his voice filled with wonder. "The tear in your wing—it's healing."

"That can't be," said pTo. "Tornwing never heals. Tornwing is devil's meat."

"But it *is* true. The sides of the tear have been joined together, and a scar is forming between them, just like on fur skin. The Old Ones have the power to make leather heal."

"Oh, Poto. Who can say now that it was wrong for me to come down to the Old Ones?"

"Boboi can," said Poto wryly.

"What do *you* say?" asked pTo.

"I say that my otherself led the way. I say that without your courage and daring and disobedience, the people would have remained strangers to the Old Ones. But now the Old Ones are our friends. And one of them is our aunt, and we are her fathers."

For Elemak, learning the language of the diggers was like a return to his youth, to the days when he braved the dangers of the road in order to earn his rightful place as his father's heir. In those days he was quick with languages, picking them up from men he hired, from guides, from hosts in the cities he visited. The first few languages took real effort, but after a while he began to find regularities, patterns in them. Bozhotz was like Cilme except that all *B* sounds became *P* sounds, and long vowels became diphthongs with terminal *U*'s. Just set your mouth right, be careful of a few words that didn't mean the same thing in the different languages—*olpoic* does not mean *home* in Bozhotz, so don't ask a man to take you to his olpoic if you don't want to get stabbed—and you could get along. After long enough on the road, it became so easy that, while Elemak took pride in his ability with language, he took little interest in it.

Now he was discredited as his father's heir, he would never be free to roam the world again—and even if he were, there'd be no place worth going—his wife had repudiated him in front of the entire human population of this planet, and all that was left to him was to learn the language of some overgrown underground rodents.

But that was all right. Even learning the rudiments of it from Oykib was all right. After all, he might be Nafai's pet brother, but he wasn't actually Nafai himself. In fact, if things had worked out differently, Oykib might at last have been the brother that Issib would have been, if he hadn't been crippled. Smart, but not smart-mouthed; obedient, but willing to take the initiative; courageous but not foolish; confident but not boastful. He liked Oykib. He wished that he couldn't tell how obviously Oykib distrusted and feared him. Well, there was that bit about throwing him around a little in the library back on the ship. A matter of temper. No use trying to explain to him that it was Nafai that Elemak was angry at, Nafai's betrayal. No use trying to suck up to him, either, explaining that if once, just once, Nafai had shown a sign of being like Oykib, they would have been friends. It was enough to learn the language from him, to help him puzzle out the hard bits, to search for the rules and patterns.

Because there *were* rules and patterns. Nothing from the languages of Harmony applied, of course, because digger language had evolved on its own, without human antecedents. But there were still constants in language. Ways of expressing time so that language could convey past and present and future, cause and effect, motive and intention. Actors and actions forced every language to develop, after a fashion, nouns and verbs. And quite quickly—almost as quickly as when Elemak was young—he caught on to the *feel* of the language, the music of it. When they went to the forest edge to converse with the observers who watched there, Elemak could see that they liked the way he talked, liked the sound of his voice, the fact that one of the gods could handle digger speech.

Elemak could see that Oykib was a little jealous. After all, he had begun as the teacher, and now, after a few weeks, it was Elemak who was teaching, if not the meanings of things, then the grammar and pronunciation, the idiomatic usage. When could Oykib have developed an ear for such things? This was his first foreign language, and Elemak's fiftieth. To Oykib's credit, though, he said nothing but praise for Elemak's ability, and there was no hint of Oykib resisting the change in their relationship or trying to get out of teaching Elemak anymore. If only Nafai had had such self-control. . . .

The time came at last, however, when he felt confident enough to try to communicate with the hostages on the ship. Four of the original nine had already been let go—the soldiers who had been prepared, at the war king's command, to kill the kidnappers. But the four kidnappers remained, and, most important of all, Fusum, the son of the blood king, the man who planned it all. "I want him rehabilitated," said Volemak. "I want him to be the one who carries human culture to the diggers, because he was the one who tried to destroy us. His friendship is the friendship that matters most."

So Elemak would make friends with him. "But I'll do it my way, Father, or not at all."

"What way is that?"

"Fusum is a man of violence and anger, Father," Elemak said.

"So we must teach him another way."

"First we must establish who is the teacher," said

Elemak. "Then we can set about teaching him another way to live."

Volemak had his doubts, but finally he gave in. "No harm to him, though, Elya," said Volemak. "Nothing to make the enmity between him and us worse than it already is."

So Elemak wouldn't hurt him. Not permanently, anyway. And in exchange for that promise, he had a free hand in every other way. A free hand, and no observers.

Except that at first he would only be able to meet with Fusum and the other diggers inside the ship, where he would be watched by the computer they still called the Oversoul, even though he hadn't even a tiny fraction of the power the real Oversoul exercised back on Harmony. Well, let the machine watch. Let it make its reports to Volemak and Issib and Nafai. There'd be no secrets. Besides, Nyef and Issya were busy worrying about their little angel twins. Nasty little creatures. Bones like twigs. But they were so pretty when they flew, and they had made nice-nice with Nafai's bitch so now they were all family. Naturally Nafai was too stupid to realize that it does no good to ally yourself with weakness. The angels were useless. Skymeat, the diggers called them. As far as Elemak could figure, the only reason the angels weren't wiped out by now was that the diggers wanted to keep a steady supply of their favorite dish. Sentient casserole, that's all the angels were, stew on the wing, and *those* were the ones that Nafai and Issib were going to befriend.

Please, Father, *don't* make me stay down here and make friends with the strongest, most courageous and self-willed of the strong, aggressive diggers! Elemak almost laughed out loud, sometimes, thinking about how Father's clever maneuvering to try to create peace was setting up a future in which it was Elemak who was the expert on the only creatures of Earth that were worth knowing, while Nafai's expertise pertained to their worthless, witless, boneless prey.

Elemak told Oykib first. "I'm going to start working with the hostages now. I'll want to meet with you every day and compare what I've learned about the language and culture from them with the things you've learned from the free diggers down here."

Oykib accepted that, and never even hinted that he might want to go with Elemak into the ship to work with the hostages. A good boy, a marvelous boy.

Then Elemak went to Shedemei. "Wake up the four kidnappers first," he said. "I want to practice with them for a while. Learn from them, hear them talking to each other, in circumstances where I'm in control so they can't just take off into the brush when the questions get hard."

"They're very strong," said Shedemei. "Stronger than you might think."

"But I think they're very strong," said Elemak. "So I don't think I'll be surprised."

"I'm just saying you might not want to be alone," she said.

"And I'm just saying that I might not want to give them the slightest hint that I fear them," said Elemak. "I've handled men more dangerous than this—men from cultures I didn't know anything about until they showed me by their actions. It's my field of study. I don't look over your shoulder on the genetics thing, do I?"

Shamed, Shedemei awoke the four kidnappers one at a time. Elemak made it a point to be the first face they saw when they woke up. He also made it a point to handle them roughly and constantly. They felt his grip on their shoulders as they were propelled along the corridors of the ship. By their ankles he pushed each one ahead of him up the ladderway to the deck of the ship that he would use as his school, his negotiating table, his prison.

Four weeks he spent with them, learning all he could. New vocabulary every day, of course, and more and more complex rules of grammar, which he scrupulously shared with Oykib every night when the diggers were locked down. But also he learned the culture, the way things worked in the underground city. How the blood king was the holy one, who gave boys the passage into young manhood. The blood king also marked the feast of the skymeat babies, taking care to assign much credit to the men with good clean kills, and most credit of all to those who brought their prey home alive, crippled but not bleeding. Thus the war king trained the young men in fighting, stalking, killing; chose their officers; led them against prey both large and small; but it was the blood king who conferred all honors, the blood king who chose which men were great and which were nothing.

Mufruzhuuzh had been a great war king, but there were men who said that his mistake was marrying Emeezem. Not that he had a choice, of course. He was forced into it. And it wasn't his fault that because of her dreams and voices she was made deep mother, master of the underground city. But her very strength had weakened him; he deferred to her too much, listened to her when he should have been listening to his men. It left a vacuum.

Fusum's father, Shosseemem, should have filled that vacuum. He should have stepped in and helped the men feel their strength instead of letting Emeezem's dominance leach it away. But Shosseemem was as immobilized by Emeezem's visions as Mufruzhuuzh was. After all, she had said that the Untouched God was coming from the sky, and he came. They saw him among the undergods and demigods, saw how he moved with confidence and power, and they dared not doubt Emeezem's authority even when she counseled weakness and passivity.

Watch, she said! Watch and wait! Learn before you act! Well, they had watched, they had waited, and then one day Fusum came to them and said, "Are you men or women? If you're women, then where are the infants to suckle at your teats? And if you're men, then why are you still waiting and watching, when you have seen where the babies are kept and how ill-watched they are? They have neither tunnels nor nests, so their babies are at ground level all the time. Why haven't we taken them to the blood king?"

"Because the blood king doesn't ask for them. And the war king doesn't command us to act."

"That is because they are ruled by women. But I am a man, and if I have no men to rule over me, then I will rule myself. These are not gods, even if they did come from the sky. Don't they piss out their urine onto the ground just as we do? Don't they eat and breathe and defecate as we do? What is there that is divine about them?"

"These are the lies that Fusum told us," they insisted to Elemak. "He deceived us. If we had known that you truly are gods, as we do now, we would never have heeded him. Forgive us, mighty one, let not the wrath of your shining fathergod strike us down," and so on and so on until Elemak wanted to strangle them for their weakness and disloyalty.

But he showed them no sign that he didn't approve of their abject betrayal of Fusum. He let them believe that he wanted them to profess undying devotion to the shining god—to Nafai, the lying little bastard. And when he had learned from them all that he could learn, he told Volemak that he thought they were ready to come out of the ship to where Shedemei and Oykib, Chveya and Yasai and whoever else was trying to learn digger ways could work with them.

Oh, Volemak and all the others were so *happy* with the work that Elemak had done with them. They were so compliant, those four. So eager to please. So rich with information and wisdom. Their wives were sent for and came up to join the conversations; they all got along so well, the humans and the four who once had stolen a baby out of Elemak's house. "I'm proud of you, Son," said Volemak. "You took those who harmed you and your family, and made friends with them. It was a good work, and well done."

Elemak knew better. It would have been a shameful thing, if it had been sincere. But he knew the truth about the four kidnappers. Disloyal, that's what they were. Cowards. Fusum had bullied them into doing what they did, and now they were eager to let Elemak bully them into doing something else. If Fusum had any sense at all, he would kill them as soon as he came into power.

For Fusum *would* come into power. Of that Elemak was certain, for the more he heard from the kidnappers, the more he felt he knew Fusum, knew how he thought, what he felt, what he wanted, and what he would do to get what he wanted.

What he wanted was simple: power.

And what would he do to get it? Whatever it took.

Elemak knew Fusum, yes, because he *was* Fusum. Or at least he might be Fusum, if this son of the blood king had sense enough to understand the situation and bide his time as Elemak was doing.

So the day came when Shedemei brought Fusum's suspended animation chamber into readiness.

"I'd like to be alone with him when he comes to," said Elemak.

She looked at him steadily. "And why is that?"

"Because I know him," said Elemak. "From what the others have said. This one is dangerous, and if he's to be tamed I have to show him who is master. If you're here, he'll see that there is some other human involved. He won't know that I'm in sole control of every aspect of his life. Do you see?"

"I see," said Shedemei. "But I don't agree."

"But you *will* leave me alone with him," said Elemak.

"I will because Volemak said to let you handle things your way." She turned her back on him and left.

After a while, the lid slid back and Fusum lay before him, blinking his eyes, trying to understand his surroundings. Elemak reached down with one hand, took him by the throat, and raised him up almost to a sitting position, screaming at him in the most fluent and colorful digger language, "You stole my daughter! You were going to eat her! Is that the warrior you are, the kind who can fight babies but you cower in front of men?"

Fusum's first response was not fear but rage. Elemak was glad to see that, how Fusum reached out with arms still weak from the suspended animation drugs and tried to rake Elemak's heart out of his chest. Very good. Not a whiner, are you? "So now you attack me, you fool!" Still gripping him by his throat, Elemak yanked him up and out of the chamber and flung him against the opposite wall.

Ah, yes, this one wasn't a weak and fragile toy like the angel had been. This one rebounded, his body unbroken, his teeth bared and his hands ready for fighting. But he had been weakened and he was groggy. It wasn't a fair fight, which was exactly as Elemak wanted it. This was about authority and dominance, not justice. If it were about justice, Elemak would have strangled him in his sleep.

Fusum leapt at him—a high, springing movement that might have caught Elemak off guard if he hadn't already had the kidnappers demonstrate their fighting technique in mock gladiatorial combats. Just to learn the words for each of the things you do, he had told them. Well, he learned the words. He also figured out the physical reply. And so it was that Fusum found his own weight used against him as he was thrown again, this time down the corridor, so that he landed skidding and sliding until he fetched up against the back wall.

With a growl he leapt back into combat, but his feet made poor purchase on the smooth floor and he could never build up enough momentum to knock Elemak off his feet or even unbalance him for a moment. By the time the drugs wore off he was physically exhausted and humiliated by his endless defeats at Elemak's hands.

Finally, when Fusum could move no more, Elemak seized him by a hind leg and dragged him along the corridor to the central ladder, then carried him up to the room where he would be kept in lockdown when Elemak wasn't with him. During the trip he made no effort to protect the digger's head and body from pain, nor did he permit Fusum to get enough leverage or balance to protect himself. And when he got to the room, he threw Fusum into it, followed him in, shut the door, and stood there laughing.

The diggers didn't laugh the way that humans did, but the message was clearly getting across. Fusum rose onto his hind legs, exposing his pink hairless belly. "Are you going to sacrifice me like a man?" Fusum asked. "Here's my belly, take my heart and entrails and eat them before my eyes—I don't care, I'll eat as much of it myself as I can get away from you!"

Elemak knew brave posturing when he saw it. "I'd sooner eat my own feces than have any of your cowardly blood on my lips."

"So you mean to give me a coward's death, then. Here's my throat. Cut it, I don't care. Life is nothing to me because now that you gods are here, men are nothing. There are no men. Only women and cowards with two tails."

Elemak couldn't help but laugh again. Such defiance! He was such a *boy*, this one. But then, it would have been disappointing if he had reacted any other way. An Obring would have been groveling and pleading for his life. A Vas would have been sullen and silent. A Mebbekew would have been trying to bargain, to strike a deal. But this one, Fusum, he really *was* a man, doing his best to take any sense of joy and triumph out of Elemak's victory.

"Fool," said Elemak in digger language. "I don't want you dead. I want you to be king."

That silenced the digger as nothing else could have.

"Your father is worthless," said Elemak. "Emeezem rules over him. Mufruzhuuzh isn't a war leader, he might as well be wingless skymeat for all the good he does. I thought maybe your conspirators, those four who did the kidnapping, I thought perhaps they were men, but they are nothing, they gladly offered to trade you for their own lives, and blamed you for everything." Elemak mimicked their voices, making them breathy and feminine. "Oh, Fusum *deceived* us. He *made* us. It wasn't our *fault*. If we'd known you were really *gods*."

Fusum hissed in reply, spraying saliva across Elemak's entire side of the room. It was the ultimate gesture of contempt. It would have provoked a deadly battle, if Elemak were a digger.

Elemak only laughed. "If your spittle were poison, it might be worth spending it on me. But there's no point in it. If you intend to save your people, to keep them out of slavery to *us*, then I'm the only hope you've got."

"If you're my hope I have no hope."

"You really are a fool, aren't you. But what can I expect from you? After all, I'm a god, and *you're* an earth-crawling worm."

"I am no worm, and you. . . ."

"Go on, Fusum, my dear little boy, my helpless lovey baby, say the rest of it."

Fusum shook his head.

"You were going to say, 'And you are no god.' Weren't you? Let's be honest with each other."

"I felt your hands on my body," said Fusum. "They were no god-hands."

"Oh really," said Elemak. "No doubt you've had many gods handle you before, so you know how *their* hands feel."

Fusum didn't answer.

"I'll tell you what *my* hands felt like. They felt like

they belonged to a man who is stronger, smarter, faster, and more filled with hate than you."

Fusum studied him. "A man, you say."

"I say a man," said Elemak. "Not a god."

"Stronger, yes," said Fusum. "Today, anyway. Faster today. Smarter—perhaps. Today."

"Forever, Fusum," said Elemak. "In ten thousand years your whole people couldn't learn what I know right now."

"Smarter," said Fusum, conceding the point. "But never filled with more hate than me."

"Do you think not?" said Elemak. "Let's compare stories, shall we?"

They did. And when that first long day together was done, when Elemak at last brought food to Fusum, they were no longer prisoner and guard, or hostage and master, or man and god. They were allies, two men out of power among their own people, but determined to use each other's friendship to gain ascendancy over their rivals among their own people. It would take patience and planning. It would take time. But they *had* time, hadn't they? And patience could be learned one day after another. Elemak was doing it, wasn't he? Fusum could do the same.

"Just remember," Elemak told him, as Fusum splunged noisily into his meal. "If there comes a time whey you think you can do just as well without me, I will see that thought in your mind before you notice it yourself, and when you turn around to put a knife in me, you'll find that my knife is already in you."

Fusum laughed, the wheezy, hissy laugh of a diggerman. "Now I know I can trust you with my life."

"You can," said Elemak. "All I'm telling you is that I will never trust you with *mine*."

When Nafai and Luet, Issib and Hushidh set out for the village of the angels, they carried their tools on their backs—or, in Issib's case, on the chair he had following behind him. Yasai and Oykib had climbed to the chosen spot the week before and placed the relay array, so that Issib could float easily up the pathway into the canyon. But his chair was there in case of bad weather, or in case someone stole some of his floats while he slept.

Their little children they left behind in the care of others. If all went well in their first contact with the village of the angels, they would build houses and then come back down to retrieve the children—along with seeds, extra clothing, and materials for teaching. They hoped to have a working farm in time for the full growing season at that elevation. If all went well.

pTo and Poto led the way up the canyon, quickly rising up into the air from time to time, then circling back down so that the humans could talk to them when they caught up. They were all quite aware that many among the angels had rejected the idea of befriending the humans—the Old Ones. But they had prepared the script that they thought would win them over, or at least win permission for the four humans to dwell among them. And when at last they reached the top of the canyon, the very meadow where pTo's bones had been broken, wing torn, blood spilt, they stopped and played it out.

pTo perched on Nafai's head, and Poto on Luet's. Their feet pressed, lightly but firmly, against the humans' jaws. And their wings unfolded, wrapped around Nafai's and Luet's shoulders, like cloaks, like tents.

"Like nests," said Luet.

Nafai nodded. For although they had never seen an angel nest with their own eyes, they had heard the descriptions pTo and Poto gave them, they had looked at the drawings they made, and finally they dreamed them and awoke from the dreams sure that the Keeper of Earth had shown them the truth. Woven and thatched out of supple twigs and grasses, the nests were really roofs sheltering the branches where the wives and young ones slept, hanging head down, wrapped in the blanket of their own wings.

Somewhere in the branches, in the surrounding trees, they knew the angels were watching them. Judging them.

Issib glided forward, his feet not touching the ground; Hushidh followed him, quietly telling him where the angels were, and which ones did not seem well connected to pTo and Poto. Those were the ones who needed to be won over, of course, and Issib, standing in the air—a trick that no one else, not even Nafai with his cloak, could do—he overawed them, the god visible, the only one who could fly.

"Where is Iguo, when her husband comes home to her?" Issib called out loudly in the language of the angels. He knew his voice would be hard to understand, pitched as low as it was, but he spoke quickly, hoping that the consonants would be enough of a guide to help them grasp his words.

No one emerged from the forest, but that was no surprise, not yet.

"His wing was torn, but now there is no tear in it. Do you think we will harm you, we who can heal the torn wing of a brave explorer?"

Still no one came forward.

"When the angry Old One harmed pTo, it was because he thought it was you, the people, who carried off his baby. We did not yet know the dark underground way of the devils."

Luet had argued against using the angels' word for the diggers, but Issib had insisted that they had to speak to them in language they would understand. "After all, Elya and Okya call the angels *skymeat* when they talk to the diggers, don't they?" Issib had pointed out. Everyone agreed then that *devils* was certainly no worse a word to use than that.

Issib went on addressing the invisible angels. "Now we know that the people do not come down the canyon to steal our children. Instead we see that when one brave man has been stricken down unjustly, his otherself, a man as brave as the first, will come down to care for him and save him if he can."

At last a few of the angels began letting themselves be seen, hopping forward to the leading branches of the trees that surrounded the clearing. Some of them stood upright atop the branches; others hung from them, head downward. It was dizzying to watch them, but Issib went on. "Now we know that the people who might have stopped brave Poto chose to let him come. These are the people who hoped for friendship with us, with the Old Ones who have been brought home by the Keeper of Earth."

There had been some argument about that, too. The angels had no concept of the Keeper of Earth, but Nafai had insisted that the name must be introduced from the beginning. "They'll find out soon enough that we aren't gods," Nafai had said. "Let it never be said we lied to them."

"As we lied to the diggers?" asked Luet mildly.

"We aren't trying to rescue a kidnapped baby from the angels," Nafai pointed out. "We're trying to make friends with people who have only seen us be mindlessly cruel. We're not going to let them see us as gods, even if we *do* get their attention by having Issib do his hovering trick."

So now Issib spoke the name of the Keeper of Earth, using the translation that pTo and Poto had given them, when they finally understood what and who the Keeper was. Or rather, when they understood as much as the humans did, as much as they could explain with their rudimentary mastery of the angels' difficult language.

"The Old Ones ask you to forgive us for our mistake. We did not know you then, but we know you now. Through these two brave and virtuous men we know you. Through the healing of pTo's wing you know us.

Let the four of us dwell among you. But first, let Iguo come forward to join her husband. Come and see, Iguo, that his body is whole, that it is truly pTo that we have brought back to you."

They waited then, doing nothing, saying nothing except for pTo's and Poto's occasional murmurs of reassurance. Patience. Have patience. This is a difficult thing, for them to decide whether to let Iguo come to us.

She came, fluttering awkwardly under the branches of the nearer trees until she reached the clearing. Her awkwardness, they soon saw, was because two infants clung to the fur of her chest, unbalancing her as she flew.

pTo gasped in surprise, while Poto sang in delight. "Sons," he sang. "The wife of the broken one gave him sons while he healed. Now his joy is doubled and doubled again, for he returns to the woman he left as a wife and finds her now as a mother."

pTo leapt from Luet's head and landed before his wife. The two of them spoke softly, rapidly, the music of their voices beautiful together even though none of the humans could make sense of the words they said. As Iguo inspected pTo's body, especially the wing that had once been torn, pTo in his turn examined the two babies that she left in the grass at his feet. They could stand, even if they could not fly, and though their words were halting and babyish, they knew to call him Father, and pTo wept shamelessly to be able to touch them with his fingertips and his tongue, to have them climb up his body and frolic under the canopy of his wings.

At last Iguo turned back to the waiting angels. "What cannot be healed has been healed," she said. "What was lost forever has been found. Therefore let that which cannot be forgiven be forgiven, and let friendship bind the guests who have come to us, weave them into our hearts and our families, our nests and our trees."

It was the formal proposal that pTo and Poto had

primed them to wait for. And now came the vote. Only a few dropped out of the trees to the ground to show their displeasure or their misgivings. And when the voting was finished, all those who had said yes by remaining in the trees now took flight, rising over the clearing, swarming and frolicking and singing, then darting down, a few at a time, to touch the humans, to see them with hands and feet as well as with their eyes, to hear their voices as they struggled with the difficult language.

"Dapai," they called Nafai, because they could not pronounce the nasal and fricative of his name. "Quet," they called Luet, now using the deep guttural plosive as their substitute for the unpronounceable *L*. "Ittib" was Issib, and "Kucheed" was Hushidh. pTo had complained that the Old Ones seemed to have chosen all their names to make them impossible for the people to say them.

But Dapai, Quet, Ittib, and Kucheed were close enough. The angels had spoken their names and welcomed them. With the chair tagging along behind, they followed the soaring, swarming angels down into the valley that was their home.

THIRTEEN

KILLINGS

Vas meant no harm. He was simply an observant man, and a compassionate one. In the months that had passed since Elemak brutalized that flying nightmare they called an angel and Eiadh repudiated him in front of everybody, Vas noticed that the chill between Elemak and Eiadh seemed not to have thawed. Indeed, as far as he could tell the two of them were not speaking to each other, and Elemak managed to spend almost no time in the same house with his wife. Not that Vas normally kept track of people's comings and goings. It was simply a matter of happening to observe that Elemak was staying in the ship with the digger hostage, learning to hum and hiss when he spoke, and poor Eiadh was without a male companion in her life.

Well, Vas was nearly as lonely. Sevet, his dear wife, who had regularly betrayed him back in Basilica, now had betrayed him again by growing thick-bellied from bearing so many children. Worse, she had none of the bright charm that he had loved back when he had contracted to marry her for a few years. In those days she had been a celebrity, a singer, popular and well-loved. It had been quite a coup for Vas to be the man on her arm.

But she hadn't sung in years. Not since that night when Kokor came home to find her husband Obring bouncing away on Sevet's nubile loins. Koya, acting more out of fitful temper than a sense of justice, lashed out at the person she hated most in all the world, her sister Sevet. The blow took her in the larynx, and Sevet hadn't sung a note since. Not that the damage was physical. She could speak, and not in a monotone, either. And she hummed lullabies to the children as they were born. But singing, her voice full out and strong, that was over. And so, of course, was the fame in whose bright shadow Vas had so reveled. So there was nothing much attractive about Sevet anymore. Unfortunately, however, she was Rasa's daughter and they all got caught up in the nonsense that trapped them into coming out in the desert and so the marriage had not ended even though any spark of love that had once been between them ended on the night she betrayed him with her sister's pathetic miserable stupid loathsome worm of a husband, Obring.

So Vas was as lonely as Eiadh, and for similar reasons—both had discovered that their spouses were moral cretins, incapable of even a spark of human decency. Vas had endured his loveless marriage and even sired three children on the bitch and no one guessed how much he hated even to touch her. And it wasn't just her thickening waist or the loss of their fame-gilt life in Basilica. It was the image of her legs wrapped around Obring's white naked flaccid hairy thighs and knowing that she didn't even do it to betray Vas but rather to spite her vicious untalented little sister Kokor. Vas no doubt didn't even enter into Sevet's thoughts at all as she. . . .

Many years ago, it was many long years ago, and a

hundred years of interstellar flight, not to mention years in the desert and another year, almost, in this new world, but to Vas it was yesterday, perpetually yesterday, and so Vas remembered very clearly the vow he had made when Elemak stopped him from killing Obring and Sevet to redeem his honor and manhood. He had vowed then that someday, perhaps when Elemak was old and feeble and helpless, Vas would put things back in balance. Vas would kill Obring and Sevet and then, the blood still fresh on his hands, he would come to Elemak and Elemak would laugh at him and say, You still remember? For *that*, so long ago, you killed them? And Vas would say to him, Elemak, it wasn't long ago. It was in this lifetime. And so it is in this lifetime that I will restore the balance. Them, for their betrayal. You, for stopping me from taking this vengeance hot. When it's cold, it takes more blood to make it work. Yours now, Elemak. Die at my hands, the way my pride died at yours.

Oh, hadn't he imagined it ten thousand times since then? Over and over again, when Elemak tried to kill Nafai or Volemak and they stopped him, battered him down, humiliated him, Vas had watched them, saying silently, Don't kill him. Save him for me. Ten thousand times he had imagined the way Obring would whimper and plead for mercy, and Sevet would scornfully disdain him, not believing he would kill her until that look of unspeakable surprise as the knife went in—oh, it would have to be a knife, a weapon of the hand, to feel the flesh break under the pressure of the stabbing blade, to feel the steel slide into the blood-lubricated flesh, probing inside until it found the heart and the blood gouted out under his hand, spasming up his arm in the last climax of Sevet's miserable life. . . .

The day will come, thought Vas. But first, why not prepare for it properly? Elemak thought that it was nothing for another man to sleep with my wife. Won't it be right and just, then, as he lies dying, for me to tell him in his last moments of consciousness that, Oh yes, Elemak, my friend, you remember what my wife did to me? Well, your wife did it to you, too, and with me. And Elemak will look into my eyes and know that I am speaking the truth and then he'll realize that I wasn't a passive creature after all, was never the mindless tool he thought I was for so many years.

The only trouble with that dream was Eiadh herself. Even if she wasn't sleeping with Elemak, that didn't mean she'd spare a thought for Vas. He wasn't a fool. He was an observant man, that's all. He knew that this was a time of vulnerability for her. Loneliness. And Vas could be compassionate. He would not come to Eiadh in anger or seeking vengeance on Elemak, no, not at all. He would come to her as a friend, offer a strong arm of comfort, and one thing would lead to another. Vas had read books. He knew this sort of thing happened. Why not to him? Why not with Eiadh, whose waist had *not* thickened despite bearing twice as many children as Sevet? Eiadh, who still sang, not with the power of a famous entertainer like Sevet, but with a lustrous intimacy, a voice that could waken all the longing in a man's soul, ah, yes, Eiadh, I have heard you singing and I have known that someday that voice would moan, that sweet throat would arch backward as your body shuddered in response to mine.

"Yes?" asked Eiadh.

He hadn't even clapped his hands. She must have seen him coming. How awkward. "Eiadh," he said.

"Yes?" she said again.

"May I come in?" asked Vas.

"Is something wrong?" asked Eiadh. He could see her taking mental inventory of her children.

"Not that I know of," said Vas. "Except that I'm concerned about you."

Eiadh looked confused. "Me?"

"Please, may I come in?" he asked.

She laughed but let him through the door. "Of

course, Vas, but I have no idea what you're talking about. Except that I'm tired all the time, but that's the same complaint that everyone else has. If you've come to cut the vegetables for supper, then I'm delighted."

"Do you really need help with the vegetables?" asked Vas.

"No, that was a figure of speech. I'm actually sewing. Volemak insists that we all learn to sew with these awful bone needles. They're so thick that with every stitch they open gaping holes in the fabric but he insists that someday there'll be no more steel ones and so—well, it makes no sense to *me*, not even in the desert did we have to—I'm boring you, aren't I?"

"I'm sorry," said Vas. "Not boring me. But I was listening more to your voice than your words, I hope you'll forgive me. Elemak is a lucky man, to have a wife whose common speech is so like music."

She looked puzzled at the compliment, but then laughed lightly. "I don't think Elemak feels very lucky," she said.

"Then Elemak is a fool," said Vas. "For him to turn away from such goodness and beauty as—"

"Vas, are you trying to seduce me?" asked Eiadh.

Flustered, Vas could only deny it. "No, I can't—did I lead you to think that I—oh, this is embarrassing. I came to *talk*. I've been lonely and I thought perhaps you—but if you think it's not proper for us to be alone in the house here—"

"It's all right," said Eiadh. "I know my virtue is safe with you."

Vas put on his best wry smile. "Everyone's virtue is safe with me, apparently."

"Poor Vas," she said. "You and I have something in common."

"Do we?" he asked. Was it possible she felt toward him as he felt toward her? Perhaps he shouldn't have denied his seductive intent so quickly and emphatically.

"I mean besides the obvious," she said. "It seems

that both of us are fated to play secondary roles in our own autobiographies."

Vas laughed because it seemed that she was waiting for him to laugh. "By which you mean . . ." he said.

"Oh, just that we both seem to be buffeted here and there by the choices that other people make. Why in the world were *we* ever brought aboard a starship, can you think of a reason? Just a matter of chance. Falling in love with the wrong person on the wrong day at the wrong point in history."

"Yes," said Vas. "Now I understand you. But can't two bit players like ourselves nevertheless make our own little plays, on a small stage in the wings, while the famous actors make orotund speeches before the great audience of history? Can't there be some kind of happiness snatched in the darkness, where the only audience is ourselves?"

"I'm not the snatch-in-the-darkness type," said Eiadh. "I married stupidly and I knew it almost at once. So did you, I'm afraid. But that doesn't mean that I'll jeopardize the future of my children, not to mention my own future, for the sake of some kind of consolation or vengeance. I take what happiness I can in the light, out in the open. Loving my children. You have good children yourself, Vas. Take comfort in them."

"The love of my children isn't the love that I hunger for," he said. He dared to be direct with her because he realized that she saw through all his attempts at clever indirection anyway.

"Vas," she said kindly. "I have admired you for so long, because you bear everything with such patience. I no longer have any problem knowing which kind of strength, yours or Elemak's, is the better kind. But part of what I admire is that you are able to bear it all without flinching. Let's not become like they are. Let's not stoop low enough that we finally deserve what they're doing to us."

Vas was not an unobservant man. He noticed right

away that she seemed to be referring to something recent, not ancient history from back in Basilica. She seemed to assume that he already knew something that he did not know. "You will never deserve what Elemak is doing to you," he said, hoping that it would prompt a certain response.

And it did. "You don't deserve what Sevet is doing to you, either," she answered. "You'd think she would have learned her lesson long ago, but some women learn nothing, while others learn everything."

Vas's head spun. He had dwelt so long on the memory of the years-ago betrayal with Obring that it hadn't crossed his mind that Sevet might be taking someone else into her bed. Yet there were many opportunities. When he was out in the fields, taking his turn; when he was standing watch; when he was off those two times with Zdorab, using the ship's launch to explore and map the surrounding country. Sevet might have—but surely even she would not—not a second time, not after she lost so much, lost her voice. . . .

But then, I wasn't the one who took her voice from her, was I? That was Kokor, and then we were out of Basilica by the time Sevet's voice healed. Sevet might know to fear Kokor's temper, but what has ever taught her to fear mine?

The time has come, Vas realized. This time there would be no patience. This time there would be no Elemak to stay his hand. Sevet and Obring would die, and then he would turn to Elemak and rid Eiadh of the burden of that monstrous husband forever. Then, with all impediments out of the way, *then* she would turn to the man who had freed her.

Or not. Who really cared whether anyone loved him or approved of him at all? He wasn't trying to win anyone's love or admiration except his own. He had been too long without it, and it was time to get it back.

"Hard to believe that she could still be taken in by Obring," said Vas. "You'd think she would see through him now, when he's outgrown his boyish charm—as if he ever had any."

She laughed, but there was a puzzled look on her face. Now, what could that mean?

It meant that it wasn't Obring. Sevet was being unfaithful, but not with Obring.

Then he remembered what she said before. About how they had something in common. "I mean besides the obvious," she said. What was the obvious? So obvious that only Vas had missed it. Everyone must know. Everyone.

She must have seen the realization on his face, because it was her turn to look stricken. "Oh, Vas, I thought you knew, I thought that's why you came here, to get even with them. But I wasn't angry, you see, because I don't want him in my bed anyway, so I don't much care where he puts his sweaty body and I thought . . . I don't know why but I just assumed that you had the same attitude but I see that you don't, you didn't know, and I'm so sorry, I. . . ."

He didn't hear her finish because he got up and left her house. Elemak's house.

"Don't do anything foolish, Vas," she said softly. And then, because she knew perfectly well that there was a very good chance he *would* do something foolish, she went in search of help. Volemak had to know that there was a quarrel brewing. He would know how to put a stop to it. Eiadh should have done this long ago. Adultery was a terrible thing in their tiny community— Elemak himself had laid down that law in the desert years before. Eiadh had never complained because she honestly was glad not to have to have him close to her, with those angry hands that had broken a helpless innocent being, those hands that had brutalized and terrorized everyone aboard the ship. Better to sleep alone and dream of the only real man she had ever known. A man who once, when he was a boy, had loved her, or at least longed for her. A man who now didn't so much as look at her with pleasure.

With all her childish longing for Nafai, it had never occurred to her that the reason Vas hadn't complained about Elemak's and Sevet's adultery was because he didn't know. How could he not know? Were men so much more blind than women? Or did he imagine that just because he might have stopped wanting Sevet, her own sexual desires would naturally just wither away?

It was going to be a mess, and somebody was going to be dead at the end of it, she knew that now, because she had never seen Vas with such a look of blank rage in his face before. She had seen Elemak like that, but Elemak was used to having such feelings and restraining them. Vas had no such practice.

On the way to Volemak's house, she passed Mebbekew, who was staking out the hide of a goat that he and a couple of diggers had taken while hunting up in the hills this morning. "What's the hurry?" he asked.

"You might want to come along and help," she said. "Vas just found out about Sevet's adultery and I think he might be dangerous."

From the way Meb's face went pale, Eiadh knew that Sevet had let more than one farmer plow in her field. "Not you," said Eiadh. "He doesn't know about you."

"Who else?" he asked, baffled.

She laughed at him. "Are all the men as stupid as you and Vas? You all think you own the moon, just because you never see anybody else looking at it."

Meb smiled. "So Vas is out to kill Elemak," he said.

"I'm getting Volemak. We've got to put a stop to it."

"Oh, and I'll be right there to help, you can be sure of it. I wouldn't miss this for anything."

But Mebbekew did not follow her to Volemak's house. Instead, still holding the heavy mallet in his hands, he tried to think where Vas might go first. The tool shed, no doubt, to get something to do violence with—Vas wasn't likely to be a bare-hands sort of fighter, not if he had killing on his mind. He knew his limitations. So did Meb. Vas would have something sharp with a long handle. And Meb would have a very large mallet. Vas, being a proud man, would speak to his intended victim, call his name, face him. Meb, having no pride at all, would come up on him from behind. Or lie in wait and take him by ambush. Meb was not ashamed of this. He knew that in an open fight he was no match for a determined enemy. Fighting wasn't a skill he had worked to acquire. He was meant to be an actor and, if there had been a real God and not just this stupid computer, Meb would still be in Basilica on the stage, making a name for himself and finding new women and new friends every night. Instead he was here in this filthy village living in dirt and covered every day with sweat and dust and mud and insect bites, and now there was a very angry husband and, whether the husband knew it or not, Meb was almost certainly the most recent man to sleep with Vas's wife.

He will go to Sevet, of course. He'll go home.

But at Vas's own house there was no one. Sevet was gone. Off with the women. Oh, yes. Teaching, this was her time of day to teach the children, as if reading mattered anymore. What were they going to read? The latest story written by a rat in a hole? But it was saving Sevet's life at the moment, so it wasn't all bad, was it? Sevet was a very grateful lover. And she had acquired some skill during her heyday, so sleeping with her was a welcome relief after Dolya's clinging, cloying, hungry, needy, selfish, clumsy. . . .

Which was not to say that Meb minded sleeping with Dol whenever she wanted. Meb was still a young man, and now that Elemak wasn't policing the adultery law anymore, nobody else seemed to catch on except the adulterers themselves. That was the nice thing about having laws enforced only by those who believed in them—they were not likely to suspect that the laws were being broken because breaking them wouldn't even occur to their innocent little minds.

If Vas couldn't get to Sevet, and if he didn't know about Meb, then he'd certainly go for Elemak. That meant he was heading for the ship, where Elemak would be working with the hostage.

On his way there, though, Meb passed Obring's house and saw that the door stood open, even though Obring would be sleeping late after having kept watch last night and—was it possible? Did Vas harbor resentment against Obring so many years after the fact? Or did Vas imagine that Sevet would ever have slept with Obring again, after that nasty evening when Kokor came in on them? Or was it simply that his wife's new adultery refreshed the memory of the old?

Even if he was safely asleep, Obring would want to see the fun and Meb wouldn't mind having another man with him for safety's sake, even if the man was Obring and therefore unreliable and cowardly. I'm unreliable and cowardly myself, thought Meb, so I can't very well hold it against *him*.

Meb stepped into the house. Obring lay on his bed, eyes wide open, hands spread across the wound in his chest, though it was doubtful he had died from that alone. It was the deep slice across his throat that no doubt finished him off. Very neatly done. The wound in the chest could have been from a pick or an axe. Definitely not a hoe. The throat wound made it definite, though, that it was a bladed weapon. One of the scythes. No. An axe. Edge enough to slice the throat, but powerful enough to crush its way into the chest. Poor Obring. Poor me, if Vas decides to take after me. An axe against a mallet? Perhaps I'd better wait until Father decides what to do, let Nafai go in with his magical cloak and give poor Vas a jolt.

What in the world will they do with a murderer?

Meb heard some loud talking far away, near Volemak's house, but he ignored it and headed swiftly into the ship. Vas is in a hurry, and Elemak is waiting. What deck does he have the digger on? Should have paid more attention. Elemak will be glad if I get there in time to save his life. And if I don't, I might still be able to set up a little ambush for Vas. That'll solve Father's problem very nicely, if the murderer turns up pleasantly dead.

Elemak and Fusum were verbally sparring, arguing back and forth, Elemak speaking the digger language, Fusum doing the best he could with the human words. It was part of the deal they had worked out with each other. Fusum would teach Elemak the subtlest nuances of language if, in the end, Fusum also understood whatever it was the humans said. "If you're not gods," said Fusum, "then your language isn't sacred and it's no sin for me to learn it, right?" And Elemak could only agree.

Fusum had nothing like Elemak's skill or practice at learning languages, however, and he had spent most of the morning being resentful and sullen about the way Elemak rattled off eloquent sentences while Fusum could only stammer his way through the most rudimentary answers. Every now and then he would erupt in a torrent of arguments in his native language, only to fall silent at Elemak's superior smile and return to struggling with the human speech. The sounds they made— like skymeat, half their sounds were. Like animals. Or so Fusum said, whenever he gave up and raged for a few moments.

Elemak enjoyed it all.

Until the moment that Vas appeared in the open doorway, a blood-soaked axe in his hands. This was not in Elemak's plans for today. "What have you been doing with that axe?" asked Elemak. The sorry bastard couldn't have killed Sevet already, could he? She'd be teaching right now—he wouldn't do it in front of the children, would he? And who told him? After all these months, why did they tell him *now*?

"I planned to kill you anyway," said Vas. "Because of how you stopped me from killing Obring and Sevet back all those years ago. I never forgot how you humiliated me, Elemak. But this—sleeping with Sevet. Why didn't you just screw one of the digger women, if Eiadh wasn't letting you into her bed? That's your style, isn't it, Elemak? Rutting with helpless little barbarian animals?"

Elemak spoke in digger language to Fusum. "I don't suppose there's anything you can do to help, is there?"

"Talk so I can understand you!" demanded Vas.

"What, haven't you been studying the diggers' language like a good boy?" asked Elemak.

Meanwhile, Fusum had figured out how to answer Elemak's request in human speech. "I'd like to help you but the crazy man has the axe."

Vas looked at him coldly. "Very good decision, rat boy," he said. "I don't much care whether your brains end up on the floor or not."

"Actually," said Elemak—again in digger language— "he'll kill you as soon as he kills me, and then he'll say that you were the one who hit me with the axe and then he struggled with you and got it away and killed *you* with it."

Fusum glared at him and answered, stubbornly, in human speech so Vas could understand him. "The axe is already bloody. He's already killed somebody outside the ship."

"Who did you kill, Vas?" asked Elemak. "Anyone I know?"

"Obring," said Vas. "I took his throat out. After I smashed into his heart."

"How appropriate. To shatter his heart as he shattered yours." Elemak laughed. Not because he didn't believe Vas would kill him. On the contrary, he was quite prepared to believe that Vas would try, and given the fact that Elemak was in a weak position, sitting on the floor with no particular leverage, there was a good chance Vas would fell him with a blow before he could attempt any kind of response.

"It's funny to you?" asked Vas.

"And sad, of course. Poor Sevet. Once I'm dead, she'll be back to having to make do with your clumsy occasional efforts at lovemaking."

"I'll kill her, too," said Vas.

"And then who? Everybody else, for instance? You're doomed, Vas. You should have been more clever. You should have bided your time."

"I've already bided my time long enough."

"You should have made it look like an accident. Or better yet, you could have made it look as though you tried to *save* my life. Take us one at a time, not all at once with an axe. And you have Obring's blood on your clothes. Very clumsy, Vas. They'll have to kill you for it, you know. Can't very well let a murderer run loose."

"You'll be dead first," said Vas.

"Oh, definitely. That'll make you feel *much* better as they—what, strangle you? Drown you? Maybe Shedemei has some drug that will carry you off painlessly in your sleep. You can dream of me as you croak out your last breath."

"I'm not afraid to die," said Vas.

"That's too bad," said Elemak. "Because I am. Do you know why? I'm afraid there might be a life after death. I'm afraid I might have to go on living, only without this very comfortable body. What if I'm reincarnated? What if I come back with a body like . . . *yours?*"

He said this last with as much loathing as he could muster. It had no effect.

"I'm not going to let you goad me into taking an unconsidered move," said Vas. "I know you're sitting there imagining ways to take the axe away from me before I can smash your head in with it. But why should I aim for your head? There are your legs, spread out like the limbs of a tree. I can chop through a five-centimeter branch with a single blow—think I can do as well with your ankle?"

"No, I don't think you can," said Elemak.

"You think you're quick enough to stop me? From a sitting position, you arrogant fool?"

"I don't have to stop you," said Elemak.

"Good thing," said Vas. "Because you can't."

"But Meb can," said Elemak. "He's standing behind you with a very large mallet, and I think he's planning to drive your head down into your shoulders like a spike."

Vas didn't even bother to turn around. "As long as you're conjuring up demons to frighten me with, why not have it be Nafai? *He's* the only real man around here anyway. I'm not afraid of Meb."

"I quite agree with you," said Elemak. "Meb is only frightening when he's behind you with a mallet. Most of the time he's a worthless little digger turd. But Meb, it won't work. You can't drive his head down into his shoulders, not a soft little head like Vas's. It'll burst open like a melon first. Splash all over the room."

"Don't fantasize about my head," said Vas. "It's your legs that are going to go." He raised the axe above his head.

"If it's any consolation to you," said Elemak, "Meb's been sleeping with Sevet, too."

Vas hesitated, not swinging the axe, not striking the blow.

Elemak went on talking. "Your poor wife is apparently lonely enough to settle for anything that pretends to be male, even Meb, who isn't brave enough to smash you from behind after all. What's the mallet *for*, then, Meb? A cure for rectal itch?"

Meb looked back at him with loathing. Elemak knew that he just *hated* being taunted and manipulated.

"Oh, Meb," said Elemak. "Just swing the damn thing and have done."

So he did. Meb turned out to have a much stronger swing than Elemak had expected. But Elemak *was* right about the splashing. It got really nasty, especially after Vas hit the floor and Meb kept right on pounding on his head with the mallet, three, four, five times, until the head was pulped and bits of brain and bone were spattered all over the room. Of course, as soon as Meb calmed down and could look at what he had done, he threw up, as if somehow Vas's head had exploded all by itself and not because he mashed it. But Elemak didn't much worry about Meb. It was Fusum who fascinated him, as he picked bits of Vas's brains off his naked body and ate them.

"Don't get a taste for that, Fusum," Elemak said in digger language.

"Not much different from peccary brains," said Fusum. "I already *have* a taste for those."

"If you ever harm a human, Fusum, I'll cut you into tiny pieces."

"Even Nafai?" asked Fusum, taunting him.

So Fusum had picked up on the conflicts within the human community—even with Nafai up the canyon most of the time, trying to teach the skymeat how to farm.

"Especially Nafai," said Elemak. "He's mine."

Meb had stopped throwing up. "What were you saying? I heard you mention Nafai."

"Oh, Fusum and I were just saying what a pity it was that the one useful act you will ever perform in your life was wasted on Vas."

"Wasted?" asked Meb. "I killed my friend to save your life and you call it a waste?"

"I would have stopped him before he touched me," said Elemak. He didn't know whether it was true, but he was fairly sure Meb would believe it. "And as for Vas being your friend—I'm not going to weep for you. Not with the smell of Sevet still on you from last night while he was on watch."

"Shows what *you* know," said Meb. "Last night I didn't have time for Sevet. After all these months of pestering, I finally gave in and let Eiadh make love to—"

Meb didn't finish his sentence. He found himself pressed against the wall with the axe handle strangling him.

"I know it's a lie," said Elemak. "But if I ever thought that it was true, you'd end up praying for me to do for you what you did for Vas. A quick finish. It'd be too good for you, Meb."

"I was joking, you ass," said Meb, when he could speak again.

"Don't waste my time with your apologies," said Elemak. "Not when we have to explain Vas's death to the people I can hear coming up the ladderway right now."

"What's to explain?" said Meb. "I saved your life."

"Ah, but why was Vas trying to take it? And why did you so sweetly care?"

"He was trying to kill you because you were humping his wife," said Meb. "And I cared enough to stop him because you're my older brother and I love you."

"Is that your best performance, Meb?" asked Eiadh as she strode down the corridor toward them. "Lucky for you that we left Basilica before you could humiliate yourself by trying to *act* in public." Volemak, Oykib, and Padarok came to the door with her, all carrying tools that would have made pretty convincing weapons if they hadn't been in the hands of such gentle, peace-loving souls. "What's all this mess?" asked Eiadh. "Where's Vas?" Then she saw the body on the floor, the ruined head still crookedly connected to the shoulders. She recoiled. "What have you done?" she whispered to Elemak.

"Actually, *I* did it," said Meb. "Just as he was about to take Elemak's ankle off."

But Eiadh paid no attention to Meb. She looked

Elemak coldly in the eye. "This man is dead because you couldn't live a month without getting *some* woman into bed."

Elemak smiled at her. "Not true. As long as I've been married to you, my love, my bed has never had a woman in it."

"You really are evil," said Eiadh. "You really do love destroying things. And not even great evil, not even that spectacular, world-wrecking kind of evil that epics are written about. No, what's in your heart is just a whiny little wormlike evil."

"Say your worst," said Elemak. "I know you're really just glad I'm still alive."

"The second most terrible thing I ever did in my life," said Eiadh, "was letting you be the father of my poor, innocent children."

"And the worst thing?" said Elemak. "Go ahead and say it—I'm brave, I'm tough. I've got Vas's blood and brains all over me, I can take anything."

Eiadh smiled at him, for she knew she was about to say the most terrible thing he could ever hear. "The worst thing I ever did was not to marry Nafai when I realized he was in love with me back in Rasa's house. I knew my mistake long before I actually married *you*, Elemak. I only went ahead and married you in order to stay close to Nafai. I prayed that all my sons would grow up to be like him, not you. And every time you made love to me, I always pretended it was him. It was all I could do to keep from crying out his name."

"Enough of this," said Volemak. "Terrible things have happened here today, and you're wasting our time with a domestic squabble."

Elemak obediently dropped the discussion and submitted to Volemak's questioning. But he heard what Eiadh had said to him. He heard, and he would remember.

* * *

It was Oykib who got the assignment of traveling up the canyon to tell about the killings. Shedemei could have used the ship's computers to tell Issib through the Index, but Volemak insisted that it had to be done in person. The first thought, then, was to send Chveya to tell her parents, but she was almost ready to be delivered of her firstborn child, and so her husband was chosen instead. He was not grateful. "I don't like leaving here right now," he said. "Not with violence in the air."

"I think the killing is over," said Volemak.

"And if you're wrong?"

"Be practical," said Zdorab. "If Elemak did nothing when he had Obring and Vas to call upon, will he do anything now, when he has only Meb as a grown man to stand beside him? The killing is over."

"The killing will never be over," interrupted Rasa, "if the adultery continues and goes unpunished."

"I would say," said Volemak, "that the penalty for adultery has been clearly demonstrated."

"I would say it hasn't," said Rasa. "I would say that your two oldest sons are adulterers by the words of their own mouths, and that my two daughters stand condemned by the same testimony."

"What would you have me do?" asked Volemak. "Put them to death? Of the sixteen original adults of our expedition, shall we end with six of them dead?"

"Which is worse, Volemak? Six dead now, and the law affirmed? Or two dead, and the law with them?"

"You're a hard one, Mother," said Oykib. "The death penalty for adultery was a measure for the desert, not for here."

"Because there are trees and streams, adultery is less fatal for our community?" asked Rasa. "I thought I raised you to reason better than that, Oykib."

"Enough of this discussion," said Volemak. "Oykib must travel up the canyon to break the news."

"I think he should take Eiadh with him," said Rasa. The others looked at her as if she were insane. "After what she said to Elemak?" asked Oykib. "Do you want to sign her death warrant?"

"Do you think that leaving her down here is any better?" asked Rasa.

"Yes," said Volemak. "For her to go up where Nafai is would be seen by Elemak as proof of some kind of liaison between them, when in fact there has never been any such thing. Rasa, are you determined to make things worse?"

Rasa was furious. "I am determined to make things better five years from now, while you seem determined to make things better for the moment and let the future go hang." She stormed out of the library.

Volemak sighed. "Every leader has his critics," he said. "Usually, though, they don't have to go home to them at night."

"She was right in everything she said," said Shedemei. "But you were also right in everything you decided."

Volemak laughed grimly. "Sometimes, Shedya, there *is* no middle way."

"I'm not taking a middle way. You were right that at this moment you can't decide any other way than the way you have decided. But she was right about the consequences. Sevet and Kokor will go on sleeping with Elemak and Mebbekew and, for all we know, every randy male digger who passes by their houses. Elemak and Mebbekew will go on betraying their wives and then hating the very women they're harming."

"And what am I supposed to be able to do about that?" demanded Volemak.

"Nothing," said Shedemei. "Nothing except watch our social order disintegrate."

"Sometimes you're too much the scientist, Aunt Shedya," said Oykib.

"Not possible," said Shedemei. "And you forget, my own children have to live in the new social order we've created here. When you think about it, this really marks the moment of Elemak's triumph over his father. Despite the oath, despite Elemak's many defeats, he has finally succeeded in undoing all his father's works. This is Elemak's type of society now, because the rest of us haven't the coldness of heart to uphold the law and put him to death."

"That's right," said Volemak. "The rest of us haven't the coldness of heart. Do you?"

"No," said Shedemei immediately. "As I said, your decisions are the only ones that can be made, disastrous as they are. Now let's let Oykib be on his way while the rest of you prepare the bodies for burning. As for me, I have a very messy room to clean up."

Oykib stood up to leave. "I'll go up the mountain, but I don't like leaving Chveya at a time like this."

"I'll be all right," Chveya murmured.

"And what worries me has nothing to do with Elemak and Mebbekew and adultery and all that," said Oykib.

"Oh, what's *your* concern, then?" asked Volemak. "I'm always happy to learn of something new to keep me awake at night."

"Fusum saw Vas die."

"We've never pretended to be immortal," Volemak said.

Oykib shook his head. "Fusum saw Vas die. Someday we'll all agree that that was the worst thing about today's events."

He went home long enough to pack up some hard-crusted bread for the journey. The way up the canyon was a path, now, and was becoming more of a road as they cut out underbrush and used picks and spades to smooth the roughest places. So it was only two hours to the saddle at the top of the canyon, and then another hour through the forest to the village.

It had been transformed in the past few months, as Nafai and the others worked with the angels to teach them ways to make their lives better. Where the angels had known the location of every useful plant within twenty kilometers of their village, they now had felled enough trees to make a field where yams and manioc, melons and maize could thrive in open sunlight. Where the angels had kept herbivores from their protected plants and predators from their houses by building traps along every path and track at the perimeter of their territory, they now had a fence around their fields, and their turkeys and goats were corralled at night. Already the angels could grow food enough to feed twice their present population, and most of the surplus could be stored.

But the agricultural revolution was not the only one. The angels seemed to want to emulate the humans in every way. Many of them now had built houses on the ground, the way the humans did, even though they hadn't the strength to build as sturdily and the first strong wind would tear the houses away. They knew this, too, and during bad weather continued to sleep hanging from branches in the trees. But it was important to them that they *have* a house in the human style, and Nafai had long since given up trying to persuade them of the uselessness of it.

Oykib found Nyef and Hushidh working with the angel toolmakers.

"What's wrong?" Hushidh said instantly. "Who is dead?"

"How did you know?" asked Oykib.

"Your face," she said. "Your fear to speak to us."

"Is it Father?" asked Nafai. And that was the most pertinent question—when Volemak died, everything would change.

"Not Father," said Oykib. "Vas killed Obring— vengeance for what happened between him and Sevet back in Basilica, apparently. And when he went to kill Elemak for more current betrayals, Meb was able to slip up behind him and kill him."

"Elemak didn't do any killing?"

"He might have, but he didn't get the chance," said Oykib. "Another thing. Fusum was watching when Mebbekew killed Vas. It happened right in front of him. With the mallet Meb had been using to stake out hides."

"And how did Vas kill Obring?"

"An axe to the chest and then through the throat," said Oykib. "Does it matter how?"

"It matters what the diggers have learned about how to kill us," said Nafai.

Oykib smiled grimly. "My own thoughts exactly."

"That's not all you came to tell us, though, is it," said Hushidh.

"No," said Oykib. And then he told them what Eiadh had said to Elemak, taunting him that she had been in love with Nafai all through her marriage to Elemak, that she wanted her sons to grow up to be like Nafai.

"Why didn't she save time and just slit my throat?" said Nafai.

"And then her own," said Hushidh. "As far as Elemak is concerned, the two of you might as well have committed adultery. And no one hates other people's adultery like an adulterer."

"Funny, isn't it," said Nafai, "how few years it took for us to change from the way it was at Basilica. Back there, Eiadh would simply not have renewed Elemak, and Sevet and Kokor would be on their sixth or tenth husbands since then, and nobody would have died for it."

"Do you think that it was more civilized?" asked Hushidh. "The same rages were just beneath the surface, the same hunger for loyalty from a husband or wife. Obring didn't die for something he did in the wild. He died for what he did back there in the city."

"But it wasn't in the city that he died," said Nafai. "Never mind. If the diggers know that humans can be killed, we'd better make sure we tell the story to the angels as well. Fortunately I've never had to play god up here, so it'll come to them as less of a shock. We'll come down the mountain for the funeral, of course. And we'll bring some angels with us. They need to see a human body going into the flames."

"Maybe that's the wrong lesson to teach them," said Hushidh.

"Why?" asked Nafai. "Do you think some angels are secretly wishing to slaughter all the humans?"

"Not at all," said Hushidh. "But I think some angels are counting on us to keep the diggers from coming up against them and stealing their infants to eat them and make pedestals out of their bones. It won't encourage them to see that we can be broken and killed."

"Especially not the way Vas died," said Oykib. Whereupon they insisted that he describe how it happened, and then clearly wished that he had not.

"Just as well to have the angels know our weakness," said Nafai. "It's their own strength they have to trust in, that and the care and wisdom of the Keeper of Earth."

"The Keeper?" asked Oykib. "They know about him?"

"Not by that name, not till we taught them," said Nafai. "But there have always been dreamers among them. And Luet has found several who respond well to the trances that she used as Waterseer in Basilica. The Keeper speaks to them. And I'm working on trying to find weapons they can use that will enable them to stand against the diggers, if it ever comes to war."

"Don't you think we'll be able to keep them at peace with each other?" asked Oykib.

"I don't think we'll be able to keep at peace with ourselves," said Nafai. "We have the first two deaths as evidence."

"Is it very awful of me," said Hushidh, "that I don't think I'm going to miss Obring at all?"

"It would be more surprising if you did," said Nafai. "But Vas wanted to be a good man, I think."

Oykib scoffed. "If he had wanted to be, he would have, Nafai. People are what they want to be."

"What an uncharitable view," said Hushidh. "Why, you'd think, from the way you talk, that people were responsible for their own behavior."

"And they're not?" asked Oykib.

"Haven't you ever seen a three-year-old when he makes a foolish blunder? He looks at whatever child or adult is nearby and screams at him, 'Look what you made me do!' That's the moral universe that Vas and Obring always lived in, and Sevet and Kokor, too."

At the funeral, Kokor kept watching Sevet furtively, matching her tear for tear and sigh for sigh. I'm not going to let the old bitch get any more mileage out of widowhood than me, thought Kokor. After all, it was *her* husband who killed mine. She drove him to it, that's what, because she was so clumsy she got found out. *I* slept with Elemak even back before the voyage to Earth, and nobody ever knew. Sevet has a habit of getting caught in her little liaisons. Of course, maybe she wants to. Maybe that's how she gets her kicks, watching people go into frenzies of misery and rage over what she did and who she did it with.

It certainly worked on me, back in Basilica. She certainly got me angry, didn't she? And then got to play the victim for years and years, never singing again even though her voice came back just *fine* within the first year. Always holding her musical silence over my head when Mother would look at her and reminisce about how she once sang the "Love Dream of Sogliadatai" or the "Death of the Poisoned Sparrow."

The funeral pyres were set alight, and the angels around them started making the most awful whining sort of sound. Nasty little creatures. What did *they* know of grief?

But their singing—if that's what it was—gave Kokor an idea, and she acted on it at once. The "Death of the Poisoned Sparrow" had been Sevet's signature song, and it would fit beautifully right at this moment, even though it was not actually about a funeral, but rather about the end of a beautiful but impossible love affair. And one of the best arrangements of the song had been a duet between Sevet and a flute. Kokor had listened to it over and over, had coveted the song with all her heart, but had never dared to sing it in public for the obvious reason that it would make it look as though she envied her sister and was trying to compete with her. Still, she knew every note of it. And, as she thought about it for a moment, she realized that she also remembered every note of the flute part.

So that is what she began to sing, wordlessly, letting her voice rise and soar in the notes of the flute. She couldn't sing it quite as high as the flute had played, of course, but then, Sevet no doubt couldn't sing as high as she had sung back when she was a girl, especially without practice. Once Kokor started singing, she did not dare even steal a glance at Sevet, or it would look like she was trying to get Sevet to do something instead of simply expressing the heartbreak she felt as she watched her husband's body going up in flame.

She sang the entire flute part and Sevet didn't join in. But Kokor could also tell from the stillness of the others—even the angels fell silent to hear her—that she had chosen to do the right thing this time, that for once the others approved of and even appreciated her. And when she began the flute part again at the beginning, Sevet's voice came out at last, singing the melody. Now the strangeness of the melody Kokor had sung began to make sense as harmony to Sevet's voice, and the words Sevet sang brought tears to people's eyes as the death of such worthless men as Obring and Vas never would have. People cried when she sang it in theaters, when nobody had died—how could they help but sob their little hearts out here, with the smell of cooking meat in their nostrils and Obring's and Vas's littlest children crying their poor little eyes out because their papas were such worthless murdering fornicating pieces of digger poo. Kokor loved the way her voice sounded with Sevet's. For Sevet's had changed, had grown richer and more mature, but Kokor's had not, had retained the flutelike simplicity and purity of youth. Kokor had no need to try to sound like Sevet now, nor Sevet to resent the similarity between them. They made different sounds, but they could be beautiful together nonetheless.

When the song ended, the appropriate action was obvious, and Sevet did not fail her. They both extended their arms at once, and weeping copiously they fell into each other's embrace. Kokor enjoyed hearing the collective sigh of the watching humans. The sisters, reconciled at last! She could imagine Mother reaching down and squeezing Volemak's hand, and Volemak whispering to her later, If only my sons could make peace as your daughters have.

While they clung to each other in their embrace of grief and forgiveness, Sevet whispered in Kokor's ear. "I'm going to be Elemak's mistress now, little sister, so don't try to stop me."

To which Kokor whispered in reply, "So am I. He's cocksman enough for the two of us, don't you think?"

"Share and share alike?" murmured Sevet.

"I'll bet I bear him a baby before you do," whispered Kokor. Of course she had no intention of bearing him a child at all, but it would be lovely if Sevet did, ruining her thick body even more than having three children already had. Let the poor bitch think we're competing to give birth to Elya's bastards—I'll just let her "win" and keep the real victory, which is my youthful body despite having let Obring sire five babies on me. If all five were really his.

They broke the embrace and pulled apart a little.

"Oh, Kokor," said Sevet. "My sister." Then she burst into tears again.

Damn. That would be hard to top.

Kokor reached out and took a tear from Sevet's cheek, then held it up as a glistening patch of wetness on her fingertip. "I will never cause you to shed another one of these, my beloved Sevya."

The sigh from the others was all the applause Kokor needed. I win again, Sevet. You're simply no match for me.

Fusum learned two things from the killing of Obring and Vas.

First, he learned that the humans were, in fact, mortal, and could be killed if enough force were applied using a sufficient weapon in the right way. He had no immediate plans to use this information, but he intended to devote a great deal of thought to it over the months and years to come.

Second, he learned that killing was a powerful device that should not be wasted. You must kill the right person, and at the right time, and always in order to achieve an important purpose. That was why, when Fusum was finally judged to be rehabilitated and returned to his people, he made it a point to become a friend and companion to Nen. As the eldest and most gifted son of Emeezem and Mufruzhuuzh, the deep mother and the war king, Nen was the bright golden hope of the next generation. He spoke the human language almost as fluently as Fusum himself, having learned it through close association with Oykib, and when Emeezem and Mufruzhuuzh coerced Fusum's own father, the blood king Shosseemem, to join them in declaring a ban on the kidnapping and eating of skymeat infants, it was Nen who came forward and swept away the pedestal of bones on which the Untouched God had rested. It was Nen who cried out, "Let friendship everlasting stand between our people and the people of the sky." Oh, Fusum had cheered along with everyone else that day. And he worked hard to win a place at Nen's side, as his most trusted friend.

Then one day they were out hunting together, carrying the traditional stone-tipped spear in one hand, knotty club in the other. They were stalking a peccary through the undergrowth, near enough to hear it grunting now and then, when suddenly Fusum saw his opportunity. A panther, too, was stalking the peccary, but as everyone knew, panthers were only too happy to make a meal of whatever meat was at hand. It had to be living meat, though, so when Fusum struck, he didn't strike hard enough to kill—or at least he hoped not. Nen dropped like a rock, but then almost immediately lifted himself up on his elbows, moaning. Fusum didn't even need to throw a stone to attract the panther's attention. It leapt on Nen and tore his throat out in a moment. Then Fusum charged, driving his spear into the panther's side under the ribs, finding its heart immediately. I *am* good at this, thought Fusum. Then he clubbed the panther in the head, over and over, so that no one would think to look for traces of Nen's blood and hair and scent on the club.

Minutes later, he came staggering and weeping into the digger city, crying out his grief at the death of his friend Nen, blaming himself for having failed the golden one, the beautiful one. "No man ever had a worse friend than me!" he cried. "Kill me, I beg you! I don't want to live with Nen's death on my hands." But when they found the scene, the men of the city cleared Fusum of any culpability, and the story of his great grief at the death of his beloved friend swept through the city. Some of Nen's glory thus lingered with Fusum, and many began to look to him as the hope of the future, now that Nen was gone.

FOURTEEN

WORDS

Nafai wasn't sure whether the dream came from the Keeper, the Oversoul, or his own concerns. Perhaps it was simply the fact that he realized that in all their teaching of the angels and the diggers, in all their teaching of their own children, the one thing they couldn't give them was a compelling reason to learn how to read and write.

What was it good for? Did it make the crops grow better? Did it keep the flocks in their pens at night? Did it ward off predators? Did it keep children from getting sick?

When he talked to Luet about it, she didn't seem worried. "Nyef, we're not recreating Basilica here. We can't. The next generation is going to lack so many things. We have to teach them the herbs that can heal infections or cure different diseases. We have to teach them the principles of sanitation, so they don't foul their own water supply. We have to—"

"We have to keep them human."

"It isn't writing that makes us human."

"Isn't it?" asked Nafai. "Then what is it?"

"The diggers and angels are sentient. They're *people*. And they don't read and write."

It was unanswerable, what she said, and the way she said it made it clear she didn't think it a problem worth worrying about. Yet hadn't they taught their own children how to read and write? Hadn't they risked destruction on the journey, teaching them how to use the computers, letting them pore over millions of volumes of human learning and history and it would all be extinguished in the next generation.

And the next generation was already here. In the five years since landfall, Chveya's and Oykib's generation had all started families. Their children were growing up and when they turned six or seven or eight would there even *be* a school for them? No, they would set to work learning the skills of survival. Side by side with diggers and angels in the fields, out gathering in the forest, building fences and walls, gleaning and weeding, planting and harvesting, tanning hides and tooling leather, carding wool and spinning it into yarn—where in all this activity was there a moment when they needed to read something? On the ship they had been preparing for a new life, learning in advance what they would need to know for subsistence in a new world. Now they were in that world, and the new generation learned from the adults, not from books.

And that was fine. No harm was done. The things that mattered for survival were taught. What else was needed?

Yet Nafai couldn't shake his uneasiness about it. In all the forty million years of history on Harmony, human beings could read and write. Languages drifted and changed over centuries and across kilometers. But there was writing. The past could be recovered. Learned from. It was writing that allowed a community to hold its memory outside the individuals who happened to be alive and present at the moment.

How long till I'm forgotten, I and Luet and Father and Mother and all of us?

Then he laughed at himself for the vanity of wanting

people to go to the trouble of reading and writing, just so they could remember that he had once lived. In ten generations it wouldn't matter at all.

It was in the beginning of the sixth year that he had the dream. He saw a man leading a great nation of angels and humans, with farms spreading on either side of a great river, kilometer after kilometer, as far as the eye could see. Angels flew here and there, and goats and dogs drew carts and sledges along roads. Boats trafficked up and down the river, some of them with diggers, some with angels as their crew. And here and there, in towers rising high above the tallest trees, watchmen kept the perimeter in view, so that no enemy could take them unaware.

The man who led this great nation was weary and afraid. Enemies were coming to beset them on every side, and within the nation factions threatened to tear apart the fabric of the community. Towns that had once been independent forgot that in those days they had also been hungry. People whose ancestors had once been rulers forgot that those ancestors had also been killed by enemies and their people only survived at all because they came under the protection of this great nation. People who longed for wealth were getting it by any means possible, plotting and cheating, bullying and sometimes even killing to get rivals out of the way. It was a beautiful land, but the struggle to keep it so seemed harder every year and the man despaired.

In his loneliness and fear, he went into his small house and opened a box he kept hidden inside a jar of dried corn. Inside the box he found a thick pile of metal sheets, bound together on one side with metal rings. It was a book, Nafai realized, for language had been inscribed in the metal, and the man opened it and began to turn the pages.

Without understanding how, Nafai knew what the words contained, what the man was seeing in his mind's eye as he read. The man was reading the story of Volemak seeing a pillar of fire on a rock in the desert and coming home to Basilica to give warning that the city was going to be destroyed. The story of Nafai and his brothers going back to the city to fetch the Index. The man saw Nafai standing over the dead body of Gaballufix and he nodded. Sometimes those who care for a whole community must act in a way that harms the individual. For a good man it never becomes easy and he avoids it when he can; but when the people need him to be harsh, he will be harsh indeed, and he won't shrink from it, he'll do it with his own hand and let it be known what he does.

From me he learned this, thought Nafai, and then he realized that he was the one who made the book and wrote in it the story of his life, of the life and acts of all the people in this community, their evil deeds and their heroic ones, their times of doubt and their astonishing achievements. And this man, this leader, this king, he looked into the book and found stories in it, tales that made clear to him what he must do, wisdom that stiffened his resolve, love that taught him compassion, hopes that led to noble actions even when the hopes themselves were unfulfilled.

Nafai awoke and thought, This dream was so clear, it must have come from the Oversoul. Or perhaps the Keeper of Earth.

And then he thought, This dream so exactly fits my own desire to keep reading and writing alive among this people that it could just as easily have come out of my own longings.

But then, where did his longings come from? Why did he want so much to preserve written language among his descendants? Couldn't those very desires have come from the Keeper?

No, he thought. Those desires came from my memory of standing over the corpse of Gaballufix. I killed him in order to get the Index from him. And what was the Index for? It was my access—*our* access—to the vast store of learning in the starship that brought us here. It was the key to all that the Oversoul knew. What would it have meant to us if none of us could read and write? To an illiterate people, the Index would be worthless and therefore no man should have had to die so Nafai could get it. I dream the dream that justifies my own actions to myself.

Yet even as he dismissed the dream, he knew that he would act on it.

Explaining nothing, he took his leave from Volemak, from Luet, and took the ship's launch out to where the survey maps showed that gold could be found. It was a rich vein, one brought to the surface of the earth through the great foldings and upheavals that had taken place in the last forty million years. Nafai was armed with the metal tools from the ship's store, and in two days of solitary labor he had several pounds of solid gold taken from the exposed vein in the mountainside. He spent a day refining it. Then he pounded it, unalloyed, into flat, smooth sheets, using the imperturbable metal surface of the launch as his anvil. The metal was very thin, but piled together it was also very heavy. It took him three days to make the sheets of gold, and during that time he only occasionally paused to gather the most obvious food that came easily to hand. He was hungry, but the work he was doing mattered more to him than food.

He found, in his first experiments, that the sweeping curves of the alphabet that had been used for so many millennia on Harmony simply did not work well when pressed by hand into the gold. He had to find squarer forms for the letters and yet still keep them different from each other. Also, some of the spellings were too complex and used too many letters to represent the sounds. So he changed them, inventing five new letters to represent sounds that had previously required two letters each. The result was a definite compression of the written language, and as he wrote, he compressed it even more, using only a couple of letters to stand for the most common words.

How do I dare to change the language like this? he asked himself. Who in the world could understand this?

Obviously, the only people who could read it easily would be people that he taught to read and write, and so they would know what his symbols meant. Perhaps just as important, though, anyone who had learned to read the script he used for pressing language into the gold would easily decode most of the letters used in the language of Harmony—the language of the ship's computer library. At least until the language changed, he would not have cut his descendants off from their literary heritage, if ever the chance came for them to recover it.

Gold. How appropriate, for such a treasure as he hoped this book would be. But it wasn't for the value of the gold as a medium of exchange that he chose it. Rather he used it for the same reasons that gold had been used for coinage in most cultures through most of human history. It was soft. It could be shaped. Yet it was not so soft that it couldn't hold its shape. And it didn't corrode or corrupt, tarnish or degrade in any way. Long after Nafai was dead, the letters would still exist on the pages of his metal book.

He put the gold leaves into the launch, along with all the leftover gold, and flew home. When he returned the launch to the ship, he explained nothing about where he had gone or what he had done. He didn't mean to deceive anyone, and it wasn't that he had no trust in Father or Mother, in Luet or anyone else. It's just that he felt shy about telling anyone. They would think it was silly of him.

No, that wasn't it. That wasn't it at all, he knew. As he sat there working by lamplight, the wick flickering as it floated on the melted fat in the clay cup, he could feel the power in what he was doing. I am projecting myself and my view of all that has happened to us into the future. Someday the only version of these events that anyone will know will be the one I wrote. Our descendants will see us through my eyes and no other. So it is I who will live in their memories. I who will whisper in the ear

of that great leader—if he ever exists, if this book sur-
vives, if there is really anything of wisdom in it.

It is the writing on these gold pages that makes me
immortal. When everyone else is dead, I will be alive
and shining. That's why I keep this secret. That's why
I hold it for myself. It's a heartless, egotistical thing for
me to do.

<No it isn't.>

I know my own heart. I'm not ashamed to admit that
my motives are impure.

<It's a generous thing you're doing. Giving your children of ten and twenty generations from now a knowledge of their past. A knowledge of why humans and
diggers and angels dwell together in this place.>

What if Elemak were writing this book? It would be
a different thing entirely, wouldn't it?

<It would be filled with lies.>

A storyteller can't help but distort every tale he tells.
Without even knowing it, I'm also lying by giving events
the shape that makes sense to me. Anyone else would
write it differently. My way isn't necessarily the best.

<What you are creating will be treated as a sacred ob-
ject. A token of authority, passed down from generation
to generation. Like the Index. It lasted forty million
years.>

Nafai laughed silently, careful not to waken Luet or
their last three little ones, born since they came up the
canyon to live here with the angels, or the twins, who
slept in the loft, dreaming of new pranks to play and ac-
cidents to stumble into in order to cause their parents
to live in perpetual terror.

<You laugh, but you know that I'm telling you the
truth.>

So, Oversoul, my dear old friend, was it you that sent
me my dream?

<No.>

The Keeper, then?

<You know that I don't know what the Keeper does and doesn't do.>

So it could be just the private fancy of a man who is reaching middle age and feels his future death breathing down his neck.

<And if it *is* nothing more than that, does that change the fact that it's a wise thing to do? A great gift to give to the future?>

I'll have to teach somebody to read my script. I'll have to give it to somebody to pass along into the future.

<You'll find someone. Perhaps one who's little now. It will be clear to you who should have the book, when the time comes.>

I'm telling everything. If they read this, my children will say, Why didn't he just shut up? Why didn't he ever leave well enough alone? My mistakes will be out in the open and they'll despise me.

<What if they do? You'll be dead.>

And if Elemak ever reads this, he'll kill me and destroy the book. You know that.

<I'd suggest that you not show it to him.>

Or anyone. The hours I spend on this—are they wasted?

<Are they?>

Nafai had no answer. Except that he kept on writing. Writing and writing, his script getting ever tinier and more compact, fitting more and more words onto the pages. His tale getting more and more spare.

What did he write? At first it was a very personal story, an account as best he remembered it of all their days in Basilica, of the journey through the desert, of the finding of the starport at Vusadka. But when the story reached Earth, it became far more general. The things they had learned about diggers and angels were set down in the order in which they discovered them or figured them out. The results of Zdorab's journeys in the ship's launch, mapping and bringing back plant and animal samples for Shedemei to study. The culture of the angels and diggers, and the way they responded to the cultural innovations the humans brought to them. The political machinations as the digger and angel communities struggled to deal with the destruction of their gods and the shattering of their equilibrium.

For the old gods were being destroyed. One cannot live with gods and still believe in them, Nafai decided. And even though after the early times of crisis Nafai had explained to them all that he and Volemak had never been gods, that their powers were all the result of technology and learning, that not a one of them had the power to duplicate even the least of the complicated machines in the starship—even though he explained this, he could sense that many resented knowing it. Emeezem most of all. When he told her that as far as he could tell the clay figure that she had worshipped and treasured almost her entire life was just a remarkably fine sculpture by a talented angel named Kiti, she didn't thank him. She acted as if he had slapped her face. "Should I break the statue then?" she demanded bitterly.

"Break something as finely wrought as that?" asked Nafai. "Break something that helped make you into the noble ruler that you are?"

But she was not to be mollified with praise; it sounded like flattery to her now, even though it was truthful and sincere. Nafai's rejection of her worship was the cruelest blow. He could see her wither up; even though she lived on and continued to lead her people with wisdom and firmness, the heart had gone out of her. It was not just faith but also hope that she had lost.

The angels had it easier. Since Elemak's rage had been their first exposure to humans, it was a relief to them to learn that none of them were gods. But the humans knew so many secrets and their wisdom, put to work for the angels, saved so many lives and improved everyone's health so much that there was still an element of worship in their relationship, and therefore a bit—or perhaps a lot—of disappointment and disillusion when some human failed at a task, gave bad advice, or predicted an outcome and was proven wrong.

As he was writing about all of this, Nafai realized that what the people needed, diggers and angels and humans alike, was someone outside themselves in whom their hopes of wisdom and rightness could be invested. They had to begin to think of the Keeper of Earth as the only one who would never be wrong.

Not that Nafai was altogether sure of this himself. He never heard the voice of the Keeper with the kind of clarity with which the Oversoul spoke to him. In fact he was never quite sure whether he heard the voice or saw the dreams of the Keeper of Earth at all. Nor did he know what the Keeper might be. That he was real enough was obvious—there was no other explanation of the statue whose face looked exactly like Nafai, carved back when Nafai was just getting on the starship to come to Earth. Nor was there any other explanation of the dreams they had back on Harmony, when so many of them saw diggers and angels when the Oversoul himself had no notion that these were the creatures that populated Earth. Yet the dreams were always ambiguous, and tinged with the dreamer's own hopes and fears and memories, so that it was never certain where the Keeper's message left off and self-deception began.

Yet, inadequate as Nafai's understanding of the Keeper of Earth might be, he knew that belief in the Keeper would fulfill a vital social function. The Keeper would be the highest authority, the one who was never wrong, the repository of Truth. When it became clear that even the wisest of humans knew very little, really; when it became plain that the most marvelous of miracles was in fact the result of working with a machine or exploiting a bit of ordinary knowledge; then there would still be no disillusionment because, after all, everyone knew that humans, angels, and diggers were all equal in the eyes of the Keeper of Earth, and all equally ignorant and weak and unwise compared to him.

Nafai explained these thoughts to Luet and she agreed. She began teaching the angel women about the Keeper of Earth, and adapting their ancient lore about various gods into a coherent story that replaced all the good gods with various aspects of the Keeper. With the angel men, Nafai was a bit more brutal, sweeping all the old gods away and keeping only a few of their ancient legends. Not that the old legends would die, of course—but he wanted them to start with a pure core of knowledge about the Keeper, even though the knowledge was really very small.

Then Nafai and Luet took Oykib and Chveya into their confidence, and soon Oykib was teaching the digger men and Chveya the digger women about the Keeper of Earth. They, too, adapted what the people already believed; they, too, were candid about how little they personally knew about the Keeper. But they did know this much: The Keeper wanted humans, diggers, and angels to live together in peace.

The trouble was that as the old religion faded, as fewer and fewer diggers took part in the annual raid to steal statues from the mating angels, the diggers' birthrate also seemed to fall off—even as the angels prospered, their population blooming at an almost alarming rate. Whispers began among the diggers that the new religion of the Keeper of Earth was really part of a conspiracy to destroy the diggers so that angels and humans could divide the world between them. Not that many people believed these tales, but enough did that it was a worry. There were those who would exploit such rumors. And, in fact, when Nafai began to hear that it wasn't all the humans but rather just Nafai and those who followed him who were plotting to destroy the diggers, he knew that someone was already seeking to turn these fears to his advantage.

In the meantime, though, the digger birthrate continued falling off, even though the nutrition levels were higher and higher all the time. And the angels had to expand constantly, burning more patches of forest to put more land under cultivation. All those twins, and none of them getting murdered now in infancy; all those healthy adults, and none of them getting culled by the marauding diggers.

They had been on Earth for twelve years when Shedemei called the adult humans together for a meeting. She had finally solved the mysteries, she said. But now there were some new mysteries, and some decisions to be made.

"We've been meddling," said Shedemei. "As you're all aware, the falling birthrate among the diggers is causing some serious worries among them."

"We're worried too," said Volemak.

"Yes, well, now I know why it's happening. We did it. We're doing it."

They waited. Finally Mebbekew said, "I didn't know you had such a flair for the dramatic, Shedya. How long do we wait for the other shoe to drop?"

"This is only the first shoe," she said. "The other shoe comes after." There was some nervous laughter. "The problem is, you see, that we've stopped them from believing in their gods. They aren't worshipping anymore. They aren't even stealing fresh statues from the angels. And that's why they aren't having any babies."

"You're telling us," said Elemak, laughing, "that their religion is *true*?"

"In a word, yes," said Shedemei. "We have a dozen years' worth of close observation of the local digger and angel tribes. Zdorab and I have also made some sampling visits to other digger and angel settlements, and we feel reasonably confident that we have uncovered a universal pattern. For one thing, there's no such thing as an angel village without a digger city nearby, nor a digger city without an angel village within a few hours' walk. This is not an accident. The diggers can't survive without the angels. Specifically, the diggers can't reproduce without worshipping the statues that the angel males create as part of their mating ritual."

"Do I get the impression that the cause is biological rather than theological?" asked Rasa.

"Of course, though it's hard to look at little clay statues and see a biological mechanism," said Shedemei. "It was Zdorab who first pointed out to me that what matters, biologically, may not be the artistry involved in the creation of the statues. It's the spit. The angel men take the clay into their mouths and mix a wet mud out of it, which they use to start the wad that becomes the statue. Every now and then they take another mouthful of mud and wet it. The saliva flows very freely."

The listeners' minds were working rapidly, trying to put things together. "You mean diggers need to rub angel spit on their bodies in order to mate?" asked Dza.

"Not quite," said Shedemei. "The first time we examined the bodies of angels and diggers, we found a little organ—a gland, actually—near the scrotum. It was identical in both species, even though they have no common ancestor with a similar organ. Very puzzling, of course. But we now know the function of the organ. It continuously secrets tiny amounts of a hormone that suppresses the production of sperm. No, let me be clear. It completely shuts down the production of sperm. While the organ is functioning, males are completely, absolutely sterile."

"What a useful little organ," murmured Oykib. Then, louder, "Why would that evolve?"

"It gets worse," said Zdorab.

"There's a tiny flatworm, a microscopic one, that lives in all the freshwater rivers of this massif. During the rainy season, when the rivers are in flood, this flatworm burrows into beds of firm clay and lays millions of tiny eggs. They don't develop as long as they remain wet. But when the dry season comes and the water subsides, the eggs develop, forming hard little coatings that hold in what moisture they have. The embryos are ready to hatch at any time. But they can't, because they can't get rid of their own confining shells. So they hibernate, living off their yolks. They use the yolks so slowly that they can live for twenty or thirty years like that. The next rainy season doesn't cause them to hatch, because water doesn't dissolve the shells. Guess what dissolves them."

"Angel spit," said Oykib.

"Amazing boy," said Shedemei. "My prize student." There was some laughter, but they were all waiting for the story to go on. "No other fluid will do it, because the angels have tiny organelles in the saliva-producing cells of their mouths, which secrete an enzyme that has no function whatsoever within the bodies of the angels—but it dissolves the shells of the flatworm eggs. So when the males bring the clay into their mouths, they're not just softening it to make sculptures. They're also dissolving the shells of millions of little flatworms. And it just so happens that the dissolved shells contain precisely the one chemical that suppresses the action of the prophylactic gland near the angels' and diggers' scrota. The fertility chemical breaks down very slowly, and the statues contain useful quantities of it perhaps as long as ten years, certainly for five."

Everybody was getting it now. "So when the diggers rubbed the statues all over their bodies. . . ." "Were the angels swallowing some of it?" "How much of the fertility chemical does it take?"

Shedemei raised her hands to damp the questions and comments. "Yes, you've got it. The angel males absorb the fertility enzyme by mouth. It doesn't take much of it to shut down the action of the prophylactic gland, and it doesn't recover and start up again for about two weeks, maybe three. So there's a window there in which reproduction can take place. And the digger males have a special absorbent patch on their lower bellies, near the groin, where the chemical can be absorbed quite directly into the bloodstream. Rubbing the statues on their sweating bellies dissolves some of the clay, whereupon the dissolved fertility enzyme is taken into the blood and, just as with the angels, it shuts down the prophylactic gland and the digger males are fertile. But because they actually get a great deal less of the enzyme, the fertility window is only a few days long for them. Doesn't matter, though. Where the angels make their statues once a year and have to score a reproductive hit that one time, the diggers are culturally able to worship the statues any time. In effect, the statues enable them to reproduce whenever they want. They just have to pray first."

"That is the most absurdly complicated, unlikely, ridiculous mechanism I've ever heard of," said Issib.

"Exactly," said Shedemei. "There is no chance that it evolved naturally. Why would the diggers and angels independently evolve identical organs that make them sterile? There's no evolutionary advantage in it. Why didn't the angels simply die out before they ever started making their sculptures in the first place? Why didn't the diggers die out before they ever discovered the virtues of rubbing angel statues all over themselves? And why would a species of flatworm just happen to require a special chemical in angel saliva in order to hatch their eggs? And why did the angels develop a chemical with no use in their bodies except to dissolve the shells of the flatworms?"

"There are a lot of strange things in nature," said Oykib.

"Of course," said Shedemei. "I shouldn't have said there's no chance it evolved naturally. It's just that for me, at least, the coincidence is too great to believe in natural causation. This was *done* to the diggers and angels."

"But that's not what matters right now," said Zdorab. "Shedya has an answer to that, but what matters is that we have to tell the diggers the truth. They need to go back to using the statues. And getting new ones."

"Maybe we can get the angels just to *give* their statues to the diggers," said Padarok. "It's not as if the angels use them after the women judge the men."

"Maybe," said Shedemei. "But it's not just the diggers who are suffering from our interference in their previous social patterns. This relationship, this connection between diggers and angels has been going on for millions of years. Forty million years, to be more precise. And in those countless generations, certain patterns have evolved. The twinning of the angels, for instance. Every pregnancy is double. This isn't accidental. It's only happened twice in all our observations, and never in our own angel village, but when a single birth takes place, the baby is destroyed and the mother is never allowed to mate again. In other words, single births are ruthlessly excluded from angel society. It looks to me as if this is a response to the fact that diggers follow angels wherever they go. The diggers have to follow the angels in order to get the statues. But then the diggers can't help but see the angels as an easy source of meat, especially when the angel infants are at that awkward age when they can't fly well at all, and yet they're too heavy for one adult to carry them alone and still fly. In effect, the twinning allows each generation of angels to have one death and one survivor. Over the years, community cooperation has enabled between two-thirds and three-fourths of the twin-pairs to survive intact. Now, though, in our village all the twins are living to adulthood. And all the damaged, weak, sick, and crippled angels are surviving, where in other villages the diggers cull them out. In short, the angels have evolved a strategy of reproducing far beyond their sustainable population in order to survive the depredations of the diggers. When the diggers no longer prey on them, their population balloons out of control."

"It's a delicate balance," Zdorab said. "I found one place where it reached a crisis. The diggers had lost discipline and were eating more than the infants and the strays. They were systematically wiping out the angels in their area. When I got there, only a few beleaguered families of angels survived. But the diggers were already paying the price. They had plenty of old statues, of course.

But no new ones. And so after about five years, their birthrate fell off. Just as it has here. Not so suddenly, of course, since they were still worshipping the statues they had, only the statues contained progressively less and less of the enzyme. Births became more and more rare. With fewer diggers to prey on them, the angel population was going to start recovering soon. When it did, eventually the few surviving diggers would also recover."

Shedemei took over again. "So there's a social balance, you see. The diggers can't harvest too many of the angels for food, because then they lose their own ability to reproduce. It's self-correcting."

"What's to stop the angels from taking off and starting a colony where there aren't any diggers?" asked Protchnu.

"Nothing," said Shedemei, "and I'm sure it's happened many times. But they can only live where they can find clay that supports the flatworms. That means that they can only live where there's a pattern of rainy season flooding, and they can only live at elevations where the flatworm can survive. It's a pretty narrow range, common enough on this massif but not elsewhere. And the diggers range far and wide. I don't think there's anywhere that angels can go without a digger finding them sooner or later. When the digger finds them, he goes home and reports that he's found a new spot that's favored by the gods, and so they send out a colony. It's actually to the benefit of the angels. Without diggers devouring their young, their populations reach climax very quickly."

"Are you suggesting," said Nafai, "that we should let the diggers go back to kidnapping and eating angel infants?"

"That's the question," said Shedemei. "That's really the question, isn't it?"

"Does any of this," asked Chveya, "have to do with the evolution of intelligence among the angels and diggers?"

"Some, I think," said Shedemei. "The way the angel females select their mates is by the intricacy, beauty, originality, and accuracy of their sculptures. Obviously, the more intelligent and creative the angel male, the better his chances of reproducing early and often. For the diggers, it's a little different. In order to kill angels, they have to be devious and smart. We don't see it that much now, of course, because the diggers are *so* smart that the angels had almost given up trying to stop them. But we've all seen the traps that the angels set at the perimeter of their villages. It may be that the stupid diggers used to get caught in such traps. Now they recognize and evade them easily. But perhaps their very intelligence evolved because only the smart ones got through the angel traps in order to steal statues and baby angels."

"In other words, intelligence evolved naturally," said Chveya. "It's this symbiotic relationship that's unnatural."

"Not just unnatural," said Shedemei. "Human-made."

"How can you know that?" asked Protchnu.

"Because we believed that it couldn't be natural. And we knew that humans ceased to live on Earth at the time of the emigration that settled Harmony and, no doubt, other worlds as well. As we searched with the Index, we found that the one part of history where the ship's library had *no* useful information was human life at the time of the emigration."

Zdorab, the librarian, took over here. "Now, we have always imagined that this was because it was such a terrible time that they tried to forget it. There were implications of wars using weapons so dreadful that they turned the Earth for a while into a ball of ice. That's what the Oversoul himself believed. But then something Nafai said to me one time made me realize that this paucity of information really wasn't believable. He said, 'How could the people who saved humanity by leaving Earth have allowed themselves to be so completely forgotten?' And I thought, Of course they couldn't. So I started searching the computers on the ship, the ones that *aren't* tied to the Oversoul. And I found what I was looking for. A database that the Oversoul has no conscious access to. It's called, as nearly as

I can translate it, *The Book of the Sins of the Human Race*."

"Sins?" asked Mebbekew.

"Well, it's the most economical translation. It's a term that means 'willful mistakes.' 'Crimes of avoidable negligence,' perhaps. I thought *sin* was a pretty good way of summing it up."

"What does the book contain?" asked Nafai.

"I only just found it. I haven't read it all, and I'd be glad to have any of you who have the time and interest help me in the translation. The language is close to several known languages but it's very very old and the Oversoul hasn't been updating it because he wasn't conscious that it was there. The thing is, one of the first things I found was the explanation for how the angels and diggers began. It was one of the 'sins,' you see."

Zdorab brought up a document on the computer screen nearest to him and began to read aloud.

"We have sinned by fiddling with the genes of animals, giving them intelligence without freedom, talent without power, desires without hope. We used them for our amusement, displaying their paintings and sculptures and music and dance while keeping the painters and sculptors, the musicians and dancers in prisons. If they escaped their freedom was worthless because they could have children only in captivity. This was an abomination, and the Keeper of Earth revolted against it, driving away the slavemakers and slavekeepers, and setting the little ones free."

Shedemei spoke up. "I think the possible connection with diggers and angels should be obvious. The angels are the ones who still do some kind of art, but that's what they were bred for, perhaps. Zdorab and I can't think what the diggers were originally bred to do."

"Dig," said Elemak.

"Possibly," said Shedemei. "Just because the *Book of Sins* mentioned only the intelligent animals created in order to entertain humans doesn't mean there weren't also animals that were genetically enhanced in order to do more menial tasks. Like seeking out underground deposits of various minerals, for instance. Or simply digging tunnels."

"Sewer work," said Elemak.

"As I said, we don't know," said Shedemei. "I think there's a good chance that the diggers' ancestors weren't very intelligent at all. Enhanced physically, but not mentally. But they survived because they *were* bright enough, or lucky enough, to live close to a tribe of angels and perhaps simply by chance they rubbed themselves with the statues."

"Or maybe they survived," said Zdorab, "because the diggers lived in burrows and the angels lived in caves, and so when the Earth went into a profound ice age they both survived underground and developed their symbiosis there."

"Or maybe they were taught to do it in a dream," said Luet.

"Well, there we are," said Shedemei. "It might all have been planned and controlled. Even as the Keeper of Earth drove out the human race, she might have been planning to replace our ancestors with new species. She might have been manipulating them both to help them both evolve intelligence."

"And in the meantime," said Zdorab, "to make them symbiotic so that they couldn't possibly survive without each other. The old humans created the flatworms and made it so that the angels' ancestors *had* to sculpt clay or they couldn't reproduce. Perhaps they didn't give any of the other captive animals a mechanism that would allow them to get a supply of the chemical they needed without human intervention. Only the diggers found their own way to piggyback on the angels' survival method. Who says the Keeper of Earth couldn't have put it all together that way? Perhaps it was because of the Keeper that humans first developed the flatworm vector for creating the chemical the angels needed. Perhaps the Keeper planned it all."

"Whatever the Keeper is," said Meb.

"I have another idea," said Elemak. "What if there's no such thing as the Keeper? Those dreams you had back on Harmony, you were all so sure they came from this supposed Keeper because the Oversoul knew nothing about the diggers and the angels. But now we find out that the Oversoul had all this information in his databanks, only he simply couldn't *consciously* access it. So those dreams could have come from the Oversoul all along, without his knowing it, right? And now we don't have to imagine some mechanism for sending dreams faster than light across the space between Earth and Harmony."

"Very good theory," said Shedemei. "But it doesn't explain Kiti making a perfect likeness of Nafai a hundred years before we arrived here."

"I don't think," said Volemak icily, "that it's very helpful to assume that just because we find the natural mechanism by which some things came to be, we have therefore proven that the Keeper of Earth does not exist. We don't know how far the reach of the Keeper might be, or what power he has; perhaps all he can do is give dreams to people. Wishful thinking gives false gods to people who hunger for gods, but those who yearn for a world with no gods are no less likely to fall victim to their own wishful thinking."

"I'll memorize that one, Father," said Meb. "That was deep."

Elemak smiled but did not speak.

"If we can set aside speculative theology," said Shedemei, "I want to lay two choices before you. The first choice is this: We can explain everything to the diggers and angels. The diggers can go back to using the sculptures. The angels can start trying to control their population by breeding less often—perhaps nothing more than each man making a sculpture only every

other year. There's no reason to go back to the slaughter of infant angels. The trouble is that while this might
work here, it will have no effect elsewhere. But perhaps
that's the reason the Keeper of Earth brought us here,
to teach the diggers and angels how to live together
without killing."

"I thought we were setting aside speculative theology," said Meb.

"The other choice," said Shedemei, "is to get rid of
that prophylactic gland."

"Get rid of it?" asked Volemak.

"I've found the gene that creates it. It's artificial—it
was inserted. By analogy with the genes of unaltered
rats and bats, we've found all the inserts and they're
quite obvious. We isolated the particular genetic word
that creates the prophylactic gland by inserting each of
the artificial words into common rats and bats and seeing which ones developed the prophylactic gland.
Knowing which gene causes it, we can uncause it."

"How?" asked Volemak.

"A bacterial infection that carries an enzyme whose
sole function is to find that genetic word and clip it out.
It's the method I use to do gene alteration anyway. I'll
just use an infectious bacterium instead of the benign
ones I usually work with. It has few symptoms. With
the diggers it's a little stuffness of the joints and some
nasal inflammation. With the angels it can also cause
weeping eyes for a few days. Once the infection has
spread throughout all digger and angel populations, reproduction will be cut loose from the flatworms. The
angels can sculpt to their hearts' content, of course, but
if they stop it won't matter. The change will only affect
those conceived after the bacterial epidemic made the
alteration in their parents, and it may cause spontaneous
abortion of male digger and angel embryos that happen
to be in the first few weeks of development when the
infection comes. But in a single generation, the prophylactic gland will disappear."

"I don't like it," said Oykib. "The Keeper of Earth set up a mechanism that kept balance here, and we'll be destroying it."

"I don't know, Okya," said Chveya. "It was humans who set up the mechanism, really. It's listed in the *Book of Sins*. It's one of the things that the Keeper hated. Maybe we've been brought back just to remove it."

"As I said," Shedemei went on. "We have those two choices. But personally I favor intervention. Removing the prophylactic gland seems to me like striking the manacles off a slave. After forty million years, it's about time, don't you think?"

"Just do it," said Elemak. "Don't waste our time with endless discussion about what the Keeper might want or might not want. You have the power to do it, and it's a decent thing to do, so just do it and have done." Elemak got up and left.

It took many hours of discussion after that, but finally Elemak's point of view prevailed. The only reason the discussion took so long was because Protchnu suggested asking the diggers and angels what *they* thought should be done. But they all realized that neither the diggers nor the angels had the conceptual framework to understand the genetic issues involved. "They won't receive it as science because they have no science," said Volemak as he reached his decision. "They'll convert it to religion and it will cause division and controversy among them and may lead to real hatred of us or civil war within their own communities. I believe in letting people make their own choices, when they're capable of understanding the choice. But you don't let your toddlers decide whether or not they're ready to play in the stream. You simply keep them away from the water and you don't even try to explain the concept of drowning. Later you can explain it to them, when they're older."

"So the diggers and angels are our children now?" asked Meb, mockingly.

"Better to treat them as our children," said Volemak,

"than to treat them as our ancestors did—as slaves, as playthings. So the decision is made. We explain only as much as they can understand. Oykib will explain to the diggers, and Nafai to the angels. I'd appreciate it if everyone else would keep their mouths shut about it. Shedemei, I'd like you to introduce the bacteria as quickly as possible into both communities."

"It's simple enough," she said. "I'll simply expose everyone here to it right now. It'll cause a bit of a runny nose, maybe a slight fever in a few cases. Just make sure you follow your normal patterns of interaction with diggers and angels, and the disease will spread naturally. Just come up here and swab the insides of your noses with this gel."

"That's disgusting," said one of the younger women.

"Only if you use someone else's swab," said Protchnu.

"What worries me," said Mebbekew, "is what's going to happen to the poor flatworms. Nobody seems to care about them. I think we have too much of a bias in favor of big animals. Don't microscopic creatures have rights?" He grinned, and the others laughed with him.

While the meeting went on, however, Elemak had a meeting of his own. He sought out Fusum, who had recently been made blood king after the death of his father.

"I have a gift for you," Elemak said.

"What could you possibly have that I want?" asked Fusum.

"Oh, we're full of ourselves, aren't we, now that we're king."

Fusum growled a little. "I have a life of my own, Elemak. I'm not a hostage anymore. I have responsibilities."

"You also have power," said Elemak, "and I think you wouldn't mind getting a little more. So here's my gift—more power."

"Really," said Fusum. "I didn't know you had any power to give."

"Knowledge is power, or so I've heard," said Elemak. "But there's a condition. You have to promise to tell your people you got the idea from me."

"What idea?" asked Fusum.

"Promise first."

"I promise," said Fusum.

"But do you really mean it?" asked Elemak.

"If you're going to mock me, you can keep your gift," said Fusum.

"Ah, now that we're the blood king, we're too important to take a little teasing from a friend."

"You've never been a friend, Elemak," said Fusum. "You've been a useful source of knowledge."

"But perhaps now we *can* be friends," said Elemak.

"Either tell me the idea you have or don't."

"Go at once to the statue of the Untouched God," said Elemak.

"You mean the one that looks like your shining brother Nafai?"

Elemak refused to be goaded. "That's the one. Go to it, and in front of as many witnesses as possible, declare that the reason so few children are being born is because this statue has not been properly worshipped. Then do whatever it is you do with it. Rub it all over yourself."

"That could get me killed."

"Not the blood king. Not right away. And not if you promise the people that now that you have worshipped the Untouched God, obliterating the face of that deceiver Nafai, the true god will send a mild plague to purge the last traces of evil among your people. A few male embryos may even be miscarried because they were not pure. All those who are alive right now will have to worship the gods in the old way until the day they die. But the new children born after this time will not have to worship any gods at all. They are born in purity and they are blessed."

"What kind of fungus are you trying to make me eat?" said Fusum. "You're the one who told me that all this religious stuff was nonsense."

"But the people believe it, don't they. So you tell them that no matter what Oykib or Chveya or anybody else tells them, *I* told *you* the truth, and it's *your* action that will free your people from having to go up the canyon and get your gods from the skymeat. You won't *need* the skymeat anymore. Your new children and grandchildren can kill them all then, and it won't matter because they will be pure and the gods won't require them to humiliate themselves by worshipping objects created by the skymeat."

"Why should I believe that any of this will happen?"

"I don't care," said Elemak. "You can doubt me and delay, and then Oykib will come out and make an announcement and all the power and influence will go to him and, through him, to Emeezem. Or you can believe me and act *now*, so that you've already done it before anybody else says a word. Then *you* and *I* will be the liberators of the diggers. It's going to happen anyway, of course. The little act you put on with that statue of Nafai won't actually do anything at all. Except make your people think you've got religious powers beyond any blood king before you. And it won't hurt that you can make hash out of Emeezem's insistence that the Untouched God remain untouched. When your prophecies come true, she'll be discredited. But you can let the opportunity pass you by, Fusum. You can spend the rest of your life wishing you had taken the chance when I gave it to you. I really don't care."

"Yes you do," said Fusum. "And you can be sure that I *will* use your name and tell them that I learned about this from you. Because if it fails, I might be able to save myself by laying the blame on you."

"And when it succeeds," said Elemak, "your people will know who is their true friend among the humans."

"And I'll know," said Fusum, "that you are a liar who is obviously planning to betray his own people and you want to have the diggers behind you when you strike."

"Any problem with that?" said Elemak.

"None whatsoever," said Fusum. "Just so you remember who is the king of the diggers when the time comes."

"I'll remember," said Elemak. "I remember everything."

So Fusum went down to the temple of the Untouched God, made his speech and performed his blasphemous worship. Emeezem had him bound and walled up in a prison chamber, but his imprisonment lasted only until Oykib called together the elders of the digger people and explained to them that a minor plague was going to come among them, but all children conceived afterward would no longer need to worship statues anymore. "The Keeper of Earth has set you free from your old gods," he said. But there were many who said among themselves, Fusum set us free. And Emeezem was unable to prevent them from releasing Fusum from his prison and restoring him as blood king.

The plague came within days, just as Fusum had predicted. But no other harmful consequences came from his having touched the Untouched God. And now the Untouched God didn't look like Nafai anymore, and people said, It was Elemak who taught us this secret, that Nafai is not a god, and that he hasn't even got the power to keep his face on the statue. Fusum is a true blood king, but Emeezem as our deep mother didn't know the truth about the Untouched God.

When Mufruzhuuzh died not long after, the people chose Fusum to be the new war king, saying, He was Nen's true friend, and killed the panther that slaughtered him. He also set our children free from the gods of the skymeat. Let him be war king and blood king, both at once.

That day marked the end of Emeezem's rule over the digger city. She still had great influence over the women, but the men belonged to Fusum, and Fusum began to train them for war.

For months, Nafai and Oykib pored over the *Book of the Sins of the Human Race*, learning from it all they could. Here were the secrets of the evolution of the human race, of the development of technologies, of the cruel uses that humans put them to. Here were the tales of wars and slaughters, of oppressive poverty that paid for the wealth of a few, of stripped and ruined land, of ancient resources burned up or thrown away.

At the end, they found these words:

"These sins came about because of rebellion, for the human race ignored the good dreams that came from the Keeper of Earth, until at last the Keeper wearied of their sins and shrugged them off. Then the great floating continents shuddered, and the earth shook, and the volcanos burst open in a thousand places. The sky was filled with smoke and the plants died; the Earth grew cold and ice covered the face of the Earth in the deepest ice age ever known. Those few human beings who survived understood that the Keeper of Earth was done with them. The Earth had no more room for human beings, and if they were to live at all they must leave. Seven fleets were assembled and seven colonies left, and of the others we have no word. We know only this: that on our new world, Harmony, we will build an Oversoul to be the servant of the Keeper of Earth, and under the Oversoul's watchful eye the human race will not remember how to sin on such a terrible scale. As for Earth, it belongs to the Keeper now, and human beings will never live there again, unless the Keeper forgives us and calls us home."

Nafai and Oykib both translated this final passage,

338 ORSON SCOTT CARD

and then reconciled their translations. "Who wrote this?" Oykib asked. "How could he know what power the Keeper had? To cause earthquakes and volcanos, to change the flow of continental drift. . . ."

"Maybe the Keeper has something to do with the convection currents in the flowing magma on which the crust of the Earth floats. Who knows how quickly it might change?" said Nafai.

"I know this much," said Oykib. "We have to teach our people about this book, the warnings in this book. We have to teach them what the Keeper expects of us, even if we don't understand exactly what the Keeper of Earth might be."

"By 'our people,' do you mean just humans?" asked Nafai.

"Of course not," said Oykib. "In fact, maybe the reason the Keeper brought us back to Earth was precisely so that we could not only set the angels and diggers free from their ancient bondage, but also could teach them how to live so that the Keeper won't feel the need to make the Earth uninhabitable again."

"I think you're right," said Nafai. "But it's going to become a religion no matter what we do or how we teach it. Even our most naturalistic explanations are going to sound mystical to them. After all, what our ancestors wrote in the *Book of Sins* sounds mystical to *us*."

"Is that bad?" asked Oykib.

"Not bad in itself. It's just that religions have a way of losing track of the truth at the core. The diggers had a religion that kept them rubbing themselves with clay that contained the chemical derived from flatworm eggshells and angel spit—but they had no idea why they were doing it, and so they were enslaved by it. All we'll be doing, then, is teaching our children and their children arbitrary rules. The true reasons will be lost, or converted into myths."

"What can we do about it?" asked Oykib.

"We can write a book," said Nafai.

"You mean like the one you're already writing?" he asked.

Nafai glared at him. "I should have known I couldn't keep a secret from you."

"Yes, you should have," said Oykib. "Especially since you talked to the Oversoul about it almost constantly for weeks when you first thought of it. I figured you'd tell me about it when you felt like it."

"Well, I feel like it," said Nafai. "Because I think our descendants aren't going to have access to the ship's computer. The skill of reading and writing will be lost to most of them. But a few of them will be taught to read and write in order to keep a record of what we've learned. We'll write it down as clearly as we can, a true history of our voyage and everything we've learned and done. We'll pass it along from parent to child, and because it's written down it can't be distorted."

"People can distort anything," said Oykib.

"But as long as the original text is there, the next generation or the one after, somewhere along the line, they can go back to the original and discover the truth. The way we learned so much from the *Book of Sins*."

"Well, fine," said Oykib. "You're already keeping a record."

"I'm keeping *one* record. But I think we need to keep another. The first one has everything in it, all the details, everything I can remember. But I had a dream last night. . . ."

"Ah, another dream."

"I know you'd like to have these dreams yourself, Oykib, but—"

"I don't need to have my own dreams," Oykib said. "Not when I have yours. You dreamed of writing a book that you would give to me and Chveya instead of to Zhyat and Netsya."

"A book," said Nafai, "that includes everything from the *Book of Sins*, written on gold so we don't need a computer to read it and so it won't corrode. We can seal up that part, so no one adds to or changes it. But the rest of the book will be a record, not of the whole history of our people, but just the story of our dealings with the Oversoul and the Keeper of Earth. Just the. . . ."

"Just the theology," said Oykib.

"To the diggers and angels it will seem like theology," said Nafai.

"And to our children and grandchildren, too," said Oykib. "They won't have lived in the starship. They won't have used the great library. They'll have no idea of what a computer is."

Nafai nodded. "So you've come to the same conclusion."

"No, I've simply seen you and Luet and Chveya all having the same dream. The ship has got to go. We have to cut ourselves off from the machinery of the past and live in the technology of the present. The ship has to go up into orbit."

"We don't have the technology anymore to hide it on the planet's surface, the way our ancestors hid it on Harmony," said Nafai.

"I'll help you with your second book," said Oykib. "You write whatever you want to in order to start it off. You have to tell the parts where I wasn't born yet anyway. I'll take over when you tell me to. But in the meantime, I can be copying out the *Book of Sins.*"

"The *Book of Sins,* yes," said Nafai. "And maybe also you should start a record of the dreams the Keeper sent us. Especially the ones that don't seem yet to be completely fulfilled. It's the only guide we have to what the Keeper might have planned for us."

"The *Book of Sins* and the *Book of Dreams,*" said Oykib. "I'll get those started. And you write the *Book of Nafai.*"

"And in the meantime," said Nafai, "I'm going to start figuring out some kind of weapon that the angels can use in flight, something that can kill a digger despite the diggers' enormously greater strength."

Oykib nodded. "So you think your dreams of war between diggers and angels, you think those are from the Keeper of Earth."

"Whether they come from the Keeper or my own fears, I have to be prepared, don't I? I have to prepare my people, just in case."

Oykib nodded. "I love the diggers, Nafai. I don't want to have to choose between them and the angels."

"That won't be your choice, Oykib. *Your* choice will be the same one it's always been. Between Elemak and me, after Father dies."

"Still? Broken as Elemak is?"

"Elemak isn't broken, Oykib. He simply learned how to be patient. How to bide his time. But Hushidh has told me that his connection with Fusum is strong, even if it's tinged with loathing on both their parts. I'm sure Chveya has noticed the same thing, with the two of you living here among the diggers all these years."

"She's noticed it," said Oykib. "But it's hard to see how he can turn it to his advantage."

"Not really," said Nafai. "They'll follow Elemak, if he leads them where they already want to go."

"And where is that?" asked Oykib.

"To slaughter angels. They don't have to leave any angels alive now, because they can propagate without the statues."

Oykib frowned. "Then we made a mistake to wipe out the prophylactic gland?"

"No," said Nafai. "It was right to set both peoples free. But now we have to help them struggle to find a new equilibrium. One that's based on respect and tolerance."

"I wouldn't bet on that anytime soon," said Oykib, "not as long as the diggers think of angels as meat, and angels think of diggers as devils."

"I know," said Nafai. "That's why we have our work

cut out for us. Many lifetimes of teaching lie ahead, for us and for those who try to serve the Keeper of Earth after us. And in the meantime, I'm going to come up with some weapons that help even up the combat between angels and diggers. Something that will drive the diggers back into their holes when they dare to make war against the angels."

"So then the angels are masters. How does that help?"

"The angels don't seek out diggers in order to eat them," said Nafai. "They don't want to fight with the diggers at all. They just want to be left alone. As far as I can see, that tips the moral balance heavily onto the side of the angels."

"The diggers aren't monsters," Oykib said. "They're children of their own genetic and cultural heritage. They don't deserve to be slaughtered from the sky."

"I know that," said Nafai. "That's why we have to teach them all as well as we can. And in the meantime, try to keep a balance between them."

"I don't want to choose," said Oykib.

"You have no choice but to choose," said Nafai. "When Elemak takes the diggers to war, you're one of the ones he'll be trying to kill. You'll be on the angels' side because you have nowhere else to turn."

"You know this from dreams?" asked Oykib.

"The Keeper doesn't have to send me dreams to tell me what I can figure out for myself."

Oykib furiously brushed away a tear that had slipped down his cheek. "None of this was necessary," he said. "Why didn't you just kill Elemak when you had the chance?"

"Because I love him," said Nafai.

"So how many of my friends among the diggers and your friends among the angels have to die because of that?"

"Elemak has his hand in it," said Nafai, "but if you think that Fusum or someone else wouldn't have stirred up the diggers to rebellion against us or war against the angels, you don't understand human nature."

"The diggers aren't humans," said Oykib.

"When it comes to hate and rage and envy, yes they are," said Nafai.

"And love and generosity, too," said Oykib. "And trust, and wisdom, and dignity, and—"

"Yes," said Nafai. "They're human in all those ways. So are the angels."

"So how are we different from our ancestors, who got driven off the planet forty million years ago?"

"I don't know," said Nafai. "But maybe, given enough time, we and the diggers and the angels can find our way to peace."

"And in the meantime, you're going to design weapons," said Oykib.

"I'm thinking of blowguns," said Nafai. "With fleched darts. What I don't know is whether they need to be poisoned or not, in order to be effective."

"It's my friends you're talking about killing," said Oykib.

"Do your best to teach your friends to hate war and refuse to take part in it," said Nafai. "Teach them to loathe the very thought of eating infant skymeat. Then they'll never be brought down by an angel's dart."

FIFTEEN

DIVISIONS

When peace depends on the life of one man, then each new day becomes a deathwatch. Each new plan must include the thought: Can this be finished before he dies? Each new child is welcomed with the prayer: Let safety last another year. Another month, another week.

Not that people talked about it much—about how old Volemak was looking, how his back was stooping, how he winced with arthritis when he walked, how he tended to lose breath when he worked hard, how he now called meetings in the schoolhouse instead of up the ladder inside the starship. It was something they saw, regretted, feared, but kept to themselves, pretending that it wasn't that bad, he had plenty of time left, no need to worry yet.

Then Emeezem died and Fusum seized full power among the diggers. She had started losing heart when her son Nen was killed by a panther while hunting. Later, the desecration of the Untouched God was a harsh blow, and her heart died then; the death of her husband Mufruzhuuzh was merely an afterthought compared to those. The world has ended, Emeezem, and, oh yes, your husband is dead and the brutal boy who *says* he tried to save your son is now both blood king and war king and when you die he will destroy all peace among your people and there's nothing you can do except teach the women to look for a day of peace in some distant day only the women seem to barely listen anymore, and the only one who does you honor is the human Nafai whose face was your salvation long ago. When death finally came to her, coughing out of her lungs as she lay in her deep chamber, in darkness, attended by silent women and a few men watching for the exact moment of death so they could begin destroying her memory—when death finally came to her, she welcomed it with bitter relief. What took you so long? And where are Nen and Mufruzhuuzh? And for that matter, where's my mother? Why has my life turned out to be so worthless?

Only just as she was on the edge of death there came a dream into her mind even though she had thought she was awake. She saw a human, a digger, and an angel, standing together on the brow of a hill as a host of people of all three species gathered round them, weeping, laughing for joy, surging forward to touch them, and each one who touched them sang out loud, the same glad song, and then the human, the digger, and the angel looked at *her*, at Emeezem the deep mother who was dying, and said to her, Thank you for setting your people on this road.

The dream did not bring Nen back to life, or give her hope that Fusum's reign would not be bloody and terrible, and it certainly did not take her from the brink of death. All it did was let her step off that brink into the dark unknown with a smile on her face and pride in her heart. It made death sweet to her.

Fusum saw to it that she was given great honor, and

in his funeral oration he praised her for preparing the people for the coming of the humans—even if she misunderstood what the gods meant their people to do. Then, over the next several days, all his rivals and opponents disappeared and were never heard of again. The message was clear: The supreme law of the digger people was Fusum, for Fusum was blood king, war king, deep mother, and, yes, god, all in one, and for all time. Most of the young men were happy with this, for he would make warriors of them once again, after so many years of being in the shadow of the humans and under the thumb of women. And if the young men were happy with him, no one else dared to be unhappy.

Fusum respectfully asked Oykib to stop teaching his silly ideas about the Keeper of Earth. Fusum took Chveya aside and told her that her presence was intimidating to the digger women and they would be happier if she stopped helping them learn about the safe storage and preservation of food. One by one the other humans were kindly asked to desist, until at last only Elemak, Mebbekew, and Protchnu were allowed to visit with the diggers.

What could Volemak do? He asked Elemak to protest to Fusum. Elemak said that he would, then came back and said that he had, and conveyed Fusum's assurance that nothing had changed except that diggers would be taking the responsibility for educating their own people. "He said that we should be happy, Father, because now we have more time to devote to our own families."

It was all handled so quietly, so politely, that it left Volemak helpless to interfere. He knew—everybody knew—that in effect the diggers were in revolt against human overlordship, even though until the revolt none of the humans had thought of themselves as overlords. They also knew that Elemak had somehow pulled off a coup, for he now controlled all access to the diggers even though until that moment Oykib and Chveya had been the dominant human presence among the digger people. Everyone was sure that Elemak had planned and worked on this for years, that in all likelihood he and Fusum had struck some kind of bargain twenty years before when Fusum was a hostage and Elemak was learning digger speech from him and supposedly winning him over to friendship with the humans.

"Fusum kidnapped Elemak's child," Chveya said, unbelieving. "How could Elemak have made *friends* with him?"

"I think," said Oykib, "that Elemak understood that there was nothing personal about Fusum's choice of kidnap victim. And I don't think that what they made between them was what you or I would understand as friendship."

It didn't matter now what any of the rest of them thought of it. It was done.

That was when they started watching Volemak's health in earnest. Even Volemak began to speak of it, quietly, to a few.

He and Nafai got together with Hushidh and Chveya and made a list of who was clearly loyal to Nafari and who was loyal to Elemak. "We're divided into Nafari and Elemaki again," said Chveya. "I thought for a while that those days might be behind us."

Volemak looked sad, but not grim. "I knew that Elemak had changed, but what he learned was patience, not generosity. The Oversoul knew it all along."

Among the humans, Nafari outnumbered Elemaki overwhelmingly, and of the adult men who might serve as soldiers, there would be no contest if it ever came to battle among humans only. But of course, everyone understood now that the battle, if it came, would be between Nafai's humans and Fusum's army of diggers. On that scale, Nafai's soldiers were the merest handful, and no one had the slightest confidence that the angels, however willing they might be, could really stand against the diggers in an open war. It could not be allowed to come to battle. Nafai and his people would have to leave.

Yet even among the children of Kokor and Sevet, more than half were loyal to Nafai—in part because of the open secret that their mothers were Elemak's mistresses. "The real complication," said Hushidh, "is that Eiadh is perhaps the most loyal of all to Nafai, and she'll want to take as many of her children and grandchildren with her as she can."

"How many of them would come?" asked Nafai.

"Most. Most of Elemak's children would come with you, though not Protchnu or Nadya and their children. But Elemak won't stand for it if you take any of them, even if you take just Eiadh. He'd follow us wherever we might go. We can't bring her with us if we ever hope for peace."

Volemak listened and listened to their discussion, and then made his decision. "You'll take everyone whose loyalty to Nafai is genuine and deep, if they want to go. You'll have to trust in the Keeper of Earth to help you."

If any of them thought to say, That's easy for you to decide, Volemak, because you'll be dead when the wars begin, they kept it to themselves.

As Volemak's health weakened, he began to call people to him, one by one. Just for a conversation, he said, but they all came away rather shaken by the experience. He would sit with them and tell them with almost brutal frankness what he thought of them. The words could sting, but when he praised the good in them, their talents, their virtues, their accomplishments, his words were like gold. Some of them remembered mostly the criticism, of course, and some mostly the praise, but each of these meetings was recorded and later, Nafai or Oykib wrote down the words on the golden leaves of the book. Someday, when they wanted to remember what Volemak said, the words would be there for them to read.

It was an open secret that Volemak was saying good-bye. And when he took sick, the pace quickened.

He met with pTo and Poto, who came down the canyon to him because even in the launch he couldn't stand the strain of traveling to their village one more time. "We will fight and die for Nafai," they told him.

"I don't want you to die, and you must fight only if they force you to. The real question, my friends, is this: Will you and all your people follow Nafai into the wilderness, to start over, to build a new colony in another land?"

"We'd rather defeat the diggers," said pTo. "We'd rather fight like men. Nafai has taught us to fight with new weapons. We can bring down panthers on the run, we can kill them while we're in flight and they can't touch us."

"Diggers are smarter than panthers," said Volemak.

"But angels are smarter than diggers," said Poto.

"You don't understand me," said Volemak. "I say that diggers are smarter than panthers because it means their lives are more precious. You should not be proud because you can kill diggers, because they're men, not animals."

Abashed, pTo and Poto fell silent.

"Will you and your people follow Nafai higher into the mountains?"

"I can tell you with perfect confidence, Father Volemak," said pTo, "that not only will the people follow Nafai to the moon or to the depths of hell, but also they will beg him to be their king and rule over them, because if he is their ruler they know that they'll be safe."

"What if Nafai didn't have the cloak of the starmaster?" asked Volemak.

They looked at each other for a moment. Finally Poto remembered. "Oh, you mean the thing that lets him glow like a firefly when he wants to?"

"That means nothing to us," said pTo. "We don't

want him to lead us because he has some kind of magical power, Father Volemak. We want him to lead us because he and Luet and Issib and Hushidh are the best
and wisest people that we know, and they love us, and
we love them."

Volemak nodded. "Then you will be my children forever, even after I'm dead."

They went home and told their people to begin to
prepare to leave. They gathered up their belongings and
decided which to take and which to leave. They packed
their seed and the cuttings of the plants that did not
grow from seed. They packed the food that they would
need for the journey and to live on until their new fields
ripened. And they began to move their children a day's
flight up the valley and over the next ridge, so that they
would already be out of the reach of the diggers if the
flight should begin in haste.

"How long will Father Volemak live?" everyone
asked them.

How could they answer? "Not long enough," they
said, over and over, to everyone who asked.

At last all goodbyes had been said, all blessings given,
all hopes and memories and love expressed, and yet
Volemak still lingered. Rasa came to Shedemei and said,
"Volya and Nyef want to see you, Shedya. Please come
quickly." She smiled at Zdorab. "This time alone,
please." Zdorab nodded.

Shedemei followed the old woman into the house
where Volemak lay, his eyes closed, his chest unmoving.

"Is he . . ." she began.

"Not yet," answered Volemak softly.

Nafai sat on a stool in the corner. Rasa left the house,
saying only, "Be quick." They understood that she
didn't want to be outside when her husband died.

"Nafai," whispered Volemak. "Give the cloak of the
starmaster to her."

"What?" said Shedemei.

"Shedemei," said Volemak. "Take the cloak. Learn

how to use it. Take the ship up into the sky, where no man can touch it or use it. Live long—the cloak will sustain you. Watch over the Earth."

"That's the Keeper's job, not mine," said Shedemei, but in truth her heart wasn't in her protests. Volemak wants me to have the cloak, me to have the ship! Volemak wants me to have the only decent laboratory in the world, and time enough to use it!

"The Keeper of Earth will be glad of any help that he can get," said Volemak. "If he could do his work alone he wouldn't have brought us here."

Nafai stood up, taking off his clothing as he did. "It will pass from my flesh to yours," he said. "If you're willing to receive it. And if I'm willing to let it go."

"Are you?" asked Shedemei.

"Tend this world as your garden," said Nafai. "And watch over my people when I sleep."

Volemak died that night, with only Rasa at his side. By dawn his passing was known from the deepest chamber of the digger city to the highest nest of the angels. The grief was immediate and real among the angels, and among all the diggers who did not lust for war. They knew that peace was ended for them all; and also, they had loved and honored the man Volemak, not just for his authority, but for the way he used it.

At Rasa's request they did not burn his body, but rather buried it according to the digger custom.

It was only two days later that the test of authority came. Nafai was preparing to go back up to the angel village, where Luet already waited for him. Elemak, flanked by Meb and Protchnu, and with a dozen digger soldiers behind him, intercepted Nafai at the forest's edge.

"Please don't go," said Elemak.

"Luet's waiting," said Nafai. "Is there some urgent business?"

"I'd appreciate it if you didn't go," said Elemak. "I'll

send word to Luet to come down here. I'd rather you live in this village now. The skymeat don't need you anymore."

His words and manner were gentle, so that if Nafai showed any resistance *he* would look like the aggressor, not Elemak. But the message was plain. Elemak was seizing power, and Nafai was his prisoner.

"I'm glad to hear that," said Nafai. "I thought I still had a great deal of work to do among them, but now I imagine I can just retire."

"Oh, no, there's still a lot of work to do down here," said Elemak. "Fields to be cleared, tunnels to be dug. A lot of work. And your back is still strong, Nafai. I think there's a lot of labor left in you."

He was taken to Volemak's house. Rasa saw at once what was happening, and she did not take it calmly. "You were always a snake, Elemak, but I thought you learned long ago that imprisoning Nafai accomplishes nothing."

"Nafai's not my prisoner," said Elemak. "He's just another citizen, doing his duty to the community."

"What, am I supposed to have the good manners to pretend that I believe your lies?" asked Rasa.

"Lady Rasa," said Elemak, "Nafai is my brother. But you are *not* my mother."

"For which I give thanks to the Oversoul, you may be sure."

Nafai finally broke his silence. "Mother, please. Keep peace. Elemak thinks he rules here, but this world belongs to the Keeper, not to him or any man. He has no power here."

In another time, Elemak would have flown into a rage at those words, would have blustered and threatened, or lashed out in fury. But he was a different man now, a tempered man, a man of discipline and quiet, ruthless wisdom. He said nothing, merely watched until Nafai went into his father's house. Then two digger soldiers were left to stand guard at the door.

Rasa went to the ship, to Shedemei. "I don't think Elemak knows that you have the cloak now, Shedemei. You could use it to stop him, to strike him down."

Shedemei shook her head. "I don't know how to use it that well yet. I'm learning. It's a terrible burden, this cloak. I don't know how Nafai bore it."

"Don't you see that he's helpless here? Elemak is going to kill him, probably tonight. He won't let Nafai live till morning."

"I know," said Shedemei. "I received a message from Issib, through the Index. I hear him directly now, you know, wearing the cloak. He says that Luet dreamed a true dream last night. In the dream she saw all the digger soldiers asleep, and all those who follow Elemak. Asleep while you and Nafai and all the loyal men and women and children journeyed up the canyon, and then onward, higher and farther, to a new land."

"And what is that supposed to mean?"

"I think—she thinks, and so does Issib, and so says the Oversoul—that it was a true dream. The Oversoul has power enough to put the humans to sleep. But since the dream came from the Keeper, perhaps we must trust that she, too, has the power to put her people to sleep." Shedemei looked away. "I'm not familiar with this sort of thing. I wasn't one to have visions. Just one dream, really, of a garden."

Zdorab was sitting sourly in a corner. "She won't take me with her," he said. "She insists I have to go with Nafai and help start another damn colony."

"You don't *have* to," said Shedemei.

"Or stay with Elemak—do you really think that's a choice?" said Zdorab. "Reason with her, Rasa. I'm a librarian."

"I'm just doing what the Oversoul advised," said Shedemei. "She says that Zdorab will be needed."

"But what about what I *want*?" demanded Zdorab. "Lady Rasa, haven't I kept my oath to Nafai all these years? Haven't I stood by him?"

"Perhaps now," said Rasa, "is your chance to repay him for his forgiveness of your mistake during the voyage."

Zdorab looked away.

"Can't you take him with you?" asked Rasa.

"I want to," whispered Shedemei. "But the Oversoul says not for now."

"Then tell him that. Tell him it's not for now," said Rasa. "He thinks that it's forever."

From the corner Zdorab spoke again, and he was weeping. "Don't you know, Shedemei, that I love you? Don't you know that I don't want to live without you?"

Tears came to Shedemei's eyes, too. She whispered to Rasa, "I never thought he'd. . . ."

"Love you?" asked Rasa. "You never think anyone will love you, but we do. Let him go with you, Shedemei. The Oversoul doesn't know everything. She's just a computer, you know."

Shedemei nodded gravely, knowing perfectly well that Rasa did not believe for a moment that the Oversoul was nothing more than a machine. "Zdorab," said Shedemei, "will you take the ship's launch, to carry Lady Rasa and the heaviest burdens up the canyon? And then use it to take Issib and his chair, and Lady Rasa again, and bring them to the new place where the Nafari will start their colony?"

"I will," said Zdorab.

"And then, when Nafai tells you he has no further use for the launch, would you be kind enough to bring it back to me here at the ship, so we can lift ourselves into orbit?"

He smiled. He embraced her.

"You know that the cloak will sustain my life," she said. "Longer than is natural. And I intend to hibernate a lot, too, so I can have the time to study many generations of life and gather a great deal of data over time."

"I don't mind dying before you do," said Zdorab. "In fact, I rather prefer it that way."

"It'll be work all the time," said Shedemei.

"So you'll need a secretary and librarian all the more."

"And the salary is low," she said.

"I've already been paid," he answered her.

When darkness fell, the digger soldiers outside the door of Volemak's house fell asleep. Nafai stepped out almost at once, and began going door to door, speaking quietly to his loyal supporters and gathering them at the forest's edge. They were not silent, though they tried to be; there was no way to keep the little children from talking or, occasionally, crying or complaining. But no alarm was raised.

Chveya stood beside Nafai, looking at the ties still binding him to the people he was leaving behind. "If they're asleep," said Chveya, "doesn't that mean the Oversoul doesn't want them to go with you?"

"It doesn't matter what the Oversoul wants this time," said Nafai. "I'm taking anyone who wants to join me."

Chveya nodded. "Well, then, I must tell you that you are still bound to Eiadh and three of her children."

Nafai nodded. "But I don't need to speak to her," he said. "See? She's coming."

And it was true. She was accompanied by the young men Yistina and Peremenya and the young woman Zhivoya, the one who had been kidnapped twenty years before. Yistina and Peremenya had their wives with them, but Zhivoya's husband, Muzhestvo, had not come. "He's asleep and I can't waken him," she explained with tears in her eyes.

"You can stay with him," said Nafai. "No one will blame you for that."

She shook her head. "I know what he is," she said. "I didn't when I married him, but I know it now. He's one of them. In his heart and soul, he's one of them." She put her hands on her stomach. "But the baby is mine."

Eiadh touched Nafai's arm. "You don't have to take us, Nafai. I know the danger it puts you in. He'll never forgive us for this. He'll believe that you and I—"

"He'll believe that you and I have done what he and Kokor and he and Sevet and probably he and Dol have already done." Nafai nodded. "But you and I know that we haven't and that we never will."

Eiadh smiled wanly at the gentle way he made it very clear that she was coming as a fellow-citizen, and not as a lover.

"Then we're all here," said Chveya.

"No we're not," said Nafai. "I have to invite my sisters."

"They're sleeping with *him*, Father," Chveya said. "Not to mention that they aren't the most trustworthy people in the world."

"Are we only taking the strong and virtuous?" he asked. "Their husbands are dead, and as you said, their morals have never been their best talent. But they're my sisters." He walked away, back into the village.

It was a ghost town, the doors standing open, the people gone or, in just a few of the houses now, deeply asleep. But when Nafai came to the door of Sevet's house, there she stood in the doorway, looking sleepy and surprised. "I had a dream," she said, when Nafai approached her. "I don't even remember what it was, but it made me get up and here you are."

"We're leaving," said Nafai. "Before Elemak has a chance to kill me, we're leaving, everyone who would rather not live under his rule. We're taking all the angels with us, and going to a new place far away."

"He'll track you down and kill you if he can," said Sevet. "You don't know how much hate there is in him."

"Yes I do," said Nafai. "Will you come with me?"

She began to weep. "Would you really take me, after all I've done?"

"Would you really come?" he asked. "Would you really stand with me now?"

"I'm so afraid of him," she said. "And my Vasnaminanya and my Umya, they think the sun rises and sets with him."

"But Panimanya is with us," said Nafai.

"So am I," said Sevet.

They went to Kokor's door. It stood open, but she was not standing there as Sevet had been. They came inside, quietly, and found that she was not alone in her bed. Mebbekew lay beside her, naked and sweating in the damp heat of the night. But Mebbekew was asleep, while Kokor's eyes were already open when they came inside.

They said nothing, for fear that Meb might come awake. Kokor looked at them in the darkness, blinking. Nafai nodded to her, beckoned, and then led Sevet outside. They waited several paces from the house. Soon she came out, still arranging her clothing. "You're leaving," she said softly. "I dreamed it."

"Will you come with us?" asked Nafai.

Kokor looked at Sevet, her eyes widening. "Us?" she asked.

"You can stay with him if you want to, Kokor," said Sevet. "I think he does love you."

"He doesn't love anybody," said Kokor.

"I didn't mean Meb," said Sevet.

"I know," said Kokor. "But can't I come with you if I want to?"

"There's no going back," said Nafai. "And in our new city, we'll respect the law."

They understood what he was telling them. "I think perhaps we've had our fill," said Sevet.

Kokor rolled her eyes. "I will never have my fill," she said. "But I know it won't be Basilica. I'll be good."

"Are you sure you wouldn't be happier if you stayed?" asked Nafai.

"Don't you want us to come with you?" asked Kokor.

"Of course I do," he answered.

"Give us some credit, Nafai," said Kokor. "We can

tell the difference between you and Elemak. We know steel from cheap tin when we see it."

"Then let's go," said Nafai. "There's a long journey ahead of us tonight."

Oykib was already leading the long procession out onto the forest path, so that only a few remained when Nafai got there, among them Rasa and Zdorab on the launch. Shedemei was there, too.

"Seal the ship," said Nafai. "They can't get in if you don't let them."

"I know," she said. "The ship will be safe."

"Don't try to be heroic," said Nafai. "We'll be fine."

"You need more than one night's head start," said Shedemei.

Nafai shook his head, obviously intending to argue further. But she reached out a hand and touched his lips to silence him. "Nyef, my dear friend, I'm the star-master now. You go lead your colony into the wilderness. I will tend the ship and decide how the powers of the cloak are to be used."

Shedemei embraced Rasa and Zdorab and then waved as the launch rose into the sky and soared over the tops of the trees, passing all the other travelers who were trudging along the road. Then she embraced Nafai and returned to the ship.

Nafai was the last to set out on the road. He thought he was alone, when suddenly he found himself surrounded by a dozen diggers. His first thought was that the Keeper had failed, that while the Oversoul was able to keep his human enemies asleep, the diggers had been able to awaken. This is how I'll die, he thought.

Then he saw that they weren't armed, and half of them were women.

"Take us with you," said one of them in digger language.

Nafai wasn't as fluent in that tongue as Oykib was, but he could understand them. "And live among the angels?" he asked. "They'll never trust you."

"We would rather be servants to the . . . angels," said the woman who was speaking for them all. Nafai noticed that she did not say *skymeat*, but rather struggled to form her lips and tongue around the strange sounds of the angels' own word for *people*. "Fusum is the most terrible god."

Nafai nodded. "It will be hard for you among the angels," he said, "but you have my protection, and I will trust you unless you teach me that I can't. Do all of you take an oath to obey me and harm none of my people, humans or angels?"

They took the oath, and so he let them follow him. There was consternation among the angels when they arrived, but Nafai's assurances and their own humble pleas won the grudging acceptance of the angels. It was still dark when they left the angel village empty, and set out into the new country to build a new city, of a new kind.

When, after many days of travel, they reached the place that Nafai had chosen years before, knowing that this day might come, pTo and Poto held a little ceremony. "A place must have a name," they said. "And since we will always be known as the Nafari—" the word their lips pronounced was more like Dapati, but they were understood "—then we think this must now be called the land of Nafai—" Dapai "—and you are the one we choose to lead us all."

The voices rang out so loud in approbation that Nafai could only smile and say, "No man could be more happily praised than to have his friends choose to name their home after him." But despite the modesty of his words, they all knew what the naming meant. Nafai was their king. Their war king. And they would gladly die for him.

SIXTEEN

STARMASTER

Shedemei heard what Issib said to her through the Index. "It's dawn, and we're well away from the village, but we're slow, Shedya, and an army of diggers could have us by noon."

To this Shedemei replied, "There will be no army today or tomorrow."

"Just remember, Shedya," Issib answered. "There's only one of you to protect all of us. Don't be noble. Don't be fair. Prevail."

"Good advice, Issya. Now let me go and follow it."

For all her confidence, Shedemei was reluctant to leave the shelter of the starship, to make the door seal itself behind her. Wearing the cloak gave her a feeling of connection and closeness to every part of the ship, but in truth she had felt not very differently before. The ship was where her tools were, her library, her work, her career, herself. Stepping out into the village—the remnant of the village, the mostly deserted human-built houses—she was becoming someone else. Nafai must have relished this, thought Shedemei, this feeling of power, of control. But I don't. I'm not interested to find out how much power can be focused through my flesh. I have no desire to know just how strong a jolt I can give someone without killing him.

To be fair, Nafai might not have loved it either. But good-hearted as he might be, he *was* a man, and men seemed to find an obscene amount of pleasure in having the upper hand, in winning. Shedemei, on the other hand, simply wanted to *know*. But maybe it wasn't a matter of men and women. Maybe it was just that Shedemei's connection to other people was never very strong, compared to her love for her work, her devotion to understanding the way life worked. Is that really different, though? she wondered. Nafai and Elemak were born to rule men and determined to win out over each other. But I feel myself also born to rule, not men or women but organisms, genetic codes, life systems, ecologies. And, like Nafai and Elemak, I *will* have my way.

The problem today would not be Elemak, not really. The problem would be the diggers. Shedemei could easily stop Elemak and his few human followers. But there was no way she could seek out and block all of Fusum's soldiers, and they were the ones who would do the killing if they reached the Nafari while they were traveling, encumbered as they were by children and infants, by supplies and flocks and herds.

So whatever Shedemei did, she would have to persuade the diggers that they must wait; if the diggers did not go, then Elemak would also have to wait.

Thus it was that Shedemei walked through the village, paying no attention to the shouting as Elemak, Mebbekew, and Protchnu searching all the houses, ransacked them, really, screaming to each other about the betrayal, about all those who had gone. Mebbekew saw her and called out to her, then went howling off to find Elemak, crying out that Shedemei had stayed, Shedemei couldn't leave the ship after all. "We have the laborato-

ries! We have the computers! We have the Oversoul!"
Time enough to disabuse him of this delusion later.

She made her way to where the digger watchmen
were conferring in terror, wondering what would happen to them when Fusum learned that somehow they
had all slept through the night, seeing nothing, hearing
nothing, as most of the humans slipped away. "Fusum
will kill you," she said in her halting digger language.

They answered her in human speech, for which she
was grateful. "What can we do? What happened to us?
Someone poisoned us!"

"It was the Keeper of Earth," she said. "The Keeper
of Earth has rejected you, because a murderer rules over
you. You have chosen a murderer to be your blood king
and your war king." Then, with some effort, she made
her skin begin to glow. "Did you think that when
Fusum desecrated the statue of the Untouched God, it
would go unnoticed?"

She hated doing this. It had taken a great deal of effort
to break them free of superstition, and here she was re-
kindling all their old fears and faiths. But how else could
she control them, given the few powers that she had?

They were supine before her, offering their under-
bellies in a gesture of submission.

"I don't want your naked bellies," she said. "Stand like
men, for once. If you had stood like men before, the
Keeper of Earth would not be so angry with you now."

"What should we do, great one?"

"Bring me the friend-killer, the liar who murdered
Nen on the hunt."

The charge was like an electric current suddenly flowing through them. "So it was not the panther! Not the
panther!" they said.

"There was a panther," said Shedemei, "but the panther killed a man who had been struck down by a blow
from a friend." Even as she said it, she wondered if it
was true, and, if it was, how she knew it.

<I'm wondering that myself.> The voice of the Oversoul was clear and strong inside her head.

Could it be true? she asked.

<I watch over the humans. You're the only ones who have been changed to enable you to hear me, and to enable me to touch your mind.>

But we set twelve satellites in orbit, she said. You must be able to see, even if you can't hear their thoughts.

<I've never been programmed to watch animals.>

Furiously Shedemei responded, Well, I program you *now* to treat diggers and angels as if they were human, too.

<They aren't human, and so I can't regard them that way.>

Then do this, said Shedemei silently. Remember that because the humans have to live among diggers and angels now, our safety and survival depend on you watching what these sentient aliens do. You must always know.

<I don't have the resources that I had on Harmony. I don't have the power, the memory, the speed, the vision to watch them all.>

Do your best.

<And when you set me to work on mathematical problems or searches and comparisons, Shedemei, I can barely watch anything at all.>

Within your limits, within a reasonable set of priorities, do your best.

<We're going to have to have a long talk about priorities before long.>

Don't pretend to be helpless. I know what you are, *who* you are, and you don't need me to explain things to you. Now do your best to help me understand Elemak.

<Don't kill him.>

Shedemei almost said, I wasn't planning to. But then she realized that in the back of her mind that was exactly what she had planned. Fusum and Elemak, both of them dead and therefore the Nafari safe.

Why not kill him? she asked.

<The diggers must be restrained. Oykib is explaining this to Nafai and Issib right now. If they aren't held in by a powerful leader, they will run rampant, slaughtering angels and humans alike. The rage and hunger for blood in them is strong, after such long restraint. Fusum wasn't causing them to lust for war, he was using that lust to maintain himself in power. He was riding the panther, but he wasn't controlling it, and now you've cut the panther free of him.>

I haven't done anything to him yet.

<All through the digger city they've risen up in revolt, because they carry the tale of how you, the woman of the tower, have come out shining and angry, condemning them all because of Fusum's treachery.>

How can you know this?

<Oykib knows it. He hears the praying and the cursing. I told you, I have no eyes to see what diggers do underground.>

So Nafai thinks that I need Elemak to keep the diggers in check.

<Nafai says that once they're safely in their new home, they can fight off any attack. Natural defenses, dangerous ascents where diggers will be exposed to the darts of the angels—those will be enough if they can get there safely.>

Nafai was planning this all along, wasn't he? When he gave me the cloak, he knew he would need me to do this.

<Yes, of course. Actually, it was my idea. If he had tried to do what you're doing, Shedemei, he probably would have had to kill Elemak because this would have been one blow too many for Elemak to submit to him again. But with you in the cloak of the starmaster, Elemak should be able to bear another defeat, especially since you're also handing him a victory.>

Victory?

<Over his only serious rival for power.>

They dragged Fusum out of a hole in the ground and spread-eagled him before her. He hissed and howled and cursed her. She gave him the mildest of jolts, and his body spasmed. "Hold your tongue," she said.

He held his tongue.

She had them bring him along into the human village, where now Elemak and Protchnu stood, with all the other humans gathered behind them.

<Mebbekew is planning treachery behind you.>

Shedemei spoke to Elemak. "Tell Mebbekew to come out in the open and join you where you stand, Elya, or I'll have to make an example of him and it won't be nice."

Elemak laughed. "So, underneath our shy and quiet Shedemei there was a queen waiting to emerge. All it took was a little bit of power, and here you are, lord of all."

In the meantime, Mebbekew had slunk out from behind one of the houses and now stood behind Elemak. "Nafai took our women," Mebbekew complained.

"I'm sure that if you ask him, Protchnu will teach you how to ease your deprivation," Shedemei said. Protchnu glowered. So did Mebbekew, when he got it.

"I see you've already seized control of the diggers," said Elemak, gesturing toward the captive Fusum.

"On the contrary," said Shedemei. "I've seized control of nothing. I have merely accused this man, Fusum, of murdering his friend Nen."

"I didn't kill him," Fusum said.

"He clubbed him down when he knew a panther was stalking them," said Shedemei. "Only when he knew that Nen was dead did he lunge forward and kill the panther."

"Why are you telling me this?" asked Elemak.

"Are you not the one that has been chosen to unite humans and diggers into one people?" asked Shedemei. "Are you not the one who will found the nation of the Elemaki?"

Elemak chuckled. "Oh, of course," he said. "Of course the starmaster has always wanted me to rule."

"The starmaster intends to take this starship into space on the day the launch returns with my husband inside it."

"And when will that happy day come?"

"When the great nation of the Nafari is safe."

"As long as I'm alive, there will never be such a day," said Elemak.

Oh, yes, Nafai almost certainly would have had to kill him. "Safe enough," she said. "Because you know and I know that you will only be able to lead your soldiers against their redoubt so many times before the people will cease to follow you. You're a born leader, Elemak. You'll know how far you can push and goad and persuade. And it won't be far enough. Nafai and his people will be safe."

"How many days?" Elemak said. He understood the bargain.

"I think it will take you at least eight days to examine the crimes of this traitor. You'll have to find witnesses among his soldiers who will publicly confess about all the others who were murdered after Emeezem died. Justice takes time."

"Eight days."

"Or until the launch comes back. You'll also be busy moving your village so nobody gets killed when the ship takes off."

"I can see my work is cut out for me."

Protchnu was furious. "You aren't going to accept this corrupt bargain, are you, Father? That snake took half your family, half *my* family—"

Shedemei interrupted him. "Everyone who went with Nafai went of their own free will."

"And we're supposed to believe that?" said Protchnu. "Maybe Father will agree to your bargain in exchange for power over *these*—" he indicated the diggers with disdain "—but *I* will track them and hunt them down and my spear will take Nafai's heart out of his body!"

"And your mother's, too?" said Shedemei. "Because the only way she'll ever come back to Elemak is if she's dead."

"She's already dead!" screamed Protchnu. "She has no soul!"

"You have to forgive the boy," said Elemak. "He's distraught."

"He just doesn't understand what he's dealing with," said Shedemei. She reached out a hand toward Protchnu.

"No!" cried Elemak. But the air was already sparking with power, and Protchnu bounced into the air, his limbs cavorting madly. Then he fell to the ground, still twitching, and he whimpered, long high sighs that trembled as they faded. "You are really a bitch after all," whispered Elemak.

"I think it's useful for everyone to see that the Keeper of Earth does not leave her servants without power," said Shedemei. "Now let everyone see how Elemak does justice. Call your witnesses, confer with the leaders of the digger people, and when in eight days or so you reach your judgment, all of us will see whether you are fit to be named the war king of the Elemaki. If the voice of the diggers and the voice of the humans are united in calling for you to lead them, then I will make you war king, and you will lead this people with authority."

Elemak smiled at her, since of course he knew full well that she was trading the freedom of these diggers for the safety of the Nafari. He bent down and helped his son rise, shaking, to his feet.

"Remember, though," said Shedemei. "I said *war* king. There will be no more blood king among the people. Do you all hear me?"

They heard.

"This one has defiled the office so that it can never be held worthily again. From now on it is forbidden to eat the flesh of angel or human. Any man who eats that forbidden flesh will be as guilty as if he ate the flesh of his own child. That is now the law of all people, through all the world! And you will enforce it over all the diggers of every land!"

"Thanks for the assignment," said Elemak softly.

"I think you'll come to see the wisdom of teaching

them not to think of humans as a snack," said Shedemei, just as quietly. "If they can eat your enemies, Elya, how long before they decide that you are also a comestible?"

"I got the point already," said Elemak. "Now are you done?"

"No diggers following the Nafari," said Shedemei.

"Do you think we won't be able to follow the trail?" asked Elemak.

"No assassins on the road," she said.

"I know the bargain," said Elemak. "I know that I've been humiliated again, and this time Nafai took my wife and half my family, and you struck down my son. But I can live with that, because you've given me a nation. A nation of ugly rodents who live in dirt, but I've dealt with worse in caravans on Harmony, even though they walked in human shape. I *will* stand over Nafai's body someday, Shedemei, regardless of what you think. But if it makes you feel better, I won't eat him. And I won't let anybody else eat him, either. Except perhaps the crows and vultures."

"I'm glad to see that you're filled with the spirit of conciliation."

He smiled at her. Then he stepped away from her and spoke to the diggers who held Fusum. "Take the prisoner into my house. And then start bringing me those who think they know of crimes this man has done." He looked again at Shedemei. "That should take up the first day, I imagine."

Shedemei turned from him to Protchnu, whose cheeks were stained with tears. "You shouldn't have done that to me," he whispered. "That was *wrong*."

"You were such a promising boy," she answered kindly. "Of all the tragedies this lifelong war between brothers has caused, you are the saddest one of all."

He went livid. "I'll kill him, Shedya. I'll kill them all. Every one of them."

"What you're saying, then, is that you're sure your father's going to fail?"

"I meant that I'd kill any he left behind."

"You know the truth, Protchnu. Stop worrying about vengeance and learn how to be a leader. These people need a king far more than your father needs to be justified. All he's ever done, he did for power. Now he's got it. You'll see. He'll go through the motions of war, but he'll lose because his hunger has been satisfied."

"You don't know Father," said Protchnu proudly. "And you don't know me."

"Nobody does," said Shedemei. "So maybe you'll surprise us all."

Eight days later, Zdorab returned to the ship in the launch. He arrived in time to watch as Fusum was executed for his crimes, his throat cut by one of his own soldiers. His body was then hung from the limb of a tree, so that no part of it was touching the sacred earth. Shedemei, her skin aglow, stepped forward then and went through the ritual of naming Elemak to be war king. The people hailed him and cheered him, then watched in silence as Shedemei and Zdorab flew upward in the launch until they entered the tower through the high wide bay where the launch was kept.

The door closed behind them, and Elemak set out at once with two hundred soldiers, leaving Muzhestvo—Mebbekew's youngest, now a man of twenty-three—to rule the people in his absence. Elemak's army was halfway up the canyon when the starship roared to life and rose into the sky.

It became another point of light in the night heaven, circling and circling, now and then changing its position. It was called *Basilica*, but in time almost no one remembered why, or what it was, or that it had once been a tower standing by the first human village on Earth in forty million years.

Elemak's army tracked the wide path of the Nafari

migration, but when they reached the stony cliff that barred the southern passage into the wide high valley of the land of Nafai, angels assaulted them from the air, shooting darts into their exposed backs. Twenty diggers died in that place, and forty more were injured. They struggled back home, and Elemak taught them to make armor so that next year they could try again.

And so it went, year after year. But between the futile wars, both nations prospered and grew, and both sent out traders and teachers to spread the new agriculture and the new modes of warfare and the new myths and legends and religions to every other digger city and angel village.

Generations passed, and the humans became hundreds, then thousands, then tens of thousands, and there was not a digger city that didn't have its human houses overhead, not an angel village that didn't have humans joining in the evening song. The term that became common for humans in both societies was *middle people*, because they stood between the angels in the sky and the diggers in the earth.

In the sky, the starship circled and circled, but it was full of life. Shedemei and Zdorab slept long and often, but then they would emerge and use the launch to explore, to gather specimens, to introduce new variations, to give shape and strength and variety to the gardens of the Earth. In time, Zdorab's body wore out, and Shedemei laid him to rest in a field of flowers she had brought from Harmony. Then, alone, she woke less often. But still from time to time she visited, she gathered, she tended, and silently she watched as the people spread across the face of the land, always cleverer each time she saw them, yet also angrier, and always at war.

What else could happen? The human race was home again.